SING IN THE SUNLIGHT

CHAPARRAL HEARTS ~ BOOK 2

KATHLEEN DENLY

WILD HEART
BOOKS

Cover design by: Carpe Librum Book Design

ISBN-13: 978-1-942265-29-0

To Leota Jones, the Wilson Sisters, the Dyke sisters, and especially my mother for demonstrating the beauty of praising our Lord in song. Also, to my beautiful daughter, Ava, without whom this novel would not exist.

*Thou hast turned for me my mourning into
dancing;
thou hast put off my sackcloth
and girded me with gladness;
To the end that my glory may sing praise to thee
and not be silent.
O LORD my God, I will give thanks unto thee for
ever!*

— PSALM 30: 11-12 (KJV)

ACKNOWLEDGMENTS

I must first thank the Lord. Though no particular event in this story is taken directly from my own life, this book was inspired by a combination of many experiences in my life, both good and bad, which God has used to reveal His unconditional love and grace. I pray He uses this story to share some of that with you.

Next, I must thank you, dear reader. Without you I would be talking to the wall. Or my cats. They're very good listeners, but the feedback is a bit one note. Seriously though, reading your reviews and especially receiving notes from those of you who have reached out to let me know that something I wrote touched your heart, helps keep me going on the tough days.

My thanks to the Kathleen's Readers' Club Members, my Armchair Adventure Krew, my SITS Launch Team, and my Super Beta Reader Squad. Your continuing support and encouragement are truly cherished.

Thanks to all my *Sing in the Sunlight* beta readers for your willingness to slog through the early draft of this novel. Your timely feedback is much needed and greatly appreciated.

I am incredibly grateful for the editorial efforts of Erin

Taylor Young, whose insight and suggestions helped make this story the best it could be.

A special thanks to the staff of the Barona Cultural Center & Museum who helped guide me to the right resources for understanding the culture of the Native Peoples living in San Diego during the 1800s. I'm especially grateful that despite our current turbulent times, they managed to find the time to read the relevant portions of my manuscript and provide sensitivity guidance.

A huge thanks to Jessica Baker whose invaluable assistance with my online presence and other backend author tasks has allowed me to focus on my manuscript. This simple sentence cannot convey the depth of my gratitude.

Thank you to Misty Beller and the rest of the Wild Heart team for working so hard to get this novel into readers' hands.

Finally, I want to thank my husband for showing me what it looks like to love someone through their dark places, to never give up, and to draw them out of themselves so that they can fully feel the light of God's love.

CHAPTER 1

*C*larinda Humphrey jammed the chair beneath her doorknob and tugged the beautiful garnet ring from its hiding place beneath her chemise. Undoing the knot, she slipped the heirloom free of the ribbon that had kept it close to her heart these last three days. She slid the ring onto the third finger of her left hand.

Or tried to.

The metal caught on the thick, hideous scar that ran across her second knuckle. With determination, she shoved it past and narrowed her attention to the stone's promise.

She was loved.

The urge to hum swelled within her as she strolled to the window. She pulled back the heavy drapes and lifted her hand to the light filtering through the thin lace curtains. Barely a glint reflected in the deep red stone.

She parted the lace, careful to remain out of view, and tilted her hand in the late afternoon sunlight below the sill. A myriad of tiny red dots danced across the walls.

This was the night. She'd never be alone again. She clapped her fingertips in a quiet patter.

Laughter filtered through the windowpane.

She froze. Had they seen her? No. The slit in the curtains was too narrow. Wasn't it? She dared a peek at the garden below.

Several of her classmates strolled the paths. The girls chattered in the late afternoon sunlight, seemingly oblivious to her observation.

Not girls. Women—despite what their parents may believe. Like her, they'd been sent to the first female college in the west to be trained—molded—into the ladies their parents wished them to become.

But they were nothing like her.

All bright, beautiful, and whole, none of her classmates had ever questioned their future. Why should they? They'd never been shunned at social gatherings, nor been asked to remain behind so as not to repel the other guests. They hadn't been told they would never marry—that no man would ever want them. They'd never lain awake at night wondering why God had abandoned them.

Nor had they ever made any attempt to befriend her.

And that was fine with her. Normally.

Right now Clarinda'd give almost anything for a confidante to entrust with her secret. She was bursting to tell someone. Not even Katie, her one true friend at this school, knew of her plans. Clarinda couldn't risk the young maid losing her position here if it were discovered she'd kept a scandalous confidence. Though, she would know soon enough. The day had finally arrived.

Clarinda's left arm grew warm. She glanced at her sleeve.

She'd been rubbing her scars through the fabric again. With a huff, she turned from the window, tugging her cuff out of habit. She pulled on her gloves and lifted her hat from its hook, pinning it in place.

She jerked the tea towel cover from the small oval mirror and examined her reflection. Her veil hung askew, allowing a rebellious blond curl to poke out the bottom. Perhaps she *should* have confided in Katie. With her friend's help, Clarinda's chignon wouldn't be falling apart minutes after it'd been created. She jabbed in another pin to hold the curl.

Clarinda adjusted her veil so the flowers embroidered on its sheer fabric hid the left side of her face. She'd grown so used to staring through the creamy-white cotton voile, she rarely noticed it anymore. If she lifted the filter, the world's colors grew bolder. The light, brighter. But she preferred her muted, hazy view. She tucked the ends of the veil into the unfashionably high neck of her bodice. The haze suited her life.

Or it *had*.

Her mouth pulled to the side, smirking at her reflection. Arnie had changed all that.

She lifted the timepiece from where it was pinned to her bodice.

One hour.

Her stomach fluttered as she sucked in a breath.

One hour until she could break free of these walls—these grounds that had imprisoned her since her parents banished her here two and a half years ago. They hadn't called it that, of course. They insisted sending her to this school was their way of ensuring she had a means of supporting herself once they'd gone. After all, it wasn't fair to expect her future brother-in-law to provide for her. He would have his own family, as well as their parents' shop, to look after. A shop she'd never been permitted to set foot in for fear she would make their customers uncomfortable.

She didn't make Arnie uncomfortable. Quite the opposite. Grinning, she pictured his bright blue eyes and wavy brown hair slicked back with oil. His goatee had tickled her face the first time they kissed, but she'd gotten used to the scruff.

Footsteps hurried down the hall outside her door. She darted across the room and yanked the drapes over the window, cloaking the room in near darkness. Only skinny lines of light peeked around the fabric's edges.

Arnie hadn't been deterred by her veil. He saw it as a challenge, as some men were wont to do. Usually, the removal of her left glove—revealing the scars beneath—was enough to send those men running for the hills. Not Arnie. He didn't so much as flinch at the sight. Nor did he laugh or mock her the way those men on the ship had when a gust of wind whipped her covering loose during her journey from San Diego.

Home. She could scarcely believe she would see it again.

When her parents had put her on that steamer up the coast, they'd bid her farewell with the expectation that, upon graduation, she would find a position as a teacher in some backwoods town where the community would be too desperate for an instructor to care about her scars.

Instead, she'd be returning with a new husband. The look of shock on her parents' faces would be priceless. And once the truth set in, her mother might genuinely smile.

At her. For the first time in fourteen years. She ran a finger through the dust on the sill. Her parents might even let her visit their shop.

After a childhood spent dusting shelves and tidying stock, she'd never imagined it possible to miss such tasks as terribly as she had after they moved to San Diego eight years ago. Again, she wondered how their new shop differed from the one she'd cleaned in Washington D.C. Father said the place was bigger. Her little sister, Lucy, claimed it was fourteen steps across and twenty eight steps deep. But Clarinda longed to see it for herself. Lucy was almost a foot shorter than Clarinda's five feet, ten inches. Did she remember to dust the tops of the shelves the way Clarinda used to?

Someone knocked on her door.

"Miss Humphrey, are you feeling better, dear?" Miss Leming's voice carried through the door. "Will you be joining us this evening?"

Aside from Katie, Miss Leming was the only one who paid attention to Clarinda outside of classes and recitals. It was her job to supervise the students housed in her section of the second-floor sleeping quarters. Since Clarinda had no roommate, she received extra attention. None of the other young women had wanted to room with her. Not that Clarinda minded. Sneaking out to see Arnie would have been impossible had she had a roommate.

Clarinda removed the chair, careful not to allow a telltale scrape. She opened the door and feigned a wince, squinting as if the light from the hall pained her. "I'm afraid not, Miss Leming. This headache is positively merciless. I can barely keep my eyes open and feel a bit light-headed." She pretended to waver on her feet. "I think I'd better rest for the night."

Miss Leming placed a hand on Clarinda's right arm—no one ever touched her on the left. "Should I send for the doctor?"

"Oh no, ma'am." Perhaps the wavering had been a bit too much. "I'm sure all I need is a restful night's sleep. I'll be good as new in the morning. You'll see."

"Well, if you're sure."

Clarinda tensed as Miss Leming peered past her shoulder, studying the room. "One of the maids brought you fresh linens and a pitcher of water, I see. Does it need refilling?"

Miss Leming tried to enter, but Clarinda blocked her way. "No, ma'am. I've plenty. The maid was just here to refill it."

"Oh. Well..." the teacher stepped back. "You will let me know if the pain grows worse or you need anything?"

Clarinda nodded and began edging the door closed.

Miss Leming took the hint and turned to go. "I'll see you in the morning, then."

"Goodnight." Clarinda closed the door and leaned her forehead against the wood.

The teacher's footsteps faded away.

She scanned the darkened interior of her room. How much of the space had been illuminated by the hall lamps? Could the teacher have seen Clarinda's traveling bag? She shook herself. Surely not, or Miss Leming wouldn't have left.

Clarinda lifted the timepiece again. One quarter of an hour had passed. She groaned. How would she ever endure the next forty-five minutes?

~

NEVADA CITY, CALIFORNIA
DECEMBER 3, 1857

*N*umbers blurred before Richard Stevens's eyes. Truth was, the Prosperity Mine's ledger had long ago lost his attention. Since the shock of his sister's letter last week, the sense that he was wasting time had hounded him. And it was only growing worse.

This office was a prison. The responsibilities of ownership, like shackles chaining him to his desk. He wanted to walk the mile to his mine and...

What?

His desire to dig had died. Buried in the collapsed mine alongside the previous owner's son. After the accident, Richard nearly walked away from the chance to purchase Prosperity Mine. But the men who worked the shafts depended on the wages they earned to support their families. He was proud of the changes he'd made, lowering the risk of another accident. But the alterations had been completed months ago. Now...

He glared at his ledger. How could owning a successful gold mine be so mind-numbing?

Female sniffling dragged his thoughts back to the office. His gaze shifted to his secretary seated at her desk across the small room. Miss Bennetti wiped at her nose. Did she have a cold? At least, instead of her dress sleeve she now used a handkerchief.

His secretary had changed in the past year. She wore a plain, brown dress, and a simple bun. Perfectly respectable. So, the yellow violet tucked behind her ear was a bit unusual. Still, her appearance was a far cry from the shocking get-up she'd been wearing when he met her. If that weren't enough, her face had been caked in powders and her eyes outlined by lampblack. He'd had trouble believing she was only eighteen until she'd wiped herself clean. Without the makeup, her big brown eyes... were shimmering with tears? Wet trails ran down her cheeks. "What's wrong, Miss Bennetti?"

"I'm so sorry."

He glanced at her tidy desk. Nothing seemed amiss. "For what?"

"I'm such a wicked woman. I took advantage of your big heart." She wrung her kerchief. "You should've left me where you found me."

Not this again.

He'd taken a wrong turn into the Barbary Coast last spring and found Bella Bennetti sobbing in an alley. Of course, he couldn't leave her there. So he'd escorted her to safety. On the stoop of the nearest church, she'd shared her tale of woe and he'd done what any gentleman would—offered her a respectable means of supporting herself. She'd eagerly accepted.

Unfortunately, Miss Bennetti lapsed into her first fit of self-recrimination within a week of arriving in Nevada City. Her dramatic episodes continued off and on for months. It had been enough to break his heart and drive him mad at the same time.

Yet three months had passed since her last fit. Richard thought she'd finally accepted his assurances of her value as a forgiven child of God and would no longer castigate herself for her past naïve mistakes. It seemed he'd been wrong.

"You're forgetting, God loves and forgives you and so do I. Besides"—he waved a hand to encompass their tiny office —"you've been doing a marvelous job. I don't know how I'd get on without you."

It was the truth. On her desk sat a stack of correspondence she'd penned and addressed for him, the wood floors still gleamed from her morning scrubbing, and the little green curtains she'd sewn for him framed clean windows. His lips tilted. There probably weren't curtains in actual prisons.

Unfortunately, his reassurances failed to make his secretary smile. Instead, she wailed louder.

"You don't understand. I'm so ungrateful." She sniffed and blew her nose. "I mean, I'm not ungrateful. Oh, no!" She leapt from her chair and rushed across the room to grasp his hand in both of hers. "Please don't ever think me ungrateful. I am *so* grateful. Truly, I am."

"No, of course not"—Richard began, but quickly corrected —"I mean, of course. I know you're grateful. You've told me repeatedly how grateful you are."

Miss Bennetti nodded. Her breathing slowed, and her face crumpled again. "Oh, but I'm not!" she wailed. "I'm so sorry." She fell into his lap, burying her face in his collar, still sobbing.

Her momentum threatened to topple them both. Richard grabbed the edge of his desk, keeping them upright.

The sensation of crawling ants traveled up his spine. He glanced at the windows facing the town's main street. If anyone looked their way, the view wouldn't do his reputation any favors. People already thought him odd for hiring a female secretary.

He patted her shoulder. "There, there. Of course you are. You're just too hard on yourself." He ought to remove her from his lap. But how to do it without further upsetting her?

She shook her head, face still mashed into his shirtfront. "Please forgive me. I didn't mean for it to happen."

Richard stilled. "Didn't mean for *what* to happen?"

"To-o-ommy!" She somehow extended his head miner's name into a three syllable whine that sent a chill through his veins. "I didn't mean to, but he's so handsome and he was so nice to me and—" A white-hot fire chased the chill away.

"What did he do to you?" He shoved her back to see her face. Images of other scenes he'd witnessed after taking that wrong turn last year, flashed through his mind. "Tell me and I'll make sure he regrets it. I'll make sure he never comes near you again."

She gasped. "Oh, no! I knew you'd feel like that. I told Tommy. He didn't believe me, but I told him ..."

Richard slid her from his lap and stood.

He guided her into his chair, vaguely aware she was still talking.

Tommy. Richard stomped to the coat rack. He and that man had worked side by side in the shafts for years. Tommy was like family. That's why he'd given Tommy the task of bringing the roster to the office each day. How could his head miner have betrayed him?

Richard ground his teeth.

Miss Bennetti sniffed, blotted her eyes with the mangled kerchief, and blew her nose. "I'll tell him the wedding is off, that's all. He'll understand. He has to."

Her words doused his burning rage like a bucket of creek water. "What?"

"I'm so sorry. I know how much you depend on me, and I knew—no matter how you denied it—I knew you were attracted to me." She pushed to her feet. "Of course, I'll marry you instead of Tommy. It's only right after everything you've done." She sniffled and wiped her nose again.

"He offered to marry you?" What was she saying? "After he took advantage of you, you mean? To stop you from telling me?"

Her hand flew to her mouth. "No! It wasn't like that at all. Tommy and I haven't..."

How could a woman with her background still blush and stammer over the subject of physical intimacy? "You haven't?"

"No." She slumped into his chair, her lower lip jutted out. "I told you I wouldn't. I promised God. I thought you..."

He grimaced and examined the floor. He *had* seen the change in her since she'd knelt at the church altar last month. He shouldn't have thought she'd...but hadn't she said...? His memory was clear as mud. But it didn't matter.

He strode across the room and lowered himself to a knee in front of her. "Miss Bennetti,"—he took her hand and waited for her to look at him—"it would be a great honor to call you my wife. But I would never ask you to give up the desires of your heart."

Her mouth popped open.

He held up his hand. "Tommy is a good man. If I cannot have you for myself, nothing would make me happier than to see you married to him. *If* that is what you wish."

"But what about you, Mr. Stevens? Once I'm married, I'll be too busy seeing after Tommy to come to the office. And won't you be brokenhearted?"

A family of his own *was* something he'd always wanted. He'd once considered solving both their problems with an offer of marriage. However, it hadn't taken him long to realize their temperaments were not well suited. And the thought perished. In fact, it was so fleeting, he was certain he'd never revealed any hint of it to anyone.

Nevertheless, Miss Bennetti believed any man who'd go to

such trouble to help her must have ulterior motives. But he'd no desire for a marriage of convenience. "I'll miss you, of course, but I'll be fine. If God's plan is for you to marry Tommy, I'm certain the Lord will see me through in your absence. Don't you worry about me." He patted her hand.

The office door opened and they turned.

Tommy stood there, a bouquet in his grip. His mouth pressed firm as his nostrils flared.

∾

*B*ag in hand, Clarinda slipped from her room, pulling the door shut behind her. The click echoed in the empty hall. She froze, listening. The barely discernible voice of the school's director addressing the students came through the floorboards. Nothing more. Clarinda released her breath and scurried to the stairs.

As she descended, the muffled notes of "When I Saw Sweet Nellie Home" filled the hall. Of course, it was Arnie's sister's rich contralto voice singing. Beautiful Mary always began the nightly musical recitations for the school. The song's melody was exquisite, and the lyrics so fitting Clarinda's current mood that she sucked in a breath—her lungs ready to release the music trapped within. But as she'd done every day of her life for the past nine years, she squelched it.

No one wanted to hear her sing. Not anymore.

A door swung open as a maid backed out of the nearest classroom.

"Katie," Clarinda whispered.

Katie jumped. Both the vases she'd had tucked beneath her arms crashed to the floor with a deafening shatter. Wilted petals and stems scattered across the wooden planks.

Clarinda tossed her bag behind a nearby sideboard as the door to the assembly room flew open.

Miss Leming emerged, eyes wide. "What's happened?"

Before either Katie or Clarinda could answer, the teacher spied the mess and moaned. "Oh, no. Not again, Katie."

Clarinda cringed. Though Katie's heart was the biggest Clarinda had ever known, and her intent was always for good, she possessed an uncanny knack for disaster. The school's director had warned Katie if the calamities didn't stop she would lose her position—a position that had rescued her from her monster of a father.

Clarinda stepped forward. "It was my fault. I bumped into her."

Miss Leming offered a sad smile. "That's kind of you to say, Clarinda, but falsehoods, even those formed with good intentions, are unbecoming a woman of God."

Clarinda ignored the twinge in her conscience. God hardly cared what she did, never mind what she said. "No, really. It was entirely my fault." She stepped back to place a hand on the banister, as though to steady herself. "I thought I was feeling better and came to join the assembly, but a dizziness overcame me just as Katie was exiting the classroom. I'm afraid I bumped her in my attempt to regain my balance."

Miss Leming looked to Katie. "Is this true?"

"I..." Katie glanced at Clarinda.

Squinting as if the light bothered her, Clarinda placed a hand over her face and directed a sideways glare at Katie. *Do not contradict me.*

Turning her gaze to the floor, Katie nodded.

"Very well." Miss Leming sighed. "Clarinda, I will assist you back to your room. You clearly should have remained in bed. Katie, please see that this mess is cleared before the assembly is concluded. I don't want the girls walking through these shards."

Clarinda's hand dropped. She couldn't return to her room. Only a few minutes of assembly remained. She'd miss her opportunity to escape.

Arnie was waiting for her.

Clarinda resisted the urge to glance at her secreted travel bag and grimaced as she lowered herself to the steps. "I think I'd better rest here a moment instead, Miss Leming. The dizziness has grown worse with all this commotion. I fear if I take another step I'll not be able to retain the contents of my stomach."

Miss Leming tisked her disapproval. "I knew I should have sent for the doctor." She turned to Katie. "Will you find one of the other maids and send them—"

"No!" Clarinda relaxed her expression to give the impression her discomfort was easing. "Please. If you'll allow me a moment's rest, I'm sure I'll be able to return to my room. You're right. I should never have left it. A good night's rest is all I need. This headache will surely be gone by morning."

The assembly room door opened again. Clarinda stifled a groan. Would the entire school be coming to see what the fuss was about?

One of Clarinda's classmates poked her head into the hall-way. She gaped at the mess on the floor. "It's time for your class's recitations, Miss Leming."

Miss Leming stepped toward the door, but pivoted. "I'll not have you climbing those stairs on your own—"

"I won't. I promise. I'll just sit here until Katie is finished cleaning. I'm sure she won't mind helping me upstairs."

Katie, who'd begun collecting the dead blooms and sharp pottery pieces, looked up from her kneeling position. "I'm happy to help Miss Humphrey, ma'am."

"Miss Leming?" The director's voice rang out from the open door.

Heaving a sigh, Miss Leming hurried away.

At last, the door closed behind the teacher. Clarinda sprang from the steps and fetched her bag.

Katie stood. "What're thee doing?" The maid's Northern

English accent thickened with confusion, making her more difficult to understand. "Shh." Clarinda glanced at the closed door. "Arnie and I are to be married tonight." She picked her way through the mess to her friend. "I'm meeting him behind the church, and then we're riding to Sacramento. He's found a preacher who'll marry us there." She pulled the precious ring from its hiding place.

"He has?" Katie's eyebrows rose toward her mobcap.

"He asked me three days ago. I've been dying to tell you, but he made me promise not to tell a soul."

"Loavin days!" Katie's hurt was written on her face. "And thee're leaving without even a farewell?"

"No." Clarinda released the ring to dangle from her neck and gripped Katie's fingers. "Never. I was coming to find you."

Katie peered through the film of Clarinda's veil, searching her eyes. Her mouth eased into a sad smile. "I know it's what thee've been hoping for, but it'll be lonesome 'round here without thee."

Clarinda pulled her into a fierce hug. "I'll miss you, too." She drew back. Tears clogged her throat, but the joy of what lay before her forbade them from forming in her eyes. "But I'll write."

"Thee will?"

"I promise." She glanced to the still-closed assembly door. The muffled recitations continued for now, but wouldn't last much longer. "I must go." She squeezed her friend's hands. "Wish me well?"

"May the good Lord keep thee."

Clarinda dashed to the front door.

"Wait!" Katie's loud whisper halted Clarinda as she gripped the knob.

She glanced back.

Katie darted closer, keeping her voice low. "What'll I tell Miss Leming?"

"Don't tell her anything unless she asks." Clarinda hesitated. Katie loathed deceit. "If she does ask, tell her I'm in my room and have gone to sleep."

Katie frowned, but nodded.

With a soft smile, Clarinda pulled the door open and raced toward her future.

CHAPTER 2

*C*larinda was going to be sick. She pressed a hand against her stomach, willing it to stop churning. *Where is he?* She peered around the corner of the tall hedge hiding her from view of the school.

The barren tree branches swayed with a gentle breeze, casting dancing shadows over the empty lawn and paths lined with short bushes. The flickering lights of her classmates' lanterns had long ago been snuffed. If she were caught out after curfew…

Clarinda ducked back into the secret alcove Arnie had told her about the day they'd met. While his sister played the piano in the assembly room, Clarinda had been helping Katie remove the evidence of another shattered platter in the dining room. Restless after his sister's performance, Arnie'd snuck away from the recitations and wandered into the dining room. He'd promised not to betray Katie's secret if Clarinda agreed to meet him here the following afternoon.

He'd been late that day, too.

She looked around the strange cave carved into the tall, wide hedges surrounding the school's garden. It had taken her weeks of secret rendezvous to get the story of its origin from him. Before the school had purchased the building and grounds, it had been home to a large family with a strict father. When the family's eldest daughter showed interest in a less than desirable suitor, the father forbid them from seeing each other. Determined not to let her father keep her from true love, the young woman had taken their gardener's sheers and carved this secret meeting place herself. Or so Arnie had told her.

Where was he?

Arnie had warned her he may be delayed and made her promise to wait for him, but...two hours? He'd often complained of his father's nightly lectures on what a disappointment Arnie was. Yet could the man be lecturing his son at this hour? What if Arnie wasn't delayed? What if he'd changed his mind?

What if he'd confided their plans to his friends and they'd talked him out of chaining his life to a social outcast? Maybe she shouldn't let Arnie go through with their plans. He was convinced that marrying her and giving her his family's name would make her more socially acceptable. But what if it made Arnie an outcast like her?

No. She shook the doubt from her mind. Arnie was right.

The Walkers were royalty in this town. Once she carried the Walker family name, people wouldn't dare continue spurning and ridiculing *her*. The idea that they'd treat the heir to the Walker fortune with any hint of disdain was laughable. Goosebumps skittered up her arms. Life would be different after tonight. After she was married.

She'd share a bed with Arnie tonight. The thought settled like a brick on her chest. Would he mind if she kept her chemise on? He'd seen the scars on her face and hands, but there were so many more he hadn't seen. Perhaps if she—

A branch snapped beyond the hedge. She caught her breath, listening as footfalls crunched across dried leaves. Someone was coming. What if it wasn't Arnie? How would she explain—

17

Arnie barreled around the corner. "Clarie!" He pulled her into his arms, thrust her veil aside and pressed his lips to hers.

She melted into him. He was here. He'd come! He still loved her. She clutched his lapel. He squeezed her until no air remained between them. His mouth trailed kisses to her left ear and tingles swept over her. Oh, to have such a man care for her. How could this be?

His fingers began fiddling with the buttons at the neck of her dress.

Alarm bells clanged in her head. She pushed back. "Not yet, Arnie." Sucking in air, she tried to catch her breath. "We aren't married."

"Close enough." His arms tightened. "Don't you know how I want you?"

He kissed her with a passion that almost undid her resolve. To be so wanted by a man who'd seen her scars. It was more than she'd ever dreamed.

His fingers fiddled again with her buttons. "Don't torture me, so."

Cool air caressed her clavicle, jarring her to her senses. She stepped away. Then farther. Her fingers sought and found three undone buttons. She'd been enjoying his advances too much.

She dropped her gaze and restored her modesty. "Hadn't we better get going? We're going to be late as it is. Are you sure the preacher will still be available?"

His pout was so adorable she almost laughed. He put her in mind of a child denied a candy at Christmas.

"I suppose you're right." He grabbed her hand and lifted her bag. "Come on."

*R*ichard lifted his hands. "Tommy, wait. This—"

"No, Richard." Tommy slammed the door behind him and stormed forward. "You had your chance. It's too late now. She's agreed to marry *me*." His gaze switched to Miss Bennetti. "Isn't that right, Bella? You have told him, haven't you?"

Miss Bennetti knocked Richard to the floor in her haste to reach Tommy. "Yes, Tommy." In two steps, she flung herself into his arms. "I just told him and he said it was all right."

Tommy's gaze swung to Richard's. "You did?"

Richard grinned at him. "I did."

Tommy released Miss Bennetti and offered Richard a hand up.

Back on his feet, Richard dusted his hands on his trousers. "Why didn't you tell me you were courting Miss Bennetti?"

Tommy winced. "I thought about it, but…well, you aren't her father and I wasn't sure she'd have me." He shrugged. "Didn't see any point in humiliating myself with telling you my intentions just to have her turn me down. Then after she said yes… I don't know." He clasped Miss Bennetti's hand. "I guess I just liked the idea of keeping things to ourselves for a while."

Richard hesitated to ask, nearly certain of the answer, but he had to be sure. "You're not ashamed—"

"No!" Tommy cut his hand through the air. "I could never be ashamed of Bella, but word had gotten round that you didn't let anyone near her. So the men were leaving her alone. I was afraid if word got out that she was accepting callers…well, I didn't want to risk someone else stealing her away."

The doe-eyed look Miss Bennetti gave Tommy said it all. "No one could ever steal me away from you, Tommy."

Richard choked on his laugh, disguising it as a cough. She'd all but proposed to Richard a moment ago, though she hadn't meant it. Her offer to marry him had been one of misguided

obligation. It was clear where her heart laid. As for Tommy...
"What about your brother? Didn't you say he's arriving next
week? Have you told him?" There would be no reason to keep
the news from a man who'd never met Miss Bennetti.

Tommy barked a laugh. "That's the whole reason he's
coming. Said he couldn't miss seeing his little brother get
married."

Richard envied such a relationship. Neither of his brothers,
nor his youngest sister had written him a single letter in the
four years he'd been in California. At least the elder of his
sisters, Alice, kept him apprised of their family's affairs, or he'd
never have known about Mother's passing.

He offered his hand to Tommy. "Then I wish you the best."

"Thank you."

Miss Bennetti wrapped her arms around her fiancé and
squeezed him tight. "See, I told you everything would work
out."

Tommy laughed. "That you did, sweetheart."

A pang struck Richard at the look exchanged between the
lovebirds. *Lord, you do have someone for me, don't you?* He turned
away as the two leaned forward, their lips meeting in a way that
made it clear they'd forgotten his presence.

He shut his ledger, revealing the unopened, black-edged
letter bearing his sister's handwriting which had arrived that
morning. No doubt it held the details of Mother's funeral. The
sight of the mourning stationary had provoked Miss Bennetti to
tears, so he'd hidden it to calm her. The excuse to delay reading
the correspondence had been convenient, but he shouldn't put
it off any longer.

A throat cleared behind him.

"Sorry." Tommy's cheeks were flushed. "I can't seem to keep
my eyes off her."

Richard smiled. "Not at all. Listen"—his gaze returned to the
letter—"why don't the two of you eat at the restaurant tonight

to celebrate? Tell Maggie it's my treat and I'll pick up the tab later."

"Why don't you come with us?"

"No, I've got some things to finish up here." He waved the letter. "You two go ahead."

~

*C*larinda peered into the darkness as a cloud passed over the half moon. Arnie's arms encircled her waist, his chest warming her back as they rode—protecting her from the cold winter's night. They'd been riding for hours. When Arnie had suggested riding to Sacramento to elope, he'd made it sound like they'd arrive shortly after the evening meal. But it was well past that now.

"How much farther is it?"

"We're about halfway."

Halfway? "But—"

Arnie turned the horse onto a narrow trail leading away from the main road.

"Are we stopping to rest?" Her sore backside rejoiced at the thought, yet... "Hadn't we better continue? What if the preacher gives up on us and retires for the night?"

Arnie said nothing as they rode farther into a dense forest.

His long silence unsettled her. "Arnie? Where are we going?"

"I'm sorry, Clarie. I can't do it."

"What?" Clarinda twisted in the saddle. She couldn't read his eyes in the gloom. He couldn't have changed his mind. Not now. Not after they'd come so far. "You don't want...?" Her breath caught on the words. She couldn't force them out.

"No. Oh, no, Clarie. That's not what I meant, sweetie." He halted the horse in a clearing and slid down. His hands claimed her waist and he lifted her from the saddle. He crushed her against him and kissed her long and hard.

21

When he pulled away, her eyes drifted open and she had to blink to regain her surroundings. The cloud had passed. His earnestness was clear in the pale moonlight.

"Of course, I want you. It's just..." His arms dropped and he slumped. "I'm so tired. I can't keep my eyes open. Father was especially...*enthusiastic* tonight. And I guess I'm...worn out." He kicked at the grass, his next words almost a whisper. "More so than I realized."

"Oh." Clarinda sucked in a breath. He was tired. That was all? She could handle that. "Well, why don't you lean against me and rest as we ride? I can takeover leading the horse and—"

Arnie turned away, cutting off her words. He stared in the direction they'd come for several seconds. His gaze flicked to hers and away again. "You don't know the way. You've never been to Sacramento. I know you're a very capable woman, but it's easy to make a wrong turn and get lost out here. We could wind up riding for hours in the wrong direction."

She craned her neck, trying to catch his eye. "But what shall we do?"

He pivoted from her, gesturing to the small clearing they stood in. "Let's rest here for a while. I just need a nap. And then we can...go."

"What about the preacher?"

"Don't worry about him." Arnie opened the bags that'd been tied to the saddle when he met her this evening. He withdrew a blanket and spread it over the soft grasses. "Come sit with me."

"But—"

"It's just for a few minutes." His gaze finally met hers, pleading. "Don't you trust me?"

She hurried to where he'd settled on the blanket.

He patted the spot beside him. "Join me."

A small voice warned her this was not wise, but she ignored it and sat beside the man she loved. "Go on. Rest." She waved for him to lie down. "I'm right here."

His hand found hers as he lay back and his lids fell shut. A moment later, a frown marred his face and he squinted at her. "Where's your ring?"

She tugged her veil free of the collar and dipped her fingers beneath her bodice to unhook the chain. She pulled the ring free and lifted it.

"Put it on." He plucked the glove from her left hand. "I want to see it on you."

Her heart trilled with the possessiveness of his command. The ring had been his mother's. Anyone who saw it would know she was Arnie's intended. She slipped it from the chain and pushed it onto her finger.

He smiled as his eyes drifted closed and he took her hand again. "I don't care what he says. I'm going to build you the biggest house in the city."

He'd told his father about her? Her thoughts tumbled even as she reassured him. "I don't need a big house, just—"

"But you deserve it. *We* deserve it." His brows crunched together. "And I *can* do it." His eyes locked on hers as his grip tightened. "You believe I can do it, don't you?"

"Of course. You're smart and talented and the most charming man I know. You can accomplish anything you set your mind to." She tipped her head. "But I thought you were tired. You said you needed a nap."

His eyes closed, his clasp relaxing. "I do."

Oh, how she longed to hear him say those words before a preacher with her by his side. She ran the gloved fingers of her free hand through his hair. "Then hush. We can talk about this later."

He fell silent and his breathing slowed.

She studied his relaxed features. The curve of his brow, the firm line of his jaw, the soft strokes of his brown lashes against his pale cheeks. Had he truly told his father about her? It didn't make sense. Arnie'd planned their elopement because his father

23

would object to Clarinda as Arnie's fiancée. If he *had* told his father, how had Arnold Walker Senior reacted? It couldn't be positive if they were still eloping instead of planning a wedding.

Would his father accept her once they were married, as Arnie claimed? What if Mr. Walker never accepted her? What if he cut his son from the family fortune? Clarinda wouldn't mind the loss, but would Arnie come to resent her after years of laboring for a living? Would he resent sacrificing the life of luxury he might have had if he'd married a woman his father approved of? She couldn't bear the thought. He was risking so much for her.

He blinked and peered at her through his lashes. "Kiss me goodnight?"

With a smile, she swept her veil aside and shifted so she could lean down. She touched her lips to his, intending a light peck.

He grasped her head, pressing the kiss deeper.

She returned his pressure, her hands braced on the ground on either side of his head.

Keeping one hand to the back of her head, he pressed the other against her back and pulled her on top of him.

She stiffened. *He wants me and he's risking everything for me. Don't I owe him that in return?* She forced herself to relax as his hand moved down her back. *We're getting married. Would a few hours make any difference?*

CHAPTER 3

*R*ichard traced his finger along the black border framing the address penned by his sister's hand. The dark bars framing the envelope were an inch wide—as thick as last week's letter. No doubt Alice would continue using the mourning stationary for the full year expected of a child who'd lost a parent.

He resisted the urge to crumple the envelope. He didn't want to open it. Didn't want to read it. If only he could shred it, burn it. He wanted to take quill in hand and let flow the bitterness her previous letter had sparked with its shocking news.

Mother had passed.

Without warning. With no opportunity to return home and say his farewells.

He'd been informed Mother was ill, but every subsequent letter praised her improved health, declared her impending recovery.

Until last week.

The envelope wrinkled between his pinched fingers.

Alice claimed it was Mother who'd asked his family not to

share anything that might cause him to leave his prosperous business.

It was no excuse. It hadn't been Alice's choice to make.

He ripped open the envelope and extracted the letter within. He was a grown man with a right to make his own decisions.

The paper crunched in his fist.

He bowed his head and closed his eyes. *Take this anger from me, Lord. Help me forgive them.* It wasn't like him to remain angry. The emotion chafed like a pair of new boots. Why couldn't he release this betrayal at the foot of the cross?

He set aside the crumpled correspondence, opened a drawer, and withdrew his Bible. A scrap of brown paper made it easy to find the verses he'd underlined in Ephesians last week.

Let all bitterness, and wrath, and anger, and clamour, and evil speaking, be put away from you, with all malice: And be ye kind one to another, tenderhearted, forgiving one another, even as God for Christ's sake hath forgiven you.

Richard found the book of Matthew and read more marked verses. Again and again, he turned the pages, seeking the words that would steer his heart toward Christ. Eventually, the indescribable peace that comes only from God covered his anger. A final prayer helped him release his hurt to God's hands. He set the Bible aside and returned to the letter.

Roxbury, Mass.,
September 5th, 1857

My dear brother,

Since I last wrote you with the dreadful news of Mother's passing, her funeral has been endured. She is now laid to rest beside Father. The loss of her tenderhearted presence grieves me more than I can express.

I do wish you had been able to return for the ceremony. I can barely keep back my tears as I think of the beautiful words the reverend spoke. You would have been pleased. I know you always enjoyed a good sermon.

Despite her illness keeping her from society this past year, her friends have not forgotten her. So many of them turned out for the ceremony, I could not count them all. Each one had kind words to say about our dear mother, of course. She will be deeply missed and lovingly remembered.

In the midst of this pain, I'm glad to have a bit of cheering news to share with you. I've had a visit from the doctor and he's confirmed that we are to expect another blessing. We anticipate this newest addition will join our small family in the coming summer. We have not told the children yet, for we anticipate quite an argument regarding whether we ought to pray for a boy or a girl.

Richard smiled, genuinely happy for his sister's blessings. Four years ago, he'd been less than certain of her future happiness, but marriage had changed her. Alice's letters reflected a maturity and contentment he attributed to her husband's influence.

As for missing the funeral... Richard's smile dimmed. Alice had known the usual months of delay between her letters being posted and their arrival in his hands—assuming they weren't lost—would rob him of the opportunity to attend. Why didn't she— No. He wouldn't dwell on that.

He returned his attention to the letter.

Now I have some news that will astound you, I think. Certainly, it astounded the rest of us when we learned of it.

27

*Father's solicitor paid us a visit today and you can imagine my
astonishment when he revealed he'd been handling financial
affairs for Mother as well.*

*Without a single one of us knowing, Mother somehow squir-
reled away some savings of her own. And who do you think she
has left it to? You! Every penny is now yours and has been
settled in an account in your name at D.O. Mills and
Company in Sacramento. We understand it is not far from
Nevada City. I cannot imagine it could be more than a very
small sum and won't come close to repaying the money Father
repeatedly stole from you. Nevertheless, it was sweet of her to
try. As Mother's last gift to you, I pray you use it well.*

Your loving sister,
Mrs. Alice Clarke

Richard leaned back in his chair and scanned the letter
again. He must have misread it. Father had been stingy during
his life and left Mother little to live on when he passed. The
bulk of his fortune went to the illegitimate offspring whom no
one was surprised to learn existed. How had Mother come by
enough funds to save anything at all?

He eyed his battered derby waiting on the rack by the door.
The hat kept his head warm and protected. That was all he
required of it, but Mother had held a fondness for nice hats. If
there were enough funds in the account she'd left him, perhaps
he'd purchase a new one in her honor.

~

The crunch of dirt beneath boots woke Clarinda from
slumber. She blinked, and the half moon illuminated
the empty blanket beside her. She jolted upright. "Arnie?"

He was tightening a satchel. "Oh. You're awake." He removed the strap holding her travel bag.

A cool breeze reminded her that only her drawers and chemise protected her lower half from the elements. Her skirts and petticoats were still bunched around her waist. She rose to her knees and tugged them down. Her body ached in a new way as she settled on her heels. Heat seared her cheeks. Why had she given in? Was it always so...? Surely not. It was only their first time. The experience would improve with practice. And there would be plenty of time for that since they were practically married. All that remained was making it official. She had nothing to be ashamed of.

Arnie held out her bag. "Here." There was something odd in his voice. "I'm sure you'll want to change." The warmth was gone.

She clutched the bag to her pounding chest. "Arnie?"

He wouldn't meet her gaze.

"What's wrong?"

Without responding, he returned to their horse.

"Arnie?" She pushed to her feet. "Arnie? What's going on? Why won't you look at me?"

"It's over." His voice cracked as the words sliced through her. "Father's won." He jammed his foot in the stirrup and swung himself into the saddle. "I've put enough coin in your bag to buy you a ticket home."

She stumbled toward him. A ticket? What was he talking about? They were in the middle of nowhere. Why wouldn't he look at her? "I don't understand. What are you—?"

"Goodbye, Clarinda."

Goodbye? "No, wait." Clarinda reached for his pant leg, but he nudged the horse sideways, evading her grasp. "Wait! Where are you going?"

"I'm sorry, Clarie." Arnie circled the horse to face the direction they'd come. "I can't do this." He kicked his mount into a run.

"Arnie!"

CHAPTER 4

*C*larinda tapped on Katie's window as a dull gray dawn lightened the wet fog that had hampered her trudge back to school. Her feet ached from hours of walking, and the hem of her dress was irredeemably soiled and frayed. She poked a finger through the hole in her skirt where it'd torn when she tripped. Her petticoat peeked through the slit. Clarinda sank further into the shadows created by the large lilac bushes lining the south side of the school building.

Why wasn't Katie responding? Clarinda lifted her hand to tap again.

Hoofbeats broke the stillness.

Arnie! She dashed to the end of the building nearest the main drive and skidded to a stop.

The milkman stood at the kitchen door with one hand holding a lantern, the other poised to knock. Behind him, his horse waited, hitched to a loaded cart.

She jumped back, slipping between the bushes. Had he seen her? She peeked around the corner as he knocked.

The door opened.

"Mornin', miss. Got yer milk for you."

The cook's voice wafted on the thinning fog. "Thank you. If you'll bring it inside…"

Their voices faded.

Clarinda exhaled. He hadn't seen her.

She scurried to Katie's window and tapped again.

You are every kind of fool, Clarinda Humphrey. You're still hoping your knight will come riding back to save you. Face it. He abandoned you.

He panicked. It was a moment of weakness.

He used you. You must have disappointed him. He doesn't want to marry you or he wouldn't have—

The blessed swoosh of curtains being drawn saved Clarinda from the voices warring in her mind.

Katie's eyes widened and she waved for Clarinda to move toward the servant's entrance.

Moments later, the door creaked open and Katie yanked Clarinda inside. "What happened?" Katie whispered.

Clarinda opened her mouth, but she couldn't push the shame past her lips.

The flicker of Katie's candle danced across the walls of the narrow hallway as she inspected Clarinda from her mud-caked hem to her tattered veil. She grabbed Clarinda's hand and led her through the darkened school, up the stairs, and into Clarinda's room.

Katie shut the door without a sound and turned. Her eyes shimmered with tears and her voice shook. "Did he hurt thee?"

Clarinda shook her head. He'd left wounds deeper than any of those her scars now covered. But he hadn't hurt her in the way Katie meant. Whatever else he'd done, she couldn't let Katie believe that of him. "I'm fine. I—" Her voice choked.

Katie set the candle on Clarinda's desk and opened her arms. "There now. Let it all out."

Clarinda muffled her sobs against Katie's shoulder until the torrent eased. At last, she pulled back, still sniffling. "I'm sorry. I've soaked your bodice."

"Nonsense." Katie eased her onto the bed. "Now, tell me what happened."

"Oh, Katie, I'm such a fool." She twisted the ring beneath her glove. "I thought we were getting married. I let him…"

"Oh, hun. And then he left thee?"

Clarinda dropped her gaze to the floor and gave a small nod.

"And thee still wear his ring?" Katie snatched Clarinda's hand, yanked the glove off, and stole the precious jewelry from her finger.

"What are you doing?" Clarinda grabbed for the ring.

Katie hid it behind her back. "That pigeon-head doesn't deserve thou."

"Give me back my ring."

"*His* ring, thee mean." She backed toward the door. "I'll not have thee pining over him. I'll take it to the coward." She jerked open the door and whispered, "Tell him where to put it, too."

Clarinda's mouth hung open as the door clicked shut.

~

*R*ichard stood in a muddy side-alley beside the bank. His hands shook as he gaped at the letter handed to him minutes before. A letter Mother had written. According to the bank owner, she'd sent it to the bank, along with a staggering sum of money, more than six months prior.

All those times she'd insisted he save his money—that she didn't need it—she'd been telling the truth. About that, at least. But what confounded him was *why* she hadn't needed it.

All his life he'd seen his mother as an angel whose trusting heart had bound her to Abner Stevens—a man so blinded by his wicked desires he couldn't appreciate the precious gift his wife was.

Never had Richard imagined his mother capable of breaking her wedding vows. But not only did she confess to doing so, she claimed to have been the *first* to do so. She swore it only happened once and with a man she'd loved long before she met Father. A man she was told had perished at sea. By the time she learned the man had survived the wreck, it was too late. She'd wed Father and meant to honor her vows. Then one night, she found herself alone with the man she loved. She'd given in to temptation.

Mother wrote that it was knowledge of her infidelity and that her love belonged to another that drove Father to find comfort in drink and the arms of other women.

Richard pressed his hand against the brick wall as the world tilted beneath him.

All his life, he'd wondered why Father hadn't offered Richard the same attention and affections he'd given Richard's two older brothers. Finally, he understood. Father had known what Richard did not.

Richard was not Abner's son.

~

JANUARY 28, 1858
BENICIA, CALIFORNIA

*T*hough her stomach had no contents to expel, Clarinda leaned over the bowl on her bedroom floor and retched again. She'd been sick every morning for the past two weeks. If her cousin, Fletcher, didn't arrive soon, Miss Leming would send for the doctor again. Clarinda wasn't certain she could fool him a second time.

The first time, she'd convinced Katie to prepare a steaming hot bath in a storage closet. Wrapped in wool blankets, Clarinda breathed in the steam until her face grew red and her body hot.

With Katie as lookout, Clarinda retreated to her room in time to greet the doctor. The effect of her steaming was enough to convince the poor man she'd caught an ague. He ordered bed rest until the symptoms passed and threatened to return if her fever didn't break the next day. Of course, the steaming effects didn't last long, but with her continued stomach troubles, Miss Leming was threatening to send for the doctor anyway.

Clarinda took a long, slow breath. She needed to get her body under control.

Someone knocked at the door. "Clarinda?" *Katie.*

"What is it?"

"Miss Leming sent me to check on thou. May I come in?"

On all fours, bent over the putrid-smelling bowl, Clarinda wore only her night shift—no gloves covered her hands, no veil hid her face. No one could see her like this. "No—" Clarinda's body heaved again.

The knob turned, but the chair Clarinda had wedged against it prevented Katie from entering. "Clarinda? Are thee all right?"

"I'm fine." She gasped between dry heaves. "Just leave me be."

"Thee don't sound fine." Concern laced her dear friend's voice. "Please let me in. I can help thou."

"There's nothing you can do."

"At least let me pray with thou."

As if that would do any good. So far as Clarinda could tell, the God who'd created the universe didn't concern Himself with the lives of His creations. She didn't understand why Katie persisted in believing He did. If that were true, He'd have saved Katie from her cruel father and Clarinda from the attack that had ruined her life.

He'd done neither.

And now she'd missed her womanly bleeding last month. She knew what it meant. The shame she'd brought on herself. She'd be facing it alone, save for Fletcher's unwavering support.

Hopefully, her cousin was even now crossing the bay from

San Francisco. She'd received no letter in response to her written plea for help, but Fletcher wouldn't waste time with such. He could arrive as fast as any letter he sent. Surely he was on his way. He must be. She couldn't ask Katie for more help. Her dear friend had risked enough to help her. Too much. Clarinda's elbows wobbled. What would become of Katie if she lost her job here?

"Clarinda?" Katie rattled the door.

"I'm fine now. Going to sleep." Clarinda's middle tightened again, but she focused all her strength on controlling her breathing. Slow breath in, long breath out.

"Yer sure thee don't—"

"I'm sure." Biting out the words threatened her tenuous control of her gut. She took another breath and gradually released it.

At last, Katie's footsteps shuffled away.

Clarinda fell onto her haunches. Her eyes drifted to the light penetrating the lace curtains. Since her return, she'd snuck away to their alcove every chance she could—hoping to find Arnie waiting. He hadn't returned to the school.

Her stomach heaved again. *Oh Arnie, how could you do this to me?*

CHAPTER 5

larinda watched as a short, narrow plank pushed out from the Benicia ferry like a tongue reaching for shore. Bright afternoon sun bounced off the waters of the Carquinez Strait. She squeezed Fletcher's hand as they stepped across the platform to the ship's deck. The minute sway of the wooden floor unsettled her stomach. She swallowed against the pressure climbing her throat. Striding to the rail, she sucked in long, slow breaths of the crisp afternoon air.

Fletcher joined her, his dark brow puckered over his green eyes. "Are you all right?"

She nodded. Speaking might break her delicate control.

Since missing her monthly bleeding, it seemed her body had declared war against her. Her breasts were swelling at a painful rate, her digestive system had gone mad, and she couldn't sleep at night, but struggled to stay awake during the day. Nausea hounded her most of every day. She never knew if the few bites of food she took would stay down, but Katie insisted Clarinda keep trying.

Of course, Katie was right. No matter how tempting it was to lie down and let death take her rather than face the fate she'd created for herself, life wasn't about Clarinda anymore.

Gripping the rail, she stared at the farthest point she could see. There was a new life growing inside her that hadn't asked to be made—hadn't asked to be given an unwed mother too hideous to be loved. This precious life had done no wrong and deserved better. A better mother. A better life than the one Clarinda could offer.

The now familiar thought pushed its way into her mind—should she secretly deliver the child to an orphanage? Bile surged up her throat. Her cheeks bulged with the effort of keeping it down.

"Quick, lean over the water." The slight panic in Fletcher's voice as he pressed her into the rail would have made her laugh under any other circumstance. As it was, she could find no humor in her situation.

"Hadn't you better remove your veil?"

She shook her head. How could he suggest such a thing with so many people around?

Fletcher made a sound of annoyance. "Why are you so—?"

"Not now." She closed her eyes, her strength too focused on calming her middle to endure another round of Fletcher's arguments against her veil. He'd never agreed with her parents' edicts that she be covered at all times. But he hadn't been the one to endure the stares, the whispers, nor—worst of all—the children who screamed and ran from her in terror. Would her own child fear her? No, her younger sister had never feared her.

"Fine. I'll see if I can find a private room or somewhere you might have a bit of privacy and remove that wretched thing." Fletcher stormed away.

What had he told his parents about her decision to leave

school? Fletcher had assured her they knew she was coming and were looking forward to seeing her, but that seemed unlikely. They'd told everyone their move to San Francisco four years ago was a business decision, but Clarinda knew gaining distance from their socially-outcast niece hadn't displeased them.

Despite her parents' letters explaining Clarinda's condition, she could still remember the look of revulsion on her aunt's face the day her family had arrived in San Diego. To his mother's vexation, Fletcher had been Clarinda's sole advocate from the day they met. Losing his companionship when his family moved left a hole in her lonely childhood no one had tried to fill.

Two men shuffled closer to her, one pointing at something on the shore. Their stench of whiskey, smoke, and sweat drove her toward the bow of the ship.

~

*S*everal feet from the other passengers, Richard stood near the bow of the Benicia ferry as it cut through the rippling waters of the bay. He squinted past the sunlight winking off the water and peered into the murky depths below. What would it be like to live his life at sea? To meet his death there?

Now that he'd given Tommy management of the mine, Richard didn't have to stay in Nevada City. He could go anywhere, do anything. But the life of a sailor held little appeal.

His natural father—a Mr. Geoffrey Childs of Boston, Massachusetts—had died of malaria on a ship in the south Atlantic less than a year after Richard's birth. In Geoffrey's will, he'd named Richard the heir to his shipping company. Since then it had been managed by Simeon Childs, Geoffrey's twin brother.

Richard rested his forearms on the damp wood railing. It was odd to think he had an uncle he'd never met.

According to his mother's letter, Simeon had been sending Mother an allowance all these years—money she'd saved for Richard. Yet Simeon had been instructed not to contact Richard until after her death. The value of the shipping company, added to Mother's savings, and combined with the profits from Prosperity Mine brought Richard's total financial worth to a staggering sum.

What would he ever do with so much?

His gaze shifted west, seeking San Francisco's wharf, though it wouldn't be visible until they rounded a bend in the bay. He pressed a hand against his pocket. The letters within crinkled. *Lord, give Mr. Davidson words of wisdom to guide me.*

Henry Davidson was the only other man Richard knew who came close to possessing such a sum—the only one he trusted, at any rate—which was why Richard had immediately written, requesting advice. He didn't disclose the full details of his inheritance. There was no reason to soil Mother's good name, even if she had passed beyond a place of caring. He merely stated that he'd received an unexpected and large inheritance. The kind entrepreneur had responded with an invitation for Richard to visit.

Would Geoffrey Childs have been so welcoming? What had the man been like? Did Richard look like him? Was that why Richard had never been able to pinpoint who'd given him the unique shape of his nose? While everyone else in his family had noses as smooth as Michelangelo's David, Richard's nose was narrow and straight with the tiniest bump that better resembled Bernini's David—though with less of a hook at the end. It was something he'd noticed in his youth, but his mother had always dismissed his question with the claim that he must have inherited it from a distant ancestor. Richard released a mirthless laugh.

How would Simeon respond if Richard requested a likeness of Geoffrey? Richard had sent a letter of introduction, but it likely hadn't reached Massachusetts yet. His uncle must have worked hard to make the shipping company such a success. If Richard returned to Boston to see the business he now owned, would his uncle resent the sudden intrusion of a near stranger? Most likely, he would.

Someone moaned to Richard's right.

Three feet away, a woman in a green traveling gown grasped the rail. Her face was clouded by an ivory veil tucked into her high collar. She pressed a gloved hand to her abdomen and moaned.

"Are you all right, miss?"

She nodded, but her intake of breath was loud and its slow exhale, deliberate.

The woman must be experiencing seasickness. It was unusual on the calm waters of the bay, but not unheard of. He wished there were something—

He blinked. The peppermint sticks he'd packed as a surprise for the Davidson and Clarke children! He lifted his bag from its place at his feet. He rummaged through the contents, extracted a piece of candy from its paper bundle and held it out.

Behind the filmy fabric, her gaze flicked from the candy to him. Her brows lifted in question.

"It's peppermint. It'll help with the seasickness."

Another second passed before she reached for the candy. "Thank you."

Her soft voice nudged something inside him. He studied her as she turned her back to him. Her movements suggested she was untucking the bottom of the beautiful-but-strange veil.

He'd never seen anything like it. If it were black, he might think it a fashionable mourning veil, but the lace was cream. And an embroidered floral pattern on the garment obscured one-third of her face. Then there was the fact she'd turned her back to him before untucking it. She must wear the garment for other reasons.

Did she fear recognition? But no, such an unusual accessory would draw attention rather than dissuade it. Disfigurement, then. She must be hiding a terrible flaw in her appearance. Yet, the part of her face visible through the thin veil was striking in its beauty. What had she been through that compelled her to disguise herself?

He waited for her to face him again.

The bay's waves slapped against the hull of the ship. A seagull cried. Laughter burst from the other end of the ferry.

She didn't turn.

He stuffed his hands into his pockets. "Is it helping?"

"Yes, thank you."

"I have more if you need them."

She nodded, still keeping her face turned away.

A tall, dark-haired man came striding across the deck. "There you are. I was worried when you weren't where I'd left you. I—" The newcomer pivoted toward Richard. "Oh, hello. I'm Fletcher Johnson and"—he gestured to the mystery woman —"this is my cousin, Miss Humphrey."

Richard accepted the man's outstretched hand. "Richard Stevens. Pleased to meet you both." He glanced to Miss Humphrey, but her body remained averted.

Mr. Johnson's attention returned to his cousin. "There aren't any private rooms available, but if you want to sit, there are plenty of chairs inside."

Miss Humphrey shook her head. "The cool breeze helps."

Again something stirred inside Richard at her soft reply.

Mr. Johnson cocked his head. "What's that you've got?"

"Peppermint." Richard forced his attention to her cousin. "She's suffering a touch of seasickness and I happened to have a bit of candy. I thought it might help."

"That was kind of you. Where are you headed?"

"San Francisco."

"On business?"

"Yes and no. I'm visiting a friend." The ferry rocked over the wake of a passing ship, and Richard shifted his weight. "What about the two of you?"

"Well, I live in San Francisco, but I just fetched my cousin from school. She"—Mr. Johnson drew out the *e* sound as if searching for his next words—"needed a break, and I'm escorting her home for a visit with my family."

"That sounds like a pleasant trip." Richard issued the expected reply, though instinct told him there was more to their story. Not that it was any of his business. He tried to catch Miss Humphrey's attention. "Are you able to stay long or will you need to hurry back to school?"

"That remains to be seen." Mr. Johnson adjusted his stance so he partially blocked Richard's view of Miss Humphrey. "What sort of business are you in?"

That was a more complicated question than the man realized. "I own the Prosperity Mine in Nevada City, and I've recently inherited a shipping business based in Boston."

Mr. Johnson whistled, his brows rising. "Is that so? Profitable?"

"So I'm told. I don't know much about it yet."

The man's green eyes held a swarm of questions, but to his credit, he didn't pry. "What about your mine? Was that an inheritance as well?"

Richard dove into an explanation of his mining experience and Mr. Johnson peppered him with questions. The man's friendly, curious nature bolstered Richard's mood. Before he knew it, the sun was dipping below the horizon and the ferry approached a dock near the foot of San Francisco's Market Street.

He turned to see whether Miss Humphrey had noticed their arrival, but she wasn't there. When had she moved away? He scanned the deck. There. Slumped in a nearby chair. Her head rested at an awkward angle against the wall and her eyes were closed. The seasickness must have worn her out.

Fletcher, as the man had invited Richard to call him, strolled across the deck and nudged his cousin's shoulder. She startled and would have fallen from her seat had Fletcher's reflexes been any slower. Richard ran a hand over his mouth to smother his chuckle.

Her head snapped in his direction.

Apparently, he'd been heard. He shrugged with what he hoped was an apologetic expression—despite the smile he could feel on his face. He couldn't help it. The crooked tilt of her bonnet was comical.

She straightened the hat and ran her fingers over her collar as if to check her veil was still secured. It was.

Fletcher said something to Miss Humphrey as the ferry settled into place, and she shrugged.

He returned to Richard. "She's exhausted. Once we've secured our belongings, I'm going to see about hiring transport to my family's home. Would you mind staying with her while I do so? I don't want to make her walk more than necessary."

That was considerate of him. "It would be my honor."

~

*C*larinda placed a gloved hand over her middle, grateful to be on solid ground once more. Well, almost. At least the dock didn't sway.

She stared into the bustling crowd as twilight settled over the restless city. *Where are you, Fletcher?* He'd disappeared several minutes ago in search of a dray, leaving the talkative Mr. Stevens to guard her and their belongings.

As if she needed a stranger's protection.

Grumpy as she was, entertaining a stranger with small talk held no appeal. And no matter how splendidly he and Fletcher had bonded aboard ship, the man *was* still a stranger to her. An irritatingly cheerful stranger whose infernal grin was apparently an insufficient expression of his good cheer.

He'd now taken to whistling.

She imagined yanking the glove from her right hand and stuffing it into his mouth. Perhaps the thought wasn't charitable of her considering his kindness in sharing his peppermint, but the image was so satisfying, she barely noticed the tickling around her knees.

Mr. Stevens leaned toward her with a silly grin. "I think he likes you."

"Huh?"

He nodded toward her skirts.

She glanced down and froze. Her lungs quit working. Every muscle in her body tensed. A large, brown beast was pressing its filthy muzzle into her dress.

She spun and ran.

Folds of fabric tangled with her legs. She snatched them up as she charged through the crowd.

A small man carrying a large crate stepped into her path. She ducked to squeeze past him.

A line of men waiting at the foot of a gangplank blocked her path.

Bark! The dog's vicious clamoring drew closer.

She shoved her way through the men.

"Hey!"

Splash!

She glanced back.

A small crowd peered over the edge of the dock.

Her steps faltered. Had she knocked someone into the bay?

The mutt squeezed through the group, its beady eyes trained on her.

She swallowed a scream and yanked her attention forward.

Someone shouted, "Look out!"

A crate-filled cargo net loomed in front of her.

She ducked. Her bonnet snagged, ripping the veil from her face. She slapped her hand over her scars as she skidded to a stop and whirled. Her hat hung from the side of the net. The veil drooped from its side.

The beast leapt atop the netted cargo, panting. *Bark!*

She spun away, sprinting again.

The crowd thickened.

She forced her way through. "Pardon me!" The stench of unwashed bodies caused bile to rise up her throat. She swallowed it down. "Let me by!"

On the other side of the crowd, she glanced back. She couldn't see the dog, but his barks indicated he wasn't far behind.

Seconds later, she reached the end of the dock. Her legs shook, threatening to drop her. She couldn't keep this up. But what else could she do?

A large pyramid of crates caught her attention, like a beacon in a storm. Darting around its base, she searched for a way up the steep stack. There was a small ledge where the crates didn't line up. She hauled herself up two layers of the stack and squeezed into a small gap between boxes.

She struggled to control her panting. Her ears strained for sounds of the dog's continued pursuit. The rumble of passing wagons, pounding hammers, yammering people, and crying seagulls drowned out all else.

She stuck her head out, scanning the ground for signs of the dog. Her stomach heaved and bile surged up her throat. She clamped her lips shut and forced herself to swallow. Willing her body to calm, she sucked air through her nose.

Passersby gave her odd looks.

She jerked back. Cringing, she clamped her hand over her scars. How could she have forgotten she was uncovered? How many people had seen her hideous face as she ran for her life? She swiped her sleeve across her mouth.

A canine whimpered nearby.

Clarinda held her breath. Would the beast find her?

"Is she up there, boy?"

Mr. Stevens? Clarinda opened her mouth to call for the man, but her throat was too tight, her breathing too rapid.

The scrape of claws on wood forced a strangled scream from her.

Several thumps followed, growing louder with each second.

This was it. She was going to die.

Her hand covered her abdomen. She couldn't give up without a fight. She needed a weapon. She scoured the narrow confines of her hiding place. Scratched at the sides of the rough crates.

There. A crack in the wood. But it wouldn't come loose. *Come on, Clarinda. Think!*

Her shoes! She shifted onto her back so her booted heels aimed at the opening nearest the approaching sounds.

CHAPTER 6

*R*ichard tossed a hunk of jerky for the large pup, who'd enjoyed the merry chase along the dock. The brown dog abandoned his search of the piled crates to snatch the jerky and dash away, unaware of the sheer terror he'd instilled in his playmate.

Richard studied the piled cargo. A bit of green fabric dangled from an opening near the top. Why wasn't she coming out? Was she hurt? He scaled the mound and peered into the gap.

Something hard smashed into his nose, shoving his head backward. Pain shot through his face and he toppled off the pile with a screech.

His body slammed into the hard-packed earth with a thud. He lay there a moment, his cramped lungs screaming for air until they relaxed. With a gasp, he surged to a sitting position. Something wet trickled from his nose. He fished his handkerchief from his pocket and stemmed the flow of blood.

Emerald skirts fluttered into view. Miss Humphrey sank to her knees in front of him. Her gentle hands came to rest on his.

"Oh my! I'm so sorry. I thought you were the—" Miss Humphrey's head swiveled to scan the area. "Is it gone?"

His gaze fixed on the thin, jagged scars crisscrossing her left cheek and disappearing into the left side of her collar. *This* was what she'd been hiding? The faded marks were nothing compared to her elegant bone structure, golden brow, and adorably rosy cheeks. Did she know how vibrant her blue eyes shone in the sunlight? His focus drifted to her pale pink lips. Would they taste of peppermint if he—Whoa! Where had that thought come from?

"I don't see it." Miss Humphrey's strained voice sobered his thoughts.

He glanced to where the pup had disappeared into the crowd. "Seems to be gone." His voice came out more nasally than usual. He gingerly prodded the bridge of his nose. It didn't *feel* broken. Like a disobedient child, his gaze returned to her face. "Why do you hide yourself?"

With a gasp, her hand flew to cover the scars. Tears filled her eyes. "Don't be cruel."

"What are you talking about?"

"You saw perfectly well the reason."

He reached for her, but his senses kicked in before he made contact. He barely knew this woman. "Miss Humphrey, you are a beautiful woman. Hiding behind that veil is doing the world a disservice."

She pushed to her feet, hand still clasped over the side of her face. "Just stop it."

"Stop what?" He rose to stand in front of her.

"Lying to make me feel better."

"I'm not. I—"

"Clarinda!" Fletcher jogged toward them. "What happened? Where's your veil?"

Miss Humphrey collapsed into her cousin's open arms. "Oh, it was awful. That horrid beast chased me. I was so sure it would catch me. And it almost did." Her voice grew muffled as she buried her face in the man's jacket. "I could've died!"

"Shh." Fletcher's expression softened as he stroked his cousin's hair. "It's all right now. It's over." He scanned their surroundings. "The dog is gone. Nothing's going to hurt you."

The fact that Fletcher knew, without asking, exactly what sort of beast Miss Humphrey was referring to spoke volumes. The jagged scarring, combined with her irrational response to the dog's attention and Fletcher's immediate understanding, could only mean one thing. At some point in her life, this beautiful woman had been viciously attacked by a canine.

Richard studied the woman through the deepening dusk. Her scars were so faint. It must've been several years since the attack. But it was clear the trauma was still raw.

Lord, heal her wounds.

He stuffed the bloodied kerchief in his pocket and wiped his hands on his trousers. With a scowl, he retrieved her bonnet and veil from a nearby crate. As he'd followed in the dog's wake, he'd snatched the items from where they'd snagged. Then he'd laid them on the box before tossing the dog his jerky. He should have left the garments where they'd come off her. She didn't need them.

He eyed the hand still covering her cheek.

But she wanted them.

Richard lifted the accessories into Miss Humphrey's view.

She seized the items and—in a move that was becoming too familiar—turned her back to settle them into place. Moments later, she faced him. The only part of her skin still visible peeked through a small tear in the right side of the garment. "Thank you, Mr. Stevens. I appreciate your assistance and hope I haven't caused you too much pain."

Fletcher's eyes widened. *"You did that?"*

Richard tried to detect the brilliant blue of her eyes through the veil. It was impossible. The fabric and shadows rendered them a dull gray. He forced his lips upward. "My pleasure, Miss Humphrey."

"Yes, well..." Her words trailed off.

Fletcher narrowed his gaze on Richard. "Is there something I should know?"

Miss Humphrey placed a staying hand on her cousin's shoulder. "Just a misunderstanding. I thought he was the beast."

Fletcher burst out laughing.

Richard tried to scowl, but couldn't stop his lips from twitching upward. "Gee, thanks for your sympathy."

Fletcher clapped him on the back. "Glad to hear it. Listen, I've enjoyed speaking with you. Maybe—"

"Weren't you finding us a dray, Fletcher?"

"Oh, right. I did and he's probably finished loading our things." He turned toward the end of the dock. "Yes. There he is. We'd better go." He faced Richard. "As I was saying, why don't you—"

"Come, cousin." Miss Humphrey dragged her cousin in the direction of the dray. "Let's not keep the man waiting."

$\sim$

The drayman pulled to a stop in an alley darkened by full night. Clarinda nibbled her lip. His lantern splashed light across loose, unpainted siding holding up shadowed stacks of empty crates beside black piles of something that reeked of rot. This was her aunt and uncle's new home? Perhaps it looked better in the light of day.

She sniffed and winced. Had someone relieved themselves nearby?

Fletcher hopped down and turned to assist her.

She accepted his raised hand. "I thought you told your parents I was coming."

"I did." Fletcher paid the drayman. "There's more for you if you'll wait here a moment. I shall be down shortly to collect her trunk."

"I can carry it up for you, sir."

"No, thank you. I think I'd better go in and let them know we've arrived first. Will you wait?"

The drayman tipped his hat. "Yes, sir."

Fletcher lifted her bag from the dray.

Clarinda whispered, "Why are we sneaking in through the rear?"

"We're not. This is the only entrance." The nearest unpainted door groaned as he opened it.

Clarinda followed him into a dingy, narrow stairway. A single candle flickered within a pierced-tin lantern hanging just inside. Perhaps someone expected them after all.

Fletcher lifted the lantern from its hook and his body blocked the light. She trailed behind in the near pitch-black. The musty odor of mold filled her nostrils.

"How long until the new shop is finished?" She'd known her cousin's family had struggled since their storefront had burned in a fire last autumn. Having lived above the shop, they'd not only lost their business, but their personal belongings and their home. Yet when they'd found this new building to rent last month, Fletcher made it sound as though their life had returned to normal.

The step beneath her foot cracked, and she froze.

Fletcher pivoted. "Sorry, forgot to warn you to skip that one. Landlord keeps promising to fix it, but he hasn't got round to it. Suppose I'll have to see to it tomorrow." He offered her a hand.

She accepted and stepped past the broken step. Moisture soaked through the fabric of her glove where she'd gripped the rail a moment ago.

"It's not as bad as it seems. Wait until we get inside. Mom's done a great job fixing up the place." He swung open the door at the top of the stairs and held it for her.

Clarinda gaped at the sight of a stove on the opposite wall. Their front door opened to their kitchen?

"Good, you're home." Her aunt's voice drew Clarinda's attention to the extraordinary number of people crammed into the small room. Far more than her cousin's family were crowded onto the settee, chairs, and an upturned crate clustered to one side of the space.

Her aunt rose and hurried to help Fletcher remove his coat. "You're later than I expected. I was beginning to worry."

Fletcher laughed and kissed his mother's head. "You worry too much." He entered a short hallway. "I'm going to put Clarinda's bag in her room and head back down for her trunk." He disappeared through one of three doors.

"Her trunk?" Clarinda's aunt's brow wrinkled as she finally addressed Clarinda. "I thought you were here for a few days. Don't you need to return to school?"

Clarinda's fists clenched. It was just like Fletcher to offer her a place to stay without seeking his parent's permission first. She should have known. "I...uh..."

Fletcher reappeared in the hallway. "She's taking a break from school, remember?"

"Yes, but—"

"Come on, let me introduce you." Fletcher grabbed Clarinda's hand and led her to the group of people who'd been gawking at her throughout the awkward exchange.

~

*R*ichard sprinted up the long dirt road, shrouded in a thick white fog. Endless stacks of barrels and crates lined both sides.

He paused to shove several boxes down. There was nothing but more fog behind them.

He spun and ran down the road. More crates toppled to the earth. Nothing there either.

His chest heaved, muscles aching. His legs trembled, threatening to give out. He'd been searching for so long. He couldn't keep this up, but he had to find...

He fisted his hair, tugging at its roots. What was he looking for?

A disembodied voice answered his unspoken question. "Clarinda."

Richard bolted upright in bed. *Clarinda?* Who was Clarinda? And why had he heard her name in his dream?

CHAPTER 7

*C*larinda checked the clock on the shelf. Almost midnight. Each member of this motley household had trickled away as the night grew long, but Clarinda's uncle remained. He'd been hunched over his accounts, quill in hand for the past hour.

Wasn't he tired? She certainly was. But she needed a private word with her dear cousin. How could he have failed to mention another family shared this apartment with his? With her aunt, uncle, Fletcher, and his fifteen-year-old sister, Ada, that amounted to eight people residing in a space that couldn't be more than fifteen feet wide and thirty feet long.

The Enrights seemed nice enough, but how could so many people live in such a tiny place? She'd heard of multiple families packed into small apartments back east, but she'd never witnessed such a situation first hand. Nor had she thought such things troubled the wide open land of California. She'd never imagined her aunt and uncle faced such poverty.

At last, her uncle stood. "I'm off to bed. See you in the morning, Clarinda. Fletcher."

She and Fletcher bid him a good night as he shambled down the hall.

"Well, guess I'd better grab my blanket." Fletcher turned to follow his father. "I—"

Clarinda snagged his arm and whispered, "Not so fast." She waited until the last door closed down the hall, leaving her alone in the main room with Fletcher, before rounding on him. "You didn't tell them I was coming. And you lied to me."

Fletcher stiffened. "I never lied to you."

Clarinda kept her voice low, suspecting sound traveled easily through the thin walls. "You told me your family's situation had improved—that you were living almost as you were before the fire."

"We are. It's just—"

"Don't tell me you shared a tiny upstairs apartment with a whole other family before the fire." She surveyed the faded, second-hand furniture, the worn, unpainted wallboards, and the ancient stove set right in the middle of it all. They didn't even own enough chairs. Mr. Enright and Fletcher had had to sit on upturned crates during their evening meal. "I know better, remember? I visited on my way to school two years ago."

"Well, we almost did." Fletcher huffed. "The Enrights owned the shop next to ours and a single wall separated our home from theirs. We could hear their daughter scampering around at all hours of the day and night."

Now that he mentioned it, she could recall the pattering of little feet in the apartment adjacent to theirs, but only when she stood in certain rooms of their home. That apartment had been a palace compared to the one they lived in now. It had consisted of two parlors, a dining room, four bedrooms, and a separate kitchen. And they hadn't shared it with anyone.

Fletcher threw his hands up. "They lost almost as much as we did when the fire broke out. Their home and shop were as uninhabitable as ours. It made sense for our families to combine what we had left in order to get on with things."

Fletcher paced to the window, his back to her. She shouldn't have mentioned the fire. It had been Fletcher's desire to set out on his own that forced her uncle to hire another man to help out in the shop. That man left a candle burning when he departed one night, causing the fire. Fletcher felt so responsible for the fiasco, he'd returned home to help his family regain their feet.

She could understand why he'd been reluctant to explain the depths of their struggles. Had she known the truth of their situation, she never would have written him of her troubles. She'd known he'd come to her rescue. He always did. Fletcher was her best friend. He would move heaven and earth to aid her.

Clarinda rubbed her left arm as she studied the inadequate space. Her aunt's attempts to cheer the room showed in the bright yellow curtains, colorful rag rugs, and overall cleanliness of the place. Yet, how could Clarinda live here?

As they'd cleared the dishes, her aunt revealed Fletcher had been making his bed in the main living space each night. For Clarinda to have a bed, Ada would give up her half of the one she shared with the Enrights' young daughter. Ada insisted she didn't mind sleeping on the floor, but her sweet cousin was under the impression Clarinda's stay would be less than a week.

She joined Fletcher at the window. "I can't stay here."

"Sure you can. Ada's thrilled to have you here."

"For a *visit*. She has no idea you invited me to stay indefinitely. None of them do." Clarinda flopped onto the closest chair, clamping her hands over her face. "What were you thinking?"

Fletcher pulled a chair closer to hers. "If I told them up front how long you were staying, it would open a box of questions I didn't know how to answer. You did ask me to keep quiet about...everything."

Clarinda stifled a moan. He was right. It would have raised loads of questions. Questions she'd still have to face if she stayed here. Which she couldn't. "Oh, Fletcher. What am I going to do?"

"You're going to have a baby." He leaned back, extending his legs and crossing his ankles. "And you'll be a fine mother."

"Will I?" She raised her face to study him. Everywhere she went, people stared and whispered about her veil. Would her child be mocked or ostracized because of her? Removing her veil only turned the whispers into horrified gasps. Sometimes screams. The frightened children were the worst. "What if my own child is afraid of me?"

"Don't be absurd." Fletcher crossed his arms behind his head. "You aren't *that* beautiful."

She should have known better than to ask the question of Fletcher. He'd never believed in her need to hide—had always insisted her scar was a sign of strength to be worn proudly. But he wasn't the one people pointed at and crossed the street to avoid. He wasn't the one who'd sent children running in terror. "Be serious."

"I am being serious. You're beautiful, kind, intelligent, and determined. You can do anything you set your mind to—including mothering."

"But I'm not married."

"So?"

"So, I don't want that for my child. It's bad enough that he—"

"Or she." Fletcher held up a finger.

"Or she"—Clarinda nodded—"will have me as a mother. To be labeled a—"

Fletcher straightened, a strange gleam lighting his eyes. "So get married."

"Right." She snapped her fingers. "Just like that."

"I'm serious."

"No, thanks." She shifted in her seat, unwelcome memories

of Arnie filling her mind. Nausea threatened to return her small evening meal. She swallowed. "I tried that, remember? Didn't work out."

"I'm not talking about a real marriage."

"What then? A marriage of convenience?"

"No. You don't need to actually *be* married. You just—"

"You're not making any sense." Her brows puckered as fatigue weighted her eyelids. "I thought you just said I should get married."

"If you'd let me finish."

She waved for him to continue, allowing her lids to lower. It had been a long day.

"As I was saying, you don't need to *be* married. You just need to *appear* married."

She squinted one eye at him. "And how do I do that? Wear a fake ring?"

"Yes. Exactly. A ring will announce to the whole world your child is legitimate and not to be shunned." He rubbed his hands together. "At least that coward didn't ask for his ring back." He looked at her hand. "Where is it, anyway?"

She ducked her chin. "I gave it back."

"You what?" Fletcher's voice rose. "You said you hadn't seen him."

"I haven't." She flinched and gestured for him to be quiet. "Katie did it for me."

"Who?"

"My friend. She...it doesn't matter. It's gone." It had taken Katie three days to catch Arnie coming out of his house. His father had followed a minute later and Arnie snatched the ring from Katie's hand. He left before she could give him the tongue-lashing she'd prepared.

He hadn't even asked about Clarinda.

"But you said it was so valuable. You might have at least sold it."

"To who? The whole town would recognize that ring. Just forget about it." Clarinda wrung her gloved hands. "What about your family? They've seen me without a ring. They'd know any marriage I claimed was fake. Do you honestly think your parents would go along with—"

"You're right. Mother's way too pious to tolerate such a scheme." He rolled his eyes. "We'll have to fool them, too."

"But—"

"Give me a minute to think."

Silence reigned so long, Clarinda's eyes drifted shut.

The snap of Fletcher's fingers woke her.

He pointed at her. "We'll say the ring's at the goldsmith's being resized and you're picking it up tomorrow."

"But where would we find a ring that fits on such short notice, let alone pay for one?"

"I'll find you one. Trust me."

"But you haven't any money." Though he'd never said as much, she knew he'd given every cent he had to his parents after the fire, and had been working for the family without pay since. It was the kind of man he was. "And what about my husband? Why isn't he with me?"

Clarinda shook her head. "No. This is ridiculous and will only cause more problems than it solves. Besides, pretending to be married won't solve the problem of where I'll live. We have to think of something else."

Fletcher rose and paced the room, keeping his voice low. "He's too busy working."

Her dear cousin was like a dog with a bone once he got an idea in his head. She might as well play along, though she'd never be able to pull off such a deception. "And how does my clearly devoted husband earn his living?"

Fletcher made a face at her. "Your *desperately* devoted and *wealthy* husband owns a successful mine. Like that man on the ferry. Stevens, remember?"

Who? Oh, right. The man who'd saved her from the dog at the wharf. "But he was traveling. So owning a mine wouldn't preclude him from accompanying his wife if he were married. Is he?"

"I don't think so. At least, he never mentioned a wife. Regardless, from what Richard was saying, every mine runs a bit differently. We'll just tell your family—"

"*My* family?"

"Yes. You're insisting you cannot live here, so returning to San Diego is the logical solution."

Return to the Grand Valley Ranch? She wrapped her arms around her middle. "But—"

"Hush!" Fletcher pivoted to point at her. "Quit interrupting. Let's see..." He tapped his finger on his chin. "Yes, we'll tell everyone your husband owns a large, successful mine and can't take time away to visit now, but *you* wanted to spend time with your family before the baby came."

"And when the baby comes? What then? Don't you think it'll be a bit odd when I give birth and no father shows up to claim his heir?"

"Not if he's dead."

"Wait a minute. Hold on." Clarinda pushed herself to her feet, despite the fatigue. "You want me to pretend, for months, that my husband is too busy to bother visiting his wife or meeting his in-laws, and then claim he died in some tragic accident? No one will ever believe it."

"They will if we offer them proof."

"What proof?" She threw her arms up. "How can we have proof of a man who doesn't exist?"

"His letters, of course."

Clarinda's mouth gaped. This was it. The strain of being her friend despite his mother's discouragement had taken its toll. Fletcher had finally lost his mind.

She set a hand on his shoulder. "Fletcher, I think you should lay down, get some rest. We can figure this out tomorrow."

He shook off her touch with a laugh. "*I'll* write the letters, of course, but I'll sign them in your husband's name."

"Don't you think our families will recognize your hand-writing?"

"Not if"—Fletcher strode across the room and settled into the chair at the writing desk—"I write like this."

He snatched the quill, dipped it in ink, and scribbled a few sentences across the page. He held the results up for her inspection.

Clarinda snatched the paper from his hand. As if holding it herself would somehow change what she saw. The words he'd written, though still elegant and smooth, bore no resemblance to his usual penmanship. Having corresponded regularly with him since his family had moved to San Francisco three years prior, she knew his handwriting.

But this...The *t*'s were crossed too high, the flourishes were all wrong, and the *b*'s and *d*'s were too skinny. If she hadn't witnessed him put pen to paper, she'd never have believed he wrote these words. "How did you do that?"

Fletcher's face took on a pink hue. "Never mind about that. Have I convinced you?"

Clarinda's hand trembled. If she could receive letters from someone who claimed to be her husband, but not actually have to get married...not only would her child avoid the shame of illegitimacy, it would put an end to the pitying looks, give her parents the pride of having their daughter married, and deter any man who found his curiosity caught by her unusual attire.

She'd still be stared at and whispered about for her veil and gloves, but with a ring on her finger, the world would know she was loved—that someone had chosen her. They didn't need to know it was only her cousin who loved her.

"I'll do it."

~

*R*ichard knocked at the door of what would soon be known as The Davidson Home for Women and Children. Henry Davidson had recruited several business partners to support his construction of a place to serve women and children in need. After several months of remodeling, the exterior bore no sign of the building's former life as a melodeon. Located on the outer edges of one of San Francisco's poorest districts, Henry and his wife had chosen this building for its size and proximity to the people they hoped to serve.

Henry opened the door. "You made it!" Morning light bounced off his glasses.

Richard blinked and laughed. "Did you think I'd get lost again?" He'd been on his way to visit this site the day he'd met his secretary, Miss Bennetti—though she was Mrs. Tommy Brigham now and no longer his secretary.

"I admit I had my doubts when you said you wanted to walk over after breakfast."

"I had some thinking to do." He'd been a terrible guest that morning. Half of him had been present and interested in the Davidsons' conversation. The other half remained at the foot of the dock, replaying the moment when Miss Humphrey had dragged her cousin away yesterday.

Her intent had been clear enough. Fletcher had been on the verge of issuing an invitation to Richard but Miss Humphrey was averse to continuing their acquaintance. What Richard couldn't understand was why. There had been nothing unpleasant in their interactions. He'd been a perfect gentleman. Her reaction made no sense, but his mind insisted on trying to puzzle it out. It had taken a long walk through the city to finally clear his mind of the mysterious woman.

"I noticed." Henry ushered him inside. "But we'll talk about that later. First, I'll give you the tour."

Several minutes later, Henry led Richard through the upstairs hallway and into the first room on the right.

"This will be our nursery. The youngest ones will be tended here while their mothers and older siblings are occupied in the classrooms I showed you on the first floor."

Richard took in the simple room painted in a pale blue. Two finely crafted toy boxes sat against the far wall beneath a row of windows, and no less than six cribs lined the walls at either side. "How many do you expect you'll be able to assist at a time?"

"At least six infants and their mothers." The answer came from behind, and Richard turned. His childhood friend, Daniel Clarke, stood in the hallway hefting a rocking chair. Richard stepped aside and Daniel carried the chair into the room. "Plus we've room for half a dozen older children in the rooms down the hall."

It was Daniel's disappearance with Henry's niece, Eliza, into the wilds of Southern California four years ago that led to Richard's introduction to the Davidsons. After marrying Eliza, Daniel returned to San Francisco to work for Henry. Daniel's talents as a carpenter showed in many of the building's recent improvements. No doubt he'd also made the chair he now placed in the center of the room.

"And you plan to pay the women to learn to cook, sew, and care for their own children?" While Richard admired their heart to help the less fortunate, how could they hope to be financially solvent with such a plan?

Henry chuckled. "It's more complicated than that. Many women lack the skills to obtain respectable work. Faced with watching their children go hungry, many make desperate decisions."

That's what had happened to the mother of Henry's adopted daughter. Richard didn't know the full details, but when the mother met a tragic end, the Davidson's took over the girl's care.

Daniel ran his hands along the top rail of a crib. "We'll be teaching the women skills needed for respectable employment"—he examined the crib's spindles as though searching for flaws in his own work—"and providing care for their children while they study, and later, while they work."

Henry plucked a small wooden duck from the rug and tossed it into a toy box. "The orphanages have been overrun with the offspring of mothers faced with either starving or leaving their children unattended while they work."

Richard waved to the space around them. "So this is the solution?"

"We hope so."

Richard surveyed the room, considering all he'd seen on the tour Henry had given him. It was wonderful how close they were to opening their doors to those in need, but what was left for Richard to help with? He'd hoped to find his own place here. Something to ease the nagging restlessness inside him. What could leave more of a mark on the world than aiding women and children in need? But beyond offering his financial support —which he certainly would—there seemed little left for him to do.

He needed more than just sitting behind a desk writing letters and issuing funds. Richard had learned the hard way that he was a man of action. Desk work *could* help others and he loved that. It was why he hadn't sold the mine. But the life-style suited him like an ill-fitted glove. He'd been designed for something different. He just needed to figure out what that was.

Henry crossed his arms. "You seem skeptical."

"It isn't that. It's just..." Richard opened his arms. "I'm happy to donate to your cause—thrilled even. But is there anything left that I can actually *do* for you?"

"I'm not going to lie. I was hoping you'd be interested in investing." Henry clapped him on the shoulder. "But as for something more to do…" He adjusted his glasses. "What did you have in mind?"

"Honestly? I'm not sure." Richard shrugged. "I finally have the freedom I've been wanting since I took over Prosperity, but I have no idea what to do with it."

Daniel patted his shoulder. "You've been praying about it?"

"Of course."

"Then He'll show you the way. You just need to be patient."

Of course what Daniel said was true, but no one was guaranteed another day in this life. If he died tomorrow, what would people say of him? 'Here lies Richard, a man who owned a mine and tormented his little sisters.' Not much of a legacy.

He burned with the desire to know that when he passed on, his life would have meant something—that he'd made a difference with the days given to him, however short or long they might be.

"Daniel?" Eliza entered the room, their one-year-old daughter on her hip. "There you are. The driver is here with the rest of the furniture."

"Oh, good." Daniel stepped forward. "I'll start unloading and get the other rooms set up. How'd the interviews go? Do we have any beds left to fill?"

"I promised our last one to the first woman I spoke with this morning. I didn't expect so many would agree to our requirements."

Richard cocked his head. "Requirements?"

"We have a set of rules for the women's behavior and things they need to do while they're here. Things like modest clothing, no gentleman callers, attending classes, helping with chores, and, of course, attending church." The toddler began to fuss and Eliza stuck her finger in the child's mouth. "They're also expected to donate a small portion of their earnings for the first year after they move out."

"Won't that be difficult?"

"Yes, but it returns a bit of their pride after accepting our help. This way they're helping others in turn." She shifted her daughter to her opposite side. "Still, I didn't think they'd all agree so readily."

Daniel placed a hand at his wife's back. "So you finished your interviews?"

"For the morning. But I promised to speak with three more women this afternoon."

Henry ran his hand through his hair. "We can't help them all. Even if we installed more beds, there aren't the funds to—"

"I know. I just want to start a waiting list in case one of the women doesn't show up when we open in two weeks." A yawn stretched her face. "I'm taking the children out back to play before the next one arrives."

"Oh no you don't." Daniel swooped his daughter from Eliza's hip. "It's time *you* took a nap."

"But they've been cooped up all day, I—"

"I'll look after the children."

"But the furniture—"

"Can wait until you've had a rest."

"Don't be silly." Richard raised his empty hands. "I can unload the furniture. I'm sure Henry will tell me where it all belongs."

Eliza pulled a handkerchief from her sleeve and dabbed at her daughters drool. "But you're our guest. We can't let you—"

"Of course you can. I was just telling your husband how much I want to be of help. In fact, I think your timing is positively providential."

"If you're sure…" Eliza glanced at her husband.

Daniel shifted the toddler to one side and pointed toward the hall. "Use one of the rooms we've finished setting up. I'll wake you in an hour so you're ready for the next round of interviews."

Eliza bit her lip. "Promise?"

67

Daniel wrapped his free arm around his wife's waist and tugged her close. "I promise." He pressed a kiss to her lips then pushed her toward the hall. "Now go."

"All right. The other two children are waiting in the school room. Thank you." Her posture wilted as she smiled. "I love you."

"I love you, too."

She exited the way she'd come.

Daniel gave the toddler his own handkerchief, which she promptly crammed into her mouth and began to chew. He shook a finger in the child's face. "You be quiet now. You kept your mama up all night with your fussing. She needs her rest." He kissed her nose before turning to Richard. "She's got a tooth coming in."

"Ouch." Richard rubbed his jaw.

The girl began to fuss again. Daniel crossed the room and pulled the wooden duck from the toy box. He handed it to his daughter, who began gnawing on its bill. "I appreciate your offer of help, Richard, but it really isn't necessary. The furniture can wait."

"I meant what I said. Just point me in the right direction."

Henry set a hand on Richard's shoulder and steered him toward the hall. "This way."

~

*A*n hour later, Richard paused beside the freight wagon to tip his face to the unusually warm sun. He let his eyes drift closed for a moment. "I hope this weather holds out. I don't know about you, but I'm enjoying the break from winter rains."

Henry grabbed one end of a wooden bedstead and Richard lifted the other.

"It has been pleasant, I suppose. Though I admit I've had

precious little time to enjoy it. Too much work to do. But work's what makes all this"—he gestured to the nearly complete charity building—"possible."

Together, they hauled the bed frame up the steps and into the front hall where they set the piece down to wait as a workman finished hanging a sconce near the foot of the stairs. "I suppose, but don't you ever get tired of being stuck indoors? Don't you ever want to..." Richard searched for the right words. "...get your hands dirty? To feel your muscles ache, not from sitting behind a desk all day, but from getting out there, making something with your own hands?"

"You sound like my brother. He's the doer of our family. Me, I'm the thinker. I find my satisfaction in coming up with new ideas and seeing them through to completion." Henry adjusted his spectacles. "I'm not as good at the doing part, but I've developed the necessary skill of distinguishing a good worker from a slothful one. I'm able to hire the right workers to execute the plans I set before them."

The workman finished his task and removed his ladder from their path.

Richard hefted his end of the furniture again. "I suppose that's where you and I differ."

"I suppose it is, and I think that's a good thing." Henry lifted his end and their conversation paused until they'd reached the top of the stairs. When he spoke again, Henry's voice was low enough to avoid disturbing Eliza. "If God made each of us doers, there wouldn't be the thinkers to create the grand ideas for doers to execute. And if he made each of us thinkers, we'd all be sitting around with wonderful ideas yet lacking the skills to make them a reality."

Richard adjusted his grip. "Well said."

They maneuvered through a doorway and set the bed down in an empty room.

Laughter outside drew Richard to the window. Daniel was

out back playing tag with his three-year-old son and Henry's eight-year-old adopted daughter. Daniel's own daughter sat on a nearby blanket, still gnawing the wooden duck.

A pang struck Richard's chest. He'd expected to be married and have children of his own by now. But how could he begin finding a wife and raising children with this restlessness within him? He may have the funds to provide for a family, but what further promise could he make when he didn't know where he'd be living in a year? His sisters had taught him women generally preferred to know things like that before agreeing to marry a man.

Henry joined him at the window. "Wherever do they find such energy?"

Richard laughed. "They're young."

"Speaking of being young, I had an idea."

"That is your specialty." Richard winked.

Henry missed it. "The lumber industry is booming, and Daniel says there's nothing like working with wood."

"I don't know that I have the talent to do what Daniel does."

"I'm not suggesting you do. But what about getting involved in logging? I know of at least two lumber companies that are poorly managed. The owners would probably be thrilled to be bought out of the business. Are you interested?"

"I don't know. I've never thought about logging before. I do have some experience as a sawyer, but as the owner wouldn't I wind up right where I am—pushing paper behind a desk?"

"Not necessarily. You could hire someone to handle the paperwork for you and spend your days out in the woods. It's not risk free, but it seems less dangerous than mine work."

Richard had confessed in his letter that he'd lost his interest in digging. "I'll have to pray about it. In the meantime, can you tell me how to contact them?"

⁓

*R*ichard lay in bed that night, staring at the ceiling as he'd been doing for the last hour or more. If he fell asleep, would he have another dream? Never in his life had he experienced a dream, a fact he knew made him odd. He'd heard enough men talk about their dreams to let him know *not* having dreams was the unusual thing. He'd even woken a few he'd shared rooms, tents, and caves with over the years from what they called nightmares. The men had cried and shouted in their sleep, making Richard thankful he didn't have to worry about such nonsense.

But now that he'd had one, he couldn't stop thinking about it.

Was it usual for people to hear names in their dreams? He'd never heard anyone else discuss such a dream. They talked of falling from the sky, showing up to school without their clothes on, and being chased by wild animals. But, to his knowledge, no one had heard a name in their dream.

Certainly not a name they couldn't place.

In a voice they didn't recognize.

He shifted beneath the covers. That wasn't true. He *had* recognized the voice. He just...struggled to accept it.

The memory of another man who'd experienced an unusual dream fluttered in Richard's mind. He fumbled for the matchbox and lit the candle on the small table beside his bed. He lifted his Bible and flipped to the book of Matthew. There, in the first chapter, he found the story of Joseph, father of Jesus. Well, he was sort of the father of Jesus. He raised him, cared for him, loved him, but he hadn't contributed his seed to the child.

Richard was struck by the similarity to his own situation. Abner, the man Richard had called *Father* all his life, hadn't contributed his seed to Richard's existence, either. That had been Geoffrey Child's doing. Though Abner had raised Richard and provided for him to a degree, Richard couldn't ever

71

remember Abner telling him he loved him. Only his mother's doting and the affection of his siblings had kept Richard from a loveless childhood.

He began to read. Several lines down, the twenty-fourth verse leapt off the page at him.

Then Joseph being raised from sleep did as the angel of the Lord had bidden him, and took unto him his wife.

And took unto him his wife. The words echoed in Richard's mind. Had God given him the name of his wife? The thought settled like truth in his soul. Yes. That must be exactly what He had done. But how was Richard to find her?

CHAPTER 8

$\mathcal{I}$ t took Richard a full week to recall where he'd heard the name, Clarinda. Not until a stray dog ran across his path did he remember Fletcher shouting the name after his cousin took her mad dash across the wharves.

It was *her*. The beautiful woman hiding beneath that strange veil was Clarinda Humphrey.

And she'd wanted nothing more to do with him.

Richard set his jaw. Well, he'd just have to change her mind.

Once he found her.

He approached the fourth door that morning. *Lord, please let this be the right Johnson family.*

When he'd set out yesterday to find the cousins Clarinda was staying with, he'd had no idea there were so many Johnsons living in San Francisco. He'd thought it would help that he knew the family owned a shop, but he'd failed to ask Fletcher what sort of goods they sold. In the *1858 San Francisco Directory and Business Guide*, there were nearly a dozen Johnsons who ran shops of some kind, and another half dozen whose occupations were unlisted.

While the Davidsons and Clarkes were busy with the

opening of their charity house, Richard had slogged his way to the doors of the first half dozen families yesterday with no success. Two families had moved away, one address was nothing but a frame built atop the ash heap of its predecessor, and the rest had no relation named Humphrey.

He gave three firm raps to the wooden door and stepped back to wait. This morning Richard had received a response from one of the logging company owners with an invitation to visit in three days. If he didn't find Clarinda soon…

A brown-haired woman answered with one babe on her hip and another child tugging at her skirts, while a third wailed from somewhere within. The harried woman pushed at the wilting bun atop her head. "Can I help you?"

"I'm looking for a man named Fletcher Johnson and his cousin, Miss Humphrey. I was told they might be here."

"Sorry. Never heard of 'em." Something crashed behind the woman. She whirled around, slamming the door behind her.

Richard sighed and crossed out the address in the directory as his stomach rumbled. The next home on the list was at least four blocks away. Perhaps he should have hired a driver as Henry had suggested, but the idea of a strange man waiting for Richard at each stop, bearing witness to his foolish behavior was too humiliating. It had been embarrassing enough explaining his plans to *Henry.*

Richard squinted at the sun. Nearly noon. Was there a restaurant in this part of town? He checked the list again. Seven more addresses to try. He needed to leave in the morning if he wanted to accept the invitation from the logging company owner. Was there enough time to find each address? What if he didn't find her?

～

*T*he stage celerity wagon rocked and rattled its way along the dirt road leading to San Diego. Clarinda fidgeted with the fancy goldwork wrapped around the ring finger on her left hand. Fletcher had come through on his promise. In fact, he'd found a matching set of rings—one fancy enough to legitimize her claim of a wealthy husband. Where he'd found the pair, he wouldn't say and she didn't press him. Fletcher had a penchant for gambling. Her gain was likely some poor woman's loss.

Clarinda tried not to think about it.

The set had served its purpose, convincing her aunt and uncle of her husband's affection, while the letter Fletcher produced convinced them of the man's existence. Naturally there had been questions. Why hadn't she waited for a formal ceremony? Why hadn't she informed them of her marriage by letter or upon her arrival? And the most difficult to answer of all—who was her husband and why wasn't he with her?

Fletcher had handled each question with alarming ease. She had no idea her dear cousin was such a smooth liar. As she listened to him assuage their every concern, awe and discomfort warred within her. Perhaps her aunt had been less than warm toward Clarinda, but the woman had never been outright cruel. Lying to her—to all of them—made Clarinda squirm. Even though she hadn't been the one doing most of the lying.

Soon she'd have to lie to her parents, too. Could she continue this deception for the sake of her child?

Her stomach rolled with another dip of the swaying vehicle. Pressing a hand to her middle, she sucked in a long breath and let it out slowly. The queasiness seemed to come and go. Thankfully, breathing through the random surges often kept her from losing what little food she managed to get down.

She lifted one of the leather curtains covering the open sides of the wagon and relished the cooler air, despite its dust. Her veil filtered most of it anyway. The familiar bright sage greens and golden browns covering the chaparral land surrounding San Diego rushed past. Her lips tipped upward even as her hand itched to yank the brake lever. Never as lush as its northern half, Southern California held its own kind of beauty in the winter. In the distance, she could make out the Robinson's large, two-story home with its wraparound porch, white paint, and green trim. Mother had written that Mr. Robinson passed away last year and his widow was thinking of selling. Clarinda couldn't recall if the woman had found a buyer.

Fletcher coughed. "Shut the curtain, will you? The dust is killing me."

She let the flap drop and stared at the lump in her glove. The kid leather hid a large diamond surrounded by six claw-like prongs that seemed to hold it captive. Could the cage of lies it had helped to confirm truly set her free?

She'd been tempted to remove the rings while they traveled, but Fletcher insisted male travelers would pay her less attention if she kept the symbols on. He'd been right. She'd caught more than one of their fellow passengers casting a furtive glance at the lump in her gloves.

The wagon slowed and came to a rumbling halt. The conveyance tilted sideways as the driver climbed down. A moment later, the door swung open and a grimy hand was raised in its place.

"Ma'am. I believe this is your stop." The driver smiled as she accepted his hand and stepped down.

Fletcher exited behind her, followed by the other men who'd shared the jolting ride with them through various stops along the route from San Francisco.

When Clarinda had first boarded, she expected to remain awake each night of their journey. Though the driver seemed proud of the "bed" he formed by folding down the passenger seats each night, the surface created was akin to a kitchen table, and the hard jolting each time the wagon struck a rut wasn't a cradle's gentle rocking. Furthermore, with male strangers as companions, she'd been certain no amount of fatigue could lull her to slumber.

She'd been wrong.

With Fletcher forming a protective wall between her and the other men, Clarinda had fallen asleep their first night of travel. Fitful, broken sleep, but sleep nonetheless.

Her muscles ached in protest of their sustained abuse as she and Fletcher waited for their luggage to be unloaded onto the handsome veranda of the Franklin House. The town's grandest hotel and tallest building, its brick first level was topped by two wooden stories. She'd heard the first floor included a fine restaurant, as well as an office where Lewis Franklin conducted his attorney and notary business. Not that she'd seen either.

She surveyed the packed-dirt plaza surrounded by mostly single-story buildings clad in a variety of wood and adobe. Only the first floor of the Franklin House and her family's store with upstairs residence had utilized brick in its construction. From what she could tell, not much had changed in the two years she'd been gone. The trouble was, in the three years she'd lived at the ranch, she'd been to town less times than she had fingers. Her parents had seen to that.

One of the doors to her parents' store opened and Father exited. He rushed toward them, his head swiveling to and fro. Probably worried about who was witnessing his daughter's shameful return. He stepped onto the veranda and snatched her carpetbag along with Fletcher's. "Come, Clarinda." He turned and hurried toward the store.

She avoided Fletcher's gaze as he hefted her trunk onto his shoulder. He'd seen her parents' indifference toward her during the years both families had lived in San Diego. He'd known what his weekend visits to the ranch meant to her. Yet somehow, having him witness that nothing had changed...she blinked back sudden tears.

Fletcher adjusted his grip on the trunk. "Clarinda, it's—"

Unable to bear the pity in his voice, she rushed after Father. Fletcher's boots crunched the dirt behind her as they crossed the plaza.

Rather than reenter any of the five doors fronting the store, Father rounded the corner—as she knew he would—leading them to the rear entrance. He passed the downstairs parlor, and tromped up the stairs to their private, upstairs parlor. Ignoring her mother and sister's astonished gasps, he dropped the bags beside the fireplace. Finally, he faced her. "What's the meaning of this? Has something happened to the school?"

"No, Father. I..." ...*came to tell you I'm married.* The lie stuck to her tongue. She swallowed and tried again as she tugged the glove from her left hand. "I—I've gotten—"

"You're married!" Lucy squealed as she leapt from the settee. Clarinda resisted the urge to roll her eyes. Reaching her eighteenth birthday last month had done nothing to tame her sister's exuberant nature. "Oooh! Let me see!" She seized Clarinda's left hand and dragged her elder sister toward the nearest window. "It's beautiful! When did it happen? How did you meet him? Where was the ceremony? Oh, I wish I could have been there." Lucy's lower lip stuck out as she tore her gaze from the jewelry to look at her sister. "Why didn't you write me you had a beau? We could have planned our weddings together."

Just what Clarinda had always dreamed of—sharing her wedding day with her vivacious sister and the man who'd bypassed Clarinda to claim the unblemished Humphrey daughter. Not that Clarinda'd ever been attracted to him. Though they were the same age, she'd only met the man twice. Being hidden out of town as she'd been tended to limit one's interactions.

"Hello?" Lucy snapped her fingers in Clarinda's face. "Did you hear me?"

"I'm sorry, what did you say?"

"She asked where your husband is." Mother glided across the room to join them. "A question I think we'd all like the answer to. Not to mention his name and occupation." She sniffed. "He is employed, I hope?"

Fletcher laughed as he slung an arm over Clarinda's shoulders. "As if this beautiful lady would settle for a no-good. Richard was simply too busy with his mine to join us on this trip."

Lucy's nose wrinkled. "He's a miner?"

"He *owns* the mine." Fletcher corrected her. "A highly successful one, too. In fact, that's why—"

"And his last name?" Father demanded.

"Stevens. He's from a well-to-do family back east."

Clarinda subtly jabbed her elbow in Fletcher's side. While she appreciated his rescuing her, they'd agreed to stick as close to the truth as they could in order to avoid getting caught in their own web. To her knowledge, Mr. Stevens had said nothing about his family. Of course, he'd said nothing about wanting to become her fictitious husband, either. Yet here they were.

Poor man.

Fletcher claimed what the mine owner didn't know couldn't hurt him, and there was zero chance of Mr. Stevens ever wandering as far as San Diego. Clarinda wasn't so sure, but she'd forgotten they hadn't settled on her fictitious husband's name until his aunt asked the question. Fletcher had jumped in with what he later claimed was the first name to come to mind.

Her parents' questions continued for more than an hour, as they had with Fletcher's. Clarinda braced for the question of whether she was with child—a usual suspicion in such hasty marriages—but it never came. Her parents either trusted in her moral strength or they believed her incapable of luring a man into lustful behavior. Undoubtedly, it was the latter.

Again, Fletcher produced the letter from her supposed

husband. It described how Richard had been too enamored with Clarinda to delay their wedding a single day and offered his sincerest regrets for not accompanying his new bride. The letter further promised Richard would visit at his earliest convenience as he was anxious to meet the wonderful family that had raised such a charming young woman.

In the end, Mother scolded and Father's frown deepened, but they both seemed to accept her marriage as legitimate.

Mother stood. "Well, I suppose we'd better get you out to the ranch and resettled in your room."

The ranch. Of course. Why had she thought being married would make them want her around? Clarinda shuffled behind Mother into the hall.

She pivoted at the top of the stairs. "Fletcher, you're welcome to occupy the guest room here, of course."

Fletcher nodded. "Thank you, ma'am. I do plan to head out with the next ship to San Francisco."

Mother blinked. "So soon?"

"I need to get back and help Father with the store."

"He still hasn't hired anyone to replace that negligent scamp?"

"I'm afraid not."

"Well." Mother picked a bit of lint from the front of Clarinda's dress. "And how long are *you* staying? More than one night, I presume."

"Actually, I haven't decided yet."

Father spoke up. "Won't that husband of yours be anxious to have you home? Where did you say that was again?"

"Uhh..." Where had Fletcher said Mr. Stevens was from?

Once again her cousin saved her. "Nevada City."

Clarinda frowned. She should have asked Fletcher to write all these details down before he left. The letter in Mother's hand caught her eye. Everything Clarinda needed to remember was in there. Perhaps she could sneak it away later and make a copy.

SING IN THE SUNLIGHT

Before they banished her to the ranch. Again.

At least it would just be their housekeeper, the *vaqueros,* and Clarinda living there. Unless one of the other partners who co-owned the ranch had decided to take over Mr. Ame's job as ranch manager.

"Is the manager's house still empty?"

Mother exchanged an odd look with Father.

"Yes, it is." Father cleared his throat. "Actually, we've been meaning to write you—"

"But we've all been so busy." Mother clasped her hands together. "You understand."

An uneasy feeling swirled in Clarinda's gut. "What is it?"

"It wasn't an easy decision, of course." Father shifted his feet.

Lucy chimed in, "Besides, you were so close to graduating, there didn't seem any point—"

Father set a silencing hand on Lucy's shoulder. "No one expected the drought could last this long. But there seems no end in sight. It was time."

Clarinda clenched her fingers. "What has the drought to do with anything?"

Father squared his shoulders. "The partners have decided to sell."

"Sell? The ranch?" They couldn't. Where would she live? "But not you, right? We're keeping our portion, of course."

"I'm afraid not."

"But you just said I could stay."

"And of course you can." Father jammed his hands into his pockets. "Who knows how long it'll be until we find a buyer? And even then the plan is to sell the shares gradually. Thompson convinced everyone that if all the partners appeared to be jumping ship, no one would buy. So of course Ames'll sell his share first. Then Thompson, and well…we were to be next, but—"

"But as your Father said, all that will take months, probably longer. And until then, your old room will do nicely." Mother started down the stairs. "Of course, I'm not sure what we'll do once your husband arrives. That bed of yours wasn't made for two."

~

$\mathscr{T}$he next morning, Clarinda awoke to the smell of sizzling bacon.

And ran for the privy.

The cold February air jolted her senses as the irony sank in that her favorite breakfast food had driven her from the house. It seemed everything she loved was destined to hurt her. Save perhaps, Fletcher. Had he boarded the ship to San Francisco yet?

She exited the privy and glanced at the sun peeking through the branches of the olive trees. Almost noon.

He was gone.

Thank goodness she'd swiped the letter from Mother's desk before Father brought her to the ranch. She'd need to make a copy before Mother came for her next visit. Then she could sneak the original into Mother's reticule. Hopefully Mother wouldn't notice the letter missing in the meantime.

Clarinda wiped her mouth on her sleeve, stumbled into her bedroom, and fell onto her bed. How could she be so tired after sleeping half the day away? How could her parents be selling the ranch? She had to find a way to convince them not to sell.

Later.

Right now, blissful sleep called to her. Her eyelids drifted shut.

Her door swung open with a whoosh.

"All right, young miss. Time to get up." Teodora's perky voice, with its thick Spanish accent halted Clarinda's return to dreamland. "I know you had a long journey, but you get up now, yes?"

Clarinda rolled onto her stomach, burying her face beneath the pillow. "Go away, Teodora." Yesterday, Clarinda's parents had dropped her off and returned to town. Alone in the Humphrey ranch house, there was no one but Teodora—their Mission Indian housekeeper—to care what Clarinda did. Why bother getting up?

Teodora tugged at her blankets.

Feeling childish, Clarinda clamped one hand onto the pillow still covering her head and clenched the blanket's edge with the other. "I don't want to get up. There's no point."

"What are you talking about? It's a beautiful day. Get up and enjoy the sunshine."

"It's too bright."

Another tug, firmer this time. "Ah, *mi hija*. What a complainer you are. They sent you away a girl. I thought you came back a woman. But still you act like a child." She made a tisking sound, and the pillow vanished from Clarinda's grasp. "Did that school teach you nothing?"

Clarinda moaned into the bed.

"What are you thinking to waste this gift God has given you?"

Which gift? The nausea, her shattered plans, or the parents who couldn't stand to be around her? She threw the blanket over her head.

A firm swat met her backside, causing her to bolt upright. She glared at Teodora. "I am not a child."

"Could have fooled me." Teodora chuckled as she left the room.

For the briefest of moments, she considered lying back down and letting sleep erase her troubles. But the attempt would be pointless. Teodora would start banging pots and scraping chairs across the floor until Clarinda joined her in the kitchen.

She dragged herself from bed and changed into an old dress, leaving her corset off. Who was here to care how she looked? No one. At least she could be as comfortable as her miserable state would allow. Still, she checked her veil was in place and tugged on her gloves.

She shuffled through the main room and made her way to the kitchen. In the doorway, she paused to swallow against another revolt of her stomach. No doubt Teodora expected Clarinda to be thrilled by the plate piled high with the thick, greasy strips, but there was no way Clarinda could manage a single bite. She could barely tolerate remaining in the same room with the steaming bacon.

At the stove, the housekeeper was finishing a golden pile of eggs. Clarinda moaned. Teodora had cooked enough to feed every hand on the ranch. In fact...

"You know, this looks far too good to keep to ourselves." Plastering on a smile, she lifted the platter of bacon as Teodora turned to look at her. "I think I'll go see if the vaqueros are hungry." Which they would be. The hardworking men her father employed to run his ranch were always hungry. "Do you want to bring those eggs as well?"

Not waiting for an answer, Clarinda swept into the small courtyard created by the u-shaped ranch home. She made a left to follow the path between their cellar and the kitchen garden. Teodora followed her across the bridge leading to the adobe barn. Hopefully there'd be a few men inside. If they'd all headed for the far flung pastures, she'd have no excuse for not eating the food she carried.

Teodora drew up beside her, plate of eggs in hand. Clarinda sensed the housekeeper's inspection, but the woman said nothing as they entered the barn.

Thankfully, there were four men inside who eagerly

accepted the surprise of a warm meal. Soon the plates were empty.

Clarinda dashed for the fresh air, leaving the offensive odors of the barn behind.

Teodora caught up as they crossed the bridge toward the house. "So. That's the way it is."

Tension trailed down Clarinda's back. "What do you mean?"

"You have not told your parents." It wasn't a question.

"Told them what?" As Clarinda neared the kitchen, the lingering grease odor reached her nostrils. She changed direction.

Teodora followed.

Clarinda stopped beneath the largest shade tree in the yard. She circled its base. Where was her swing? She'd spent hour after hour soaring beneath the branches on the simple wooden swing that an old hand had hung for her here. "What happened to my swing?"

"A big storm took it away last winter. I did not see the point in replacing it now that you are grown." She planted her hands on her hips. "Have you calculated yet when the baby is expected?"

Clarinda fell against the wide tree trunk. "What?"

The housekeeper studied Clarinda's middle. "You do not seem far along, so not soon, I think. Summer? Fall?" Teodora raised her brows. "What did the doctor say?"

"I haven't seen a doctor. I mean..." Clarinda hugged herself, covering her stomach. "Why would I? I don't know what you're talking about." The lie tasted sour in her mouth. How could she do this? It was one thing to deceive her parents, but to fool Teodora? The one person in all the world who'd never treated her as anything but a normal, beautiful, beloved child? It was unthinkable. Her arms fell. "You're right. I'm with child."

"And the baby? When do you expect it?"

"Umm. September, I think."

85

"And where is the father? Your mother said you are married." She pointed to the bump in the glove covering Clarinda's rings.

Her head sank. "Not really."

"Ohhh..." Teodora began to mutter in Spanish. Clarinda had picked up on a enough phrases over the years to gather the gist of what someone said, but right now she didn't care to listen. The housekeeper wandered toward the kitchen, shaking her head and still muttering.

Clarinda sank to the base of the tree as tears burned her eyes.

Some time later, Teodora returned, a tray of toast in hand. "Do you think you can keep this down?"

Clarinda nodded, feeling too guilty to reject the kindness.

The woman handed her the tray and settled onto the ground beside her. "I sent Eduardo to fetch some *trigo sarraceno* roots. The women at the mission swore by its tea when I was a girl. It helped me during my time. When he gets back, I'll brew you a pot. Maybe it will help settle your stomach."

"What do you mean, 'during your time'?"

"When I was blessed with child, of course. What else would I mean?"

"But..." Clarinda stared at Teodora. "You don't *have* any children. I mean...you've never spoken of any. Where are they?" A terrible thought occurred to her. "Did they...die?" She whispered the last word as if doing so could remove the sting from the question.

"Die? No, thank the good Lord." Teodora's smile persisted, but there was sadness in the depths of her deep brown eyes. "No, my daughter is alive and well. All grown up now, with a family of her own."

The idea of Teodora having her own family—a daughter and even grandchildren—was mind-boggling. "But where do they live? Have you ever gone to see them?" Clarinda couldn't remember a time when Teodora had ever left the ranch, nor anyone coming to visit her. "Wait. Are you married?"

"My husband left for Mexico City when my daughter was not two years old. Never saw or heard from him again. I have not seen my daughter in many years. I have never met her husband or her children."

"But why? Does she live so far away?"

"The *ranchero* said she was a distraction from my duties. He made me send her away. She lives with my sister. In those mountains." Teodora gestured toward the range rising along the northeast edge of the wide valley. "It takes too long to travel. I am needed here. So here is where I stay."

Clarinda ducked her head. She'd only thought of Teodora as their housekeeper, but she must have been close to thirty years old when Clarinda moved to San Diego in 1850. The woman had lived a whole life before coming to work for their family. Why had Clarinda never thought to ask her about it before now?

"Don't be silly." Clarinda set aside the tray of toast. "Of course we can spare you for a visit to see your family. In fact"— she took Teodora's hands in hers—"I insist you take a holiday and go see your family."

The housekeeper patted Clarinda's hand. "You are sweet, but your mother would not like it. Years ago, I asked her. Can I go and see my daughter? She was very upset. She said she'd sack me if I go. I did not ask again. I need this job. My family needs the money."

"But how are they helped if you do not see them?"

"Eduardo knows my family. When he goes to their village, he takes my money."

"You mean, your daughter lives in the same village our vaqueros do?" Each night about half of the men who worked the ranch bedded down in their bunkhouse while the others disappeared into the hills and returned before daybreak. She'd never pondered the villages they went to.

Teodora shook her head. "No, he does not live in her village. It is too far. He visits sometimes."

"Well, this simply will not do." She squeezed Teodora's hands. "How long would a trip there and back take?"

"Eduardo says it takes a half day each way."

"If it's that close, why don't you sneak away? Mother is in town for such long stretches, she'd never notice you were gone."

"Fernando."

Clarinda's face scrunched at the name of the foreman who reported to her parents all the goings on at the ranch. If a cow went missing or Clarinda got so much as a skinned knee, her parents would learn about it at their weekly meetings. "Argh. This isn't right. Mother cannot keep you from your family. I will speak to her myself."

"No!" Teodora's eyes grew round, her grip tight. "You mustn't do that. Please promise me you will not say a word. I would not have told you if I thought you would."

She and Teodora had always spoken openly with one another—far more like a mother-daughter relationship than anything she'd experienced with her true mother since the attack. She and Teodora kept one another's confidences. If the housekeeper did not want Clarinda to speak with her mother, Clarinda would respect her wishes. "All right. But I'll find another way to get you to your daughter. It may take more time, but I will make it happen. I promise."

CHAPTER 9

"I'm sorry, sir. Without permission from the young lady's family, there isn't anything more I can tell you." The director of the Young Ladies' Seminary eyed Richard with a single lifted brow as he stood on the front step, rain drumming against his umbrella. "Even if she *were* in attendance, the young ladies of this school are not permitted gentleman callers."

"I understand. Thank you for your"—the door closed—"time." Another dead end. He retraced his steps toward the street.

The door swooshed open again and he glanced back.

A young woman in a maid's uniform pulled the door shut behind her and darted toward him. Did she know something about Miss Humphrey's whereabouts? He straightened, his breath catching.

She drew to a stop close enough to share the covering of his umbrella. "Thank heavens I caught thee. I heard thee speaking about Miss Humphrey. Have thee seen her? Is she well?"

Richard exhaled. The maid's strange accent was thick—was it English or Scottish? Either way, he understood her well enough. "Not for days. I was hoping she'd returned here."

"She's not coming back. Went to live with her cousin in San Francisco." She tucked a stray hair behind her ear. "I hoped thee knew how she was fairing. She ought to have written by now, but I've heard naught."

So, her trip wasn't a short visit. Why had Clarinda left school in the middle of the year? "I'm sorry I couldn't be of more help."

"That's all right." She tipped her head, squinting at him. "How do thee know her? I don't recall her mentioning a right smart man named...what did thee say yer name was?"

His cheeks warmed and he shoved the umbrella into her hand. "Here." He stepped away, ignoring the raindrops splatting against his wool coat. "Is there any particular reason you were concerned for Miss Humphrey?"

"Oh, no. Just um...missing her, is all. We're friends. My name's Katie Mizedale, by the way." She raised her brows. "And thee are...?"

"Running late for the ferry, I'm afraid." He made a show of checking his pocket watch. If he introduced himself, she'd expect him to explain his connection to Clarinda. That was far too complicated to ponder. Besides, he didn't want to encourage the spark in the young woman's eyes.

"Oh. Sorry." Katie's cheeks pinked. She pushed the umbrella into his hands and turned to go.

Hopefully he hadn't hurt her feelings. How well *did* she know Clarinda? Did she know how to contact Miss Humphrey's parents? Dashing through the rain-slogged yard, he reached her before she turned the knob. "What about her parents? Wouldn't they know where she is and how she's doing? Perhaps we should ask them."

The girl looked back at him, something sad in her eyes. "Not likely. They're a way down in San Diego. It'd take ages to get a letter there and back again." Twisting the knob, she grinned. "I'm sure she'll write before that. Have a good day!"

Before he could think of another question, she slipped inside and the door closed in his face. Again.

He crossed the yard once more and paused beside the road. What was he to do now?

A wagon roared through a large puddle, drenching him with muddy water from head to toe. Eyes closed, he fumbled for his pocket and withdrew his handkerchief. He wiped it across his face.

"Ha." He looked like a pig rolled in the mud. At least it had happened after he'd spoken with the school's director. The stern woman might not have spoken to him at all, had he arrived in such a state.

He'd have to find somewhere to change before his meeting with the logging company owner this afternoon.

Sighing, he looked heavenward. *Lord, what am I doing here? Did* You *send me that dream or am I chasing a fool's errand?* Had his longing for a wife and family to fill his home caused him to misunderstand the Lord's will? If the dream *had* come from the Lord, He sure wasn't making the path clear. None of the Johnsons he'd spoken with were related to or knew of Fletcher Johnson or his cousin, Clarinda Humphrey. The school director would only tell him Miss Humphrey was no longer a student there. Which left only her parents as a possible source of information, but they lived hundreds of miles away.

Several minutes later, Richard stepped into the office for the Benicia Ferry.

A portly man with thinning blond hair approached. "How may I help you sir?"

"I'd like to purchase a ticket for the ferry."

"Certainly." The man rounded a desk and took a seat. He motioned for Richard to take the seat opposite him. "Where to?"

"S—" About to respond, *Sacramento*, Richard battled the sudden urge to declare San Diego as his destination. Not that the ferry could take him that far, but once across the bay, he could catch a steamer headed down the coast, or purchase a ticket for the new Overland Mail Route and go by stage.

He rubbed his hand across his face. What was he thinking? He had an appointment to keep. He didn't have time to chase a woman he barely knew all the way to San Diego. Especially when he had no idea if she'd returned there. Her friend said Miss Humphrey intended to live with her cousin. In any case, what would he say to her parents? *Hello, I met your daughter on the ferry one afternoon, had an odd dream about her and now I've spent the past several weeks obsessed with finding her?* They'd have him arrested and consigned to the nearest sanitarium before he could blink.

~

Clarinda dropped in the last carrot seeds, covered them, and rose to her feet. She lifted her veil and wiped the chilled sweat from her forehead. Leaving the garden behind, she wandered toward the creek that ran between the barn and house. The babbling waters seemed loud in the quiet of the ranch yard. The vaqueros were all out tending to their duties in distant pastures. Only she and Teodora were around to make noise.

A horse whinnied in a corral near the barn.

All right, so there were a few animals around, too. Still, amid the constant chatter of girls and teachers, not to mention the noisy goings-on of Benicia's residents, she'd longed for the quiet of this ranch life. Now that she'd been here a month, though, it felt odd. Lonely. As much as she loved having Teodora's company once more, it wasn't the same as having someone her own age—like Katie—to confide in.

Crouching by the water, she plucked a stick from its banks. She dipped the fractured tip into the stream, and water flowed around it.

She was like the stick. Life was moving on around her—without her—but she remained unchanged. Well, not unchanged, but still in the same place. Yes, she had a baby coming. And yes, her parents believed she was happily married. But the reality was, she was still alone and unwanted.

As she'd always been.

She tossed the stick into the creek. *Stupid, Arnie. Why'd you leave me? You were supposed to love me.* She kicked the water, and splashes drenched the hem of her skirt. *Why couldn't you love me?* She rubbed her scars through her sleeve. *You said you didn't care —that I was enough. Why'd you lie?* Where was he now? Did he know she'd left school? Clarinda hadn't worked up the nerve to ask in her letter to Katie, and Katie hadn't mentioned him in her response.

So many times Clarinda'd picked up a pen to write him, tell him about their child. Each time, she'd remembered the sight of him riding away—leaving her stranded in the middle of nowhere—and she'd set the pen down. He didn't deserve to know and probably wouldn't care if he did.

And if he did care?

She shook her head and turned toward the house. Arnie's father would still stand between them.

Dust rose along the drive. Who could be coming to visit in the middle of a Thursday afternoon? Her parents weren't due until tomorrow evening, and Lucy rarely came to visit these days. She preferred to spend her free time with her betrothed at his family's home.

Arnie. The hope came unbidden. *It can't be him. He doesn't know where the ranch is.* But he did know about her parent's store. What if he'd come after her?

Her breath caught. If Arnie had come, her lie was uncovered.

She fisted her hands in her skirts and shook them. If she *had* to invent a fake husband, why hadn't she used *his* name? Then everything could be fixed.

Assuming he hadn't told them too much.

But the pain had been too raw at the time for her to even speak his name. Fletcher had known that, so he'd picked another name. One that would be safe, meaningless.

She lifted her chin. If Arnie *had* come for her, all would be well. She'd find a way to explain things to her parents. Somehow.

A wagon emerged from a break in the large oaks lining the drive. Her parents rode the wooden bench with her sister beside them. Clarinda's eyes burned.

Arnie hadn't come for her.

Blinking rapidly, she pivoted toward the house and the safety of her room.

Why had her family come early? Who was minding the store? She froze. Her father never closed the shop or left it unattended if it could be helped. Something must be gravely wrong. She spun back.

As they drew nearer, every one of her family members appeared somber. Lucy seemed on the verge of tears.

Clarinda rushed forward as the wagon drew to a stop in the yard. "What is it? What's happened?"

Ignoring her questions, Mother waited for Father to descend and assist her from the wagon. Once she and Lucy were both on the ground, Mother addressed Clarinda. "Let us go inside."

Stifling a pointless protest, Clarinda followed the rest of them into the house.

Teodora emerged from the kitchen, her eyes wide. "Mr. and Mrs. Humphrey. Miss Lucy. I wasn't expecting you until tomorrow."

"Urgent matters dictated we come early." Mother nodded. "Please prepare the tea. We have private matters to discuss."

Teodora retreated to the kitchen as Clarinda shuffled behind her parents.

What if they'd sold the ranch and come to tell her to pack

her things? What if they'd discovered her deceit? Fletcher's letters these past several weeks had seemed so convincing, *Clarinda* almost believed her husband would arrive soon. Yet perhaps he'd slipped up somehow. Her aunt and uncle might have discovered his fake letters and demanded an explanation. If so, they'd have written to her parents immediately.

She studied Mother and Father as they took their usual positions in chairs flanking the large adobe fireplace. Were they preparing to throw her out? Raising her chin, she forced herself to lower to the edge of the settee beside Lucy.

Clarinda waited several seconds, but no one spoke. "Will you please tell me what's going on? What private matters do we need to discuss?"

Father nodded to Mother and she pulled something from the hidden pocket in her skirt. Mother's expression crumbled as she held it out.

It was a black-edged envelope. The kind only used to deliver grim news.

"Who..." Clarinda swallowed. "Is it Fletcher? Or Ada?"

Her mother waved the paper. "Take it. Read for yourself. I didn't feel right opening it."

She didn't feel right opening it? Whyever not? Clarinda accepted the letter. *Mrs. Richard Stevens* was scrawled in unfamiliar handwriting on the front. Grim understanding slipped through Clarinda. Though it matched neither Fletcher's usual handwriting, nor the style he employed for the falsified letters from her husband, it must be from him. This was it.

She ripped open the letter and skimmed the brief words that confirmed her suspicions. No one had died. No one real, anyway. Fletcher had finally sent the promised letter announcing her widowhood. The letter was signed by a solicitor Clarinda had never heard of. The man was likely as real as her husband had been. Her charade of a marriage was at an end. "Thank you, Fletcher," she whispered.

Mother leaned closer. "What did you say, dear?"

Think of something sad. Clarinda scrunched her face, trying to conjure tears. No moisture gathered. *I'm finally free.* It was all she could think of. Her lips twitched upward. She slapped a gloved hand over them.

Think of Arnie's betrayal. He doesn't want you anymore. Finally, the tears came.

"Well?" Father pointed to the letter. "What does it say?"

She lifted her gaze to her parents. "It says I'm a widow, but Richard did not suffer. The cave-in was so large and happened so quickly, they are certain he was killed instantly."

Beside her, Lucy broke down in sobs. "It isn't fair. You've only just gotten married and now he's gone." No doubt thinking of her fiancé, Lucy threw her arms around Clarinda. "You're all alone again."

Clarinda patted her sister's back. Did this count as a hug? It felt more like a heavy blanket was soaking her shoulder. She pressed her face against Lucy's shoulder and forced shuddering breaths along with sounds she hoped would convince them all she was sobbing.

Lucy sobbed louder.

Teodora returned a few minutes later, bearing the tea tray. Clarinda lifted her head and made a show of wiping her face as the housekeeper set her burden on the table before them. Her gaze fluttered from one distressed family member to the next. It snagged on the black envelope in Clarinda's grip.

Teodora sent Clarinda a questioning look.

Clarinda gave a slight nod. "My husband's dead."

Lucy withdrew her handkerchief and blew her nose.

The housekeeper's lips lifted on one side. "At least you have something to remember him by. That must be a comfort."

Mother stiffened. "I beg your pardon?"

Lucy balled the handkerchief and nodded. "The rings he gave you *are* beautiful."

"I do not mean jewelry." Teodora sniffed.

Mother glared at Teodora "Did you forget the biscuits?"

"No, ma'am." In a rare show of boldness before Mother, Teodora held her ground. "I am talking about the heritage and reward God has blessed your daughter with."

"Yes, well. The tea is growing cool, so perhaps you can fetch those biscuits, now."

Clarinda cringed as Teodora finally left. It was awful how cold Mother always was toward their housekeeper.

Mother's smile was stiff. "You will, of course, inherit your husband's assets. I suppose you must hire someone to oversee his businesses now. Your father is much too busy with his own business to handle yours as well. Of course there's the mine to be managed—assuming it can be re-dug and made to produce ag—"

"No!" Clarinda struggled to moderate her tone. They couldn't hire someone to manage nonexistent businesses. "The solicitor writes that the accident occurred too far below ground and left the earth too unstable. They have decided to leave...his —" Clarinda set the letter in her lap, withdrew her handkerchief and held it to her eyes. She strained her voice as if fighting off tears. "To leave *Richard* buried where he is with the other two men who died." She dabbed her eyes and lowered the kerchief. "The mine is permanently closed."

"How can they do that?" Mother's hand flew to her chest. "It isn't right. Those poor men deserve a proper burial."

Clarinda fisted the handkerchief. "Would you have them risk the lives of living men to exhume those to whom it cannot possibly make a difference where they lie?" She folded the letter and slipped it back into its envelope. "No, mother. I agree with their decision."

"I suppose you're right, but..." Mother leaned forward. "What about the gold?"

"The gold? I..." Mother mustn't be allowed to believe

Clarinda was now a wealthy widow. Oh, why hadn't they thought of this when they'd concocted the lie? "I didn't want to worry you, but Richard recently wrote that the vein had petered out. That was how the cave-in happened. They were exploring a new section of the claim, hoping to find more."

"Well...at least that wasn't your only source of income."

"Yes." Father nodded. "What other businesses did you say he owned?"

Clarinda rubbed her left arm. What had Fletcher told them about her husband's business holdings? She couldn't recall, and her copy of the Fletcher's first letter was hidden in a box in Mr. Ames's old house. It was the only place she could think of that Teodora wouldn't find it. Fat lot of good it did her there.

Teodora returned from the kitchen. "I was not speaking of earthly wealth. I was speaking of the baby." Her message delivered along with a tray of biscuits, the housekeeper deserted the room.

How could she? Clarinda collapsed against the back of her chair. Teodora had been after her for days to tell her family, but the timing had never been right. Apparently, the housekeeper had decided the death of Clarinda's fake husband was the perfect time to spring the news.

So much for keeping one another's confidences.

"The baby?" Mother's brow knit in confusion.

Father frowned. "What baby?"

The first to catch on, Lucy squealed. "You're with child? Why didn't you say so?" She peered at Clarinda's middle. *"That's* why you've been eating so much and grown thicker around your middle. I thought it was because you were melancholy without your husband."

Lucy didn't mean to be cruel. She was just...thoughtless sometimes.

Father straightened. "Is this true?"

Clarinda nodded, flashing a glare at the kitchen door.

"Of course you told Teodora first." Mother's lips pinched.

"Actually, she—"

"Well, don't you worry dear." Mother leaned forward, her hand extending as if to touch Clarinda. She drew back without making contact. "We'll take care of you." Her gaze fell to her lap where she folded her hands.

Father pounded a hand against the arm of his chair. "Of course, we will. Just as we always have."

Just as they always had. Why did those words cause more tears than the letter?

"Does this mean you won't sell the ranch?"

Father leaned back. "I'm afraid that's not an option. We've been losing money for too long. If we can find a f—" Father tugged at his collar. "Someone willing to buy the place, we'll have to sell it. But don't you worry. We'll find somewhere to put you."

Father strode to the writing desk. "Now, what's the name of your husband's solicitor? I think it best we get a clear picture of what he's left you as soon as possible."

~

*R*ichard pushed through the front door of the Prosperity Mine office.

Tommy looked up from the ledger he'd been working on. "Something wrong?"

Richard shook his head as he removed his coat and hung it on the hook near his chair. "Just another wasted afternoon."

"The owner wasn't interested in selling?"

"Oh, he was." Richard slumped into his seat. "I just wasn't interested in buying."

"Sorry to hear that. What was wrong with this one?"

"Nothing a smart investor and new leadership couldn't fix." Both of Henry's contacts had proven to be exactly what the experienced entrepreneur had claimed—poorly managed logging companies with a wealth of unrealized potential. On paper, everything checked out. Both businesses had their positives and negatives, but both offered the opportunity to be extremely successful. So why did the idea of investing in either business leave him with a feeling of dread? Why couldn't he commit?

He drove his hands through his hair and tried to picture himself striding through the woodland, saw in hand. The way the light had poked through the branches to the forest floor had been beautiful. The rumble of men at work, familiar. The snap and thunder of a falling tree, intimidating. But it hadn't scared him. There'd been potential there but...it just hadn't felt right. Like it wasn't where God wanted him.

He looked up and caught Tommy staring at him.

"I don't understand. Isn't that what you were hoping for?"

Richard laughed. "Honestly, I don't understand myself." For the millionth time, a pair of bright blue eyes set within a frame of golden blond tresses flashed in his memory. Though he'd glimpsed Clarinda's face for only a minute or two before she retreated beneath her veil, the vision had been seared in his mind's eye.

At least, he believed it had.

Perhaps his memory was playing tricks on him, enhancing Clarinda's beauty when truly her eyes were an average blue and her hair an ordinary blond. Yet something within him refused to accept the idea.

He'd spent a full twenty minutes in the Benicia Ferry ticket office debating whether to keep his appointment or head south to San Diego. He'd made the right decision. Yet since returning home, he caught himself pondering Clarinda's whereabouts at the oddest times.

Like right now.

Where was she? What was she doing? It had been nearly two

months. Was she still unattached or had she met someone and become engaged? For that matter, she may have had a beau when they met. He and Fletcher hadn't ventured into such personal topics.

No. There couldn't have been. The school director clearly stated their students weren't allowed gentleman callers.

Still, anything could have happened since he last saw her.

An envelope on Richard's desk caught his eye. The handwriting resembled Henry's. "When did this come in?" He lifted the letter.

Tommy glanced up. "Bella stopped by earlier and brought the mail."

"That was nice of her." Richard lifted the envelope and carefully slit it open. "How's she doing?"

Tommy's chest puffed out. "Happy as a clam in high water."

Richard glanced at the bottom of the letter. Sure enough, Henry's signature graced the page. Richard returned his gaze to the top. The note said Henry'd recently learned that a successful ranch was for sale. Mr. Thompson, an acquaintance of Henry's, was responsible for finding a buyer. He thought Richard might be interested in the property if the logging companies didn't satiate his need to get his hands dirty. Henry joked that there was bound to be plenty of dirt on a cattle ranch.

Richard skimmed the rest of the letter until eyes snagged on two words—*San Diego*. He reread the sentence and felt a silly grin stretching his lips.

CHAPTER 10

*W*et sage ground beneath the wagon wheels, releasing its scent as Clarinda guided the team along the rutted road leading to town, a reluctant Teodora at her side. It had taken a lot of talking and a bit of mulish insistence to convince the housekeeper to join Clarinda on this adventure, but she was tired of being corralled on the ranch like one of the cows.

And she needed to convince her parents not to sell the ranch. Her idea for making it profitable again could work. It wasn't without risk, but it could work. It *would* work. She just needed to convince Father to listen to her. She wouldn't let him dismiss her like he had during his last visit to the ranch. This time, she'd make him listen. Somehow.

As the first town buildings came into view, Clarinda's hands tightened on the reins. She could do this. It would be different this time.

When her family had first arrived in San Diego, Clarinda stepped off the ship excited to exchange the daily rejection of former friends for the acceptance of new ones. But before she even left the beach, people began pointing and whispering.

Worse yet—in her parents' minds, at least—Clarinda's appearance had affected Lucy's ability to make friends. So Clarinda was sent to the ranch and Teodora was hired to raise her while her parents remained in town with Lucy.

At least they had visited every weekend.

The back of their store came into view as the wagon rounded a clump of large shrubs. Clarinda squared her shoulders. Another mile and they'd be there.

A shop Clarinda was finally going to enter.

Although her new widow's veil dimmed her view far more than her usual white veil, the commonness of the garment meant she wouldn't draw the attention she usually did. It was a wonder she hadn't thought of it before. Between her dark veil and the large, wool cloak that concealed her condition, she could fade into the shadows.

Surely her parents couldn't object.

∾

*R*ichard struggled to maintain an interested expression. Everett Thompson's prattling about San Diego's supposedly grand history seemed as incessant as the rain pattering against the roof of the man's office.

Richard expected any shrewd businessman to present biased information. So before his appointment, he'd struck up a conversation with some men in town. He'd not given his full name or any personal details. In towns as small as this one, it wouldn't be unusual for word to spread of an investor's plan to visit.

The conversation had proved a wise use of his time, revealing many local ranches were on the verge of bankruptcy. The economy of this small town was shrinking instead of growing. Not a situation Richard wanted to tangle with. He'd knocked on Mr. Thompson's door, fully planning to beg off the appointment, but the man was very persuasive. Next thing Richard knew, he was sitting in the man's office, listening to a long list of reasons San Diego was the best little city in the nation. People just hadn't recognized its potential yet.

"...which is why Humphrey and I decided it was time to—"

Richard coughed. "I'm sorry, did you say, 'Humphrey?'"

"Yes, Neal Humphrey, along with Patrick Kelly, Frederick Ames, and I chose to purchase Rancho Gran Valle—that's the Grand Valley Ranch—several years ago with the understanding that Mr. Ames would manage the affairs of the ranch while the rest of us would be silent partners in the venture."

Mr. Thompson continued on about the ranch's history, but Richard struggled to focus on the businessman's words. Did Neal Humphrey have a daughter named Clarinda? How many Humphreys could there be in such a small town?

"Unfortunately, Mr. Ames suffered an injury last year that never fully healed. He wishes to give up ranching and move into something less physically demanding."

Richard tapped a finger against the chair arm. "So, it isn't the entire ranch that's for sale, but Mr. Ames's share of it?"

"That's correct." Mr. Thompson shuffled some papers around. "It's not the largest ranch in the area, but we've received ample return on our investment and are reluctant to let it go."

That was a good sign. If the ranch were in dire straits, all the partners would want out. Perhaps this ranch had something going for it that others in the area did not. On the other hand, Richard hadn't been looking for business partners. And there was still the local economy to consider. If businesses and ranches in the area continued to fail, the price of any goods they didn't produce on the ranch would increase.

Mr. Thompson withdrew a map from the stack. "Here you can see how the ranch is situated relative to town." He pointed to a small wiggly line on the map. "There's a strong creek that runs from a spring on the property. You'll never want for water, and there are beautiful, large oak trees that surround the main house, as well as the manager's home, the bunkhouse, and the barn. They also run here along the creek and the drive. Some were natural, others were planted years ago by the original owners to provide shade for the various buildings."

"It seems a fair distance from town. How long does it take to reach the ranch?"

"Oh, not much more than an hour, I'd say." Everett scooped up the map and tucked it away. "Of course, it depends on how fast your horse is."

"And the other partners, do they visit the ranch often? Do any of them live on the ranch?"

"Not any more. Mr. Ames did live in the manager's home, but he's moved into town since the accident. If you decide to invest, that can be your residence, if you like."

"Why not the main house?"

"Mr. Humphrey's daughter has domain over the house. That was part of the agreement when we partnered up." Mr. Thompson scratched his tidy beard. "Of course, if you prefer the main house, I suppose we could—"

"His daughter lives there without her family? Is she married?" How many daughters did the Humphreys have?

"No, Miss Humphrey isn't married. Uh—" Mr. Thompson shifted in his seat. "Hers is an unusual situation."

"How so?" Could he be referring to Clarinda's veil? Yet, why would she live alone and so far from town?

"I'd best let her family explain it. In fact"—the businessman stood—"why don't we head over and speak with him before we drive out to see the ranch? I'll need the approval of each partner before we can strike a deal." He rounded the desk and held the door for Richard.

At the end of the hall, Mr. Thompson opened the front door and pointed across the sodden plaza. "That's the Humphrey's store, there. Neal will be inside at this time of day. Wait a moment while I find my umbrella and we'll walk over so I can introduce you." He turned toward an umbrella stand, but Richard set a hand on his shoulder.

"Do you happen to know his daughter's name?"

Mr. Thompson's brows lifted, a twinkle in his eye. "He has two daughters. The eldest's name is Clarinda. She's the one that lives on the ranch. Her younger sister is—"

"I'm sorry. Can we continue our business later? There's something personal I need to see to."

The man shoved his hands into his pockets. "Well, I suppose, but—"

The rest of the man's words were lost as Richard sped through the door and into the rain.

~

*C*larinda growled at the unexpected rain washing away her plans to explore the town. Once she entered her parents' shop, she'd have to confront the consequences of defying their desire that she remain hidden.

Oh well, with her new widow's veil, this needn't be her only visit to town. Whether her parents approved or not, she intended to exert more control over her life. She was a grown woman, about to become a mother. It was past time she quit acting like a child afraid of her mother's shadow.

Nevertheless, she drove the wagon in a wide circle around the plaza before reining to a halt at the side of the building, out of sight from the front doors. She stared at its brick walls as rain soaked through her thin gloves. She should go in. Too bad her knees wouldn't straighten.

Teodora shoved her, almost toppling Clarinda from the seat. "*¡Ay Ay Ay!* All that fuss and ruckus about seeing your family's store. Now we're here and all you want to do is sit in the rain?" She pushed her again. "Get out. Go. See what keeps your father so busy, and be quick about it. I may not be sugar, but I'm no happier sitting in the rain."

"All right. All right." Clarinda clambered to the ground and started toward the front of the building. "I'm going."

No sound of footsteps followed her.

She turned.

Teodora remained on the wagon, her hands folded beneath the wool blanket covering her lap.

"Aren't you coming?"

"I'll wait here."

"In the rain? Why?"

"Your parents and their customers won't like an Indian in their shop."

Clarinda frowned. Teodora was correct. As idiotic as the town's citizens were about Clarinda's veil, they were more obnoxious about associating with Indians. "But you can't just sit in the rain. You'll get soaked. Why don't you wait in Mary's quarters?" Her parents' maid surely wouldn't mind.

Teodora squinted at the sky. "The rain won't last much longer."

Clarinda followed her gaze westward to a stretch of blue sky chasing the gray clouds. "You're probably right, but I don't feel good about leaving you here."

"Should have thought of that before you dragged me with you on this fool's mission." Teodora's chin lifted.

There would be no persuading the housekeeper. Clarinda may as well go in.

She shuffled toward the front of the store and rounded the corner.

A tall, blond man with an athletic build was stepping onto the first stair leading to her parents' store.

Her breath left her chest as she jerked to a halt. "Richard!"

CHAPTER 11

Clarinda charged forward and seized Richard's arm. She dragged him from the front steps of her parents' store.

A quick glance through the doors showed Father's back was to them and none of the patrons inside paid them any mind.

She had to get Richard out of here.

He didn't resist or protest as she hauled him around the corner. Teodora's mouth fell open.

Clarinda didn't have time to explain. She towed him past the wagon to the back of the house and around the corner to where they were safely hidden behind the kitchen and privy. "What are you doing here?"

"Why are you dragging me?" Richard stared at her, his brow furrowed as he extracted himself from her grasp.

"Did Fletcher send you? Why would he do that when you're dead?"

Richard blinked. "Did you say, 'dead?'"

Clarinda began to pace. "Oh, this is a disaster. You were never supposed to come here. Fletcher was certain you had no business here, no family." She spun on him. "Unless you lied.

Are you a liar, Mr. Stevens? Did you trick my cousin into believing you had no reason to come to San Diego when secretly you planned to come all along?"

The man sputtered and laughed. Not a gentlemanly chuckle, but a full-belly, loud-as-you-please laugh that made his eyes sparkle and his shoulders bounce.

She crossed her arms. "Or maybe you just followed me here. Is that it?"

His laughter ceased, and his gaze darted around the yard, never meeting hers.

Chills ran down her spine. He hadn't actually followed her here, had he? What kind of man did that? *Oh, no.* She'd told her parents she was married to a madman. Or rather that she *had* been married to him. But she wasn't anymore. Because he was dead.

Except the handsome man standing before her looked far too alive for her peace of mind.

She stepped away.

Which of them was unhinged?

"I came to learn more about some ranch property for sale in the area." He shrugged. "I didn't know until I spoke with Mr. Thompson a few minutes ago that the property belonged—at least in part—to your family."

He was here to purchase her ranch? Her breath lodged in her throat. He couldn't have it! It was her home. If he bought it, where would she live? She placed a hand on her burgeoning belly. Where would she raise her child?

"You've been misinformed. The Grand Valley Ranch is not for sale." She reached a hand beneath her large black cloak and checked the watch fob pinned to her bodice. "If you hurry, you should be able to catch the stage for Los Angeles. I've heard there are several ranches for sale in that area." It was not as far as San Francisco—nor the moon, which is where she'd prefer he remove to—but at least it would get him out of town. Immediately.

If she led him to the Franklin House via the backside of the buildings surrounding the plaza, no one should see him. No one could ask his name. It was bad enough he'd spoken with Mr. Thompson. She'd have to deal with that later. First, she needed to get him away from her family.

She reached for his hand.

He drew away. "Wait a minute, I—"

A nearby door crashed open.

Hurried footsteps drew nearer.

Mother rounded the kitchen. "Clarinda! I thought I heard voices back here. What on earth are you doing in town?" She examined Richard head to toe. "And who is that man you're speaking with? What are you thinking, standing here unchaperoned where anyone might see you?"

Richard emitted a noise that sounded suspiciously like a smothered laugh.

She cast him a glare. "We are only speaking, Mother." Never mind that she'd been about to take the man's hand. Again. "We've done nothing to warrant such a fuss. Besides, he was just—"

"A proper young lady does not converse with a strange man in an alleyway."

As if their wide open backyard was an alley. As if they were still in Washington D.C. where alleyways were filled with windows where nosy gossips spied. Clarinda took in their surroundings. Not a single other person was in sight.

～

*T*he tension between Mrs. Humphrey and her daughter was palpable.

Richard stepped forward. "If it helps, ma'am. We are not

entirely strangers. My name is Richard Stevens and—"

All color drained from Mrs. Humphrey's previously red face. She swayed, and he reached for her, his arms tangling with Clarinda's around the now-limp form.

He stared at Clarinda. "What happened?"

"You wouldn't believe me, if I told you." She grunted as she shifted her mother's weight. "Just let go and I'll take her inside."

"Don't be ridiculous." He shifted his hold so one arm supported the older woman's torso, then stooped and slipped his other arm beneath her knees. Straightening with his load, he grinned. "Lead the way."

Clarinda didn't budge. "But—"

He retraced the matron's path. A door stood ajar at the rear of the building.

Clarinda hurried after him. "You can't go inside."

He paused before the threshold.

She squeezed past him, blocking his entrance.

He adjusted his grip on her mother. "Why not?"

"Because..." She darted a look over her shoulder.

He followed her gaze. The hallway held a doorway on either side, a set of stairs near the back, and a curtain at the end. That must lead to the store.

She faced him again. "You just can't."

What was her problem? He hadn't expected an eager reception, given her reluctance to continue their acquaintance in San Francisco, but neither had he expected this cold urgency to be rid of him. Hadn't he been kind to her when she'd been sick on the ferry? Hadn't he rescued her from that over-eager pup? And here he was carrying her unconscious mother. Didn't his helpfulness count for anything?

"Please"—Clarinda extended her arms—"just give her to me and go."

Apparently not.

Richard pushed past Clarinda into the house. He peered

through the first doorway on his right. A dining room. He looked left. The formal parlor.

That would have to do.

"What are you doing?" Clarinda hovered like a gnat.

He settled her mother on the nearest settee.

"You shouldn't be here." She wrung her gloved hands.

Mrs. Humphrey's eyes opened and she peered at Clarinda. "What do you mean?" She shifted her gaze to Richard. "It's a miracle." The older woman surged upward, threw her arms around his shoulders, and squeezed. "You're alive! It's so wonderful that you're alive." She pulled back to clasp his face between her hands, much the way his aunt had done when he was a child. "I thought I'd never get to meet you, but here you are."

Clarinda had mentioned him to her parents? That was a good sign. Wasn't it? But why was her mother so excited to meet a man Clarinda had known less than a full day? What could she have told them to elicit such a reaction? And why was she so adamant that he leave?

Richard tried to catch Clarinda's gaze, but she seemed inordinately fascinated by the pattern in their rug. Something fishy was going on.

Mrs. Humphrey released him and twisted toward the parlor door. "Neal! Neal, come quick. It's Clarinda's husband. He's alive! He's here."

Clarinda's husband? Yes, he'd harbored the hope that someday he might make that claim, but Mrs. Humphrey could have no idea of that. And she spoke as if he and Clarinda were already married. "I'm sorry, ma'am. There seems to have been some misunderstanding. I—"

Clarinda intertwined her left arm with his right one and a tingling sensation zipped over him. Her hand clamped onto his forearm, smothering the pleasant—if shocking—sensation. "Of course, there was." She beamed up at him through her veil.

"Obviously, you're not dead." She turned to her mother. "Isn't it wonderful?"

Before either Richard or Mrs. Humphrey could respond, a younger woman who bore a striking resemblance to Clarinda entered. On her heels came an older man of average height and build with graying hair at his temples. He must be Clarinda's father.

~

Just keep your mouth shut, husband. Clarinda resisted the urge to dig her nails into Richard's arm. Not that she could do any damage with her gloves on. Why couldn't he have left when she told him to?

Lucy rushed forward and threw her arms around him. "Oh, I'm so glad you're alive."

Clarinda refused to let go, forcing Richard to awkwardly pat her sister's back with one arm.

Lucy stepped back, eyes wide. "But what happened? We received a letter from your solicitor that you'd died in a terrible mining accident three days ago."

Clarinda glared at her sister. "Don't pester him with silly questions. No doubt the accident is a terribly painful subject. Let's just be grateful he's alive."

"And he's come to San Diego at last." Mr. Humphrey stepped forward and offered his hand. "It's a pleasure to finally meet you, young man."

Clarinda released Richard's arm but stayed at his side.

Richard slowly accepted her father's hand, clearing his throat. "A pleasure to meet you, sir."

Father's eyes narrowed. "Now, would you care to explain why you eloped with my daughter only to send her back into our care?"

Richard's face blanched as he tugged at the hand Father hadn't released. "I don't—"

"Father! He's only just arrived." She grabbed each man's wrist and wrested poor Richard free of her Father's grip. She tugged the bewildered man toward the parlor door. "Please excuse us. As you can imagine, Richard is fatigued from his journey and we've a lot to discuss before he can get some rest."

"Now just a minute," Father protested. "He and *I* have some things to discuss—"

"Later, Father, I promise." Clarinda yanked Richard into the hall.

"Oh, let the newlyweds have their reunion." Mother's voice followed them toward the stairs, causing Clarinda's cheeks to flame. "There'll be plenty of time for questions and getting to know the boy later."

Rather than take Richard to the upstairs parlor where Lucy was bound to interrupt them, Clarinda turned left at the top of the stairs and entered the sewing room. She began to shut the door, but Richard laid a hand on her shoulder.

"I think that'd better stay open." His light-hearted tone sounded forced. "Whatever the misunderstanding, you and I are not yet married."

She closed the door and pivoted. "Did you say, 'not *yet* married?'"

"Why does your family believe we *are* married?"

"I tried to warn you." Clarinda paced toward the window. "Why couldn't you just leave?" She spun to glare at him. "Why did you have to come at all? Aren't there any ranches for sale near San Francisco?"

"You're avoiding the question."

"You don't really want to know the answer. You just want a reason to laugh at me." She tugged the curtains shut. That was unfair. She didn't know this man well enough to have any idea how he might react to her situation. Then again, could she predict how any man would react in such circumstances? It wasn't as if things like this happened every day.

Why wasn't Fletcher here? He ought to be the one answering to Richard. This whole thing was her cousin's idea after all. She'd never have had the nerve to try such a deception if it weren't for him.

No, that wasn't fair either. Fletcher hadn't left her alone and with child.

"Miss Humphrey, I assure you, I will not laugh." Richard stepped closer. "But if you do not start explaining soon, I may decide to question your family instead. An action I've gathered you'd rather I not take."

Clarinda studied him. If she told him everything, what was to stop him from marching downstairs and sharing every humiliating detail with her family? Then again, if she did not explain, there seemed no doubt that he would—if nothing else—make it clear that he was not, nor ever had been, her husband.

That would ruin everything equally as well.

Hands shaking, she expelled a breath and lowered herself to the closest chair. "You may as well sit. It's a complicated story."

He settled into the chair nearest hers. "I enjoy a good story."

Clarinda searched for the words that would convince this near stranger not to betray her.

An uncomfortable silence filled the room. The rattle and crunch of a passing wagon filtered through the walls. Somewhere, a seagull cried. The wooden chair creaked as she adjusted her position.

Still, nothing she thought of seemed a strong enough argument.

"The beginning is usually a good place to start." His voice was soft and his sea-blue eyes gentle, reminding her of the kindness he'd shown her when she'd been sick on the ferry.

The beginning... What was the beginning?

~

*R*ichard reclined in his chair. If he affected an air of calm, perhaps it would set Clarinda at ease.

When he'd received Henry's letter, Richard recognized the opportunity as guidance from the Lord. The coincidence of such an investment prospect arising in the small community of San Diego was too much to be ignored. Yet he hadn't expected *she'd* find *him*. He hadn't imagined she thought of him at all—let alone that she'd told her family they were married. He resisted the urge to share in the chuckle God must be having over Richard's astonishment.

Clarinda clutched her left arm through the thick cloak. "Ever since the...incident when I was eleven"—she gestured toward her shrouded face—"my parents have treated me like a leper. They banished me. First from town, then from the ranch when they sent me to Benicia. All for my own good, of course." Bitterness seeped into her voice. "My sister, Lucy, could expect to make a good match and be a wife and mother someday, but my parents informed me that no man would ever want a disfigured woman for his wife."

Anger pulsed through him and he clenched his fists. "They actually said that to you?" What kind of parents would say such a thing to their own child? His initial impression had been of a family concerned for their daughter's welfare. This information painted an entirely different picture.

"More or less." She crossed her arms. "They sent me to get a good education, expecting that after graduation I would find a position as a teacher or tutor somewhere far from San Diego and they would no longer be burdened with my care."

"They called you a burden?"

"They didn't have to. I know I am." She turned her face away, the fabric of her veil twisting around her neck. "It's why they wanted to sell the ranch. Traveling back and forth from town was never what they wanted. With me so close to graduating, they thought they no longer had need of it."

"Your father wants to sell? But Mr. Thompson said—"

"Mr. Thompson said whatever you needed to hear to encourage your interest in buying our land." She turned back to Richard. "He's a good man, to a point. And that point is whatever stands between him and a lucrative business deal. He's been good to our family, but you don't ever want to be on the wrong side of business with that man. I've never caught him in an outright lie, but that man can stretch the truth farther than anyone I know."

"I see." Richard's mind scrambled to piece together all the new information. He'd known Thompson was holding back information, but had he lied as well? "Then, Mr. Ames wasn't injured?"

"Oh, no, he was. And he does want out of the ranching business, but so do the rest of the partners. Mr. Thompson convinced them that if they tried to sell the ranch altogether, it might spark concern in the mind of a potential buyer that all is not as profitable as it seems on the ranch."

"And is it?"

She hesitated, her eyes searching his. Was she attempting to discern which answer would most benefit her?

She shrugged. "That depends on how you look at it."

"How so?"

"The drought stole last year's crops, and many cattle have died. But we're among the fortunate few whose lands include sections of mountainside. So we've been able to keep more cattle alive than most."

"But the men I spoke with said the cattle market is down. So your ranch *is* still failing like all the other ranches in the area, isn't it?"

"It's not failing. It's struggling. But there's a way to save it. In fact, I planned to speak with my father about the solution today."

Richard tried to keep the skepticism from his voice. "You have a solution?" What could she possibly do about a drought and a depressed market? "Does this have to do with what you told your parents about me?"

"Yes and no."

"Huh?"

"The solution has nothing to do with you. We can save the ranch by switching to sheep. So I'm sorry, but you'll have to find another property to purchase."

She seemed so pleased with her idea, he hated to disappoint her. "I'm sorry, but wool prices have begun to drop as well."

"That's true. With the increased competition from ranches along the Mississippi switching to raising sheep and driving their herds to California markets, local ranchers have had to lower their prices. On top of that, our shipping costs are higher, so to compete in the larger eastern markets they've had to take a cut in profits there as well."

She was more educated on the topic than he'd given her credit for. "Then how will switching to sheep instead of cattle help?"

"Sheep eat different feed than cattle, and the things they eat handle drought better. So we have more of it. That means we can raise and sell significantly more sheep than cattle right now." She tugged at the cuff of her left sleeve. "It won't bring in the huge profits we saw in years past, but it will certainly be an improvement over the losses we're seeing now."

"If it's so simple, why are your father and the other owners still selling?"

"Although we've always kept a small herd of sheep, it will take time and a bit of reinvestment to make the switch to raising mainly sheep. And as I said, even after the switch, the profit won't be what it once was. The investors want to move their money to industries with greater potential for wealth."

Her understanding of the ranching industry was impressive. Could his new shipping business help lower the ranchers' transportation costs? He smoothed his hand across his trouser leg. That was a question for another time. He'd exchanged less than a handful of letters with his uncle and wasn't yet in a position to negotiate business deals. Best to focus on the situation before him. The ranch owners wanted to invest in something with greater profits... "So they're looking to invest in something like the logging industry up north."

Her eyes widened behind the black lace. "Why, yes, they have been discussing purchasing a logging company. How did you know?"

"Never mind that. We're getting off topic. You were supposed to be explaining why your family believes I'm your husband." Had she deliberately steered the conversation in a different direction?

Her cheeks and nose flushed a charming shade of pink. "Right. Well...I think it'd be easiest to show you."

"Show me what?"

Clarinda rose, and Richard stood out of habit.

She turned her back to him, beginning to remove her cloak.

They'd been inside for several minutes. Why remove the garment now? Was she stalling again? He gritted his teeth. "May I hang that somewhere for you?" He glanced around, but there was no coat rack, nor any hooks in the room.

Of course, there wouldn't be. Under normal circumstances, the maid or butler ought to have greeted them at the door and whisked their outer garments away. Assuming they had servants. He wasn't sure what the Humphrey's financial situation was. They weren't destitute, but could a struggling ranch and a store in a small town provide enough income for a proper staff?

Clarinda draped her cloak over the dress form standing in the corner and pivoted to face him.

His eyes were drawn to her figure. Either his memory was playing tricks on him, or the woman had gained several pounds since they'd last met—most of it near her waist. What was he doing staring at her waist? He jerked his attention to the window. "It's stopped raining."

"Teodora!"

Richard looked back, careful to keep his attention above her neck.

Clarinda's hand covered her mouth, pressing her veil against her face. She dashed toward the door.

"Oh, no you don't." Richard caught her arm. "We're not leaving this room until you finish explaining what's going on."

Clarinda huffed, smoothing the fabric of her skirts in a way that accentuated the pronounced bump forming at her middle. "You mean you haven't figured it out yet?"

The truth slammed into him. No, she couldn't—

"I'm expecting, Richard—er, Mr. Stevens." She pulled her arm from his grasp, her face flushed once more. "I needed a husband and, well, yours was the first name Fletcher thought of."

"Mr. Johnson?" Richard gaped at her, his mind struggling to catch up with what she was saying. "What has he to do with this? He's not the child's—"

"No! How could you even think—" She shuddered. "This is...a problem of my own making. Fletcher was only trying to help, that's all."

"Then who's the father?"

"You are." She tipped one shoulder, having the good sense to appear guilty. "At least, that's what my parents believe. And my sister Lucy. And my aunt and uncle and—"

"Me?" Richard drew himself to his fullest height. "I would never disgrace a woman in such a way. How could you—"

"We're married. Remember?"

"No, we're not." And if the woman could stomach as many lies as it must have taken to concoct such a story, he began to seriously doubt everything he'd thought the Lord had been speaking to him about their future.

"You're right. But my family and everyone else believes that we are, and that's all that matters."

"All that matters? What about me? What about *my* life? My reputation?" He paced the closet-sized room, his fingers dragging through his hair. "What if I'd arrived in San Diego with my real wife on my arm?"

Clarinda'd been rubbing the sleeve of her left arm, but stilled at his words. Her eyes rounded as she whispered, "You're married?"

"No," he admitted. "But I *could* have gotten married since we last met. You had no way of knowing." He stomped toward her. "What were you thinking? You did have other options. What about the child's real father?"

Her nose crinkled. "He doesn't want anything to do with us."

Vile names for the man entered Richard's mind. Words his mother would be ashamed he knew. What kind of man seduced a woman and then abandoned her?

There had to have been other options. If she knew about the Davidson Home for Women and Children, would she have applied? No. That wouldn't keep her secret. "What about an orphanage, then? Many women have their children in secret, then let the orphanages find them good homes." Or so he'd heard. He didn't personally know of anyone who'd done it, but isn't that what the orphanages were there for—to help children in need of families? "Did you even consider that?"

Rather than back down in the face of his fury, she lifted her chin and glared at him. "Of course I did. But I don't want my child to grow up wondering why his mother didn't love him enough to keep him. Nor do I want him carrying the weight of being called a bastard because his mother was foolish enough to believe"—her voice cracked and the rest of her words came out in a whisper—"to believe a man loved her enough to marry her."

A layer of anger slid off him. She'd been betrayed and done what she could to protect her child from the consequences. What was the reputation of a near stranger compared to the fate of her baby?

He clasped her shoulders. The wretched veil prevented him from seeing her as clearly as he'd like, but he held her gaze. "He's a fool, whoever he is. To let a woman as special as you slip from his grasp only shows how stupid *he* is. His choice has nothing to do with your worth."

She sniffed and slipped her hand beneath her veil to wipe her eyes. "You're doing it again."

His thumb rubbed up and down her shoulder. "What?"

"Telling me things that aren't true just to make me feel better."

She'd said something similar at the wharf when he'd declared her beautiful. The response made far more sense in light of her revelation regarding her upbringing, and the more recent betrayal by her child's father. Even if her assumptions were still untrue. "I meant every word I said then, and I mean every word now. In fact..." He gently tugged at the black lace shrouding her beauty. "I'd like it very much if you'd take this thing off."

She jerked away. "Why?"

"Well, for one, it's a widow's veil and I think we've established"—he gestured at himself—"you're not a widow." He returned his hands to her shoulders. "For another, I much prefer to see my wife's eyes clearly when I speak with her."

"But I'm not your wife."

He grinned, hoping to elicit a smile from her. "That appears to be up for debate."

"Do be serious." Her lips twitched, but did not turn up. "This is my life we're talking about."

He sobered. "And mine."

She peered at him through the black fabric. "Do you mean you'll go along with it? You won't betray me?"

It was on the tip of his tongue to reassure her. He wanted nothing more than to erase the fear in her voice. But caution restrained his words. What was he agreeing to? Dishonesty held no place in his life. Look what it had done to his parents. Could he agree to continue such a monumental falsehood—even to rescue such a beautiful damsel in distress?

What were Clarinda's feelings for the man who'd betrayed her? To wind up in this predicament, she must have felt strongly for whoever he was. Did she care for him still? Or had the man's betrayal erased her affection?

Richard opened his mouth to ask, but closed it again. Whatever her answer, it wouldn't change his course. Abner Stevens had raised another man's child, knowing his wife loved that other man, and it had destroyed him.

But Richard wasn't Abner. Richard didn't derive his value from someone else's esteem, but from *God's* view of who he was. Not even his wife could take away the fact that he was a chosen son of the one true God. And that same God had led him here, to this woman, with a clear directive that she was to become his wife. But He also expected Richard to be honest. "I won't pretend to be married to you. It isn't right."

"But—"

"But I will marry you."

Her soft gasp made him smile. He'd not expected the words himself, but they were right. It was why God had brought him here. His handiwork was too clear to be in doubt. "That is, if you'll have me."

"You barely know me. Why would you propose marriage?"

"Do you believe in God, Clarinda?" He held his breath. It

was a question he should have asked before proposing, but he'd never imagined God would direct him to marry an unbeliever.

"Of course, I do. Why?"

Relief flooded through him. "This may seem hard to believe, but I believe God has sent me to you. I believe He has chosen you to be my wife."

She looked down. "And my child?" Her tone was guarded, wary.

"Will be mine as well."

Her head lifted. "Except he's not."

Richard smirked. "You seem awfully convinced it's a boy."

She blinked. "Not really. I got tired of saying he-or-she all the time and I refuse to call him *it*. So I picked one and stuck with it."

"Then you won't mind if the child's a girl?"

"Of course not. Will you?"

"I'd be delighted. Especially if she has your beautiful blond hair."

"What if she resembles her father?"

Richard frowned. "I'll be her father."

"You know what I mean."

Recalling his own nose and the questions it had raised, he nodded. He did understand what she meant.

Would it bother him to raise a child who looked nothing like him? He searched his heart, but could find no indication that it would bother him at all. In fact, this could be his chance to rewrite the wrongs of the past in some way. Where Abner had been cold and distant, Richard could be warm and engaged. He'd teach their child to fish and ride a horse, to tell time and study the Bible. And he'd make a point to tell his son or daughter how much they were loved every day and never let them doubt it.

He smiled at Clarinda. "Whether she resembles her father or

her mother, our daughter will know love and acceptance all the days of her life, so far as I can help it."

Clarinda bit her lip. "But how can we marry without my parents finding out? The visiting preacher is good friends with Father and I don't think the priest—"

"Wait a minute. I didn't say we wouldn't tell them the truth. I'm offering to marry you—to take care of you and your child— not to help you deceive your parents."

She broke away from his touch. "But if you're going to tell everyone the truth, what's the point in getting married?"

Her words stung, driving home exactly how she viewed the idea of marrying him—as the sacrifice she was willing to make for the sake of her child.

Her gloved hands fisted at her sides. "My child will be a bastard either way. The people of this town will judge our whole family for my mistake and my parents. Even Lucy will suffer for it."

"You don't know that." He tried to take her hand, but she stepped out of his reach.

"Yes, I do. I've seen it happen. First the customers will find somewhere else to shop, then invitations to social events will fail to arrive, and eventually friends will stop coming to visit." Her breathing increased to a point of hyperventilation. "I can't do it. I can't put them through that again. I won't."

"Easy, Clarinda." He held his hands out as he would to a star-tled horse. "Take a deep breath. Here"—he inched forward and gripped her forearms—"have a seat and bend over." He guided her head toward her knees. She had to adjust herself to manage the position. How far along was she? He mentally stored the question for another time. "Deep breaths."

She took one deep breath and shook free of his touch. "You don't understand what it was like. My parents will lose every-thing. We'll have to move again. They can't start over now. Not at their age." She stood again and began to pace.

Her distress battled with his conscience. Though he did have some idea of what it was like to be ostracized by parts of society —his father's indiscretions had not gone unnoticed back east— he'd never lost the esteem of his true friends. What must it have been like to leave behind everything and everyone you knew at such a young age and for such a tragic reason? He could well understand her aversion to reliving the events, but to aid her in her deception went against Biblical instruction.

"There has to be something, some way…" Clarinda spun toward him. "I'll give you the ranch."

"What do you mean?"

"You came to buy a ranch, right? Give me one year to convince my parents we're happily married—though you'll be too busy working up north to visit often, of course—and I'll convince the partners to switch to sheep. By the end of the year we'll be making a nice profit and I'll see that the ranch is yours. You're an investor. Consider keeping my secret an investment."

"How could you possibly accomplish that?"

A sad smile lit her expression. "There are some advantages to being pitied by kind and generous men."

He didn't like the sound of that. "And at the end of the year? What happens then?"

She tipped her head. "You'll have your ranch, like I said."

"I mean, with us." He wagged his finger between them.

"Oh. Well, nothing. That is, I'll tell my family that you've decided you cannot continue to live with me so far away and have insisted that I come and live with you in…where's your mine again?"

"Nevada City."

"Right. I'll tell them I'm moving there to live with you, but truly I'll find somewhere else to live. A year ought to be enough time to figure things out, I think."

Absolutely not. There was no way he'd let her go once he had her. He only intended to make marriage vows once in his life, and he intended to keep them. Still…how far had she thought this through? "How will you live?"

"Oh, I'll think of something. I completed enough of my education that I should be able to find a job as a tutor for a family somewhere."

"What about the child? Most families aren't interested in having their tutor bringing along their infant to lessons. I imagine they're rather distracting."

"I—uh. I'm not sure, but as I've said, a year should give me enough time to figure things out." She clasped her hands behind her back. "Does that mean you'll do it?"

"No. I'm sorry, but I don't want to lie to your parents, and if we marry, I intend to keep my wedding vows."

"Then I won't marry you."

CHAPTER 12

*R*ichard closed his eyes. *What should I do, Lord?*

He waited, but no answer came. Great. Only the most important decision of his life, and the Lord was choosing now to go silent.

And wasn't that the point?

Up until now, every nudge the Lord had given him had driven him toward Clarinda—had brought him to this moment. But her insistence on maintaining the lie sowed doubt in his mind. Had he misunderstood? Had God only meant for Richard to offer his assistance or had he truly intended them to marry?

Richard recalled the verse the Lord had directed him to after his odd dream.

"Then Joseph being raised from sleep did as the angel of the Lord had bidden him, and took unto him his wife"

God had already provided him with his answers. Richard was meant to marry Clarinda and he wasn't meant to lie.

He just needed to help her see that.

Would she compromise?

He opened his eyes and held Clarinda's gaze. "If I'm asked, I won't lie for you, but if I promise not to offer the truth about our wedding date unless they ask first, will you agree to marry me?"

Her expression softened and she took his hands in her gloved fingers. "Yes. Thank you, I—"

"Hold on, I have some conditions."

"Conditions?" She dropped his hands.

"Yes. The first is that you not wear this thing when we're alone together." He pulled at her veil, but it must have been pinned.

She lifted a hand to hold the garment in place. "What else?"

He frowned, but let it go. "You must also agree to allow me to court you."

"Court me? But we'll already be married."

"In name, perhaps, and before the eyes of the law, the church, and God. But I want more than a marriage of convenience for myself and our child. I want friendship, companionship, and hopefully, someday love will grow between us."

"What if it doesn't?"

It was a valid question. God hadn't promised Richard sunshine and rainbows for the rest of his life. Marrying Clarinda might mean sacrificing his chance at finding the kind of love Daniel and Eliza had found. The bond between them showed how marriage was meant to be. He'd wanted that for himself and his future wife. What if he and Clarinda never found that kind of love?

Fear squeezed his throat like a snake coiled around its prey. *Delight thyself also in the Lord and he shall give thee the desires of thine heart.* The snake vanished. If Richard delighted first in the Lord, his desires would align with God's and he would find peace and joy, regardless of his circumstance. He refocused on Clarinda's eyes, shadowed behind the veil. "I will leave our love in the Lord's hands."

"Anything else?"

"Eventually, you need to tell your parents the truth."

"I thought you agreed to keep my secret."

"I agreed not to betray your confidence. But keeping your parents in the dark isn't right. I'll give you time to work up the courage and come to terms with the possible repercussions, but you need to be honest with them, even if no one else ever knows."

"You mean, you won't make me shout it from the stage at the next fiesta?" Sarcasm dripped from every word.

"No. What you've done in your private life is your business. The world isn't entitled to every detail. But your parents— however flawed they may be—do care about you, and they're your family. They ought to know. More importantly,"—he took her hands in his—"I think keeping this secret from them will hurt you more than it will hurt them."

She snorted derisively.

He squeezed her fingers. "I'll give you some time to think about it and pray." He turned to go.

"Wait. What will you tell my family? They'll be waiting for you downstairs."

"I won't say anything about our relationship for now. Your parents invited me to stay so I'll tell them I'm going to fetch my belongings from the hotel."

"Is that really what you'll be doing?"

"Yes. I told you, I dislike lying. But whether I stay here will be up to you, and I promise to take my time fetching my things. I want you to have plenty of time to consider your decision. Our marriage will be for life."

⁓

At the base of the stairs, Richard paused to draw a deep breath. *Lord, guide my words. Help me to be honest while keeping my promise.* Had he made the right decision in giving her time to confess?

A few steps down the hall brought him to the open door of the lower parlor. Inside, Mrs. Humphrey and Lucy shared one of two settees near the center of the room. They turned at the sound of his approach.

"Mr. Stevens. I didn't expect to see you again so soon." Mrs. Humphrey indicated the settee across from theirs. "Come, have a seat. My husband needed to return to the store and tend customers. Did you get enough rest?"

He stayed in the doorway. "Actually, I'm headed to the hotel to do exactly that. Clarinda and I were busy catching up, but I'm afraid I am quite fatigued."

"The hotel? Oh yes, I did wonder about your things after you'd gone up. I was so surprised by your resurrection at first, that I didn't realize you weren't carrying any bags."

Lucy leaned forward. "But why would you take a room at the hotel? Surely Clarinda told you that you could use our guest room."

"I wasn't sure what my reception would be, given the circumstances." It was true. He hadn't known how her family would react to a stranger asking about Clarinda's whereabouts. He took a step backward.

Mrs. Humphrey nodded, her eyes losing some of their warmth as her expression sobered. "Mr. Humphrey and I *were* less-than-pleased to learn Clarinda had married so quickly and to a man we'd never met."

"I completely understand." He had to get out of here before she demanded an explanation he could not give. "I deeply regret that that was your first impression of me, but now that I'm here,"—how long *would* he be here? Would Clarinda accept his terms?—"I hope you will give me the chance to improve on that impression. I promise, my intentions are to do my absolute best for your daughter and..." He caught himself short of mentioning Clarinda's child. No one else had mentioned her condition. Did her family know? The signs were still subtle enough she might have kept it from them, living separately as they did. "...and to make her happy." Richard turned toward the door. "For now, though, if you'll excuse me, I need to go."

~

*T*he murmur of voices below stopped.

From her perch at the top of the stairs, Clarinda leaned forward. What was happening?

Footsteps hastened across the lower hallway.

Clarinda raced to the sewing room and crossed to the window.

Richard rounded the corner and tipped his hat to Teodora, who still waited in the wagon. Thankfully, the rain had stopped. Something he said made her smile, then he dashed away.

Her gaze returned to Teodora. Clarinda ought to go down and insist the housekeeper come in now that everyone knew she was here.

As if sensing her gaze, Teodora glanced up and caught Clarinda watching her. The housekeeper lifted one eyebrow, her lips pressed tight as she shook her head.

Richard hadn't told her of his proposal. He hadn't spoken to Teodora long enough to have conveyed such a message, but the dear woman recognized trouble when she saw it.

Clarinda opened her mouth to respond.

What she was going to say, she wasn't at all sure. And Teodora couldn't hear her from here anyhow. So it didn't matter much that the housekeeper turned away before Clarinda could utter a sound.

She followed Teodora's gaze and spotted her parents' maid, Mary, standing in the side yard. She seemed to be waving for Teodora to come inside. A moment later, the two servants disappeared from view.

Clarinda paced the room. Was she seriously considering

marriage to a man who wouldn't be content with living separate lives, but wanted friendship and love from her?

At least he'd been upfront with his expectations. From everything she knew about him, he was kind, honest, hard working, and far more understanding than she'd ever dared hope. All qualities that promised he'd make a good husband and father.

Still, she wouldn't open her heart to him. No matter how sincere his blue eyes appeared. How could she when her heart still lay in pieces, scattered somewhere along the road to Sacramento? And that's where it needed to stay. Putting it back together...she wasn't sure she could, but she knew she didn't want to. That traitorous organ was what had gotten her into this mess. Hearts were weak, vulnerable.

Yet that was exactly what Richard wanted from her—vulnerability.

Could she place her heart on the line for the sake of her child?

Clarinda pictured holding her own babe to her chest. How could she not risk everything for something so precious?

Still, there was no way she would agree to his request that she not wear the veil when they were alone. Living together—which it seemed he would insist upon—they were bound to be alone much of the time. The idea of wandering around uncovered...she may as well be naked. It was unthinkable. Would he be open to compromise? Or perhaps he had servants in his Nevada City home. Surely he wouldn't expect her to be unveiled in their presence. That would significantly reduce the amount of time they spent alone.

They couldn't move right away, though. Clarinda had yet to help Teodora visit her daughter. How would she accomplish that if they lived in Nevada City? She'd have to find a way to make it happen before they left.

Richard seemed a reasonable man. He wouldn't expect her to

pick up and leave tomorrow. Then again, they needed to find a way to marry without her parents learning the truth, and traveling to a large city like San Francisco would accomplish the task. If they remained here, her parents would expect them to share a room, but she had a suspicion Richard wouldn't accept such arrangements until after their wedding.

Not that she was eager to share her bed, either. Would he expect...? She shook her head clear of the thought. Richard would take her wishes into consideration. He'd proven himself too kind not to. In fact, once she explained Teodora's situation, he'd probably insist on helping.

As for the wooing, perhaps she'd been thinking about this the wrong way. He'd only asked that she promise to let him court her. He hadn't required a promise to actually love him—had acknowledged that it might not happen. According to Lucy's letters, courtship involved parlor-room conversations on a shared settee, picnics on sunny afternoons, and long walks around town. Surely she could manage those things without losing her heart.

That left her with the requirement that she tell her parents the truth. Again, he hadn't been specific. He'd given no deadline for confessing her sins, only asked that she tell them once she'd worked up the courage. Well, she would never work up enough courage to share that particular truth, so agreeing to his request wouldn't be a problem.

She pressed her fingers to her lips. Was she truly going to marry a man she barely knew?

CHAPTER 13

*R*ichard gripped the side of the wagon bench as it rumbled along the road from town and glanced behind them. He looked past the housekeeper riding in the bed to the mare tied at the back. Mr. Humphrey had insisted Richard could choose a horse from those at Grand Valley Ranch, but Richard wanted a mount of his own.

It was bad enough he'd be moving into property his future father-in-law owned, eating the man's food, and being waited upon by the man's housekeeper. All at a time when the ranch was doing poorly, and the Humphrey's store couldn't be thriving, given the state of the local economy. Temporary or not, sponging off his in-laws didn't set well with him. He'd need to work hard to show his new family he had more to offer than deep pockets.

He'd spent as much time on his knees in prayer as he had packing at the hotel. When he returned to the Humphrey's town home, Clarinda was waiting in the downstairs hall. "Yes" was all she'd gotten out before her father interrupted and escorted them back to the parlor. The questions from her family had begun the moment he and Clarinda stepped into the room. He kept his answers to the truth, only withholding those details that would reveal Clarinda's deception. Censoring his words didn't come naturally, so he let Clarinda answer as much as she could.

When it came to his family, business, and finances, however, Clarinda knew next to nothing. So he'd spoken up. He'd informed them that his parents had passed on and his two elder brothers and two younger sisters all lived back east. Then he'd steered the conversation to his business holdings.

Still a tricky subject, he refrained from explaining his ownership of the shipping business back east. He'd stated only that a relative was overseeing the day-to-day operations on his behalf. For the most part, Richard was able to keep their conversation focused on the success of Prosperity Mine and the dangers of working in it.

When they questioned him about his supposed death, Clarinda told them there'd been a misunderstanding between the solicitor and Richard's manager when the facts of the accident were reported, but that everything was cleared up now. He'd had to bite the inside of his cheek to keep from protesting.

In the end, her family had seemed satisfied with the answers given. They encouraged Clarinda to take Richard to the ranch and get him settled.

Clarinda shifted on the bench beside him, her skirts pressed against his thigh. She'd fidgeted more and more the last few minutes.

"Are you all right? Should we stop so you can stretch your legs?" Though she'd assured him the trip from town took less than three hours—a fair distance farther than Thompson had claimed—an unpadded wagon bench was less than comfortable under normal circumstances. He couldn't imagine what it was like in her condition. He'd have to see that leather padding was added before their next trip to town.

"No, I'm fine, thank you." She shifted again.

"Are you certain? You seem uncomfortable."

Her cheeks pinked. "I'm fine, it's just..." Her head swiveled as though scanning the large valley and surrounding hills. "I suppose we had better stop for a moment."

"Of course." He brought the wagon to a stop and jumped down. He hurried to help her descend, but she was on the ground before he reached her.

"If you'll excuse me a moment." She dashed toward a large bush.

What was she—? *Oh*. Richard turned his back. Hadn't she visited the privy right before they left town? He sincerely hoped she wasn't ill. Or perhaps it was something to do with the child she carried. He'd no way of knowing. He'd been in California by the time either of his sisters had carried their children. Not that they'd have discussed such personal matters with him.

The snap and rustle of tiny branches alerted him to her approach. "Is it safe to turn?"

"Yes, thank you."

There was a bit of plant snagged on the side of her veil. He reached to pluck the debris away.

She stumbled back, her eyes widening as though he'd drawn a knife on her. "What are you doing?"

"I was trying to remove—"

"But you said I could keep it on unless we were alone."

She thought he was trying to take off her veil? "I was just trying to get that bit of plant that's stuck to your veil, but..." He glanced around. With the exception of Teodora, they *were* alone among the chaparral and grasslands. Not another person or even another building was in sight. "Now that you mention it, we *are* alone."

"Teodora is here."

"And she's never seen you without your veil?"

She cut around him to the wagon. "We only *seem* to be alone.

137

Anyone could happen upon us at any moment, out on the road as we are."

He assisted her into the conveyance and climbed in himself. He stared at the narrow wagon ruts she'd said were the main road heading east. It didn't seem likely anyone would happen upon them. How long had it taken the baby's father to convince her to remove her veil? Couldn't she give Richard an ounce of the trust she'd obviously shown the swine who'd gotten her into this fix?

He took up the reins, then hesitated. That swine had squandered her trust. No doubt it would take Richard thrice as long to earn any part of it. To say nothing of winning her heart. It wasn't fair, but... He peeked at her from the corner of his eye. Yep. She was worth it.

He glanced at Teodora, hoping for some hint of how to continue, but the woman appeared to be dozing. Wait. Was that a suspicious quirk to the older woman's lips? *Pretending* to doze, then. Clearly he'd receive no aid from her.

He returned his attention to Clarinda. "If you will not take it off entirely, will you at least lift the front? You can fix it to your hat somehow so I can see your beautiful face. Then if someone does come, you can easily flip it down before they get close enough to see you."

Her head swiveled in every direction before she reached for the front edge of her veil. Slowly, she tugged it free of her collar and paused. "Why is this so important to you?"

"You use that thing to hide from the world. With what you've shared of your past, I now understand and can accept your desire to hide from others—even if I think you shouldn't— but I'm asking you not to hide from me."

At last, she lifted the fabric and tucked it atop her hat, though her eyes remained downcast.

He wished she'd look at him, but at least she'd accepted his compromise. "Thank you." He'd pressed her enough for now.

~

a little more than an hour later, Richard followed Clarinda's direction to steer the wagon off the main road. Clarinda lowered her veil as they splashed through a wide creek.

Broad, old oaks lined the long drive to the ranch house, which was also circled by trees. More oaks scattered the yard and shaded the corrals near the barn that was situated across the creek from the house. Beyond their immediate area, there didn't seem to be many other trees in the grass-covered valley.

The ranch house itself was made of whitewashed adobe. It was larger than Richard had expected.

He drew the team to a stop where Clarinda indicated and assisted her down. Teodora scooted to the back of the wagon. He rushed to assist the housekeeper.

She offered him a stiff smile. "Thank you."

He hefted his trunk. "Where should I...?"

Clarinda had disappeared and the front door stood open.

Richard followed the housekeeper inside.

The house was warm, despite the brisk March breeze blowing outside. The room they entered was modest. It held a small dining set for four near one corner, and a writing desk with a chair nestled in another corner. A worn, brown settee faced the large fireplace with a rag rug at its feet before the hearth. Cheerful floral curtains hung at two windows, adding a bit of charm to the simple room.

Unlike his parents' home, neither paintings, nor samplers, nor any decor at all interrupted the smooth, white adobe walls. The difference was calming.

"I'll make coffee." Teodora disappeared through a door to his left.

Clarinda appeared in a doorway across from him. "This way." Without waiting for a response, she stepped through.

He hurried to follow.

Rather than the hallway he'd expected, Richard found himself in another room. Even smaller than the last, this room held a narrow bed, a wardrobe, and a washstand bearing a green bowl and pitcher. A small chair was the only other piece of furniture.

He shifted the heavy trunk to look at Clarinda. "Is this..?"

She was stepping through yet another door.

Again, he hastened after her.

This time, she stopped in the center of the room.

"This is Lucy's room, but she won't need it until my family comes to visit."

So he was to use her sister's room. He'd nearly forgotten her family lived in town while she lived on the ranch. He set his trunk down, inspecting his temporary quarters. This room was identical to the first, except the pitcher and bowl set were blue, and there was a door in the wall to his left instead of ahead of him. "When do they come?"

"My family comes Friday afternoons and leaves Saturday afternoons.

"They only visit one night per week?"

"We may not have a regular preacher, but people still gather to worship at the courthouse in town. It's a long drive from here." She opened the window curtains and surveyed the room. "That's better."

Her words from earlier replayed in his mind. *They banished me from town.*

This ranch was her parents' choice for her. She seemed passionate about preventing its sale, but did that mean she wanted to live here? His new wealth would afford them accommodations anywhere she chose. He opened his mouth to ask, but she continued speaking.

"We don't have a guest room on the ranch since my parents rarely invite people here, and never to stay overnight." She gestured to the room. "I hope this will do. The only other options are the bunkhouse or the manager's house, but word would get back to my parents if you slept there."

"What about your housekeeper? Won't she find it odd that I'm sleeping in here rather than in your room?" Where *was* Clarinda's room? Was it the one they'd passed through or somewhere else in the house?

"Teodora knows the truth about our relationship."

He stiffened. "And you trust her not to tell your parents?"

A small smile lit Clarinda's face behind the black lace. "Teodora basically raised me once we moved to San Diego. She keeps my secrets."

At least his future wife had one ally. How isolated her childhood must have been. No wonder she was so guarded. To be rejected and pushed aside at such a young age—he couldn't imagine it.

He tapped a finger against her veil. "We're alone again."

Her smile vanished. "I should see if Teodora needs help in the kitchen." She tried to step past him.

He caught her arm. "I doubt your housekeeper needs assistance making coffee." He waved to a spindly chair in the corner. "Stay with me while I unpack my things."

"There are eight men who work this ranch besides Mr. Ames, you know. It isn't just Teodora who might walk in at any moment."

Was she afraid to be alone with him? Or only afraid someone might see her if she complied with his request to remove her veil? One way to find out. "So lock the door."

"We have no locks on our doors."

Well, that wouldn't do. *Hmm.* There were two doors and only one chair, but his trunk was heavy.

He released her and shut the door they'd come through. He shoved his trunk against it. Another few seconds and he had the chair wedged against the other entrance. It wouldn't stop a determined intruder, but it should prevent unannounced company.

He faced her with a raised brow. Would she remove the veil, or demand to be let out? He'd let her leave, of course, if that was what she truly wanted. He hoped she'd trust him enough to stay.

Three long seconds passed before she reached for the black lace.

He exhaled and began removing the things from his trunk that he would need between now and tomorrow.

He cast a glance over his shoulder.

She stood in the center of the room, her face turned down, but the veil tucked up.

He set his Bible on the pillow. "Where do you sleep?"

She pointed toward the room they'd passed through to reach this one. "Just there."

He recalled the small bed and frowned. They'd need to do something about that. He didn't intend to pressure her into intimacy, but neither did he intend to spend his nights sleeping on the floor once they were married.

As if her thoughts followed a similar vein, Clarinda said, "When I agreed to your conditions, you promised you knew a way for us to get married without traveling far and without my parents finding out. What is it?"

Finished settling in, Richard turned to face her. "Some friends of mine have family living in the nearby mountains. They have a neighbor who was a preacher."

She looked up. "I've never heard of a preacher in the mountains. There's no church up there—save the one the priests established for the Indians."

Without the veil shading them, her eyes were blue as a summer sky. When her brows lifted, they made faint wrinkles on her forehead he hadn't been able to see before.

She ducked her chin again and turned away.

He must have stared too long. "This man hasn't led a church

for many years, but four years ago he performed a wedding ceremony for those same friends I mentioned. I figure he can do the same for us."

Clarinda placed a gloved hand over her middle. "Then, we'll need to travel to the mountains?"

"Yes, but it isn't far. He rarely leaves them, and I'm not certain he'd be willing to come to the ranch to perform the ceremony. His visit would raise too many questions, in any case."

"Yes, it would." She peered at him from beneath her lashes. "Teodora will need to come with us."

"If that's what you want." It would probably help Clarinda to have a trusted friend along.

"Then I think going to the mountains is a wonderful idea." For the first time, Clarinda grinned at him. The force of it struck the air from his lungs.

That settled it. He'd do everything in his power to see that she grinned as often as possible. And without that stupid veil to hide it.

⌁

The next morning, Clarinda shoved another stocking into the small bag she was packing for their trip into the mountains.

Teodora plucked it out. "This isn't wise. You do not know this man. Tell your parents the truth and be done with it."

"No. You know how they'll react." She snatched the stocking from Teodora's grip and shoved it back into the bag. "Besides, if word gets out, imagine what that will do to their business. No one will want to associate with the family of a disgraced woman. They'll lose customers, the store will fail, and you'll lose your position."

"Don't be foolish." Teodora set a hand on her hip as Clarinda collected her comb and mirror from the small stand holding her

143

bowl and pitcher. "People still need goods. No reason they should stop buying them just because you are with child and unmarried."

"You don't understand." No one could understand who hadn't lived through what her family had lived through in D.C. No one wanted to believe that strangers, friends, and even family could be so cruel. "Trust me when I say this is my best option. It's the only way."

"What if this man is not who he seems? You know nothing about him but what he has told you. Maybe he's not rich at all and does not own a mine like he claims. He could be a gambler, a thief, or an angry drunk. What if he hits you or your child?"

Clarinda carefully folded her wrapper and placed it in the bag. "He has not had a single drop, nor smelled of alcohol since I have known him."

"And how long is that? At least write to your cousin. Ask him to go to Nevada City and see if this man tells the truth. Fletcher can ask his friends what Mr. Stevens is like and write to you. Then you can make your decision."

"Richard spoke with Fletcher at length about the mining industry while we were on the ferry. From what I recall, Richard was extremely knowledgeable on the subject and he has been nothing but kind to me. Even when I was less than friendly in return. He didn't have to keep my secret and he'd no obligation to offer to marry me."

"Yes, that worries me, too." Teodora scowled as Clarinda threaded the straps through the buckles and cinched her bag. "What kind of man proposes marriage to a woman he barely knows? There's something not right about him."

The question had been swirling in Clarinda's mind as well, but she'd pushed it aside. If she didn't choose to trust and marry Richard, what alternative did she have but to confess everything to her parents and face society's rejection once more?

Clarinda lifted her bag and stiffened her spine. Her choice

was made. "I'm getting married, Teodora, and I would like you with me when it happens. Will you come or not?"

"I can see you will not change your mind." With a huff, Teodora flung open the wardrobe and retrieved a book from its bottom. "Here, you're going to need this." She shoved the Bible at Clarinda's chest and stormed toward the door. "I suppose I had better pack my things. Stubborn girl."

CHAPTER 14

*T*eodora was right. Clarinda had lost her mind.

She guided her mare behind Richard's as they followed a winding trail through the mixed oak forest that covered the tops of the mountains. Teodora followed in the deepening twilight.

The horses and riders all ambled along as if what they were doing was completely normal. As if it weren't crazy to follow a man you barely knew into the wilderness. As if planning to marry a near stranger wasn't something that ought to consign her to an institution.

It wasn't supposed to be this way. She was supposed to be married to Arnie now. Why hadn't she insisted they keep riding that night? Why did she let her emotions take control? She should have resisted. They'd been so close. If only she'd waited a few more hours. None of this would be happening now.

Instead of returning to the school, she should have walked straight to the Walker's home and demanded to speak with Arnie's father. He'd never even spoken with her. If he'd gotten to know her, maybe he'd see she was more than the freak in a veil. Maybe.

Then again, why should he be any different than the hundreds of people who couldn't see past her scars?

What made Richard so unique? She reined her mount to an abrupt halt. Rocks skittered across the path.

Richard glanced back. "What's wrong? Do you need a rest? We're nearly there, but if you need to stop that's fine." He lifted a leg to dismount.

"Why?"

Richard rested on the saddle. "There's no rush. If you need—"

"No. I mean, why..." *don't my scars bother you?* The foolish question caught in her throat. Of course they bothered him. It was just an act. The same way Arnie had pretended to love her. Or *had* he actually loved her? Had she ruined it all in those last moments? Had he been so displeased—

"Why, what?" Richard's brows knit.

She swallowed hard. "Nothing. It's nothing. Never mind. Let's keep going." She nudged her horse forward.

"You're sure?" Richard glanced from her to Teodora and back. "I really don't mind—"

"You said it's not far. I can rest when we get there."

Richard glanced at Teodora a final time before prodding his horse forward.

Less than an hour later, the trees parted and a cabin came into view. The small, L-shaped structure sat in the center of a clearing.

Richard slowed his horse, bringing them all to a stop several yards from the clearing. "Hello, the house!"

What was he doing?

"State your business." A deep voice to their right made them all jump in their saddles.

One of the largest men she'd ever seen stood beside a broad oak tree. He held a rifle at the ready, but not raised. Had the man been there the whole time? Or had he been spying on them from behind the tree?

Richard appeared unsurprised by the man's sudden appearance. "My name's Richard Stevens. Daniel sent me with a letter. Are you Mr. Brooks?"

The man grinned and his posture relaxed. "Richard!" He strode forward. "It's wonderful to finally meet you. Yes, I'm Jim Brooks. How's everyone up north? Is my granddaughter still whining about her teeth coming in?"

Richard laughed as he slid from his horse. "And then some."

The two men shook hands.

"I suppose she's walking now."

"She is at that, though not very steadily or swiftly." Richard turned and assisted Clarinda from her horse.

"Mr. Brooks, may I introduce Miss Clarinda Humphrey and"—he walked past her and assisted Teodora from her horse—"Mrs. Teodora Hernandez."

How did Richard know Teodora's last name or that she was married? When had they spoken?

Mr. Brooks grinned at them. "A pleasure to meet you both."

"Ladies, this is Jim Brooks, father-in-law of Daniel Clarke, a childhood friend of mine."

The big man slapped Richard's back. "More than a friend now, I'd say. More like family."

"True."

Clarinda raised a questioning brow at Richard. This strange mountain man was family?

"My sister married Daniel's brother a few years back, just after Daniel married Jim's daughter, Eliza."

Mr. Brooks waved toward the cabin. "Let's head over so I can introduce you to my wife, Ysabel, and my son, Ashur."

~

148

*R*ichard bounced the ball on the Brooks' cabin floor, scooped up nine jacks, and caught the ball again.

Four-year-old Ashur's mouth fell open. "Wow. You're really good."

The child took his turn, but missed catching the ball before it bounced a second time. Richard played again, scooped up all ten jacks and caught the ball in time.

Jim looked up from the letter he'd been reading and laughed. "Guess you'll have to practice more to beat him."

"I will!" Ashur cried, a look of determination making him appear older. "When you coming back?"

Richard rose from his place on the floor and dusted off his pants. "I'm not sure."

Andrew Cooper set his steaming mug on the table. With his cabin located just beyond a shallow wrinkle in the mountainside, the pastor had heard the commotion. He joined them at the Brooks' cabin within minutes of their arrival. His wife, Maria, had yet to make an appearance, however. She was off gathering plants of some kind. The older, red-haired man hadn't said much beyond a friendly greeting. He seemed content to sit back and watch the goings on.

Until now.

"Mr. Stevens hasn't told us why he's here today." Mr. Cooper's questioning brown eyes surveyed Richard, Clarinda, and Teodora. "While these lovely ladies clearly make good company, I don't see why they needed to accompany you to deliver Daniel's letter to Jim. Are you on your way somewhere?"

Richard adjusted his stance. "Actually, sir, I was hoping you'd be willing to marry us."

Andrew's bushy eyebrows lifted, his attention darting between the women.

Richard's face warmed. "Miss Humphrey and me, that is."

The man appraised Clarinda. "That so, young lady?"

"Yes, sir."

Andrew scowled at them and turned to Jim. "At least these two have a chaperone."

Jim pointed toward the cloak Clarinda had clung to, despite the heat of the fire blazing in the tiny cabin's hearth. "Something tells me, that hasn't always been so."

Though Richard couldn't see her face clearly through the white veil she'd insisted on wearing that day, he could imagine Clarinda's embarrassment. She'd removed her rings at the foot of the mountains and claimed the cloak would disguise her condition until they were ready to reveal it. Apparently, Mr. Brooks was more observant than Richard and had put two-and-two together quickly. Unfortunately, the man didn't have all the facts, so he'd drawn an erroneous conclusion.

Andrew glared at Richard. "Seems to me this situation ought to have been handled by the pastor or priest in town. What's the young lady's parents have to say about this?"

"They don't know." Clarinda's quiet whisper brought the angry man's attention to her.

"How can they *not* know? Even I can tell that Jim's right, despite that heavy cloak you're wearing."

"Of course they know she's with child." Richard stepped between her and Andrew. "But they think we're already married."

"What?" Andrew's roar was probably heard from miles away. "What kind a no-good, lying, dishonoring—"

"Please," Clarinda whimpered from behind him. "Don't blame him. It isn't his fault."

"Not his fault?" Andrew shifted to look past Richard. "Young lady, I don't know what nonsense this boy's been feeding you, but the only woman who ever got herself into this situation without a man's assistance was the blessed Mary, mother of Jesus. And even she needed God's help. You saying you're like her?"

"Of course not."

"Didn't think so."

Jim stepped in front of Richard, his fists clenched. "Give me one good reason I shouldn't sock you in the face for taking advantage of this girl and lying to her parents."

"No!" Clarinda gripped Richard's arm, dragging him to her side. "He did nothing wrong. It—it wasn't him."

Why did those words sting? She was defending him.

Jim's posture relaxed.

Andrew shook his head. "Then what are the two of you doing here? And why do your parents think you're married?"

It was mostly Clarinda's story. She should control how much was shared. Richard took a seat at the small table and gestured for her to answer the questions.

By the time she'd finished explaining their situation, the steam no longer rose from Andrew's coffee mug. Leaning back in his chair, the pastor lifted his drink and took a sip. Frowning, he set it down. "So Richard isn't the father, and the two of you barely know each other, never mind love each other, but you still want to get married?"

Richard nodded, as did Clarinda.

Andrew lifted his hands with a shrug. "I'm sorry. I can't help you."

CHAPTER 15

*R*ichard reared back. "Why not?"

"Marriage is a sacred bond. The two of you will become one flesh, inseparable for all your lives. No matter how noble your intentions"—he looked from Richard to Clarinda —"or how desperate your situation, you should not enter into such a covenant without a better understanding of the person to whom you are committing your life."

Richard stood to his full height. "My life is committed to the Lord, and I intend to honor my vows."

Andrew nodded. "I understand that, but—"

"Sir, may I speak with you in private?" Praying the man would follow, Richard strode to the door.

Clarinda rose, but Richard waved at her to be seated. "Give us a moment."

After only a second's hesitation, Clarinda returned to her seat.

Once outside, Richard paced several feet away from the cabin. He paused near a laundry-line.

Andrew joined him. "I know this isn't the answer you wanted to hear, but—"

"Please." Richard held up his hand. "I understand your concerns, but if you'll hear me out. There's something I haven't told you."

"Oh?"

"This decision isn't just about rescuing Clarinda from the consequences of her actions. God led me here."

The man's brow furrowed. "What do you mean?"

Richard explained his unusual dream and his search for Clarinda up north, as well as the letter he'd received from Henry. "Don't you see? There are far too many coincidences here for it to be anything but God's handiwork. And I feel something"—he pounded his fist to his chest—"in here. I know this what God wants for us."

Andrew scratched his beard. "I see what you're saying, but are you certain? What happens when some day you meet some other woman and—"

"That won't happen. I intend to guard my heart. More than that, I intend to give it to Clarinda." Richard rubbed the back of his neck. "The truth is, I'm already attracted to her, and there's something...something I can't explain that draws me to her." He squared his shoulders. "I'm asking you to have faith with me that God can work out our marriage for good."

Andrew sighed. "Why don't you go back inside and play some more jacks with Ashur? I'm going to need some time to pray about this."

~

*A*n hour later, Andrew poked his head through the cabin door. He signaled for Richard to join him outside.

Richard followed him out and squared his shoulders as he faced Andrew. "Have you made your decision?"

"I think so, but I have a few more questions for you."

If Andrew had decided not to help them, he wouldn't need to ask any more questions. "Yes?"

"You said you intend to give Clarinda your heart. Have you considered that hers may not be free to give to you in return?"

Andrew was right. To have done what she did, Clarinda must have deeply cared for the scoundrel. Did she still? Before Richard had proposed, he'd told himself it didn't matter. The longer he considered it, though, the more it rubbed at him.

Andrew leaned forward. "Do you know the man?"

Richard shook his head. "It happened before we met."

"Has she told you his name or anything about him?"

"Only that he wants nothing to do with her or the child." On the one hand, it bothered him that she didn't trust him enough to be open about what had happened. On the other, he wasn't certain he wanted to know the details. If he knew the man's name, Richard might be tempted to hunt him down and—

He put a halt to those thoughts. He would not become his father and express his rage through violence. No matter how badly the man deserved the sock in the face Mr. Brooks had offered Richard. "She can't still care for him, though. Not after the situation he left her in."

"A woman's heart can be a strange thing. Many a man has tried to figure it out and failed." Andrew set his hand on Richard's shoulder. "I think it best you seriously consider what you'll do if she is unable or unwilling to love you in return."

With his mother and Abner's relationship, Richard had witnessed firsthand the destructive force unrequited love could become—the neglect, lack of respect, verbal attacks, adultery, humiliation, and ultimately, the physical abuse. Neither of them had been innocent in the demise of their marriage. But Abner's response to his wife's betrayal went beyond anything Richard could comprehend. He would never sink to such depths, no matter the pain.

He lifted his chin. "Although I maintain hope that she will

find room for me in her heart, I vow that I will do what's right for her. I'll love her, cherish her, and protect her as the Lord instructs husbands to do, regardless of her affection for me or lack of it. I'll do it not for her sake, but for the Lord's."

Andrew studied him. "If your devotion to the Lord is that strong, what about this deception you're helping her with? Do you think deceiving her parents is what's best for her—what the Lord would have you do?"

Richard flinched. "No, sir. But I don't believe it is my place to tell them the truth. I think Clarinda needs to do that herself and I've made her promise to do so."

"Then why are you here and not being married in town?"

"She is still working up her courage to confess, and we do not want the entire town to know her truth. I agree that her parents should know, but I see no reason the world has a right to her private decisions."

"You have a point." Andrew rubbed his beard. "But do I have your word that either you or she will tell her parents the truth as soon as possible?"

"Yes, sir."

Andrew tilted his head toward the house. "Well, then. Let's get on with it."

"early beloved, we are gathered here in the sight of God..."

Aware of Richard at her side, and the others gathered close by, Clarinda resisted the urge to snort as Mr. Cooper began the wedding ceremony in the small clearing outside the cabin. As if the almighty God would deign to pay attention to their insignificant lives. So far as she could tell, He set her on this earth and then washed His hands of her—only waiting for her death to deal judgment.

If God were to pay her any mind, the time to do it would have been before Arnie decided to abandon her. Or even better, He ought to have been paying attention when she'd tried—in her childish innocence—to comfort a wounded dog cowering in the alley behind their Washington D.C. home. Stopping the creature's attack would have been so easy for Him. There were any number of ways He might have accomplished it, but instead He'd been busy doing...what? Keeping the stars aglow? Definitely not paying attention to her.

Or perhaps He had paid attention and simply hadn't cared.

"...and is therefore not to be entered into unadvisedly, lightly, or wantonly, to satisfy men's carnal lusts and appetites..."

Was that what Arnie had done with her—satisfied his lusts? Her stomach soured. If only she'd resisted his pleading, his kisses, for a few hours more. Perhaps they would be married now and all of this might have been avoided.

Would Arnie have been a good and faithful husband to her if she'd waited? The worst part was that she'd never know.

"First, it was ordained for the procreation of children, to be brought up in the fear and nurture of the Lord, and to praise His holy name."

She sneaked a look at Richard from the corner of her eye. Did he expect to raise her child to praise the Lord? Did she want him to?

When she'd stopped attending church, her parents had suggested she study her Bible in solitude on Sundays rather than attend services with them, but it wasn't long before she'd given up reading Scripture altogether. What was the point? No one but the maid had heeded her desperate screams for help when that vicious beast tried to kill her. Nor had anyone listened to her whispered prayers for the scars to disappear and her friends to return. God didn't care about her. Why should she learn about Him?

"Thirdly..."

Woops, she'd missed the second thing. Oh well.

"...it was ordained for the mutual society, help, and comfort that the one ought to have of the other, both in prosperity and adversity..."

As terrifying as it was to be marrying a man she barely knew, there was some comfort in knowing she would not be alone in the months and years to come. The provision and well-being of her child would not be her burden alone to bear. For whatever else she did not know about Richard, she was confident he was goodhearted and would do his best by her and her child—their child. He'd insisted the child would be as much his as hers.

"Will you, Richard August Stevens, have this woman to be your wedded wife, to live together after God's ordinance in the holy estate of matrimony? Will you love her, comfort her, honor, and keep her, in sickness and in health; and forsaking all other, keep thee only unto her, so long as ye both shall live?"

Richard's voice was clear and strong, with no hint of doubt. "I will."

"Clarinda Melissa Humphrey, will you have this man to be your wedded husband, to live together after God's ordinance in the holy estate of matrimony? Will you obey and serve him, love, honor, and keep him, in sickness and in health; and forsaking all other, keep thee only unto him, so long as you both shall live?"

Clarinda opened her mouth to reply, but her lungs wouldn't move—her voice caught in her throat, holding her promise hostage.

Forsaking all other. What if Arnie changed his mind again? What if he came after her, begging her to give him another chance? Marriage was forever. A divorce or affair would be as scandalous as an illegitimate child. Was she about to make a worse mistake than the night she spent with Arnie?

Her legs burned with the urge to run.

Her mind held her in place.

It no longer mattered what she wanted or what Arnie might someday wish for. Marriage to Richard was her only hope of a safe and happy future for her child.

Richard looked at her. "Clarinda?"

Mentally laying her own happiness on the altar for the sake of her child, Clarinda lifted her chin. She caught and held Mr. Cooper's gaze. "I will."

Richard's exhale was audible as he faced her to recite his vows. Clarinda followed suit, only stumbling a moment on the word *love*.

It isn't a lie. Love comes in many forms. It didn't have to be the mind-altering passion that had left her blind. She didn't need to set herself up for more betrayal and heartache. She could love Richard as a fellow human being and maybe someday as a friend. That counted, didn't it?

Taking her hand, Richard slid the rings onto her finger. Before they'd left the sewing room, he'd offered to buy her a new one, but she'd pointed out how odd it would seem to her parents and the limited selection he was bound to find in San Diego—most of which were sold by her father. So he'd agreed to let her continue using the rings Fletcher had found for her.

Mr. Cooper said a short prayer and joined their right hands together, saying, "Those whom God has joined together let no man put asunder. I now pronounce you, husband and wife." He raised a brow at Richard. "You may now kiss your bride."

~

*R*ichard plucked another flower from the field Maria had directed him to after the ceremony. His breath fogged the cold night air, barely visible in the light of the lantern he'd set on a nearby log. A cheerful whistle escaped him as he worked to gather a surprise for his bride. The silky feel of

Clarinda's thin veil pressed between his lips and her cheek was not the wedding kiss he'd hoped for, but he would not let such a small matter dampen his spirits.

He'd known it would take time for Clarinda to soften and open her heart toward him. They needed to get to know one another, to learn to rely on each other, and figure out how to live life together. Once they'd travelled down that path long enough, feelings of friendship and love were bound to blossom.

He just needed to be patient.

Still, when would be better than their wedding night to begin wooing his wife?

He brought the bundle of bright yellow, white, and purple flowers closer to the flickering light. Inspecting the cluster, he picked out a few broken buds. Was it big enough? Green enough? His sisters had always harped about bouquets needing the right amount of greenery. He lifted the lantern and searched the bases of nearby trees until he found a few ferns. He added them to the mix. Did that make it better or worse? Well, it'd make more of a mess to pull them out now. Might as well leave them.

He settled his gift in the small pail Maria had loaned him and lifted his gaze to the moon above. Was Clarinda finished with her evening preparations? Sensing her desire for privacy after the evening meal, he'd left her to settle into Ashur's room which had been built off the side of the Brooks' main cabin. Ysabel and Jim had moved their four year-old into the main room with them for the evening to give the newlyweds a private place to spend the night. Teodora was sleeping on a cot the Coopers' had set up in their lean-to.

Would Clarinda be pleased by his gift? He knew so little about her. Every woman liked flowers, didn't they?

Richard lifted the lantern and pail of blossoms, then picked his way through the dark to the Brooks' cabin.

He paused at the entry. Should he knock or simply enter? If

159

he *should* knock, how was he to accomplish it with a lantern in one hand and a pail in the other? Before he could decide, the door opened.

Jim grinned at him. "Good, the lions didn't take you. I was beginning to wonder."

Richard laughed and glanced toward the door leading to his and Clarinda's temporary quarters. "Has she come out?"

"No. But I didn't expect she would." Jim took the lantern and gave him a firm shove toward Ashur's room. "Best get on in there and see if she needs anything. We'll be turning the lights out soon."

Richard glanced toward the corner where a full-size bed held Ysabel and Ashur.

Jim's wife smiled softly at him over the crown of her sleeping son. "Good night."

Richard dipped his chin. "Ma'am." He faced the closed door and knocked. "Clarinda? May I come in?"

Even in the relative stillness, Richard strained to hear her soft reply. "You may."

Richard hid the bouquet behind his back and glanced over his shoulder at Jim. "Well, good night."

"See you in the morning."

Richard tugged the latch string and stepped into a room blanketed in darkness. The faint light of the lantern behind him illuminated an unlit candle in a holder sitting on a nearby shelf. He wrapped his free hand around it and nudged the door closed with his boot. Blindly, he set the bouquet on the shelf and lifted the candle. "May I light a candle?"

"Why?"

The question caught him off guard. Why didn't she want any light? "I have something I'd like to show you."

"Can it wait until morning?"

Richard winced. *Don't take it personally. She's just nervous.* "It won't be the same then. I'd like to show it to you now."

Blankets shuffled on the small bed. "All right."

He lit the candle and lifted the pail of flowers.

Clarinda sat on the bed with the blanket pulled to her nose. Her blue eyes were wide above the well-worn cotton quilt. The hat and veil gone, her beautiful golden curls cascaded down her back and around her shoulders. Had any woman ever been so beautiful?

He thrust the blooms toward her. "These are for you."

She looked at the bouquet, at him, and back at the bouquet.

Rather than the hoped-for crinkles around her eyes, indicating a smile, her gaze narrowed. "We need to talk."

His arm lowered. "We do?"

"Yes. I—" Her voice shook. "I've had a realization and I think it's only fair I share it with you."

He stilled. They'd been married less than a handful of hours and already she was thinking of backing out? He forced a jovial tone. "Have you decided what you want for breakfast? Go ahead and name it. If it's available anywhere in these mountains, I'll see that you have it." He exaggerated a grimace. "Just don't ask for mountain lion steak. My shooting skills are a tad rusty and I'd rather not refresh them under that much pressure."

Not a hint of a smile ghosted her lips.

So much for the lighthearted approach. "Listen, I meant what I said. Our marriage is permanent. It's too late to back out now."

"I don't want out."

The weight on his shoulders merely shifted. She may not want out, but whatever she did have to say wouldn't be much better. Her expression was too grim.

"I just need you to know that I can't love you." She worried the edge of the quilt with her fingers. "Not as a wife is meant to love her husband, I mean. I can love you as a fellow human being and I hope we'll be friends, but that's all. I'm not interested in loving anyone else."

Her words were like a physical blow to his chest, shattering any delusion that he'd prepared his heart for this reality. Her honesty dripped like acid, searing his hope. She *was* still in love with the man who'd abandoned her. Andrew had tried to warn him, but Richard still couldn't believe it. How could she continue to hold affection for someone who would use her and toss her away like yesterday's newspaper?

Richard ran a hand over his face. It didn't matter. Whatever her reasons, the truth was the truth. At least she'd been honest with him.

After the wedding.

Would knowing for certain that she still loved the other man have made a difference in his decision to marry her? Closing his eyes, he searched his heart. No, it wouldn't have changed the guidance the Lord had clearly given.

Lord, what am I to do now? He waited, but no clear answer came. He opened his eyes and met her gaze. "Thank you for being honest with me."

Her brows rose.

Had she expected him to be upset? Well, he was. But he'd gone into this marriage knowing she didn't love or particularly care for him. He was her rescue from scandal, humiliation, and probable poverty. Nothing more. She hadn't chosen *him*, she'd chosen the life he represented. He'd known that and married her anyway.

Still, she'd agreed to his conditions.

"However, I must remind you that you agreed to allow me to court you—that you would be open to the possibility of something more growing between us."

She lowered the quilt a few inches and opened her mouth, but he forestalled her obvious protest.

"I'm not expecting anything right now except that we spend time getting to know one another." He lifted the small pail and set it on her lap. "And when I bring you a gift, I'd like you to accept it. If you don't like it, say so—"

"Oh, it isn't that. I—"

"And if you do like it, let me know that as well. It's part of us getting to know one another. I want to know what pleases you and what displeases you. I want to know what fascinates you and what drives you crazy. And I know I can't learn it all in a single night or even a week or a month. But that's all right." He lifted one side of his mouth in a half-smile. "We've got the rest of our lives to figure this out."

Her eyes softened as he spoke, and at last a small smile played at her lips. She buried her nose in the blossoms. "Thank you. These are beautiful. Silver Lupine are some of my favorite flowers." She caressed the delicate purple petals.

His own smile grew. "I'm glad to know that. Maria showed me a meadow with several large bushes of them."

"That sounds beautiful. Too bad we'll be going home tomorrow."

"I can show them to you before we go, though." He hesitated. "If you'd like to see them, that is."

"Yes, I would."

He glanced to the empty space beside her in the bed and swallowed. "Speaking of tomorrow. We'd better get some sleep before the long ride back to the ranch. Do you think..." His throat tightened, cutting off his words.

Her cheeks pinked. "I won't ask you to sleep on the floor, if that's what you're asking, but..."

He nodded quickly. "We'll just be sleeping." Or trying to. Something told him drifting off to sleep beside his new wife wasn't going to be easy.

CHAPTER 16

*C*larinda held her breath as Richard slipped into bed beside her. Clutching the covers, she kept her gaze fixed on the ceiling. Shadows flickered across its surface in the wavering candlelight.

He rose onto his elbow, blew out the candle, then lay down.

He shifted, and the blankets moved with him.

She tensed. *You're being silly. He's just trying to get comfortable.* Still, she couldn't relax.

His shoulder brushed hers and she flinched.

He froze.

Gentle snoring drifted through the wall from the main room.

"I'm a man of my word. I won't lay a finger on you unless you welcome it."

The hurt in his whisper formed an ache in her chest. Of course he'd keep his word. He'd been nothing but kind to her from the moment they met. "I believe you." If she'd had any doubts, she'd never have married him.

Another pause stretched her nerves.

Finally, his soft voice broke the stillness. "I can move to the floor, if you prefer. I don't want to make you uncomfortable."

On the floor or on the bed, what did it matter? His mere presence made her uncomfortable. She'd just married a man she barely knew. What had she been thinking?

Married.

The word was so final. So heavy.

When she'd imagined marrying Arnie, the thought had lifted her. She'd felt lighter than air, picturing herself as Arnie's wife. That was something she could never be now. If he came for her, she couldn't go with him. She belonged to someone else. This stranger in bed beside her.

"Clarinda?"

Richard'd been so kind, she couldn't ask him to move to the floor. "You can stay."

He sank into the mattress. "Thank you." His shoulder bumped hers.

This is wrong.

The heat of his thigh warmed hers through his nightshirt and her chemise.

She couldn't breathe.

Her vision blurred.

It should be Arnie's shoulder brushing hers, Arnie's thigh beside hers. It should have been Arnie she'd married today.

She rolled to her side, turning her back to Richard and gaining an inch of separation. What had she done? How would she bear a lifetime of this?

～

The next morning, they shared a meal with the Brooks and Coopers, then Richard whisked Clarinda away to visit the field where he'd picked her bouquet.

He paused out of sight of the clearing. "Wait. Will you remove your veil, please? I couldn't see it clearly last night, but I think this is going to be a sight you'll want to see without fabric dimming your view." Besides, he wanted to see her again. As soon as she'd awakened, she'd asked him to leave so she could dress. She'd emerged with her veil and gloves in place.

"I suppose we are alone." She reached for the sheer fabric.

He placed a hand over her gloved fingers. "May I?"

She gave a jerky nod, so he proceeded to tug the fabric free of her collar. He lifted the front and waited for her gaze to meet his.

Her eyes remained downcast. The faded scarring on the left side of her face was easy to see in the bright morning light. Though nothing more than thin, pale markings now, they must have been dreadfully red and painful once. He reached to smooth a finger over the lines, but she jolted back.

The veil ripped free of the bonnet as she stepped away. "What are you doing?"

"I just..." He fisted the fabric and stuffed his hands in his pockets. "I'm sorry. You're so beautiful...I wasn't thinking."

"You truly believe that, don't you?" There was a slight tremble to her voice.

He let himself drink in the beauty of her. "I wish you knew how much."

The apples of her cheeks pinked and she ducked her head. "How much farther is the field?"

"We're nearly there." He motioned for her to follow. "Come on."

They stepped around a large oak into a meadow of blue, yellow, and white blossoms lit by the early morning sun. The flowers' scents floated toward them on the breeze.

Her biggest smile yet spread her cheeks, revealing dimples. He wanted to sweep her into his arms and kiss them. But based on last night's conversation, such an action would drive her away.

Instead, he held out his hand and, thankfully, she accepted it.

He led her through the blossoms to the log where he'd set his lantern the night before. They both sat and admired God's creation for several minutes in silence.

"Thank you for bringing me here. This is beautiful."

A stray curl dangled beside her cheek. He couldn't resist tucking it behind her ear, though he was careful not to let his touch linger. "My pleasure, Lindy."

She blinked but didn't flinch. That was progress, at least.

"Do you mind my calling you Lindy?" He'd come up with the nickname as he lay awake beside his slumbering wife last night. The warmth of her body next to his was impossible to ignore, so he forced himself to consider other things. Eventually his thoughts wandered to her tragic childhood. He liked the idea of having a name for her that no one else used—a name not associated with the ridicule and betrayal she'd experienced so much in her life.

With her gaze fixed on something across the clearing, she shrugged. "I guess not. Though, it'll take some getting used to."

He plucked a flower near the base of the log and examined one of its petals. "Isn't it incredible how much beauty and detail the Lord puts into each one of these flowers? They wither and die so quickly. Yet He still cares enough about them to make each one unique and lovely." Like the care and detail He'd put into bringing the two of them together. Richard needed to keep God's faithfulness in sight as he waited for his wife to open her heart to him.

She snorted. "You think God cares about flowers?"

The flower fell from his fingers. "Don't you?"

"No."

He waited for her to expand on her thoughts, but she held silent, not looking at him. He wanted to press her for more explanation. Clearly her view of God didn't match his. Why hadn't he asked her more questions before they'd gotten married? Then again, the knowledge wouldn't have changed his course.

At least their marriage assured he'd have all the time he needed to get to know her and where she stood in her relationship with God. Did she even have a relationship with the Lord? Her comment brought forth so many questions, but as with so much of their relationship, he sensed the need to be patient.

It could hardly be surprising that someone who'd been through as much trauma in her life as his new wife would have doubts or questions. But opening up about something that deeply personal wasn't likely to happen on their first full day as husband and wife.

First, he'd need to help her be vulnerable in other areas. That she sat beside him with her face uncovered and tipped toward the sun, her gloved fingers laced in his, was progress enough for the moment.

~

*I*t was still early as Clarinda followed Richard into the clearing outside the Brooks' cabin. Teodora was chatting amiably with Ysabel as they hung laundry on the line.

"Back so soon?" The housekeeper pinned another shirt to the rope.

Richard grinned at Clarinda. "Yes, my bride couldn't wait another moment to share her surprise with you."

"More surprises?" Teodora set her hands on her hips. "I think we've had enough of those lately."

"Not that kind of surprise." Clarinda glared at Richard. This was not how she'd intended to share their plans. She held her hands out to Teodora. "This is good news. For you."

Teodora's brows furrowed. "What do you mean?"

"We spoke with Eduardo and he gave us directions for

finding your daughter's village. We plan to take you there on our way back to the ranch."

Teodora's arms sagged as her mouth fell open. "I get to see Graciela? Today?"

Clarinda nodded as she drew her caretaker into a hug. "I packed an extra bag of belongings for you so you can stay until Thursday. Richard and I will return to—"

Teodora lurched from Clarinda's arms. "No. I cannot."

"But—"

"I told you. Fernando will report my absence to your parents and they will sack me."

"I still don't believe the Humphreys are so unreasonable." Richard stepped closer. "But Clarinda and I discussed it before we left the ranch. If they do sack you, I will hire you myself."

Teodora took Clarinda's elbow and pulled her far enough away to avoid being overheard. "You may be fool enough to marry a stranger, but I will not gamble my position on the word of a man I do not know."

"Please, Teodora. I know how much you want to see your daughter. Richard is a good man. You can trust—"

"No. Too many people depend on the money your parents pay me." Teodora's lips trembled and a sheen covered her eyes. She blinked it away. "I cannot do it. Don't ask me again."

"All right. I won't." Clarinda hated seeing Teodora cry. "You *will* see her today, though. If we leave now, you should have at least a few hours to visit before we would need to leave for the ranch."

At last, Teodora smiled. "Thank you."

~

A few hours later, Clarinda straightened in her saddle. They approached the small Indian village situated on both banks of the creek.

Eduardo's directions had been easy to follow once they'd left the Brooks' cabin and returned to the main trail. Though the path they'd ridden through the foothills couldn't be called a road, it was obviously well traveled and cut a clear, if narrow, line through the chaparral. Despite this, it had taken seven long hours of navigating the hilly terrain covered in thick shrubs to reach their destination.

The early afternoon sun warmed Clarinda's back as the trail opened to a wide, packed-dirt clearing speckled with dome-shaped huts made of curved willow branches and adobe lean-tos.

A group of six Indian men dressed in well-worn western-style clothes gathered to stand between the strangers and the village. Most of them appeared too old or too young to work, but their somber stares were no less intimidating.

"Hello." Richard pulled his horse to a stop several yards away, gesturing for Clarinda and Teodora to do the same.

"Hello." The man who appeared closest to Clarinda's age stood in front and replied in surprisingly clear English. "What brings you to our village?"

"We've brought a friend whom we think has family here." Richard motioned for Teodora to come up beside him.

She nudged her mount past Clarinda.

Richard tipped his head toward Teodora. "This is Teodora Hernandez. She's looking for her daughter, Graciela."

The spokesman's eyes lit and Spanish words flew from his mouth too quickly for Clarinda to follow.

Teodora responded. After a moment, she tipped her chin to indicate Clarinda and Richard.

The man shook his head and pointed at Clarinda as he spoke.

Teodora laughed and shook her head. She said something that made the man join in her laughter.

Clarinda shifted in her saddle. Were they laughing at her? Surely Teodora wouldn't.

Yet, Teodora was *paid* to care for Clarinda and her family. The housekeeper disliked Mother, yet was pleasant to her mistress's face. Was it possible that Clarinda had been mistaken in Teodora's affection for her? Did the woman only pretend to care in order to keep her position as housekeeper?

Teodora slid from her horse and motioned for Clarinda and Richard to do the same.

Clarinda dismounted and led her horse forward, coming to a stop between Richard and Teodora.

The housekeeper beamed at her. "Clarinda, this is Alvaro, my daughter's husband. He thought you were sick because of your veil."

Clarinda blinked back tears. Of course Teodora hadn't been laughing at her. She ought to have trusted her caretaker more than to doubt her loyalty.

Clarinda offered the man a smile. "I'm glad to meet you."

Still speaking English, Teodora introduced Richard as Clarinda's husband. The words sent a tingle across her skin.

Though Clarinda hadn't had the heart to make Richard sleep on the rough cabin floor the night before, she'd expected sleep to be impossible with him sharing her bed. Yet she stared at the wall for only minutes before fatigue forced her eyes shut and she'd drifted to sleep. When she awoke this morning, he was already dressed and sitting on the rug, his Bible open in his lap.

"Come, I will take you to Graciela and the children." Alvaro turned to lead the way.

Richard took her hand and led her behind the others through the scattered structures. Though she didn't fear Graciela's people, she appreciated the protective nature of his grip.

Several people stopped their work to stare at the strangers.

Some—especially the children—offered smiles, but no one spoke to them.

Alvaro's fluency in both Spanish and English was unusual and impressive. Most of the vaqueros on the ranch spoke only Spanish and understood little English, if any at all.

Alvaro stopped beside a small fire in front of one of the small huts. A young woman sat beside the fire, an infant asleep in her lap. A short distance away, a young girl played with a pile of sticks. Upon spotting the strangers, the girl flew to her mother's side.

The young woman looked at Teodora and gasped, her face lighting. Carefully, she rose and handed the sleeping babe to her husband. Then she threw herself into her mother's arms. Words flew between the women as tears flowed down their cheeks.

Clarinda glanced at Richard. Should they leave?

He caught Teodora's attention and spoke in a voice soft enough not to wake the child. "If you're all right here, I'm going to take Clarinda for a ride and leave you to visit with your family. We'll be gone for several hours, so take your time."

"Wait." Teodora turned from her daughter to clasp Clarinda's arm.

Clarinda sensed the housekeeper's alarm in her grip. "We'll return for you in time to reach the ranch this evening. I promise."

"Good." Teodora's hold relaxed. "I want to introduce you. Clarinda, this is my daughter Graciela."

The pretty young woman smiled at Clarinda, her cheeks still damp with tears. She said something in Spanish, which Teodora translated. "She says it's nice to meet you and she thanks you for bringing me here."

"It's a pleasure to meet you as well. Your mother is..." She paused, searching for the right words. "A dear friend. Thank you for sharing her with me. I hope we can bring her for visits more often."

Again, Teodora translated. She indicated the sleeping babe. "That sweet one is Modesto. He is just one year old." Teodora bent to peer around Graciela's skirts and spoke softly in Spanish. The little girl poked her head out to stare at Clarinda. "And this is Noemi. She's five."

Clarinda smiled and waved at the child. "Your family is beautiful."

"Thank you." Tears glittered in Teodora's eyes.

Clarinda drew her into a hug. "You sure you won't change your mind and stay for a few days?"

"*Sí.* I'm sure." With a sniff, she pushed Clarinda away. "Now, go get to know your new husband. I can see he is eager to have you to himself again."

Clarinda turned to find Richard behind her, a blush staining his cheeks.

~

*T*hirty minutes later, Clarinda reined her horse to a stop beside Richard's. He'd paused at the edge of a large, flat rock that bordered the creek.

"Why are we stopping?"

Richard pointed to the stone. "This looks like the perfect place for a game of checkers."

She laughed. "If only we had a set to play."

Richard waggled his brows. "Who says we don't?"

"You're joking."

Richard dug around in his saddle bag and produced a small, patchwork sack. He tossed it to her.

It landed in her hand with a rattle. Her eyes widened. Several round, flat objects slid around inside. "What about a board?"

"You're holding it."

She looked more closely at the patchwork and realized it

was made of alternating squares in brown and faded black. "But how...?"

Richard slid off his horse and lifted his arms to assist her down. "Come on, I'll show you."

Minutes later, the bag was laid across the rock and several wooden discs of pine and cedar were stationed at either end of the fabric board.

Richard waved for her to make the first move. "Ladies first."

She pushed one of her cedar pieces diagonally forward one square.

Richard did the same with one of his. "I've been thinking about your idea to make sheep the priority at the ranch."

"You have?" She moved another piece.

He pushed his first piece closer to hers. "I think the plan has merit."

Her finger froze on the piece she'd been about to move. "Then you'll help me convince my parents to make the change?"

"Perhaps. I need to do more research. It's no small investment we're talking about. If it doesn't work out—"

"It will."

"Well, I just wanted you to know I appreciated you sharing your idea with me. I'm taking it seriously."

She nodded. It was more than many husbands would do. From what she'd heard, most believed a woman had no right to concern herself with business matters. As if the consequences of a man's business decisions didn't affect the whole family.

Richard tipped his head toward the board. "It's still your turn."

"Oh, right." She moved a new piece up to guard against Richard's advancing piece.

Would Arnie have seriously considered her opinion? She tried to recall ever sharing an idea of her own with Arnie, but couldn't. Most of the time, he'd been the one talking. Sometimes he shared stories about the practical jokes he and his friends played. But mostly he complained about his father's unreasonable expectations and talked about the things he'd improve once his father let him take over some of the family's business interests.

"I've been thinking about the shipping company I inherited." Richard finally moved a second piece. "I'm sure I can negotiate lower rates for shipping our sheep if we agree to ship exclusively through my company—especially if I can convince some of the other ranchers in the area to agree to the same thing."

She pushed a new piece ahead of her rear flank.

"That's one of the reasons I'm not quite ready to agree to purchase the ranch or try sheep farming. If the ranchers around here aren't open to negotiation and change…" He jumped one of her pieces, snatching it from the board. "That won't bode well for a new sheep ranch."

"They can't control what we do with our own land." She frowned at the board. It was impossible to concentrate. She shoved one of her front pieces farther ahead. Maybe she could get it crowned.

"True, but out in the country like we are, we can't afford to alienate our neighbors." Richard neatly jumped her advancing piece. "Who do you run to for help in time of fire or Indian attack?"

Perhaps it would be better to bring the whole army of pieces ahead together. "Most of the nearby villages are peaceful." She prodded another rear piece forward.

"Yes, but you know as well as I do that not all of the Indians have accepted the Americans' presence here. Even if everyone in the nearest villages are kind to us, there are other groups still wanting to fight and kick us off this land." He moved another piece.

He was right of course. Out here, neighbors depended on each other. Well, most of them did.

"Clarence Smith made the switch to sheep last year, but

don't bother talking to him or anyone whose land borders his." She jumped one of his pieces.

"Why not?"

"The Smith Ranch sits several miles that way." She pointed north. "But Smith is notorious for running his sheep wherever he sees fit, regardless of who owns the land."

"Don't his neighbors complain?"

"Oh no. They support his every whim. He controls the only consistent water source in their area. He's practically the uncrowned king of the northern ranches."

"Good to know." He jumped two of her pieces and landed at her end of the board. "Speaking of crowns." He grinned at her.

She capped his sneaky piece with the only one of his pieces she'd managed to take. She needed to quit talking and start paying attention to the game.

Several minutes later, Clarinda cornered Richard's last piece. "I win."

"Nice work." He began repositioning his pieces for a new game. "If I can find a way to make the ranch profitable again, is that where you want to live?"

She paused, her fist filled with cedar discs. No one had ever asked her that before. *Did* she want to live on the ranch? She shook her head. That was a dumb question. "Of course. Where else would I live?" She positioned her pieces on the board.

"What about somewhere up north?"

Up north? Was this his way of asking her to go back to Nevada City with him? That was out of the question. "No, the ranch is my home. I'm happy there." It wasn't a lie, exactly. The ranch was beautiful and the vaqueros were used to her. No one gawked or whispered about her there. If not happy, she was at least content to be left alone. Which was the closest to happiness she'd felt in years.

The months when Arnie had secretly courted her didn't count. That happiness was a lie.

In fact, the more she considered it, the more it seemed all happiness was nothing more than an illusion. Like a sandcastle washed away by the first crashing wave—it appeared majestic and splendid, but in reality was nothing more than a pile of dirt.

CHAPTER 17

I t was past dark by the time Clarinda, Richard, and Teodora reached the ranch that evening. After a quick meal, Teodora heated water so they could bathe, then retreated to her room beside the scullery off the kitchen while Richard settled onto the settee before the fire.

Clarinda paused at the threshold of her room. A new, larger bed had replaced her old one. Had Richard instructed one of the vaqueros to install it during their absence? That seemed rather high-handed of him. Then again, they couldn't have continued sleeping in separate rooms without causing talk. Even if it was only for a few days.

Using the tub Richard had carried to her—no, *their*—room, Clarinda washed away the dirt and grime of the past two days' travel. She redressed and moved to the front room to allow Richard a chance to bathe.

In the quiet of the house, it was difficult to ignore the sloshing of water in the next room. He'd likely listened to similar sounds as she bathed. The growing warmth in her cheeks had nothing to do with the fire at her feet.

Needing a distraction, she grabbed the closest book and

opened it. She stared at the page for several seconds, but her mind remained in the other room. She forced her eyes to focus. *For I know that through your prayers and God's provision...*She snapped the book shut and returned it to the small table beside her chair. How had her Bible wound up in the front room?

After a while, the sloshing stopped, and the exterior door to her room scraped open. The sound of water splashing into dirt came through the walls.

He must have dumped the bathwater.

The outer door clicked shut again, and soft thumps pattered around her bedroom.

Richard entered the front room, his damp hair glistening in the flickering firelight. He took a seat beside her, his stockinged feet stretched toward the fire. "It feels good to be home."

Home? What about Nevada City? "Do you own a large home up north?" She wished the question back. It sounded as if she were concerned with the size of the home, when she was just curious if he'd invested in his own dwelling or was leasing one.

"No. Actually, I've been renting a room in a house across the street from my office."

Renting a room? When he could easily afford to own multiple homes? It didn't make sense. Had Teodora been right? Could he have been lying about his wealth this entire time? Did he expect her to share a single room with him? Maybe that wasn't so bad. They'd have to continue sleeping together at night, but if they shared their living space with other renters, there'd be precious little privacy during the day. "You mean, you don't own your own home?"

He shrugged and leaned against the settee, his shoulder brushing against hers. "Haven't seen a reason to purchase one. It's always been just me. Plus, the widow who owns the house needs the income. She's a great cook, keeps my room tidy, and has a hot cup of coffee waiting for me when I wake up."

Something pinched inside as his expression took on a warm

glow that revealed his fondness for the widow. "If she's that wonderful, why not marry *her?*"

Richard's gaze shot to hers and she snapped her attention to the fire.

Had she sounded jealous? No, she couldn't have, because she wasn't. She was just curious. A man as handsome, intelligent, and wealthy as her new husband surely could have had his pick of women, even amid the high competition for ladies in female-scarce California. What dirt-poor muckman could compete with a successful, kindhearted entrepreneur whose pale blue eyes sparkled when he was pleased or amused?

She glanced at him. They were sparkling now. An answering flutter unsettled her stomach.

"She wouldn't have me."

The flutter vanished. "You mean, you asked her?"

Richard's white teeth flashed in the flickering firelight. "If you'd ever had a bite of her cinnamon rolls, you'd understand."

Did the man go around proposing marriage to every woman he met?

He heaved a dramatic sigh. "Alas, she insisted I was far too young for her—what with her being close to five decades my senior."

Clarinda chuckled. He'd confessed to being twenty-five during their ride earlier. Which meant he'd proposed to a seventy-something-year-old woman. She bet it had made the woman's day.

"What's her name?"

"Mrs. Kipling."

"Mrs. Kipling? You proposed marriage and you don't even know her Christian name?"

"You should have tasted those rolls." He lowered his head in mock dejection. "No matter how many times I asked, though, she wouldn't budge."

"How many times *did* you propose?"

"Oh, at least a dozen times. She knew those rolls were my favorite, so she made them at least twice a month, and I made sure she stayed stocked with all the ingredients."

"Now, I understand your reluctance to move to your own home." She picked at a loose thread on the settee's cushion. Why *had* he married her? The question continued to plague her in the still moments, popping up when she least wanted to consider the possibilities. Surely there'd been other options for him if he'd simply wanted to marry. Was there a young woman eagerly awaiting his return to Nevada City? "You must be anxious to return. No doubt, Mrs. Kipling will have a batch waiting for you."

"I do miss those rolls." He took Clarinda's hand and warmth travelled up her arm. "But I'm not going anywhere."

She lifted her gaze to his. Was he saying that no young lady waited for him? "Don't you need to return to manage your mine?"

He shook his head. "I have a competent manager whom I trust to keep things running in my absence." He squeezed her fingers. "I may need to travel north to check on operations now and then, but I intend to make my home here, with you."

Cold washed over her like a bucket of creek water. He meant for them to live on the ranch with only Teodora to keep them from being completely alone together? How was she to guard her heart with him constantly around, charming her with his wit, compassion, and kind consideration? Richard's allure was entirely different than Arnie's, but she felt it just the same.

Richard's thumb stroked across the back of her hand, sending sparks flying down her spine.

She jerked her hand away. What was wrong with her? Was she still so desperate for acceptance? Did her foolish heart never learn? Apparently not. But her heart wasn't in charge any more.

She stood. "I'm tired. Good night." She rushed into their bedroom. She would *not* be beguiled again. She couldn't be. There weren't enough pieces of her heart left to shatter.

~

*T*he next morning, Richard crossed the bridge leading toward the barn and corrals. Several vaqueros were at work saddling horses and checking gear.

Fernando took note of him and strode forward, battered hat in hand. "*Señor* Stevens, what can I do for you? Is the bed not to your liking?"

"The bed was fine." The fact he'd not had room to turn over with the huge roll of quilts his wife had installed down the middle of the bed wasn't Fernando's fault. "I'm hoping you can teach me about the day-to-day workings of the ranch."

"I'm happy to help, but Mr. Ames, he handles the books and things. I'm not sure—"

"Not the ledgers. I mean the things you and the men do." Richard threw his hands wide. "In fact, I figure the best way to learn what it takes to run this place is by doing a little of everything myself. So this morning, I'm here to help."

"*You* want to help me and the men?"

"Exactly."

The man took in the mining garb Richard had donned this morning. The worn trousers, patched shirt, and scuffed boots were a far cry from the tailored clothes he'd been wearing since his arrival. The change must have convinced Fernando that Richard was serious, because he slapped his hat on his head and said, "*Gracias.* This way."

An hour later, Richard finished the tasks Fernando had given him, washed up at the pump, and hurried to the house. He needed to fetch Lindy and be on their way to church. Teodora must have their morning meal packed and ready to go by now. What would she make for them to eat in the wagon? Sandwiches, most likely.

He scraped his boots on the rock set outside the kitchen door for that purpose and stepped inside. A basket sat on the table, but the housekeeper was nowhere in sight. He lifted the cloth covering. The expected sandwiches were inside.

Whistling, he went in search of his bride.

Teodora sat near a window in the front room, Bible in her lap. "Done already?"

"Yes. Is Clarinda ready?"

Rather than answer his question, she set a piece of ribbon in her Bible and closed it. "Did you speak with her about your plans for today?"

"Should I have?"

Teodora made a clicking sound with her tongue as she rose from her chair. "I'll move to my room."

"Why? We'll be gone in a few minutes. No need for you to leave."

Shaking her head, she shuffled from the room.

What odd behavior. Richard shrugged it off and knocked on his and Lindy's chamber door. "Lindy? You ready?"

The door opened and Lindy appeared in a faded brown dress with fraying at the hem. Why hadn't she put on her best dress? The blue one she'd worn for their wedding was pretty and far better suited for attending church. Oh well, no time to change now. At least her veil wasn't black. During their ride, she'd confessed to owning at least a dozen veils in several variations of white and cream, as well as two black veils.

He took her gloved hand and led her toward the kitchen. "Come on. I had Teodora pack our morning meal so we can eat it in the wagon. I didn't want to rush you since you said you like to wake slowly."

"But where are we going?"

She must be more tired than he'd thought if she'd forgotten what day it was. "It's Sunday." He snatched the basket from the table and strode toward the door, her hand still snug in his.

And then it wasn't.

The loss of her warm fingers stopped him, and he turned to face her.

Her posture was rigid, her voice cool. "Are you saying we're going to church?"

He stared at her. What else would they be doing on a Sunday morning? "Yes, and if we don't hurry we're going to be late."

"You'd better leave, then." She walked toward the front room.

"Aren't you coming?"

She didn't even pause. "Of course, not. I never attend church. But don't worry about me. I'll spend my morning reading as I usually do and see that Teodora has a meal ready for you when you return."

She never went to church? But...didn't she tell him she believed in God? Her words about God not caring about flowers returned to him with new clarity. How could she know who God was if she didn't attend church? She didn't study her Bible. He'd found it covered in dust on a shelf at the base of their wardrobe.

He studied his wife as she took her usual place on the settee. "Why don't you attend church?"

"I'm too much of a distraction."

She said the words as if she was quoting someone, and they implied she *had* attended church at some point in her life. "Who told you that?"

"Hadn't you better go? You don't want to be late your first time in attendance."

He stepped closer, trying to catch her eye as she stared into the fire. "You're right, but I'd much prefer it if you came with me. It would mean a lot to have my wife at my side as we

184

worship our Lord." How was he supposed to help her grow closer to God if she refused to enter His house?

"I'm sorry to disappoint you."

The words were delivered with such cool indifference, they stole his calm. After everything he'd done for her? Keeping her secret, marrying her, establishing his home here so she wouldn't be forced to adjust to somewhere new when she was already experiencing so much change. None of that mattered? She wouldn't budge on this small request? He gritted his teeth. "You can keep your veil on. We can even sit in back, if that's what you want."

She shook her head, still not looking at him. "I'm sorry."

He reached for her hand.

She shied away.

Something broke inside. "You're sorry?" He stormed between her and the fireplace. "You're sorry? That's it?" He snapped his fingers. "No explanation. No compromise considered. Just your way or no way at all." He cut his hand through the air. "Why am I surprised? That's how it's been from the moment I met you. It's all about what *you* want, what *you* need. Never any consideration for *me*."

"That's not true." She shot to her feet and wobbled, her girth throwing her off-balance.

He reached to steady her.

She sent him a searing glare.

He jerked away. "Oh, no? I've wanted to tell your parents the truth from the beginning. You refused and I compromised. You wanted our wedding performed in secret. I arranged it. You love it here on the ranch, so I abandoned my own life to—"

"I never asked you to do that! Go back to Nevada City. I don't need you here."

Is that what she wanted? For him to leave? That cursed veil hid the nuances of her expression. Yet another thing she'd refused him. "*I* want to see your face when we're speaking, but no. You insist on wearing this wretched thing." He yanked the offensive cloth free. A horrific rip rent the air.

She cried out, her hands flying to cover her face.

Air rushed from his lungs. What had he done?

She fled to their room.

He followed. "Lindy, I'm sorry."

The door slammed in his face.

He tried to open it, but something heavy pressed against the opposite side.

"Go away!" Her muffled voice was strained, as if she were holding back tears.

Richard buried his face in his hands. What had he been thinking? He hadn't. That was the problem. He'd let the frustration build up and take charge. And what had they been arguing about? Attending church. A mirthless laugh escaped his lips as he slid to the floor, his back to the door. If this weren't proof that he needed a Savior, he didn't know what was.

~

Clarinda leaned against the door, fighting tears. She would not cry. Tears changed nothing.

On the other side of the wall, Richard's footsteps faded, and the front door clicked open and closed.

She sank to the hard tile floor and covered her face with her hands. He was right. Every decision she'd made since his arrival had been about her and her child. He'd given up his future for her—his chance at true love—surely she owed him something. But not attending church. He didn't know what he was asking of her.

She could still hear the click of the reverend's cane as he passed through the foyer of their D.C. home.

Alone in the library, Clarinda had been laying on the settee, staring at the stenciled ceiling, when a knock came at their front door. It was an unusual sound since the attack. Clarinda shot up and dashed from the room. Who had come to call?

Perhaps Victoria's mother had changed her mind and allowed her daughter to come for a visit. Clarinda hadn't seen her best friend since Victoria's little sister ran screaming from the sight of Clarinda's mangled face several weeks ago.

For that matter, Clarinda hadn't spoken with any of her friends since the incident. They always seemed in a hurry after church services.

Clarinda's shoes pounded down the hall rug, echoing off the walls. She dashed past the covered hall mirror and reached the foyer as the butler opened the door.

It was not Victoria on their doorstep, but Reverend Pennyworth. He only visited when he wanted Clarinda to sing in front of the congregation. She clapped her hands with a squeal. She missed performing at church. The arched ceilings seemed to lift her voice to the heavens.

The reverend's eyes ran straight past the servant to connect with Clarinda's. He flinched and looked away. She didn't blame him. Even she didn't like looking at her scars.

"Would you be so kind as to tell Mr. and Mrs. Humphrey that I'd appreciate a moment of their time?" He handed his card to the butler, who ushered him inside. The butler disappeared into the front parlor where Mother awaited callers every afternoon, even though they hadn't had a visitor in weeks.

She would be pleased the reverend had come to call.

Clarinda tugged at the reverend's sleeve. "I've been practicing. Want to—"

"Mr. and Mrs. Humphrey will see you now." The butler gestured for the reverend to proceed into the parlor.

Reverend Pennyworth left Clarinda without a word.

The butler pulled the door shut.

Clarinda puffed out a breath that ruffled the curls at the side of her face. She'd have to wait for Mother or Father to tell her why the reverend had come. She shuffled back to the library.

If the reverend had come to ask her to sing, why didn't he invite her into the parlor?

Was Mother right?

No one asked Clarinda to sing anymore. She used to sing at all the parties in town, but her family hadn't even been invited to one since the attack. She'd asked Mother to be sure their friends knew Clarinda's singing voice hadn't been damaged, but Mother patted Clarinda's head and told her they already knew that.

As nicely as possible, Mother had explained that no matter how talented the singer, audiences only wanted to watch *pretty* girls sing.

Clarinda slumped onto the library settee. No one wanted to watch a monster sing. And that was what she was now.

A monster.

That's why all the mirrors were covered and no one ever came to see her.

She could never be a famous singer now. The only people who ever heard her sing anymore were her family, and even they didn't want to look at her. Every time she asked if she could sing for Mother, Mother started crying and ran to her room. The few times Clarinda had been to church were the only times she'd gotten to sing where others could hear her since that awful day. But she hadn't been invited to sing at the front since the attack.

She straightened. The reverend had always praised her singing. And wasn't he always preaching about a person's insides being more important than their outsides? Maybe he just needed to hear for himself that her voice hadn't changed.

She darted down the hall once more, coming to a stop outside the parlor door as a loud whack echoed from the room.

She eased the door open a few inches and peered through the crack.

The reverend lifted his heavy wooden cane and slammed it into the floor. The repeating whack cut off whatever Father had been saying.

"You are not listening!"

"I am. I assure you, but—"

"No!" The reverend whacked his cane again. "You are hearing only what you wish to hear. I know this is a difficult thing I'm asking of you, but I truly believe it's in everyone's best interests."

"But how can you ask us—"

"Your daughter's presence is a distraction."

Clarinda covered her mouth. Were they speaking of her?

The reverend poked his cane toward the door, and she ducked, lest anyone should look her way. "She's keeping the other members of our flock from receiving the spiritual nourishment they desperately need. Would you have the loss of their souls on your conscience?"

"No, of course not, but—"

"Good." The reverend rapped his cane once more. "I'm glad you understand. I was hesitant to come here, but I told myself I could depend on your charitable hearts and sound reasoning to understand that this is the only solution."

Footsteps approached and Clarinda ducked beneath a sideboard, praying she wouldn't be seen. What was the reverend saying?

He entered the foyer and took his hat and cloak from the hooks rather than wait for the butler to attend him. He slipped on his gloves and his gaze caught hers. He shook his cane at her. "Do not cry. It's a useless behavior and it won't change a thing. Small sacrifices must be made for the betterment of the flock. You'll understand when you're older."

He pulled open the front door, stepped out, and shut it firmly behind him.

Small sacrifices. Blinking back tears, Clarinda willed away the memory. She pressed her palms to the cool tile floor and rose to her feet. Much as she wanted to give something in return for Richard's sacrifices, attending church was out of the question. She would never present herself at the altar again. She was no one's sacrifice.

CHAPTER 18

*T*hree days later, Richard parked the wagon beside the Humphrey's store. Was he doing the right thing?

"Mr. Stevens!"

Richard turned.

Everett Thompson strode across the plaza. The man wasn't much older than Richard, yet he'd established roots in this town and achieved a level of success few their age could lay claim to. How much of it was a result of the truth-stretching Clarinda claimed the man practiced, and how much was due to the astute intellect Richard had sensed behind the man's dark brown eyes?

The businessman drew to a stop beside the wagon. "I'm glad I caught you. I've just received a letter from another investor, interested in purchasing the property." He waved a piece of paper too fast for Richard to see anything but a blur of hand-writing. "Have you given any more thought to whether you'd like to purchase Mr. Ames's share of the Grand Valley Ranch?"

Richard relaxed against the newly padded backrest as if he had all the time in the world. "I've considered it some, yes. I'm not sure I want to go into business with so many partners. I'm used to being my own man."

Like a fish to a worm, Everett swallowed Richard's hook. "Well, I suppose I could speak with the other investors—see if any of them are willing to part with their share. I'm not sure I can convince them to part with such a profitable investment, but"—His bushy brown brows lifted as a gleam entered his eyes—"if I *could* convince one or more of them to sell, would that help with your decision?"

"It might."

"I believe your *wife* is partial to the property."

So Thompson had learned of Richard's connection to the Humphreys.

"I was surprised you didn't mention the connection." Curiosity danced in the man's brown eyes. He waited for Richard to explain.

The man could wait all day. The situation was none of his business.

Finally, Thompson tucked the paper into an interior coat pocket. "It'd be a shame for Mrs. Stevens to lose the home she's grown up in. I understand you've taken up residence there, yourself."

"True." Richard climbed down from the wagon. "But I regret I cannot make my decision today. I have other business to attend to."

The letter Everett had flapped around was probably not from a legitimate buyer—San Diego wasn't what one would call a popular real estate market. Even if it were, Richard had little doubt he could convince the supposed investor to sell out later on.

If that's what Richard decided he wanted. He'd spoken with each of the men working at the ranch. All seemed in agreement that Clarinda's plan of raising sheep would work. But he needed to speak with other ranchers in the area and send a letter to Henry about the market for sheep up north. He also needed to figure out if his idea for using the shipping company was even possible. All of that had to wait, though. Right now, he had a more important mission to complete.

"If you'll excuse me." Richard started toward the steps leading to the store's five open, double-wide doors.

Mr. Thompson stepped into his path. "What if I could guarantee the sale of the entire property—free of any business partners? You'd own it all yourself. Would you be able to make your decision today?"

Clarinda had been right about the other investors wanting out. Biting back an irritated reply, Richard forced himself to maintain a calm expression. "While that does sound ideal, I cannot discuss such matters at this time. I really must go."

Richard stepped around the annoying man, ascended the steps, and entered the store. Directly in front of him was a table display of soaps, perfumes, and fancy stationery meant to catch a female customer's eye. He paused to lift a bar of soap and sniff it. The citrusy scent reminded him of Clarinda. She must already have some. Besides, soap wasn't what he'd come for. He returned the bar to its display and strolled farther into the store.

On his right and left, shelves as tall as him were lined with everything from hammers to lace gloves. Near the back, a long counter ran the length of the room with an opening in the middle that allowed Mr. Humphrey to pass through. Directly behind the opening was the dark green curtain Richard had spotted past the base of the stairs when he'd let Clarinda drag him up to the sewing room.

His gaze flicked to the ceiling. Were either of the Humphrey women at home? Mr. Humphrey was busy helping a customer retrieve pickles from one of several barrels lined against the south wall of the store.

Richard made his way toward the fabric display. A modest variety of fabrics lined the shelf. He recognized the cottons, linens, and wools in practical browns, blacks, and grays. Two others that looked like the fancier fabrics women used for their best dresses. Beneath them he found a few bolts of something softer. Had Mother called it flannel? Four others bore the bright colors many Californios seemed to prefer. He moved those aside. There, at the bottom. Three bolts of fabric that looked like the stuff Clarinda used for her veils. Which would she prefer?

The pickle customer left and Mr. Humphrey joined Richard. "Richard, my boy. I didn't expect to see you here today. How's Clarinda?" He looked past Richard. "She isn't with you?"

"No, I came alone." Richard shifted his stance. "I'm hoping to surprise her." He swallowed. This wasn't what he wanted, but she hadn't spoken to him in three days. He needed some way to get through to her. "Do you have any of that special fabric she uses for her veils?"

Mr. Humphrey frowned. "I was hoping you'd talk her out of those things."

"I thought they were your idea. Or at least your wife's."

His father-in-law sent a quick glance around the store.

Richard followed his gaze. They were alone.

"They were, at first." Mr. Humphrey wiped his hands on his utility apron. "Susan thought it'd help Clarinda be in town without having to deal with...well, people can be cruel, as you probably know. And it did help some, but it wasn't enough. The stares and whispers really upset Clarinda. So we thought letting her stay at the ranch would give her time to adjust to her new appearance. Instead, she took to wearing those things at home as well as in town."

"Did you ever suggest she stop?"

"She was so adamant about wearing them..." Mr. Humphrey shrugged. "I just wanted her to be happy." His father-in-law faced him with a pained expression. "Truth is, I couldn't protect her. Not from that mongrel, not from the whispers and stares. The veil and gloves...the isolation...it seemed to help her in the beginning. But after a while we realized she was using them to keep people at a distance—even to keep *us* from getting too close." He set a hand on Richard's shoulder, tears forming in the older man's eyes. "I've never been so grateful as I was the day she came home and told me she was married."

"I thought you were upset. After all, you didn't know a thing about me."

The older man chuckled. "Oh, I was that, too. But mostly, I was grateful someone had seen in my girl the treasure I've always known she was." He sobered. "As you know, I'm not pleased with how you went about it, but I've been watching how you look at her. I can see you care about her. You're a gentleman and you're kind to Teodora. That's important because those two have grown close—something my wife resents, but which I admit I'm grateful for." He winced and shrugged. "At least she talks to someone. Clarinda wouldn't get on with anyone who didn't treat Teodora right."

Richard relaxed. "I agree. Your daughter is special, and I'm glad she's had Teodora."

"Yes, well…" Mr. Humphrey wiped the backs of his forearms across his face.

It was clear the man cared more for his daughter than she believed he did. Why hadn't her family made more of an effort to mend the relationship with their daughter instead of sending her away?

Mr. Humphrey's gaze darted around the store again as he shuffled his feet. The man had obviously revealed more than he intended.

Rather than press for more answers, Richard took pity on his new father-in-law. "I promise, I'll do everything I can to make your daughter happy." There was nothing he could do about this family's past, but perhaps there was hope for their future.

Mr. Humphrey's hands rested on his hips. "You think another veil will make her happy?"

"I don't. But..." Richard cringed. "I made a mistake and I need to make it right. I think a new veil will help."

Wordlessly, Mr. Humphrey pulled a bolt of sheer, cream-colored fabric from the shelf and rolled a length on the table. He pulled scissors from an apron pocket, cut the piece free, folded it, and held it out.

Richard grasped the fabric, but his father-in-law didn't let go.

"I like what I've seen so far, but don't think I trust you completely. I've hired a man to look into your claims—to see if you're as wealthy as you claim and whether you treat your family right. If you've lied to me... If you do anything to hurt my girl... I'll send you packing so fast your head will spin and you'll never see Clarinda again." A muscle ticked in the man's jaw. "And I'll see that you regret ever meeting her."

Richard swallowed. "I understand, sir." He'd better write to Tommy and his family as soon as he returned to the ranch. He wasn't worried about what they'd say about him or his business, but if they wrote anything that revealed Clarinda's secret—that they hadn't been married for as long as she'd led her family to believe—she'd never forgive him.

～

Clarinda froze.

Four feet ahead, a small bird perched on a low branch. Its yellow-olive feathering created a striking contrast with the dark reddish-brown bark of the big berry manzanita tree. It tipped its tiny pointed beak toward the sky and released a trilling song. Its entire body quaked with the passion of its enchanting message.

What was the bird saying? Did it call for a mate or warn others to steer clear of its territory?

If only her life were so simple that a song could set things right.

She'd locked Richard out of her bedroom the night after he tore her veil. And each night since. By spending her days riding or taking long walks, she'd managed to avoid talking to him for three days. It couldn't continue. But what could she say to him?

Crash!

Clarinda spun. A medium-sized brown bird had landed in a pile of dead leaves near the base of a nearby bush. It hopped noisily about, scattering dry leaves in its search for a meal. A moment later, the little intruder launched itself into the sky and disappeared into the distance.

Clarinda turned back toward the tiny warbler. It was gone.

Hooves clopped across the hard-packed trail she'd been following. She shielded her eyes against the setting sun.

Richard rode toward her. So much for her solitude.

He dismounted, pulled the hat from his head, and held up a small brown paper package. "I got you something."

She folded her hands at her waist. "Thank you. If you'll leave it on my bed, I'll see to it when I return." She pivoted to continue walking.

"Wait. Please."

She paused.

"I'm sorry for what I did. I...there's no excuse for it."

She faced him.

"I promise you, it will never happen again." He lifted the package. "Won't you please open it?"

His sincerity plucked at her defenses. Gone was the frustrated, angry man from their argument. In his place stood the humble, kind man she'd chosen to marry. He wasn't demanding obedience as many husbands would. Nor did he demand an explanation—though he certainly deserved one. Most women were happy to attend church. She couldn't blame him for his confusion. She ought to explain.

But the words wouldn't come.

Instead, she accepted the package. She peeled back its outer layer to reveal a folded section of her favorite fabric for constructing veils. Tears blurred her vision. Why would he buy this? Was he already weary of seeing her scars?

"I still don't want you to wear veils. I think you're beautiful and I hate not being able to see you." His boots scuffed the dirt. "But it ought to be your choice. I never should've tried to take that from you. I hope you can find it in your heart to forgive me."

She squeezed her eyes shut and two tears ran down her face. He'd done it again—called her beautiful. Would it ever feel true? She opened her eyes and held the fabric against her chest. "Thank you. And of course, I forgive you."

He crushed the brim of his hat. "I didn't mean to make you cry."

She forced a smile. "I'm told women in my condition weep often and over the silliest things."

He cupped her shoulder. "Your tears don't seem silly to me."

She stepped away and pointed to the large manzanita. "You just missed the most beautiful bird. It was such a pretty yellow and its song seemed so joyful."

Richard stared at the setting sun. "Make a joyful noise unto the Lord...come unto his presence with singing."

"I beg your pardon?"

"Nothing. I just..." He hooked his thumbs through his suspenders. "Attending church is such a special part of my week. I've figured out you're not fond of being around people you don't know well, but is there some other reason you don't want to attend church?"

She turned away. "I don't want to talk about it."

"All right. I won't press you, but what about studying the Bible with me here at home? Is that something you might consider?"

"I don't see the point."

"Well, it would mean a lot to me." He sidestepped and caught her eye. "You wouldn't have to do any reading yourself. You could just sit with me while I read aloud. And if you had any questions—"

"I won't."

"That's fine, but if you did, I'd be happy to talk them over with you." He shrugged. "We could do it on Sunday mornings. What do you think?"

"You mean, instead of attending church?"

He nodded.

"But you just said it was the best part of your week."

"I said it was special to me. But spending time with you, studying God's Word together...that would mean the world to me."

Sounded like a waste of time to her. But if it meant that much to him... "Can I sew while you read?"

"Sure."

She shrugged. "I guess that'd be all right, then."

The rush of air from his lungs about bowled her over. "Thank you." He nodded toward the trail. "May I join you in your walk? Perhaps we'll hear another bird sing."

"Your horse will scare them away."

He plopped his hat on his head and reached for her gift. "May I?" She gave the parcel to him and he tied it to the saddle. He pointed his mount toward the main buildings and removed the reins. "We're less than a mile from the barn. He'll find his way home." He slapped the horse's rump. "Besides, I have another surprise for you."

"You do?"

Richard held out his hand and nodded toward the trail. "Shall we?"

She stared at his open palm.

"I promise I don't bite."

She grabbed his hand. Heat rose in her cheeks and she led him along the path. He was right. She was behaving foolishly. It was just a hand. What harm could come of holding his hand?

Arnie had taken her hand and kept it the first time they'd met in their secret alcove. When he left, he'd pressed a kiss to her gloved knuckles.

Clarinda yanked her hand free.

Richard stopped. "What's wrong?"

"You said you had another surprise."

He cocked his head. "I did. But…?"

"So, what is it?"

"Well, I…" He ran a hand over his face. "I understand if you don't want to, but I was hoping to see your expression when I told you."

He was asking her to remove her veil. The tall mesquite and chamise *did* provide good cover at this point on the trail. No one but the vaqueros ever used it, and they were all busy at their different tasks. It wasn't likely they'd come this way. She tugged her veil free and pinned the front to her hat.

The way he looked at her…she could almost feel his caress on her face. Something fluttered inside.

She should pull her veil back down. Instead, she clasped her hands together. "Well?"

His expression sobered. "I was wondering how you'd feel about my purchasing the ranch."

"You're going to try the sheep?"

"If you still think it's a good idea."

She stepped toward him. "I think it's a great idea. But what about the partners? How will you convince them?"

"I considered buying them out." He flicked a leaf from her sleeve. "But since I'm new here, having more connections in the community might prove useful." His hand slid down her arm to clasp her gloved hand. "No doubt, they'll find a way to let me know they're ready to sell once they're confident I'm attached to the place."

"And letting them make the first move will put you in a better position to negotiate." She laughed. He was brilliant.

"Exactly." He tugged her closer. "In the meantime, I think I have enough information to put together a convincing argument for the sheep."

She searched his eyes. "Then you're doing it? You're going to save the ranch?"

"We'll save it." He wrapped his arms around her, and something flipped inside. "Together."

Her breathing kicked up with the intensity of his gaze. She ducked her chin, her forehead resting on his chest. He smelled of sweat and citrus and... What was she doing?

She jerked away. "On second thought, I'm tired. I think I'd better go take a nap."

His brow furrowed. "What about the birds?"

She spun toward the house. "I'm sorry. Some other time." The words were automatic, polite. The second they left her tongue, she wished them back. Because even as she hurried away, the warmth of his arms lingered in a distracting manner. As though she were attracted to him. But that couldn't be. Not when Arnie—scoundrel though he may be—still held her heart. There wasn't room for anyone else.

⁓

Two weeks later, Clarinda scrubbed the wood floors in the clapboard house that once belonged to Frederick Ames. When Richard had told her it was to be theirs as part of his purchase of Ames's portion of the ranch, Clarinda was thrilled. Until she'd opened the door. The former manager had vacated the home more than a year ago and it showed. Cobwebs had taken over the ceilings, dust coated every surface, and tiny droppings gave evidence that the home had not gone unoccupied in Mr. Ames's absence.

This morning, Teodora had rid the house of its cobwebs and droppings, while Clarinda washed the walls and dusted the shelves. But her parents were expected this evening, so Teodora left shortly after the noon meal to begin preparations for their evening meal. She'd told Clarinda to leave the rest of the work for the next day, but Clarinda just wanted it done.

The new bed she shared with Richard took up so much of her old bedroom, there was hardly room to turn around. She had to wait for him to leave each morning before sneaking out from the blanket and dressing herself. Their new home may have only one bedroom, but it was large enough to allow a dressing screen to shield one corner. If she angled it just so, she might be able to slip out from her side of the bed without him glimpsing her chemise.

A lump formed in her throat and she froze. It wasn't supposed to be like this. She shouldn't have to hide from her husband. *Arnie, how could you do this to me? Why did you have to leave? We were supposed to be happy together. What did I do wrong?* Why couldn't anyone love her for who she was?

Tears dripped from her cheeks to join the suds on the floor. She swallowed hard and scrubbed them away.

She would not cry for him. She dried her cheeks on her shoulders. Not anymore. He didn't deserve it.

And it wasn't fair to Richard.

Her husband had been more than patient with her these past weeks. She'd kept him at arm's length while he'd been working hard to learn the ways of the ranch. Yet he still made time to fill their home with bouquets of wildflowers and leave little notes at the kitchen table for her. This morning's note had read, "You are far more precious than jewels and I am very blessed." Beneath that he'd written, "Proverbs 31:10."

Curious, she'd gone in search of Richard's Bible. He'd left a ribbon marking the page. The verse he referenced was sweet, but other words had leapt at her from the page. They taunted her as she scrubbed. How could she ever live up to such a description?

"Clarinda?" Richard's shadow blocked the sunlight streaming through the open door. "What are you doing? Where's Teodora?" He rushed forward and pulled her to her feet. He took the scrub brush from her hands and dropped it into the bucket. His hand came to rest on her cheek. "Have you been crying?"

She twisted away. "I'm just tired."

"But—"

"I'm going to take a nap." She couldn't face his gentle concern, not with her nerves so raw.

CHAPTER 19

*R*ichard planted his shovel in the dirt. Six hard weeks of building fence and they were nearing the end. Eduardo and one of the other vaqueros lowered the final post into the hole they'd just finished digging.

The setting sun streaked the sky with shades of orange, red, and yellow. They'd need to string the barbed wire tomorrow. He let his gaze follow the line of new posts marking the western border of their new paddock.

Eduardo stepped up beside him. "It looks good, Señor."

"So far." Richard tossed his shovel into the small wagon that had been used to haul the posts. "We need the fencing finished by next week to quarantine the new sheep."

Convincing his new partners to make the switch to primarily raising sheep had been less difficult than Richard expected. Of course, offering to pay for all necessary improvements and purchase the new flock with his own funds probably had something to do with that. In exchange, the men had agreed that Richard would claim seventy percent of the profits until his investment was paid off.

Eduardo tossed his shovel in with Richard's. "How many sheep are coming?"

"Seventy-five. Give or take a few, depending on how well the animals handle the drive." He'd considered ordering more, but decided starting with a modest herd was wise. If he had any hard lessons ahead of him, better to learn them on a smaller scale.

He wiped the sweat from his brow with the back of his wrist. His skin felt rough. He scrunched his forehead. Something grated his skin. He tugged one hand free of its glove and ran a finger across his brow. It came away muddy.

He laughed. If Henry could see him now...

Richard had found plenty of dirt on this ranch. He surveyed the rolling valley of pale greens and golden browns fissured by wandering canyons. He'd found beauty and peace here, too. Saving this ranch and nurturing his marriage...they gave him a sense of purpose and belonging. A sense of home.

He climbed into the wagon seat and took up the reins. "Let's head back. I want to see how the lambing is going." And then he'd see his wife.

Several minutes later, he found Fernando in the lambing corral, overseeing the ewes and newborn lambs. Everything seemed to be going well there.

Richard scrubbed his face and arms in the creek and waved goodbye to the vaqueros who were headed to the bunkhouse. He crossed the bridge toward his and Lindy's home.

He leapt past the front two steps and paused to stomp the mud from his boots. The smell of braised mutton assailed him as he stepped inside. He rubbed his hands together. Another of his favorite dishes.

Since they'd moved out of her parents' home, Lindy had begun cooking their evening meals. She claimed she needed something to keep her occupied while he was working the ranch all day. She fixed his favorite meals so often, though, he suspected it was her way of showing her care for him. He wasn't about to complain.

At first, she'd tried to do all the things Teodora was accustomed to doing for the Humphrey family, including cleaning, bringing in water and wood for the cook stove, and a host of other tasks. But the stalwart housekeeper took offense. She insisted Lindy being married didn't change a thing about Teodora's responsibility to care for her. Lindy had argued that Teodora shouldn't be expected to take on the care of a second household.

In the end, they'd compromised.

Lindy took on the mending duties and evening meals. Teodora handled the rest. This suited Richard fine since he didn't want his wife working at all—especially in her condition —but he understood the madness of feeling idle. Besides, safety forced Lindy to remove her veil while she cooked, and his wife had become skilled in the kitchen. It was a win-win. He couldn't wait to taste the braised mutton and whatever else she was preparing for this evening's meal.

He shucked his boots, left them by the door, and padded up behind her. He slid his arms around her waist, his forearms resting above her expanding bump. It was something he'd done the first time he came home to find her busy at the stove. He'd been unable to resist taking her in his arms and giving her a good hug. He caught himself before pressing a kiss to her cheek, though. He half expected her to protest, but she didn't. So he'd made a point to greet her the same way at the end of each day.

He dipped his head low and murmured, "How was your day?" He wanted to nibble her tender earlobe. He bit his lips instead.

She hummed. "It was fine. How was yours?"

Disappointment smothered his amorous thoughts. She answered him the same way every day—even the days when he'd come home to find her eyes red-rimmed and cheeks shiny. Would she never trust him enough to be vulnerable?

He wasn't her parents, and after his conversation with her father, Richard had paid close attention to her interactions with her family. What he'd seen convinced him they weren't as cold-hearted as Lindy believed. They just didn't know how to handle a daughter who'd been far more wounded than her scars revealed.

He released her and took his seat at the table. His nose told him a pile of warm bread slices waited beneath a fabric covering at the table's center. "I think the last ewe will deliver soon. Fernando said the rest that were showing signs gave birth this afternoon without any trouble." His sisters would be shocked by his choice of topic, but ranch business seemed to fascinate his wife.

"That's wonderful." She transferred the mutton from its warming pan at the back of the stove to a delicate serving platter and poured over it the contents of the pan she'd been tending. "What does that bring our total to?" She brought the steaming dish to the table.

"With these new ones, we've got twenty-one, and most of them ewes, only a handful of rams."

She returned to the stove and retrieved the coffee pot. "What does Fernando think of our total?" She filled his mug, then her own.

"He seems pleased, and I've checked the numbers recorded for previous years. It's an increase over last year. With the new flock arriving next week, we'll be in a good position for next year's sales."

She returned the pot to the stove and took her seat.

They clasped hands across the table and bowed their heads. "Heavenly Father, thank you for a positive outcome to the lambing and that no ewes were lost this year. Thank you for this warm home and the food that we are about to receive. And I especially thank You for this beautiful woman I am blessed to call my wife. In Your name we pray. Amen." He gave her fingers a quick squeeze, then released them.

She cut into her meal and began eating. Her chewing drew his gaze to her lips. They'd been married more than two months and he still didn't know what it would be like to kiss her.

He forced his attention to his own meal and cut into the meat with more force than necessary. The knife slid across the plate with a painful screeching sound. "Sorry." He needed to be grateful for the peaceful companionship they'd established since their wedding. Having married while knowing so little about one another, it easily could have gone the other way. She might have been hiding a shrewish nature. His personal habits might have driven her mad. Instead, they seemed to get along fine.

For the most part.

He sensed she wasn't thrilled with his request to pray before each meal and before they went to sleep each night. But at least she hadn't protested like she had about church. Their argument regarding that issue only solidified his suspicion that his wife's relationship with their Savior was tentative at best.

His food turned over in his stomach. His behavior that morning had been shameful. Taking a cleansing breath, he shoved the weight aside. Lindy had forgiven him and so had the Lord. He wouldn't let past mistakes dampen his present happiness.

She'd kept her promise, as well. Each Sunday, she sat in the rocking chair beside the fireplace and sewed while he read. At first, she simply listened. After a couple weeks, though, she began to ask questions and share her thoughts on the Scripture he shared. It was the one time a week he got a glimpse into his wife's heart.

Though they spoke of other things the rest of the week, the topics were always practical and unemotional. Things like how the ranch was faring, whether they were expecting rain, and what supplies needed to be brought from town—these were all safe topics on which Lindy would speak with him at length. Anytime Richard asked how she was feeling, though, she shut down, answering him in as few words as possible. If he dared ask about her past, she would leave the room entirely.

He finished his meal and reclined in his seat. "Thank you. The mutton was especially delicious. Did you add something new to it?"

She smiled. "Cilantro."

"Really? Well, I loved it. Thank you."

She rose and began gathering the dishes.

He jumped to his feet and whisked the plates from her hands. "Here, let me do that." He made his way to the tub where he plunged the dishes into the waiting cold water. "You go rest. I know how tired you get." He added hot water from a pan warming on the stove.

She appeared beside him and bumped her hip against his, moving him away from the sink. "I'm fine. Besides, I know you're dying to get out there and check on the new lambs one more time."

It was true. Most nights during the lambing season he'd been unable to resist checking on them before heading to bed. The vaqueros laughed at him for it, but he couldn't shake a sense of awe whenever he looked at those small creatures that hadn't existed mere months ago and hadn't been seen by human eyes until that day. It made him want to camp out beside the stalls with a rifle to scare off any potential predators. If he was this affected by baby lambs, what would the birth of his and Lindy's child do to him?

He glanced at her. Her pink lips were turned down, shoulders sagging. "I honestly don't mind doing the dishes. The lambs can wait."

"I told you, I'm fine."

"You're frowning."

"Not about that."

Richard searched his mind for what else might be bothering her. "Are you worried about what your parents said yesterday?"

"About the last of the military leaving the mission last week?"

"Your Mother seemed pretty upset about it." Before her family departed, Lindy's father had confided in Richard that there were rumors of a planned Indian revolt and reports of desperado gangs attacking outlying ranches, stealing their livestock. "Your father suggested I post guards to assist the night shepherds."

"Is it that serious?"

"Your father seems to think so." Richard grabbed a towel and stole the clean dish from Lindy's hand. "I've been trying to decide if the extra protection is worth overworking the hands." He set the dry dish on the shelf.

She nodded as she handed him another dish. "Whoever stands watch at night can't be expected to perform his usual daytime tasks. Their work will need to be picked up by someone else." She washed a few more dishes before speaking again. "We could hire more men."

"True. But I'm not sure I like the idea of having strangers on the property."

"Most of our *vaqueros* live in the same village. Maybe there are more who'd be willing to work for us. Surely we could trust them."

"Perhaps. We might ask some of the men from Graciela's village as well. It's a longer journey, but we have a few extra beds in the bunkhouse they could use." He caught her with a serious look. "In the meantime, I don't want you wandering far from the house without an escort. All right?"

"All right." Her lips tipped up on one side. "I thought you were going to check on the lambs."

"I figured if I helped, you'd finish more quickly and could come with me."

"Thanks, but I can handle this. You go on. I'm looking forward to settling down with my book once I'm finished here."

Richard swallowed a sigh and headed outside. Would his wife ever long for more time alone with him?

~

larinda set her book aside and checked her watch. Richard had been gone for more than two hours. Usually he visited the lambs for a few minutes, then came inside to spend time with her before they retired for the evening. Her eyelids were growing heavy. Where was he?

Clarinda pushed to her feet and crossed the room to peer out the front window. Across the creek, the lambing corral was dark, but flickering light pierced the cracks of the barn.

That was odd.

She grabbed her shawl and threw it around her shoulders and over her head. It wasn't her veil, but none of the men should be out at this time of night. She could adjust the fabric to conceal her face if she encountered a vaquero.

She stepped into the cool night air, scurried across the yard, and thumped over the bridge. She pulled open the barn door and cringed at its loud protest. Fernando ought to oil those hinges. "Richard?"

"Over here." His voice came from somewhere toward the rear, near the source of the light.

She closed the door behind her and proceeded down the aisle.

Richard stood in an empty stall, his arms crossed atop one wall as he watched something in the next stall over.

"There you are. What are you doing in here?"

He glanced at her. "Watching." He returned his attention to whatever he'd been looking at. "Come and see."

She walked to his side and followed his gaze. In the next stall were a ewe and two lambs. "Twins?"

Richard nodded. "But this mama hasn't figured that out yet."

One of the babies made an attempt to nurse, but the mother shifted away. The same lamb tried again, but this time the mama ducked her head and butted the poor thing.

Clarinda's hand flew to her chest. "What's she doing?"

"She's accepted that one." He pointed to the lamb sleeping peacefully in a corner. "But that one"—he pointed to the lamb who was again trying to nurse—"she won't let nurse."

"That's awful."

"It's heartbreaking to watch, but Fernando assured me earlier that this sometimes happens. All we need to do is convince the mama she has two babies, not just one. Right now, she thinks that guy belongs to someone else. See how it's still dirty while that one over there looks relatively clean?"

"Do you mean the mother cleaned one but not the other?"

"Yep."

The ewe butted the little guy again, this time hard enough to knock him over. Clarinda grabbed Richard's arm. "You have to do something. She's going to hurt him."

Richard's expression firmed. "I think you're right." He entered the stall that held the sheep. "I was hoping this smaller space without the other sheep would convince her this little guy was hers as well, but it doesn't look like it's working." He opened the gate and stepped inside, closing it again behind him. Approaching the ewe, he slowly corralled her into one corner. He grabbed her leg and held her still.

"What are you doing?"

"I'm keeping her still so the other one can nurse." As he spoke, the rejected lamb slowly approached its mama and began to suckle. The ewe struggled for a few minutes, but Richard held firm. After a while, the mother calmed, but Richard didn't release her until the baby had sucked its fill.

At last, he rejoined Clarinda in the adjacent stall.

"Will she accept the lamb, now?"

"Maybe. Fernando said sometimes one forced feeding is all it takes. Sometimes it takes a whole night of them. And sometimes it doesn't work at all."

The poor little guy. The rejected lamb sidled up to his mother and was pushed aside again. If only there were something Clarinda could do. Why was the mother rejecting one and not the other? Other than a dark brown spot on the rejected one's back, Clarinda couldn't see any significant difference between the two.

Clarinda rubbed her left arm. Rejected for something he couldn't control and couldn't change. It was something she understood far too well. "It's so unfair."

"I know."

"How can the mother do that? How can she push her baby away because of something so small and superficial?"

Richard faced her, his brows raised. "What are you talking about?"

Clenching her jaw, she pointed to the offending spot. "That lamb couldn't help being born with a spot on his back. It's not fair for her to reject him like that."

Richard's head tilted. "I don't think a sheep cares much about something like that."

"Then why reject one and accept the other?"

"It's likely that this one"—he pointed to the lamb who'd just nursed—"was born second."

"That's all?" Her voice cracked as tears blurred her vision. "She rejected him because he wasn't her firstborn? How is that any better?"

"It isn't." Richard laid a hand on her shoulder, gently pulling her into his arms. "It's never right when anyone is rejected by their parent." His hand circled slowly up and down her back, his eyes fixed on hers. "That's why the shepherd keeps watch over his sheep. When he sees a parent not doing their duty, he draws that lamb close, spends time with him, and nourishes him. He loves him even when no one else does and—when he thinks they're ready—he reintroduces them to the flock and helps them find acceptance and affection."

A weight pressed hard on her chest as tears sprang to her eyes. She clamped her lips against the sobs but they shook her shoulders and escaped. Why did the plight of this animal touch her so deeply? It was just a lamb.

Yet she couldn't stop crying. Several minutes passed with Richard rubbing her back. Eventually, her tears slowed and she managed to collect herself. What must Richard think of her? She tried to step away, but he held her close, still stroking her back.

"Lindy,"—his voice was low, soothing—"I don't think your parents have rejected you the way you think they have."

She jerked against his hold, and this time he released her. He was trying to make things better, but he couldn't fix what he didn't understand. She pivoted on her heel and took a step toward the aisle.

"I'm not saying they made the right choices."

She spun, fury burning in her gut. "The right choices? They abandoned me. They stuck me on this ranch in the middle of nowhere and went on with their lives as if I didn't exist. But that wasn't good enough. They were still burdened with planning for my future care—because no man would ever want me—so they shipped me as far away as they could afford to send me. They practically made me promise never to return. I wasn't supposed to disgrace myself and come crawling home. I was supposed to find a job somewhere far away from here so they wouldn't have to think about me anymore."

He held his hands up, palms facing her. "I know that's what

you believe, but I've been watching and listening. I don't think it's them who's rejected you. I think they were honestly trying to protect you and *you've* rejected *them* for their misguided efforts."

"*I* rejected *them?*" Her fingers curled into her palm, her nails cutting into her skin. "How dare you?"

"Did you know your father hired someone to investigate me?"

Clarinda fell back a step. "He what?"

"He had someone send letters to my family back east, asking about my character. That same person made a visit to my offices and that widow I told you I rent a room from, asking them whether I pay my rent on time, how I treat my employees, and whether I was a man to be trusted." Richard glanced around and stepped forward, his voice low. "Don't worry. None of them mentioned anything to cast doubt on our wedding date."

"Are you sure it was my father who did that?" She shook her head. "*Why* would he do that?"

"He told me himself that he sent them. Warned me that if I hurt you, he'd see that I regretted it." Richard stepped toward her. "Your father was thrilled when you told him you were married, not because you were no longer a burden, but because someone else saw you for the treasure you are."

"But..." That couldn't be right. Clearly Richard misunderstood. Her parents were happy to see her married to *anyone*. It meant someone had taken her off their hands. If they'd hired an investigator, it must have been to verify Richard's claims of wealth. They'd want to make sure they'd rid themselves of their burden, not gained a new one.

CHAPTER 20

a week later, Richard crossed the yard to the main ranch house. He knocked at the front door, and a few seconds later, Teodora opened it.

"Ah, Mr. Stevens. Please, come in." Teodora stepped aside, revealing Mrs. Humphrey seated near the empty fireplace, carding wool.

His mother-in-law looked up with a smile. "You don't have to knock. You're family. This is as much your home now as it is ours. I hope you'll feel free to come and go as you please."

Richard scraped his boots and stepped inside. "Thank you. I suppose I'm still getting used to the idea."

The woman's smile faded as she addressed the housekeeper. "Go and fetch Richard a cup of coffee and some of those cookies you made yesterday."

"Yes, ma'am." Teodora disappeared into the kitchen.

Richard took a seat across from Mrs. Humphrey.

Her smile returned. "Sometimes I forget the two of you have only been married five months."

He bit his tongue. He and Lindy had been married only thirteen weeks. Thirteen long weeks in which he'd been unable to convince his wife to be honest with her parents. The longer the deception continued, the heavier his burden grew.

There was also his promise to Andrew to consider. The next time they met, Richard needed to be able to look the man in the eye and tell him the truth had been revealed.

Which was exactly why Richard had come here. If he could understand why her parents had made the decisions they did, it might help him determine how to move forward.

The carders scratched as Mrs. Humphrey dragged them through the wool. The two rectangular paddles bore countless needle-looking hooks that passed between each other as the cards were stroked in opposite directions. He'd been reading about the process. The hooks caught the fibers and more-or-less aligned them in preparation for being rolled into a rolag and later spun. To Richard, they resembled nothing so much as two hair brushes having a disagreement about which way to go.

Much like the differences in how he and Lindy viewed the idea of confessing to her parents.

He shifted in his seat. Where to begin? He picked a bit of runaway fiber from his pant leg. "Can I help?"

"If you like." She didn't pause in her strokes as she nodded toward a basket near her feet. "You can take a lump of wool from here. There are a pair of carders in that box in the corner."

He gathered his materials and returned to his chair. He placed a large pinch of wool atop the tines of one of the carders and began stroking the other carder across its surface. As he did, tiny voices took up an imaginary conversation in his mind.

Let's go this way.

No the little fibers should go that way.

No, they need to go this way.

That way.

This way.

That way.

And on they went, arguing with each stroke of the carders.

"What are you chuckling about?"

He looked up to find Mrs. Humphrey smiling at him. "Oh, I was just thinking of how these things"—he paused his strokes to hold up the carders—"seem to be arguing about which way to go." He continued stroking, vocalizing the voices he'd been imagining in high, mouse-like tones. "This way. That way. No, this way. Uh-uh, it's that way."

Mrs. Humphrey burst out laughing. "You know, I've never thought of it that way, but you're exactly right." She continued chuckling as she looked down at her own carders. "I don't think I'll ever see these the same again."

They continued carding in silence for several minutes. Every now and then a smile would grace his mother-in-law's face and she'd shake her head.

How should he broach the subject he'd come to discuss? "Has Clarinda ever helped with the carding?"

"She did when she was younger. Of course, for the past few years she's been away at school." Mrs. Humphrey rolled off the wool she'd been working, set it aside, and added a new tangled lump to her carder. "It's nice having her home again. I missed her. I saw her out in the garden this morning, pulling out weeds. I told her she oughtn't be doing such work in her condition, but she didn't pay me any mind. So I told Teodora to go out and take over the weeding. She'd just returned to tell me the job was done when you knocked." She frowned. "I hope Clarinda didn't hurt herself. Where is she now?"

"She's napping. I think you were right. The work wore her out." Hopefully she wouldn't wake and wonder where he'd gone. He'd better get to the point. "Was it Clarinda's idea to attend the Young Ladies' Seminary?"

"No, that was Lucy's idea. As soon as she heard of the school opening, she told me and I told Neal we needed to save enough money to send Clarinda." Sadness entered Mrs. Humphrey's eyes. "She was shriveling up here on the ranch. She needed something to inspire her, to restore her joy."

"Why *was* she out here while the rest of you lived in town? Pardon me for asking, but you must admit it's a bit unusual. Your husband said the attention in town bothered Clarinda, but I'm still not sure I understand the decision."

"I wouldn't expect you to. It isn't typical for a family to live as ours has. And as I said, you're family now. As her husband, you have a right to know." She stopped carding and held his gaze. "You have to understand what it was like for our dear girl. People gawked and pointed everywhere we went. They would whisper as we approached, then abruptly grow silent when we drew close enough to hear." Her lower lip wobbled. "The worst, though, was when they didn't realize she was around. They said such awful things, calling her a freak and a monster." A tear slipped from her eye. "Before we left Washington, we took Clarinda to visit a young lady who'd been her friend for years." Mrs. Humphrey shook her head, covering her lips.

A moment later, she took a deep breath and continued. "Clarinda's friend had a little sister who was playing in the yard when we arrived. That girl took one look at Clarinda and screamed as if the devil himself had come for her. She ran into the house and, a moment later, her mother was on the front porch demanding we leave and never return. Clarinda hasn't been the same since. We'd hoped moving to San Diego—a place that put less concern into appearances than the high society circles we'd enjoyed in Washington D.C.—would help her find more acceptance. By the time we arrived, though, no one could convince her to leave her room without her veil and gloves on."

Richard couldn't imagine the pain his young wife had experienced. To not only be rejected, but to know your mere presence terrified a child... No wonder she wore the veil.

"She told me the coverings were your idea."

"Yes, it was the only way I could think of to protect her.

People still stare and whisper, but at least their looks are more curious than revolted and no more children have run away from her." She paused her carding again. "Still, I'd give anything to see her face clearly once more."

"She won't reveal herself to you?"

"I haven't seen my daughter uncovered since she recovered from the influenza seven years ago."

Yet, Lindy had revealed herself to him. Had gone along with his request to remain uncovered when they were in private. The size of her sacrifice—the level of her trust in him—was much larger than he'd believed.

"Your husband said you sent Clarinda to the ranch to get away from the stares and whispers. Please forgive me if this sounds critical. But I don't understand. Why not move out here with her?"

"Well, my husband needs to be close to the store of course, but also, you have to understand Lucy is a gregarious and viva-cious child and always has been. Raising her on this isolated ranch would've been like trying to grow a sunflower in a cellar." Mrs. Humphrey's gaze dropped to her hands and she resumed her carding. "Besides, Clarinda has Teodora. She doesn't need me. Not like Lucy does." She paused, her gaze lifting to his. "As horrible as it sounds, we believed we'd already failed Clarinda. We couldn't risk failing Lucy, too."

∾

*C*larinda pressed her back against the cold wall in her former bedroom and slid to the floor.

Richard had been right. Last week, when he'd claimed her parents cared more than she thought, she hadn't believed it. But she couldn't deny the longing in Mother's voice a moment ago when she'd told Richard she wanted to see Clarinda's face without the veil. Emotion squeezed her throat. Mother *wanted* to see her. All these years, she'd believed her mother was repulsed by her appearance—had provided so many veils and gloves to ensure she never had to look upon Clarinda's hideous scars again.

Could it be true that her mother had been trying to protect her? Did Father feel the same? She'd assumed their explanations were no more than a disguise—something they told themselves to avoid the guilt of banishing their own child. And didn't they deserve to feel guilty? They *had* chosen Lucy over her. Weren't parents supposed to love all their children equally?

Clarinda glanced around her childhood room. What had she come here for? It didn't matter. She crept toward the door leading to the courtyard and eased it open. She didn't want to hear any more.

~

*C*larinda lay perfectly still, staring at the ceiling. Though she couldn't see Richard on the other side of the horse-hair-stuffed six-foot-long bolster she'd created to divide their bed, his presence seemed to fill the room. Along with his peaceful, even breathing. He'd meant well in speaking to Mother. He had. But why couldn't he let things alone? Why did he have to try to fix everything? Some things were just too broken to be fixed.

She ought to know.

Shame weighted the blankets, pinning her to the bed. She didn't deserve Richard. He was kind, handsome, considerate, and hard working. He was even wealthy. If he hadn't lost his temper over church, she might have believed him perfect.

Then again, she'd believed Arnie was perfect. Look where that had gotten her.

What was she thinking? Arnie had courted her for more than a year. She'd only known Richard a few weeks. He was probably still hiding his darker side. Everyone did that—put on their best show when they first met someone. It was human nature. So why did her heart want to believe Richard was exactly who he pretended to be? She was thinking childishly. It didn't matter that she felt like she'd instinctively known Richard from their first meeting on the ferry. Feelings lied. Men lied. Why was she so gullible?

～

Clarinda scooped the eggs into a split roll and wrapped the warm sandwich in brown paper. "I appreciate you letting me sleep late, but you could have woken me." She handed the bundle to Richard, who tucked it into his saddlebag. "I know how excited you are to see the new sheep."

She turned away and blinked against tears. How could she have overslept? Fernando and several other vaqueros had left at dawn to meet the flock being driven in from Mexico. But thanks to her, Richard was late.

"You needed the sleep and Fernando will see that everything goes smoothly until I arrive. I'm only a couple hours behind."

Thundering hooves came to a skidding halt in the yard.

Richard hurried across the room and grabbed the rifle above the door.

Someone banged on the other side. "Señor!"

Clarinda met Richard's confused gaze. "It's Eduardo." He'd left with the others. Why was he back?

Richard threw open the door. "What's wrong?"

Eduardo spun away. *Venga conmigo. Date prisa!*" He gestured for Richard to follow him. "The men. They've been taken."

CHAPTER 21

"Wait! I'm coming with you." Clarinda dashed toward her room. She needed her hat, veil, and gloves.

Richard hurried after Eduardo. "What are you talking about? Who's…"

She couldn't hear the rest of his words as she threw on her coverings. It'd been a few years since one of their vaqueros had been arrested. Whoever had taken them must be new to the area. Otherwise they'd recognize the men who worked for the Grand Valley Ranch. She grabbed Richard's saddlebag and rushed into the yard.

Richard was leading two saddled horses from the barn, one of which was her usual mount. He said something to Eduardo, and the vaquero galloped to the southeast.

Clarinda took her reins. "Where's he going?"

"I told him to take all but one of the guards and meet the team bringing in the flock." He ran his free hand through his hair. "I hate leaving the ranch so vulnerable, but it'll take several men to bring in the sheep, and Eduardo said Smith would only release our men to a white man claiming to be their employer."

Clarinda gasped. "Smith has our men?" Clarence Smith was known for his harsh treatment of Indians. He regularly sent his favorite vaqueros in search of allegedly unemployed Indians that could be hauled off to jail and charged with vagrancy. Smith would pay the court-ordered "fines" in exchange for their labor on his ranch. The service terms were meant to be finite, but he always found a way to extend them. Few of his victims escaped their legalized slavery.

She and Richard had to find their men before Smith could get them before a judge. "What about Manuel? Was he taken, too?" The thirteen-year-old boy employed to tend the animals kept near the house had been as excited as the rest about the new arrivals and received special permission to join the group meeting the flock that day.

Richard took his saddlebag and lifted her into the saddle. "He was. Eduardo only escaped because he'd lingered behind to inspect his mount's hoof." Richard attached his saddlebag, mounted his own horse and looked at her. "Eduardo said Smith and his men were driving ours north toward their ranch. He said you'd know the route."

"This way." She urged her horse into a fast trot, wishing they could gallop. But the terrain was too varied and Smith's ranch was more than a day's ride away. The horses would tire quickly if she pushed them too hard.

Richard rode beside her. "Shouldn't they be headed to the jail in San Diego?"

"Smith likes to round up a large group of Indians before taking them to the judge. He'll force the men to work his land until then."

"Is that legal?"

"No one stops him."

"Why don't the Indians just run?"

"Smith would shoot them."

"Unarmed men?"

"And women and children." She scowled. "In the back. With a smile on his face."

"And no one protests?"

"Oh, he's been put on trial a couple of times. But he always walks away a free man."

Richard pulled up short. "I've changed my mind. You're waiting at home."

"Don't be silly. Smith won't touch me. Especially with you at my side."

"Because we're white?"

"And land owners."

Richard shook his head. "It's not right to judge people on such things. A person ought to be valued for their character and what's in their heart. Not their appearance or pocketbook."

"That's what you were talking about last night."

"Exactly. *For man looketh on the outward appearance, but the Lord looketh on the heart.*"

They'd been reading the first book of Samuel. The story of how the Lord instructed Samuel to pass all of David's older, stronger brothers and anoint the youngest, least likely candidate as the future king of Israel. Richard had said it was because the Lord could see David's heart and knew that he would make the best king.

She'd pointed out that David made many mistakes as king, including adultery and murder. But Richard replied, "I said God thought David would be the *best* king, not a perfect one." He went on to list a bunch of imperfect people whom God had chosen over the course of history and whose stories were recorded in the Bible. Some she'd heard of, others were new to her.

She leaned back as they descended into a canyon. "Well, the first part of that verse is true enough. Most people do only care about a person's appearance." Arnie's father had seen her at church but never spoken with her. Her appearance was the only thing he knew about her. It had been enough to reject her as a potential daughter-in-law. Somehow, the thought didn't sting quite as much as it once had.

Richard reined his horse closer. "Most people are fools. But God is wise. He sees our broken, sinful hearts and loves us anyway. More than that, He sent His Son to live a sinless life and die a painful death so that we could be washed free of our sins."

Why would anyone sacrifice their child for her? She was broken inside and out. Clarinda shifted in her seat. How had they gotten onto this topic? "When we find Smith, make sure you stay calm. He's generally civil to people of our class, but he hates losing free labor and has a hot temper. We don't want to rile him."

"I understand."

She didn't like the double meaning she detected in his tone, but kept silent.

A few minutes later, they ascended the other side of the canyon. Not far away, a group of riders surrounded a smaller group of men on foot. At their center, stood Smith. Facing him, with squared shoulders and a red face, stood a defiant Manuel.

Richard and Clarinda urged their mounts into a gallop.

Smith reached for the whip coiled at his waist.

"No!" Clarinda vaulted from her horse and leapt between Smith and the boy.

"Stop!" Richard seized Smith's arm.

Smith roared. "How dare you!"

The two men tussled for control of the weapon.

"Richard!" Clarinda leapt forward, hands outstretched, heart pounding in her ears. If she could just grab Smith's arm, maybe Richard could gain the upper hand. But they were moving too fast.

Smith's men jumped from their horses. One tugged her arm. "You'd best get out of the way, Miss Humphrey."

She couldn't just stand there while Richard got hurt. She jerked free and yanked the man's pistol from his holster. She cocked it, pointed it in the air, and fired.

Everyone froze.

~

*R*ichard stared at his beautiful wife waving a gun in the air like a valiant warrior. Her hat had been knocked sideways. Locks of golden blonde hair peaked from beneath her veil, catching the sunlight. She was the most beautiful thing he'd ever seen.

And he loved her. The force of that revelation stole the air from his lungs.

Lord, what am I going to do? Should he tell her? He knew she didn't love him in return. Not yet. But maybe—

"Miss Humphrey?" The man with the whip gaped at Lindy. "What are you doin' here?"

Richard jerked the whip away and scrambled to his feet. "She's here because you've taken our men." Glaring at the man clearly in charge of this group, Richard wiped the blood from his quickly-swelling lip. He nodded toward the riderless horses strung together at the back of the group. "And our horses."

"Don't know about that." The leader sneered. "I caught 'em tryin' to hightail it to Mexico. Bunch of horse thieves is what they look like to me."

Lindy's face grew bright red. "You know very well these are our men." She shook a fist in the shorter man's face. "Clarence Smith you turn them loose or I'll ask Mr. Thompson to take another look at the contract for that loan he made you last year. Maybe find a way to call in your payment."

Smith sputtered. "Now listen here—"

"I'm sure that isn't necessary, darling." Richard took Lindy's shoulders and pulled her back against his chest. He wanted to

227

spin his fiery woman and kiss her soundly. But first he needed to fix the damage she'd caused by threatening Smith in front of his men. "This has clearly been a giant misunderstanding. Mr. Smith was only doing what he thought was right. You can't fault a man for that."

"He—"

Richard squeezed Lindy's arms in warning. "I'm sure now that he understands the situation, he'll be happy to return our men and horses. Right, Smith?"

Smith muttered something and stomped to his horse.

Richard tipped his head. "What was that?"

"I said, just take these animals and git!" Smith mounted up. "I ain't got time to jaw all day. There's work to be done. Let's go, men."

Smith's men mounted their horses and rode away with their boss.

Fernando strode forward and clapped Richard's shoulder. "Am I glad to see you."

Richard returned the gesture. "You all right?"

Fernando frowned. "I'm fine, but what about the sheep?"

CHAPTER 22

A few days later, Richard waved goodbye to Teodora as he and Lindy departed Graciela's village. As far as those at the ranch were concerned, Richard and Lindy were taking the day to explore the countryside with Teodora tagging along to cook for them. Which was basically true.

Before they'd left Graciela's village, Teodora had assisted her daughter in preparing a meal with the supplies they'd brought from the ranch. Now that the meal was finished, he and Lindy were heading out to allow Teodora some private time with her family.

The hot summer sun beat down on them an hour later as he led their horses up a winding path on the side of a mountain. The peak was covered in large boulders, piled one atop of the other, as though God had pinched a pile from his barrel of boulders and dropped them right there.

Richard pulled his horse to a stop and dismounted. Lindy lifted the veil from her face and pinned it up without his asking. She'd begun to do so more and more. Was she beginning to trust him? To believe in her own worth? *Lord, let it be so.*

As he helped her from the saddle, Lindy scanned the off-white rocks marked with brown and burnt-orange speckles and stripes. "What are we doing here?"

Her feet touched the ground, but he kept his grip on her waist, waiting for her gaze to meet his. "I have a surprise for you."

"A surprise? Out here? How did you manage that?"

He laughed. "All right, technically, it's God's surprise, but I get to show it to you because Eduardo told me about it."

"He told you about these rocks?"

"I asked him if there was anywhere special he might take a lady—someplace you may not have seen before." He studied her. "You haven't been here before have you?"

She shook her head.

"Good." He released her waist and took her hand. "Come on, it's this way."

Richard led her around the pile of boulders, keeping a close eye out for visitors of the four-legged or slithering kinds. It took a few seconds, but eventually he spotted the small opening Eduardo had described.

"Just a moment." He released her hand and stepped forward to check that the cave was unoccupied. It was.

He took Lindy's hand again and ducked through the gap.

Her soft gasp was magnified in the large cavity created by the boulders. "It's so cool in here."

She was right. It had to be at least ten degrees cooler in this hidden place than it had been outside. And that wasn't the best part.

Crouching low to avoid hitting his head on the rock above, Richard maneuvered around a smaller rock standing almost center in the room. On the other side, he discovered what Eduardo had promised.

He gestured to Lindy. "Come, you have to see this."

She joined him at an opening in the rocks that created a window facing southwest. Through it they could see the entire valley below. Pointing into the distance, she smiled. "Look, there's the river."

Richard stepped up behind Lindy, wrapped his arms around her and settled his chin on her shoulder. He followed her finger to the meandering line of large green bushes and trees that cut through the valley. They marked the path of the river as it flowed toward San Diego and the ocean beyond. "So it is." He turned his head slightly, his lips a hair's breadth from her cheek. "Do you like the surprise?"

She turned toward him. A word forming on her lips, her breath dancing with his.

He forced his gaze to hers.

The dancing stopped as her eyes rounded.

He waited.

A moment.

Two.

She didn't lean forward. Didn't move away.

Her gaze flicked to his mouth. Her eyelids fluttered closed with an exhale.

At last, he pressed his lips to hers. Gently, he explored their sweet softness.

She held still as he tasted her—not stiff—but not responding, either.

Then she lurched away, stepping out of his embrace. "I—that wasn't...it isn't what we agreed upon."

Richard's arms fell. "You didn't like it?"

"That isn't the point." Her cheeks turned a delightful shade of pink.

He tipped his head. "Isn't it?" He reached for her again, but she sidestepped him and tripped in her haste.

He lunged forward, catching her fall. "Careful. These rocks are rough. I don't want you to hurt yourself."

"It isn't the rocks I'm worried about." She tugged free of his grasp and sat.

"What does that mean?"

She looked away and flicked at a loose pebble on the floor of the cave. "Nothing."

He lowered to a spot across from her, careful to give her space. "Lindy, you know I'd never hurt you. I'd never force you to do anything you didn't want to."

She didn't answer, just kept flicking at pebbles, one after another.

"You do know that, don't you?"

"Of course, I know that."

He released his breath. "Then what's the problem?" If she knew he wouldn't force her and she had enjoyed the kiss—and all signs pointed to that being the case—then what was she so afraid of?

She couldn't be worried he'd abandon her like the man who'd fathered her child. They were married, and Richard had told her time and again that he was in it for life. So then, what?

"Lindy, talk to me." He hated the whine in his voice, but he was growing desperate to bridge the gap that kept them from making theirs a true and complete marriage. Not because he desired her physically—though of course he did—but because he yearned for a different kind of intimacy, one that joined their hearts and minds.

Knowing Lindy was like attending a party where the hostess would only allow you into the foyer and the front parlor, but never beyond that into the family's personal rooms. The front rooms of Lindy's heart were beautiful and endearing, but it was in those back rooms where people were most themselves, free of guile, free of the need to impress. He didn't need his wife to impress him. He needed her to...be her.

She flicked another pebble. "What do you want me to say?"

"Can you tell me what it is that's between us? What's keeping you from being open with me?"

"You won't like it."

His stomach dropped. Was she still in love with the man who'd fathered the child she carried? She'd yet to tell Richard the scoundrel's name. So far as he knew, she'd hadn't thought of the man since their first conversation about getting married.

Although she'd begun to open up about her childhood, her years at the seminary remained a mystery. How long had the relationship gone on? What had induced her to make that ultimate concession? Why had the man been fool enough to let her go?

Thank You, Lord, that he let her go. Please help me to find my way to her heart.

Swallowing, he held her gaze. "Whether I'll like it or not, I want to know. I want to know everything about you, Lindy— the good, the bad, the funny, the beautiful. I—" He hesitated. Was now the moment?

"I don't trust you."

The words struck him hard, and, for a moment, he couldn't speak. Of all the things he'd expected her to say, those were not words he'd braced for.

"I know you've done nothing to deserve it, but it's the truth. I'm damaged goods. Not just on the outside, but the inside as well." She placed a hand on her belly. "The consequences of my actions run so much deeper than this child I'm carrying. I can't trust you. I've lain awake at night, long after you've fallen asleep, reminding myself of all the ways you've proven yourself trust-worthy. But I can't do it. You're still a man and...I don't trust myself enough to trust you with..." Her voice trailed off as a tear trailed down her cheek.

"Your heart." Richard choked on the words. "You're afraid I'll break your heart like he did."

She nodded, more tears coursing down her cheeks.

His fists clenched. How he wished he knew the man's name so he might knock some sense into him. But no, that would do no one any good. He bowed his head. *Lord, take this anger from me. Help me to see how I can help her. Please heal her. Only You can cover the wound that vile man left behind.*

"I'm sorry."

Her whisper was his undoing. Warmth gathered behind his eyes, his vision blurring. He did nothing to conceal his pain from her. He wanted no secrets between them. He scooted across the rough rock and took her hands in his. "Lindy, I love you."

She gasped and started to pull away, but he held firm to her fingers.

"I understand you don't feel the same." *Lord, give me strength.* "But I had to tell you how I feel because I want you to know, I'm prepared to wait. For as long as it takes for you to heal. To someday trust me. I'll be here. I'm not going anywhere. Not now, not ever."

Lindy leaned forward and buried her face in his chest. "I don't deserve you."

He wrapped her in his arms. "Yes, you do. You just don't know it yet."

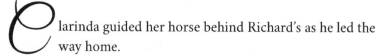

Clarinda guided her horse behind Richard's as he led the way home.

The problem was that he didn't know her. He couldn't. If he did, he wouldn't love her. Arnie spent a year getting to know her. He'd thought he loved her. But once he'd seen all of her—knew everything about her—he'd left. If she let Richard in, he'd do the same.

Her parents had known her far longer and look how little they cared for her. Even God didn't care for her.

That's not what Richard says.

Some of the Scripture Richard had read to her, and the stories he'd told her about how God had worked in his life…

they made her wonder. Richard's whole being seemed to glow when he spoke of God. It made her doubt...everything.

But Richard was wrong about that too. He had to be. Or maybe God only cared about people like Richard.

He twisted in the saddle to look at her. "You doing all right?"

She nodded, but he didn't turn away. His gaze dropped to her mouth.

She ducked her chin.

The memory of his kiss reignited on her lips. What was she supposed to do with that? She'd seen it coming. Had wanted him to kiss her. That was the most confusing part. Until that moment, she'd been certain she never wanted to kiss another man as long as she lived. But then he'd done it and...she'd wanted so badly to kiss him back. But she couldn't move. Couldn't breathe. What if she did something wrong?

So she'd done nothing. Until the warmth of his caress melted the ice in her veins. And she fled.

Still, he'd begged her to bear more of herself. She tried to evade him, but he wouldn't let her be. He just kept pressing for more. So she did the only thing she could think of. She'd hurt him with the truth. Wielded the shattered shards of her heart like a weapon

And still, he'd said he loved her.

But it couldn't be true. Because she could never love him back.

CHAPTER 23

The bright summer sun hung directly overhead as Richard guided his horse out of the eastern pasture and toward home. He didn't always have time to return to their house for the noon meal—some of the pastures were too far from the main structures for it to be practical—but whenever he could, he did. Sharing a meal with his wife invigorated him to face the second half of his day.

Lindy had slept late this morning and was still in bed when he left with the vaqueros to move the sheep to a new pasture. She'd been quiet on the way home yesterday. How would she respond to him now? Had his honesty in the boulder cave pushed her further away or opened the door to a new beginning for them?

He dismounted in front of the barn and handed his reins to Manuel. "See that she gets a good drink. There's no water where we're working today. I'll be back for her after I eat."

"Sí, Señor." The boy led the horse away and Richard hurried toward the house.

He pushed through the front door. "Lindy?" A glance at the

kitchen showed it empty, the stove cold. The rest of the room sat quiet, with no sign she'd been there recently.

Was she napping?

He strode to their chamber. Before they'd gone to sleep, he shared his plans to stop by today. She assured him she'd have a meal ready and waiting.

The bed lay empty, its blanket neatly tucked.

He spun around, hands on his hips to survey the front room once more. Where could she be?

"Lindy!" His shout bounced off the open-beam ceiling.

Back on the porch, he paused to scan the yard. "Clarinda!" There was no sign of her in the garden, near the cistern, or near the large pit Teodora sometimes used for cooking in the court-yard. *Teodora.* Perhaps she would know where his wife had disappeared to.

He burst into the kitchen of the main house.

Teodora jumped. "Oh, it's you, Señor Stevens." She stirred something in a pot on the stove. "Do you need something?"

"Sorry I startled you. Have you seen Clarinda?"

Her eyes widened. "No. Is something wrong?"

"No." He forced himself to sound calm. "I'm sure everything's fine. I just came home for the noon meal and she isn't at home."

"Have you checked the barn?"

The barn? "Why would she be in there?"

Teodora set the spoon aside and bent to check something in the oven. "I don't know, but I've seen her going there every morning for almost two weeks now."

"Thank you." Richard marched toward the barn. What was this? Another secret?

He yanked open the door. Its hinges didn't grate. Fernando must have had someone oil it.

He entered the relative gloom of the structure and singing met his ears. He stopped short. The voice was undeniably feminine and indescribably talented. Growing up, he'd been blessed to attend concerts by several of the nation's most renowned singers, and this voice, this singer, would have held her own among them.

Could it be?

Richard crouched low and inched forward. He paid close attention to every step. Instinct warned him the singer meant not to be overheard. He paused outside the stall where Lupe, the rejected lamb, had been housed and bottle-fed since his mother refused to be coerced into accepting him. Richard slowly rose until he could peek over the wall.

Inside, Lindy sat on a pile of hay in the corner. The little lamb was snuggled beside her, sucking from a large bottle. As Richard had suspected, the incredible voice belonged to his beautiful wife.

He sank out of sight. With his back pressed to the wall, he focused on the lyrics she sang.

> *And nursing the dew drop bright*
> *Ah! May the red rose live alway,*
> *To smile upon the earth and sky!*
> *Why should the beautiful ever weep?*
> *Why should the beautiful die?*

Richard frowned. Tranquil and elegant the melody may be, but the song's words were horribly depressing. *Why should the beautiful die?* Why should *anyone* die? It was because of sin entering the world that there was death and suffering. Yet the song gave no answer to its mournful question. It failed to share the amazing and wonderful news of Christ's gift of forgiveness and eternal life for all who would accept Him as their Lord and Savior.

> *Long may the daisies dance the field,*
> *Frolicking far and near!*

Why should the innocent hide their heads?
Why should the innocent fear?
Spreading their petals in mute delight
When morn in its radiance breaks,
Keeping a floral festival
Till night loving primrose wakes
Long may the daisies dance the field,
Frolicking far and near!
Why should the innocent hide their heads?
Why should the innocent fear?

The song's questions echoed his sentiments about Lindy's veil and gloves. She was not responsible for the scars she bore. Nor was she responsible for the cruel words and actions of those who mocked and excluded her. Nevertheless, she chose to hide herself from the world.

It should not be. How he longed to wrench the grip of fear from her heart and cast it upon the Lord. Yet it was not in his power to do so. Only his dear wife could cast her cares upon her Maker. Would she ever find the faith to trust Him?

Silence filled the barn, save for the slurping and sucking noises made by Lupe. So far as she knew, she was alone. Yet, even here she covered herself. He cleared his throat. "Your voice is heavenly—a true gift of God."

A startled squeak emerged from the stall behind him. "You frightened me. How long have you been there?"

"Long enough to learn yet another of your secrets." He rose to his feet and smiled to show he wasn't upset. "Why didn't you tell me you could sing so beautifully?"

Her cheeks pinked. "I don't."

"Oh, no. You cannot argue with me after what I just heard. Admit it or not, your voice could rival that of angels."

She lifted a brow, amusement sparkling in her eyes. "You've heard angels sing?"

"Every time I look into your beautiful blue eyes."

She groaned.

He chuckled. "Seriously, though. I've heard some of the best singers in the country perform, not to mention several from Europe. You could hold the stage with any one of them. You'd probably even outshine a few."

Her smile faded. "That will never happen."

"You never know." He winked. "I heard they're making plans for a big Fourth of July celebration in town. We ought to let the organizers know you're available to give a concert. I bet they'd—"

"No!" She shot to her feet. Poor Lupe startled and scurried into a corner. The milk bottle fell to the floor. "I told you I don't do that anymore." She stormed to the stall door.

He stepped aside to let her out, but caught her arms as she went by.

"Hey, hey," he cooed. "I was only teasing. I know how you feel about being the center of attention. I would never ask that of you. I'm sorry my joking upset you." When would he learn not to poke fun at such things?

She studied him a moment in silence. "That wasn't funny."

"I know. I'm sorry."

She sighed. "Fine. I forgive you. Come on, you must be starving." She led him out of the barn and across the yard. "I'm sorry I lost track of time and don't have a hot meal ready for you. I'm sure I can put together a cold sandwich if you're in a hurry. Otherwise I can heat the leftover stew I was planning to feed you."

"I'm not in a hurry, but the sandwich is fine. I'd rather sit and talk with you than have you busy at the stove the whole time I'm here."

She glanced at him as she pushed through the front door, a pretty smile in her eyes.

In minutes, she'd assembled two cold sandwiches and joined

him at the table. He said grace and took a few bites of his sandwich, mulling the wisdom of continuing their previous conversation.

The question wouldn't quit pestering him, though. "In the barn you said you don't do that *anymore*. Does that mean you used to give concerts?" He set his sandwich on his plate to hold his hands up. "You don't have to answer if you don't want to, but I had to ask." He held a hand to his heart and pulled a face. "The curiosity was killing me."

She laughed. "You poor thing." She took another bite of her sandwich and was quiet a long while. "Yes, I did."

"Was it before the...incident?"

"Yes."

"So...you gave concerts in D.C.? Like on stage?" He wasn't certain he liked the idea of his wife being on stage—the focus of attention for so many men—but he had to admit he was impressed. To perform for an audience at such a young age was remarkably brave.

"I sang at parties. Sometimes there was a stage, a small one that people had built for the occasion. Most of the time I stood on the floor at the front of the room."

"How many times did you perform?"

"I started singing when I was very young—as soon as I could talk, according to Mother. By the time I was four, she'd bring me out during her parties and ask me to sing for her friends. As I grew older, her friends started asking me to sing at their parties, and my parents hired a tutor to help me improve. By the time I was eight, I was being invited to perform in strangers' houses all over the state, and even traveled out of state two or three times on special request."

A sudden memory of a young girl hyperventilating at one of Mother's parties flooded his memory. Alice had taken the girl out to the garden, and they didn't return until the girl's turn to perform. She sang a beautiful song that Richard barely paid attention to—distracted as he was by slipping a frog into Alice's pocket—but the tone, the clarity of the singer's voice, her beautiful golden curls... "It was you."

Lindy's eyes widened. "What?"

"You came to our house to perform! You were so nervous, my sister, Alice, took you out to the garden to calm down."

Lindy's sandwich fell from her fingers, splattering on the plate. "That was *your* house? *Your* sister?"

Richard laughed. Only God could arrange such an unlikely reunion. "Oh, but you were magnificent that night. Everyone raved about you for weeks afterward. Mother was positively thrilled by all the compliments she received for having been clever enough to invite you."

"That was my first performance out of state." Lindy frowned. "I don't remember you."

"It's all right. I would hardly expect you to, you were so young. I'm five years older, and I didn't recall the event myself until your words just now reminded me."

"You haven't talked much about your family." She retrieved her sandwich, stuffing the roast beef and sliced manchego cheese between the bread. "You've told me about your brothers and your sisters, but haven't shared much about your parents. You told Father they'd passed on, right? We don't have to talk about them if it's too painful a subject, but since we're supposed to be getting to know each other..."

She let her sentence dangle unfinished. He was tempted to grab at the excuse she'd handed him for avoiding the subject, but this was his wife. She should know about his family. "Yes, my parents have all passed away." He cringed at his slip and hurried to continue. Perhaps she wouldn't notice. "Mother was a dear, though. I was closest with her. She's the one who tended my wounds whenever I got into scrapes, even though we had governesses who could've done the job. And she always laughed at my jokes."

"Sounds as though you loved her."

"I did." Richard took another bite of his sandwich. If only Mother could have met Lindy.

"You said *all.*"

He froze mid-chew. Maybe if he didn't move, didn't blink, she'd forget he was here.

"Did you have more than one mother and father? Was your mother a widow who remarried?"

He took his time chewing. As his wife, he ought to have confessed this part of his past to her long ago. How could he expect her to confide in him when he hadn't trusted her with his biggest secret? Still, he hesitated.

He'd not yet shared the truth of his parentage with another living soul. What if it upset her? Would she look at him differently once she knew? Many people would, especially those he'd associated with back east. There, many still held to the English ideologies of pedigree and class determining a person's worth.

And what did that matter?

Whatever or whomever his earthly parents may be, *he* was a child of the King of all Kings. An heir to the Kingdom of God. Nothing else mattered so long as he held firm to that truth.

Besides, if anyone would have compassion for his situation, it would be his wife.

He held Lindy's gaze. "In a manner of speaking, you could say I had two fathers, yes. But my mother was only a widow for the last year of her life and she did not remarry during that time."

Her lips twisted to one side. "Then how—?"

"My mother had an affair." He braced himself for the impact of his words on her expression. "I am the product of that relationship. Though I only learned that truth mere weeks before you and I first met."

Her sandwich halted midway to her mouth. "Then you're—"

"Illegitimate."

~

*C*larinda's appetite fled. She set the sandwich down and laid a hand atop her belly. There'd been pain in Richard's voice as he spoke that word. Would her child feel that same pain? "I'm so sorry. How did you find out?"

Richard spent the rest of his noon break explaining about the letter he'd received following his mother's death. He revealed that the shipping company he owned had been inherited from his birth father.

"My uncle has invited me to visit and meet the rest of his family—"

"Your family, too."

"I guess that's right." He squeezed the back of his neck. "In any case, the invitation is on condition that I be discreet about my relation to them."

"I'm impressed they want to meet you at all."

Richard flinched, and she set her hand on his. "Not for anything to do with you, but to risk such a scandal...it shows a great deal of care for you."

"I hadn't thought of it that way."

"Then you've never met your uncle or been back east to see how the company is being run?"

"I'd considered it, but then I found you."

"Aren't you curious?"

"Of course." He took her hand and squeezed it. "But I have more pressing matters here."

She looked at her belly. All this time, part of her had suspected he was lying about his ability to love her child—if not to her, then to himself—but... "You truly understand, don't you?"

"I do. And I promise you again that I will love *our* child with all my heart. He—"

"Or she."

"Or she, will know nothing but love and acceptance if I have anything to say about it."

The baby gave her a firm kick. "Oh!" She grinned. "I think this little one heard you. Here." She pulled Richard around the table and placed his hand on her belly. "Do you feel it?"

Their child kicked again.

Richard stilled, not seeming to breathe. "Is that...?"

She nodded, her eyes stinging with happy tears. "Our child is saying hello."

Richard's eyes rounded. "Has he or she done this before?"

"Many times, but never when you've been around. Or at least, not when you were awake. This little one sure likes to squirm when I'm trying to sleep."

"Next time, wake me up."

Clarinda nodded, the lump in her throat preventing her from speaking. She couldn't have picked a better father for her child. Richard would say it was God's doing—a sign that the Almighty cared for her. But how could that be true after what she'd done?

❧

*R*ichard helped Lindy into the wagon behind her parents' store, climbed up beside her, and took the reins. He signaled the team to start the long journey home and glanced at his wife. Despite the white veil she'd insisted on wearing to town, he could see her wide smile. "Happy?"

"Very. Thank you."

Yesterday, Fernando had mentioned that Lupe might be ready to return to his flock in a few more days. The idea had sent Lindy into a melancholy state until Richard had suggested she keep Lupe as her pet. Instantly, she resumed the singing she'd taken to doing as she tidied after each evening meal. His world was right again.

Today, they'd visited the store to order supplies for building a special corral and mini barn for Lupe to live in. At Lindy's request, Lupe's domain would be built just outside their back door.

As was usual of their infrequent trips to town, Lindy requested that Richard stop about halfway home so that she could wander into the brush and relieve herself.

He waited in the wagon as she disappeared behind a clump of large bushes.

Less than five minutes later, she let out a shriek.

His heart leapt as he sprinted toward her.

"What is it? What's wrong?" Colt in hand, he rounded the bush.

Blessedly fully dressed, Lindy hopped from foot to foot and made little squeaks of distress as she pointed at something in the dry grass. "It made a noise. What is it?"

He followed her direction. A tiny, brown, furry something lay on the ground, half-hidden by weeds. It didn't move. Richard holstered his gun and knelt down for a closer look. "It's a puppy." A filthy one at that. The mite didn't appear old enough to have left his mama.

Lindy shuffled back. "What's a puppy doing way out here?"

Richard surveyed the area. How had this tiny creature found its way to this remote location? A lumpy burlap sack lay several yards away. *Oh no.* "Clarinda, turn away."

"Why?"

"Just look away."

She turned her back to him. "What's going on?"

He stepped toward the bag. *Please, Lord, let me be wrong.* "There's something here I don't want you to see."

She peeked over her shoulder. "What is i—?"

"I said don't look!"

She whipped away.

"If it's what I think it is, this isn't something a lady should see." He reached the bag and paused to take a deep, bracing breath. An act he regretted as the stench of decaying flesh filled his mouth and nostrils. He gagged. "I don't even want to see it, but I need to be sure..." He grabbed one edge of the bag and glanced at Lindy.

She wasn't looking.

He lifted the fabric and peeked inside. The remains of four small puppies filled the sack, the state of their bodies leaving no doubt they were beyond help.

He dropped the fabric, marched to the survivor, and scooped the little thing up for a quick inspection. The pup wasn't as young as he'd initially thought, just malnourished. He fit in the palm of one of Richard's hands. "He's a boy. And I think he's a Pomeranian. One of Mother's friends had a whole pack of these that came with her everywhere she went. She was obsessed with the things."

Lindy turned. "But what did you see over...?" Her gaze drifted toward the bag. "Oh. Why, that's terrible. Who could be so cruel?"

Richard pressed his free palm over his eyes. At least her fear of the species hadn't destroyed her compassion for them. "Here." He plopped the pup into her arms. "Hold him while I grab the shovel."

"But..." She tried to push the puppy back to him, but he strode off.

It was just a pup and couldn't hurt her, especially in its weakened state. More to the point, the poor little fellow needed someone to comfort him while Richard saw to a proper burial for his siblings. He'd never been so thankful for the small shovel they kept in the wagon for emergencies.

While he dug a hole, laid the puppies to rest, and covered them, Lindy waited in the wagon. He set the shovel in the wagon bed and climbed up next to her. The little guy slept in her lap.

Richard stroked the pup's filthy fur, then set the team in motion.

"Wait!"

"Why? Did you need to...?" He let his question hang, hoping she'd figure out that he was asking if she needed to relieve herself again.

"No, but"—she scooped the puppy up and held it out —"Don't *you* want to hold it now?"

"Him."

"Huh?"

"He's a boy."

"Fine, then. Don't you want to hold *him?*"

"No, I think you're doing a fine job."

"But—"

"Besides, you'd better get used to holding him."

"Why?"

"Well, that little guy has had a rough start in life. He's going to need to be bottle fed for a while, like Lupe. *I* can't do it. I'm out in the pastures most of the day and in my study when I'm not." He scratched his chin. "I suppose I could help some in the evenings, but most of the time, his survival is going to depend on you."

CHAPTER 24

*C*larinda gave the wooden spindle another twirl and the fluffy wool fibers twisted into a neat yarn. Beast came bounding across the room and nipped at the spinning tool. She gasped. "Stop that." She held the spindle above her head, lifting her feet off the floor. "Go away."

In the four weeks since they'd found him, he'd doubled in size. Thankfully, Richard had assured her that even at maturity Beast's particular breed wouldn't be taller than her knees.

His tiny teeth still looked sharp, though.

The black furball yapped at her spindle. *He's just a puppy.* Richard had said Beast just wanted to play when he acted like this. *He won't hurt you.* She shifted her roving to the hand with the spindle and waved at him. "I said go." Rather than deter him, her action turned his attention to her fingers. His little tail wagging, he barked and snipped at her.

She screamed and jerked her hand away. She stomped hard on the wooden flooring with the low growl Richard had taught her.

Beast's ears drooped and he backed away. He slunk to the corner where he'd left the knotted rag toy Richard had fashioned for him. The pup picked it up and began to shake it. He clamped his toy to the ground with his paws, the scolding clearly forgotten. She took a deep breath and returned to her seat. Maybe now she'd be able to spin her wool in peace.

She'd settled in her chair by the empty fireplace almost an hour ago to accomplish this task and had just one yard of yarn to show for her labor, thanks to the annoying creature who'd insisted on getting into everything he wasn't supposed to. First, it had been the slop bucket, then her basket of rolled yarn, and then he'd decided the apron hanging on its hook near the stove was a varmint that needed vanquishing.

She ought to return the tiny terror to the crate Richard had made for it, but every time she did, the pest would whine and whimper until she set it free. If she weren't afraid a large bird would try to snatch the thing for lunch, she'd loose the pup in the yard. But if anything happened to the little ball of black fur, Richard would never forgive her. After all he'd done for her, the least she could do was ensure his precious Beast stayed alive.

She drafted more wool, gave the spindle another spin, and parked it between her knees. Richard would be coming for lunch any minute now, and she'd wanted to have this basket of wool spun before he arrived. The stew simmering at the back of the stove was ready, but she still needed to slice the bread and fetch the butter crock from the cellar.

The pup lost interest in his toy and pressed his nose to the ground as he wandered toward the back door. He stopped at the crack between its base and the floor and started barking.

Ignoring him, she gave the spindle another turn. She'd taken him out to do his business not a quarter of an hour ago. If he needed to go again, he could wait. She had wool to spin.

Beast's barking grew more insistent. He bounced up and down on his hind legs.

She drafted more wool and spun the wooden tool. He ought

to take a nap. He'd been playing long enough. Didn't puppies ever run out of energy?

The ungrateful creature lifted onto his hind legs and started scratching at the back door. His barks and yips were enough to wake the dead.

Gritting her teeth, she tied off her yarn and set the spindle aside. "For Pete's sake, that isn't even the door you're supposed to go through." She stomped across the room. "If you have to go that badly, why aren't you at the front door?" Dumb mutt. She scooped the animal up, but as she straightened, her own words echoed in her mind. Why *was* he barking at this door? He was never permitted through this door because it led directly into Lupe's corral. No matter what Richard said, she didn't trust the furry bundle not to harm her lamb.

Lupe.

She clutched the pup tightly to ensure it couldn't wiggle free, opened the back door, and peered outside.

In the far corner of the small enclosure, Lupe slept peacefully on a mound of hay.

Clarinda exhaled and began to turn away, but something moved in the shadow of the fence mere feet from where Lupe slept. Her eyes narrowed. Was that a snake?

She tossed Beast into the room behind her and stepped outside. The pup barked and scratched at the closed door. She snatched a shovel from where it leaned against the house. Thank heaven she'd been too tired to put the tool away after cleaning Lupe's mess that morning. Heart pounding against her ribs, she crept forward.

The snake coiled faster than she could blink, its tail rattling.

Clarinda slammed the edge of the shovel down on the snake's neck with a mighty scream. Again and again she slammed the blade down. "No! No! No!"

"Lindy!" Richard vaulted the fence. He dragged her away from the bloody remains. He pried the shovel from her tight grip and tossed it to the ground. His arms wrapped around her trembling body as she panted.

Her eyelids fluttered closed and she leaned into his comfort.

He pressed a kiss to her temple "Are you all right?" He drew back to cup her face and study her head-to-toe. "What happened? Did it bite you?" He knelt and began lifting her skirts.

The press of his fingers against her stocking-clad shin jarred her senses. She stepped away. "I'm fine. It didn't bite me."

Rising, Richard looked between the dead snake and her several times. "Thank God." His brow furrowed. "What were you thinking going after a rattlesnake with a shovel? Why didn't you call one of the hands or get your pistol?"

"I—I don't know. I didn't think. I just grabbed the shovel. I've seen Fernando—"

"Fernando isn't my wife, and he certainly isn't carrying another precious life inside him." Richard's voice rose as he gripped her arms. "You could have been killed. Our child could have been killed."

A cold chill swept through her. She pressed both hands to her growing middle. A soft thump assured her the little one remained unharmed, but what if she'd missed? What if the snake had bitten her? The reality of the risk she'd taken took the starch from her knees.

Richard caught her as she sank toward the ground. He pulled her into his arms and buried his face in her neck. "Don't you ever take a risk like that again. Do you hear me?"

She nodded and clung to him, as if doing so could erase the image of life without her child.

*T*wo weeks later, the family gathered at the main house for supper. Clarinda fidgeted with her veil as she followed Richard into the front room. Each week she told herself to confront Mother about her conversation with Richard—Mother shouldn't be allowed to lie as she had. But each week the same thought stopped her—if she demanded Mother tell the truth, Richard would likely demand Clarinda do the same.

Father handed Richard a stack of letters. "These came for you."

"Thanks." Richard set the mail on a side table and helped Lindy into her seat. "How's Beast doing?"

"Beast?" Mrs. Humphrey looked up from her seat at the table.

Richard sat beside Lindy. "That's what we've decided to name the puppy we found."

"What *you've* decided to name him." Clarinda squinted her eyes at him, but couldn't keep her lips from curling upward.

He raised both hands in self defense. "What else would you name a dog being raised by such a beauty?"

Mother beamed at him. "I think it's perfect." Her gaze shifted to Teodora as the housekeeper came in carrying a large, steaming pot. Mother scowled. "You can't possibly intend to serve us from that. Return to the kitchen at once."

Teodora froze in the doorway, her gaze flying to Clarinda. *I told you so* was written all over her expression.

Clarinda cleared her throat. "It's my fault, mother. I broke the large tureen this morning and told Teodora to use the pot until we can get a new one."

Mother sniffed. "We have more than one tureen. Surely—"

"The others are too small to hold enough for all of us. She'd have to use at least three. I didn't think you'd want her running back and forth to the kitchen to fetch them." Not that Mother had ever shown the least bit of concern for Teodora's welfare. For reasons Clarinda couldn't understand, Mother had never been fond of Teodora.

Teodora started to return to the kitchen. "I don't mind. I'll—"

"Whyever not?" Mother ignored the housekeeper. "That is what we pay her for."

Clarinda pressed her lips together as she silently counted to five. "Aside from the unnecessary work it creates for Teodora, our food would likely grow cold."

Richard's hand found Clarinda's beneath the table. "Speaking of growing cold, I believe the food is growing colder as we speak. Why don't we discuss this another time and let Teodora serve for now?"

Mother's cheeks reddened as she lowered her gaze to the empty bowl in front of her. "Oh, very well."

Teodora stepped forward and finally began serving their stew.

Richard took up his spoon and spoke as if he couldn't sense the lingering tension in the room. "So? How is he?" His gaze held Clarinda's with a grin that had her grinning back for no reason at all.

"How's who?"

"Beast."

"Oh, right. He's getting more active by the day. This morning I set him down for only a second while I moved the coffee to the back of the stove. When I turned around again, he'd crossed the room and was tugging on the strings of the new seat cushions I made." She'd been irritated with him at the time, but in hindsight she ought to have been more careful with him. He was too young to know any better.

Father laughed. "That reminds me of a dog I had as boy. He used to get into such mischief." Father shared story after story of his childhood dog. It was remarkable. He'd shared more about himself in these last four months than he had in all her growing-up years.

For that matter, *everyone* in her family had changed in some way since Richard's arrival. Although she wasn't here this weekend, Lucy did come to visit more often now, sometimes bringing her fiancé with her. Mother smiled more freely, though still not at Clarinda. She *had* patted Clarinda's right shoulder when they left last weekend.

Had Richard said something to encourage it? The gesture wasn't the warm hug she remembered from before the attack, but it was the first show of physical affection she'd received from her mother since that horrible day. Still, with the lies between them, the pat was like drinking the last drop of water from a canteen after a long hot ride, only to discover the water had turned sour.

Eventually, the food was gone and the hour grew late. They bid her parents goodnight and began the short stroll to their house. Richard took her hand and she didn't resist. She'd grown used to his frequent displays of affection and—in spite of herself—she'd begun looking forward to them. She hadn't let him kiss her again, though. It wouldn't be fair.

But was it fair to let him hold her hand? Or hug her at the end of each day? Where was the line between friendly affection and encouraging a hope that would only hurt them both in the end?

As they neared the front door, plaintive yapping met their ears.

"Sounds like Beast is missing his Beauty." Richard planted his hands on his hips. "Should I be jealous?"

She scoffed and opened the door. "Don't be ridiculous." She scooped the furry bundle from his crate and nuzzled her face into his neck. "How's my boy? Did you miss me?" The child in her womb seemed to turn somersaults. Clarinda laughed and pivoted to invite Richard to feel the commotion inside her. The words caught in her throat.

He held a letter open, his handsome features pale as the sheet of stationary.

Her chest tightened. "What is it?"

"There's been a fire."

She gasped. "Where? Was anyone hurt?"

"In Nevada City. The Propriety Mine office is gone. Tommy and his wife lost their house—"

"That's your mine manager?"

"Yes."

"But he and his wife weren't injured? They're all right?"

"It seems so."

"What about your miners?"

"Two were injured battling the blaze, but no one died. Thank the Lord." Richard looked up from the letter. "I'm sorry. I need to go and see what I can do to help."

No. Schooling her expression, she folded her hands over her belly. "I understand." She was being selfish. His workers were in need.

Besides, when had she come to depend on his presence? He was going to leave eventually. Once he realized he didn't truly love her. Better he leave now than later. She shouldn't have allowed his touches. After his words in the cave—after his kiss —she'd let herself get soft. Had she begun to hope that he might stay?

Foolish girl.

She turned away and settled Beast in his open-top crate. "I'm feeling a bit tired now. I'll help you pack in the morning." She slipped across the room and reached for the knob on their bedroom door. "Goodnigh—" The word died as his hand covered hers.

He pulled her away from the door and turned her to face him. He clasped both her hands. "I want you to come with me."

Her breath caught. He did? Why? This was his chance to leave her. To leave behind the mistake he'd made in marrying and declaring his love for her.

He squeezed her fingers. "Will you come?"

She ought to pull away, but couldn't find the strength.

Should she go with him? The ranch was where she belonged. Besides, what would she do in Nevada City? Where would she sleep? Mrs. Kipling probably wouldn't appreciate a strange woman moving into what was supposed to be a bachelor's room. The bed probably wasn't big enough for two of them. She was foolish to even consider it. "I can't. Who'll look after Beast and Lupe?"

"I'm sure Manuel can take care of them while we're away. We won't be gone long." He raised her hands to his lips and pressed a kiss against her knuckles. "Please? I don't want to go without you."

CHAPTER 25

*C*larinda let the strong river winds blow the stray hairs from her face as their ferry pulled up to the dock in Sacramento. Richard's hand settled at her back, steadying her. She ought to have told him no and remained on the ranch. It would have been the kind thing to do. The hope in his eyes when she'd said yes haunted her whenever she tried to sleep. Saying yes had been selfish. But being with Richard was a sweet sort of torture she didn't want to stop. What kind of wife did that make her?

She scanned the buildings lining the waterfront. How far was the Orleans Hotel? Richard had said they'd stay the night there before continuing on to Nevada City. Though this last leg of their journey was short, he insisted she needed a night of rest in a bed that didn't rock and sway before moving on. After almost five days of travel and restless nights, she was too fatigued to disagree.

When the ferry was secured and the plank extended, Richard offered his arm. "Shall we?" He escorted her to shore, and they waited as their luggage was unloaded.

A young lad almost dropped her trunk, and Richard hurried to assist him.

As she waited, her legs wobbled—a result of so many hours on the boat. Searching for a place to sit, she spotted a ticket office nearby. Surely there was somewhere to rest inside. She caught Richard's attention with a wave, then pointed toward the building.

He nodded and returned to helping transfer luggage.

She entered the ticket office and found four long benches, crowded with waiting passengers. As she approached, she let her girth sway her gait and pressed a hand to her back.

Two men jumped to their feet. "You can sit here, ma'am."

She sank onto their vacated space. "Thank you, sirs. That's very kind of you."

"Think nothing of it."

"It's our pleasure."

The two men wove their way through the limbs crowding the aisle to take the last remaining seats at the far end of the room.

Two children sat with their mother across from Clarinda. They kept darting glances at her veiled face and whispering to one another. After a few seconds, their weary-looking mother hushed them, but their eyes continued to stray in Clarinda's direction.

She turned so she couldn't see them.

Thankfully, her seasickness had not returned. However, days of traveling—first aboard the steamship that brought them to San Francisco, then aboard the ferry—had left her more fatigued than she'd been in weeks. Her eyelids drifted closed as she waited for Richard to fetch her.

She was in Sacramento at last. Almost eight months after she was meant to have come here with Arnie. Was the church with the preacher who'd agreed to marry two young lovers located nearby? Did Arnie ever think of the morning he'd abandoned her? Had he ever checked with the school about whether she'd made it to safety? Did he even care what became of her?

She closed her mind to the useless wonderings. Last Sunday, Richard had read from Philippians chapter four, and they'd spent a long time discussing its eighth verse. It was all about keeping one's mind from sinking into the mire and, instead, focusing on the good things in life. With Richard's help, she'd discovered many things in her life for which she could be thankful.

How had the verse started? "Finally, brethren, whatsoever things are true, whatsoever things are honest, whatsoever things are just..." That one had been difficult for Clarinda to embrace. Whenever she'd tried, all she'd thought of were the many times the Lord had allowed injustice in her life.

"I'd like two tickets to Benicia, please." The voice of a man behind her near the ticket window, interrupted her thoughts. There was something strangely familiar about it.

"Yes, first class."

Her eyes flew open, her back stiffening. That voice! But no, it couldn't be. Not here. Not now. Everything within her wanted to turn and see if her memory tricked her, or if Arnie Walker truly stood in this same room. But she didn't dare. What if he saw her? Would he dare speak to her? What if he ignored her? Which would be worse?

Without moving, hardly daring to breathe, she searched the room.

Three solid walls met her gaze. She remembered seeing one door on the wall opposite the way she'd come in, but both doors were behind where she sat, beyond her peripheral vision. She couldn't reach them without risking him noticing her. What was she to do?

Footsteps approached from behind and rounded the bench. She ducked her head.

A pair of polished, if slightly muddy shoes topped by a pair of neatly pressed dark gray trousers came to a stop before her.

"Mrs. Stevens?" This man's voice was different than the one of a moment ago. It didn't sound anything like Arnie's.

She peeked up. A man she didn't recognize stood there holding a mug.

"Are you Mrs. Stevens?"

Oh, how she longed to turn and peek at the ticket window. Was Arnie still there? Had it even been him? She kept her eyes on the stranger before her and her voice quiet. "Yes, I am."

He offered her the mug and the scent of ginger tickled her nose. "Your husband asked that I bring you this tea and let you know he's arranging your lodging. He'll return for you shortly."

Accepting the mug, she smiled at the messenger. It was so like Richard to see that things were arranged before asking her to move again. But to have a cup of tea brought to her...it reminded her of the words of love he'd spoken to her in the cave. How could she have questioned his love for her? Everything he did showed how thoroughly he considered her needs and wants. The tea was even cool, rather than hot, so it wouldn't increase the temperature of her already overheated body.

"Thank you." She searched her immediate surroundings for somewhere to set the mug so she could fetch a coin for the messenger from her reticule. There seemed no good place. She'd have to ask the man to hold her mug while she retrieved the coin. "I'm sorry. Would you mind—" She looked up, but the man was gone.

Twisting toward the entrance, she glimpsed his back disappearing outside. She lowered the mug to her lap. How odd that he hadn't waited for his tip.

"Clarinda? Is that you?" Arnie gaped at her from another bench.

She whirled away, sloshing tea onto her gloves. What now?

Leave. She jumped to her feet.

The mug shattered on the floor. Tea spilled across the floorboards.

Everyone turned.

Her face warmed as she stooped to clean the mess she'd made.

"No, stop." Arnie's hand came to her shoulder. "Let me." Before she could answer, he was on his knees, picking up the shards of mug.

Another man had found a towel somewhere and was mopping up the ginger tea.

Her eyes strayed to the door. She should go. But what kind of woman made a mess and ran from the scene?

Shards in hand, Arnie rose and strode toward a garbage bin. The man with the towel also stood, the floor now dry, and she thanked him.

"My pleasure, ma'am." He tipped his hat and left.

Arnie'd be back in a moment, demanding answers. It was a miracle the spilled tea had distracted him this long. He can't have missed her condition. Surely he'd put two and two together. What would he say? What would he do? She didn't want to find out.

She made a beeline for the exit and darted into the hot July sun.

"Clarie!" Arnie chased her.

How dare he use that name! She rushed down the street as fast as her cumbersome middle would allow.

It wasn't fast enough.

His hand gripped her arm, dragging her to a stop in the middle of the road. "Clarie, wait! Please."

Panting, she scanned the street for any sign of Richard. Which way was the hotel?

Arnie turned her to face him. "Clarie, what are you doing here?"

Her gaze snapped to his. *That* was what he wanted to

know? After all this time? With the evidence of her condition undeniable to any who cared to look? He wanted to know why she was in Sacramento? Her blood cooled. "Stop calling me that."

"Calling you what?"

"That infernal nickname. I hate it, and my name is Mrs. Stevens now. I'm here with my husband."

His fingers leapt from her arm like he'd been singed. "That's right. That man with the tea called you Mrs. Stevens. So it's true? You've married another man?"

"What did you expect?"

A wagon rattled around them, the angry driver shouting, "Move along, would ya?"

She marched to the side of the road where they'd garner less attention.

Arnie followed her. "I expected you to wait for me. To miss me. Not to jump into bed with the next—"

She slapped him. "How dare you!" She pivoted on her heel, then spun back. "You know, I almost forgot to thank you."

He rubbed his cheek and glared. "For what?"

"For not letting me chain myself to your sorry hide for the rest of my life. What a fool I was to think you would make a good husband, a good father." She laughed bitterly even as tears blurred her vision. What a fool she'd been. Arnie could never have truly cared for her if that was what he thought of her. "Richard is ten times the man you'll ever be. Our child will be blessed to call him Father." She turned to go.

"Hey wait." Arnie caught her shoulder.

She jerked free. "No. I'm through waiting for you, Arnie Walker. You're a coward and a liar and I never want to see you again."

"You can't just walk away."

She made a beeline for the ticket office. Richard would look for her there. She should have waited for him and not let her fear of Arnie's reaction chase her away. Who cared what he thought? He clearly couldn't care less about—

"That's my child you're carrying, isn't it?"

Her steps faltered, but she didn't look back. She wouldn't give him the satisfaction. The confirmation. His tone held suspicion, but it held doubt, too. If he knew for certain, would he care?

Maybe waiting at the ticket office wasn't such a good idea. She needed Richard. Now.

She rounded a corner and spotted the sign for the Orleans Hotel a few buildings down.

"Clarie!"

Why was Arnie following her? He obviously didn't want her. Did he want her child?

She broke into a lumbering run.

~

*R*ichard thanked the hotel manager and turned toward the front door. Lindy would've finished her tea by now. She'd be anxious to change and rest. His poor wife had looked ready to sleep on her feet as they'd disembarked. He was glad she'd thought to wait in the ticket office. He'd meant to suggest it himself, but then he'd gotten caught up with supervising the unloading of their belongings.

At least he'd found that tea house willing to deliver her a cup of cool ginger tea. He'd had to purchase the mug at a steep cost and tip the delivery man in advance, but it was worth it to make up for his blunder in not seeing her properly settled before tending to their luggage.

As he stepped out of the hotel, a woman bowled into his side, nearly knocking him over. His arms instinctively came around her as his back banged into the doorframe. A jolt ran through him as he recognized the feminine form he held.

"Lindy?" He stared at her flushed face. "What is it? What's wrong? Why aren't you at the ticket office?"

"I—" She tried to answer, but was too winded. Pinching the fabric of her veil, she held it out to keep from sucking it into her mouth with each breath. Her panting reminded him of when they'd first met and the dog had chased her down the wharf in San Francisco.

He looked in the direction she'd come from. Neither dog nor man chased her. He drew her inside to a chair and helped her sit.

The manager hurried to join them. "Does your wife require a doctor, sir?"

She shook her head, still breathing heavily.

Richard assessed her from head to toe. There was no sign of injury, nor any indication of illness. "I don't think so, sir. Thank you."

"Very good. I'll have someone fetch her something to drink, then." The manager disappeared through the door to the dining room.

Richard rubbed a soothing hand in circles on his wife's back.

After several seconds, she seemed to catch her breath.

He moved his hand to her shoulder. "Can you speak now and tell me what made you run like that?"

She glanced up as a server brought a tray with a glass of water. "Thank you." She accepted the glass and took a sip, then another.

Meeting her gaze over the rim, he sensed she didn't want to speak where others might overhear. "I've secured us a room. Would you like to go there and lie down?"

She set the empty glass on a small side table. "Yes, please."

CHAPTER 26

*T*he moment the door closed to their private room, Clarinda sank to the edge of their bed with a moan. "Oh, my feet are killing me."

Richard dropped to his knees and began undoing her boots.

As she'd known he would.

It was terrible of her to take advantage of his loving heart, but she wasn't ready to talk yet. She didn't know what to tell him. Why *had* she been running like that? It wasn't as though Arnie had threatened her. Only her imagination had truly terrified her.

Arnie's father was a powerful man with connections at every level of government. If he wanted custody of his grandchild, there'd be nothing she could do to stop him. Yet, the idea that Mr. Walker might be persuaded to take such action when he had been vehemently opposed to Arnie marrying her, didn't make sense. Not only was she not acceptable mother material, she and Arnie weren't married. Worse yet, she was married to another man. For Arnie to pursue custody would create a scandal Mr. Walker wouldn't even consider associating himself with.

Which meant Arnie would be on his own if he wanted to claim his heir. Which was a big assumption, considering the consequences of such an action. He hadn't been willing to pay the price of marrying her. Surely, he wouldn't risk poverty and scandal for a child he'd never met.

Richard finished removing her boots, set them aside, and motioned to her veil. "Don't you want to take that off?"

For the first time in months, she was reluctant to remove her covering for him. What would he see in her expression? Yet *not* removing it would be more telling. So she untucked the cotton voile, removed the bonnet, and dropped the items on a small side table. She lifted her feet, swiveled to lie flat on the bed, and closed her eyes.

Her heartbeat had almost resumed its normal pace after her mad dash through the city. She smothered a laugh. What a sight she must have been, large as a barrel of pickles and running like a pack of wolves chased her. *Silly woman.* She'd panicked over nothing.

"I'm glad to see you relaxing." Richard's voice brought her eyes open. He removed his own boots and walked around to sit on the opposite side of the bed. Scooting over until his hip touched her arm, he leaned against the headboard. "Care to tell me what happened?"

She let her eyes fall shut again. "I saw Arnie."

"Who?"

Oh, that's right. She'd never told Richard the name of the man whose child he'd promised to raise. He'd never required the information from her. What a patient and kind man she'd married.

She pushed herself to a sitting position and Richard helped her adjust the pillows to support her aching back. Once she was comfortable, she took a deep breath and finally confessed all to her husband. She explained how Arnie had found her helping

Katie, how they began to meet in secret, and how he begged her to elope with him.

"And you said yes." There was no question in his words, nor any judgment. He understood that she'd cared for Arnie—or at least the man she'd thought he was—and had told Arnie that she loved him. Three words she'd yet to tell Richard.

She studied her husband's expression—guarded, yet still somehow inviting, reassuring. *Did* she love him? Seeing Arnie hadn't hurt the way she'd expected. Was it possible her heart had begun to heal itself? She shook her head. Now wasn't the time to ponder that question.

Richard's brows furrowed. "You turned him down?"

"No, you were right. I accepted his proposal." She looked away, burrowing her hands in the blankets. "I was so foolish."

"You were..." Richard's voice wavered, revealing the toll this conversation was taking on him. "...in love with him."

"Yes." Or she'd thought she was. Looking back...she wasn't sure anymore. *Could* you love someone you didn't really know? Had her heart truly been broken, or only her pride and trust?

"Are you still?"

Her gaze shot to his. "No."

Is that what he thought? All this time, did he think she still loved Arnie? *Lindy, I love you.* His words in the boulder cave echoed in her memory. How could he have made such a decla-ration if he believed she loved another? He'd said he knew she didn't feel the same—that he'd wait for her. What kind of brave, self-sacrifice must that have taken? This man had given her everything, no matter the cost. He held nothing back.

And then she knew.

"I love *you.*"

His eyes widened. "Me?"

"I only just realized it, but it's true. I love you. You are brave and kind, and selfless and so handsome. I—"

He cupped her face and claimed her mouth with such tender

passion, the air left her lungs and she was floating. Every ounce of his love for her came through in how his lips caressed hers, how his hands slid into her hair, cradling her. She'd never felt more precious.

Eager to give him as much pleasure as he was giving her, she kissed him back as her arms wrapped around his shoulders. She tried to pull him close, but the size of her belly interfered. Her lips trailed along his jaw to his ear. "I love you, Richard Stevens."

With a moan, he recaptured her lips and tugged her down so they lay atop the covers, entangled in each other's arms.

"Say it again." He whispered between kisses.

She drew back to hold his gaze as her hand cupped his cheek. "I love you."

"I love you, so much." His beautiful blue eyes sparkled.

She stroked her fingers along his hairline. "I know."

He leaned forward and pressed another lingering kiss to her lips. Against them, he whispered, "And I *love* kissing you."

She giggled and kissed him briefly. "I had a suspicion."

His expression sobered as he drew further away. "But I don't want to rush into anything you aren't ready for. And if we don't stop right now...well, I can stop any time you say to, but I'd rather know now how far you want to take this." The look in his eyes radiated more desire than anything he'd revealed to her before. "Because I'm ready to make you my wife in every way. Please be clear about that. But I don't want you to have any regrets. So if you have any doubts, tell me now."

Her face was on fire. If she had an egg, it could cook on her cheeks. She was sure of it.

No one had ever spoken to her so openly about such carnal desires. Not even Arnie. Oh, he'd communicated his wants clearly enough, but not in words. There was such vulnerable honesty in Richard's words, it made her want to kiss him again. And again.

That kind of passion... Was she ready for where that led? The heat of her body shouted that she was, but what if she didn't please him?

She pulled back, untangling her legs from his.

Arnie had never said whether she'd pleased him in that way. He'd seemed happy when they fell asleep together.

But then he'd left.

What if he'd left because she'd done something wrong?

She scooted to the edge of the bed.

Would Richard still love her if she were terrible at the intimacies of marriage? No, that wasn't a fair question. Richard was too good of a man to stop loving her over something like that. But if he didn't enjoy it, he wouldn't want to do it. If they didn't enjoy intimacy together, would he seek that sort of pleasure elsewhere? No, the Bible expressly forbid it. She couldn't imagine him going against his wedding vows. So, what would he do? Would he grow to resent her? Would she become a burden to him, too?

She wanted so badly to please him, the thought of disappointing him was like a sodden blanket, smothering the flames of her desire.

She dropped her stocking feet to the floor, avoiding his gaze. "I need to eat." She inwardly cringed at her stretch of the truth. There wasn't an ounce of appetite within her churning gut, but she hadn't eaten in hours and she was growing a baby. She should eat.

Ignoring the discomfort such a move involved, she bent to retrieve her boots and shoved them onto her feet. "Do you think the restaurant is serving the evening meal yet?"

~

*A*s the sun set in Nevada City the following evening, Richard stepped through the front entrance of the National Exchange. Though the hotel's brick construction had helped spare it from the fire, the scent of smoke and ash still permeated its elegant lobby. The staff would no doubt find a way to rid the building of its smell long before the new Prosperity Mine office was completed, however.

Richard had been blessed to secure an order for enough bricks to rebuild the formerly wooden office and to add a new second floor that would serve as a home for Tommy Brigham and his wife. Unfortunately, it would take three weeks for the bricks to arrive.

In the meanwhile, the Brighams would be working and living out of the large tent Richard had procured during his stop in San Francisco. It wasn't much, but it was a step up from the lean-to they'd been camping in since the fire. The new stove and furniture he'd ordered for them should arrive in two days.

He'd instructed Tommy to send Richard the medical bills for the injured men and to see that both were well cared for until they could return to work. Thankfully, their injuries were minor and they should heal quickly. Additionally, each man who worked the Prosperity Mine was to receive a one month advance on the condition that they sign a contract promising to work at least two more. Hopefully the funds would both aid the miners who'd lost their homes and encourage them not to leave town. After all, a mine without miners was just a hole in the ground.

Richard started up the stairs. Would Lindy be awake? Despite the urgency of his business here, memories of their time in the Orleans Hotel room had pestered him throughout the day. Why had he been fool enough to open his mouth? He should have kept on kissing her and let things proceed as they may. She'd been as eager as he to move forward.

Until he encouraged her to think on it.

Then fear and doubt had crept into her eyes as clearly as the sun sinking below the horizon. His hopes had sunk with it.

Not that she was afraid of him. He was certain she trusted

him now. But she'd been afraid of *something,* and so long as that fear remained, he wouldn't press her.

Still, it had taken every ounce of his self-control to let her walk out of that hotel room. It had seemed like the right thing to do at the time. Should he have pulled her into his arms instead? What did she need from him?

He sensed the walls she was rebuilding between them now. How was he supposed to tear them down? *Lord, grant me wisdom.*

He unlocked the door to their room and stepped inside.

Lindy sat in the chair opposite him, hands on her hips, as a low moan passed her lips.

Richard dropped to his knees in front of her. "What's wrong, darling?"

She shook her head. "It's nothing."

She'd been grimacing and her face was flushed. It wasn't nothing. "Where does it hurt?"

"It doesn't. Honestly, I'm well." She braced her arms against the chair to stand.

He set a staying hand on her shoulder. "Where?"

With a huff, she used her open palm to trace a swath around her belly. "It just gets a little tight and sore sometimes. That's all. Like I'm being squished. But it only lasts for a few seconds."

"This has happened before?"

"It started last night."

"Why didn't you wake me?" Richard wiped sweat from his brow. Could it be her time? She'd seemed so sure they had a few weeks left. He leapt to his feet. "I'm sending for the doctor."

"I don't—"

Richard didn't wait to hear the rest of her argument. What she was describing couldn't be normal. She needed a doctor.

CHAPTER 27

a week later, Richard slid from his horse and handed his reins to Manuel. The boy turned to lead the mount away, but Richard held his hand up. *"Uno momento, por favor."* He untied the bag holding Lindy's surprise, then waved for the boy to continue with his task. "Gracias."

Richard's Spanish was still limited to a few key phrases, and his pronunciation made Manuel chuckle, but with the help of the vaqueros, Richard was learning. So many people in San Diego were bilingual or spoke only Spanish. It seemed prudent to learn the language of his new neighbors.

With an extra bounce to his step, Richard scurried across the yard, praying Lindy was still awake.

Since their return from Nevada City two days ago, Teodora had fixed their meals while Lindy spent nearly all her time reading in her chair beside the empty fireplace. Or so Teodora told him.

When he returned for their noon meal both days, he'd found his wife sleeping. He appreciated the notes of apology she left for him. But he missed their time together. She'd even been asleep before he returned home at night.

Not that he blamed her. The practice labor pains the Nevada City doctor had described as "perfectly normal" didn't seem like any picnic. Not to mention, it must be exhausting carrying around all that extra weight while growing a new life inside your body. Last week, she'd also admitted to frequent back pains, and she'd quit bothering with a corset. She didn't even wear the special one her mother brought from town last month. Yesterday, her ankles were too swollen to fit her boots, which had made her cry.

The sight of her little bare toes peeking from beneath her skirts was cute, but he hated seeing her unhappy. So this morning he'd gone straight to town to find a solution.

Would his gifts make her smile? He pushed through the front door.

"Oh!" Lindy lurched upright in her chair beside the fire and glared at him. "You startled me."

Richard winced. "I'm sorry." He let his gaze travel down her disheveled braid to her wrinkled dress. "Were you sleeping?"

"I think I had fallen asleep, yes." She started the rocking motion that preceded her attempts to stand these days. "Soup's on the stove. I think I'll go—"

"Wait." Richard closed the distance between them to place a staying hand on her forearm. "I've brought you something." He lifted the prettily patterned fabric sack Lucy had provided to hold Lindy's surprise. The moment Lindy's sister had spied him in the store, she hadn't let him alone until he explained his purpose there. The young woman's penchant for chatter was a wonder. Thank goodness his wife was no such magpie.

Lindy tipped her head as she peered up at him. "You went to town? I thought you went with Fernando out to the east pasture."

"I decided this was more important." He set the bag in her lap and knelt before her so his eyes were level with hers. "Go ahead. Open it."

She traced her finger along the red flowers and green stems swirling across the fabric. "This is so pretty. Thank you."

"Your sister gave me the bag."

"She did?"

"She said you'd like it. But the gift itself is from me."

Lindy untied the sack and removed an over-sized pair of boots, as well as a larger size of house slippers. "These are for me?" Her wide blue eyes shimmered.

Please let those be happy tears. "After what happened with your boots yesterday...well, I thought these might be more comfortable."

She set the shoes aside. Cupping his face, she brushed his lips with hers.

He returned her kiss with a soft moan, but she broke away.

"Thank you." Pink tinged her cheeks and she wouldn't look at him. "For the shoes I mean."

It was the first kiss they'd shared since the day she declared her heart was his. And his simple gift had prompted it.

He was sorely tempted to turn right back around and buy every pair of shoes the town's stores had to offer.

Lindy retrieved the slippers from her small side table and struggled to reach past her belly to put them on. Tears spilled onto her cheeks.

"Here, let me." The sensation of her lips on his lingered as he slid the new slippers over her stockinged feet.

Her slippers on, he helped her stand. "These are so comfortable. Thank you." She stepped around him and padded to their chamber. "I do think I need a rest, now, though. Don't forget about the soup."

∼

*T*hat night, Richard lay beside his beautiful wife, listening to the soft, rhythmic breathing of her deep sleep. As their child had grown, Lindy had taken to sleeping on her side with the extra winter blankets crammed beneath her abdomen for support. Her back faced him.

As always.

But the bolster she'd insisted on keeping between them had slipped off the foot of the bed. As she shifted in her sleep, the damp, cotton of her chemise brushed against his shoulder. Like a firebrand touched to his skin, it launched him from bed. The muggy air of their chamber was suffocating.

He rushed through the pitch-black house and crashed into the front door. He fumbled for the latch, flung it open, and stumbled onto the porch. He gulped in hot night air. Where was a cold winter's night when a man needed one? A good snow mound to throw himself into would sure help right now. Instead, they were having a heat wave. In September.

Lying beside his wife, unable to touch her, had always been uncomfortable. But since her declaration of love in Sacramento, it was nothing short of torture. The urge to touch her, to caress her soft skin, to pull her close, was so overwhelming that at times it nearly overpowered him as it had tonight. But he would not give in.

He reached for the folded blanket waiting on one of the chairs they sometimes sat in to enjoy the sunset. He laid the rough wool across the worn planks of the porch floor and settled in for another long night.

He awoke to the sounds of the vaqueros beginning their day as the dark of night lightened to the gray of dawn. More than a few of the men cast him odd looks as he straightened and tried to work the kinks from his neck and back muscles.

Only Manuel dared approach him. Leaning close the boy whispered, "Get her flowers."

"What?" Richard blinked.

"When Mama is mad at Papa, he brings her flowers." Manuel adjusted the floppy hat protecting his young face from the sun. "You've been out here three nights. You need lots of flowers." He pointed toward the creek. "There are *muchas flores* down there." Manuel laughed and dashed off to the barn.

Richard opened his mouth to shout after the boy that Lindy wasn't mad at him, but what other explanation would he give? Better to let the hands think he'd done something to earn his wife's ire than to admit the truth. It wasn't anyone's business but his and Lindy's.

He lifted the blanket and gave it several good whacks before folding it. He dropped it on the bench. With a groan, he stretched his aching back again.

How his sisters would fuss if they knew he was sleeping in such a state.

But what else could he do?

He loved Lindy more than he'd ever thought it possible to love anyone, and she'd declared her love for him in return. Yet her actions made it clear she wasn't ready to take the next step in their marriage and he wasn't interested in moving forward unless her whole heart was in agreement. Every night, every morning, and—if he was being honest—many times during the day, he prayed that his wife would find the courage to open up to him and share what it was that held her back.

She hadn't found it yet.

∼

*S*everal hours later, Richard ran a sleeve across his forehead as he guided his horse along the trail leading up the hillside. The clip-clop of Lindy's horse followed behind. He twisted in his saddle to check that she was holding up beneath the hot afternoon sun. "It's not much farther. Are you doing all right?"

She smiled at him through the thin cloud of dust their mounts kicked up. "Yes, I'm fine, though I'll be glad when we get there." She patted Beast, who rode in a specially-made bag tied to her saddle. "You said there'll be shade, right? I think Beast is getting too hot." She opened her canteen and poured a little water so the pup could drink.

"Yes. There's a large grove of oaks that'll provide plenty of shade."

He looked past her to the flock grazing at the bottom of the hill under the watchful care of Fernando, Eduardo, and four other guards. The men weren't much bigger than Beast from this distance. The sheep, even smaller.

But it was a respectable flock, healthy and strong. If things continued as they were, and the market held, the ranch would make a nice sized profit come next year. Especially if his uncle agreed to the shipping contract Richard had proposed in his last letter. That would go a long way to recovering the additional expense they'd incurred with the military's departure. Hiring the new vaqueros and adding on to the bunkhouse hadn't been cheap, but Richard felt good about giving work to so many hard-working men trying to support their families. Like the mine, there was paperwork involved, but here it was easier to get out and work alongside his employees—to see projects completed by his own hands. Not to mention the pride it would restore in Lindy to see her idea succeed.

He scanned the landscape up the trail. Where were those trees? He'd come across them while trailing a stray sheep yesterday. As soon as he saw the grove, he'd known it was the perfect place to bring Lindy for a special meal.

As they ate this morning, Richard had suggested the two of them take their usual Sunday Bible study outdoors. With less than a month to go before the baby's arrival, he hadn't been certain she'd like the idea of riding horseback, but Lindy had brightened and hurried to change into a riding skirt. Well, she'd hurried as much as a woman in her condition was able to. Which was more energy than he'd seen her exert in days.

As they crested a rise, the shaded grove of California black oaks appeared a few yards away. Richard led them into its center. Though the heat was milder than any they'd experienced in recent weeks, the cool breeze drifting beneath the widespread branches was a welcome change.

Lindy drew up beside him, pinning her veil to the top of her bonnet as she surveyed the small wood. "Is this where we're stopping?"

"This *is* the place I had in mind, but if you don't like it, we can ride on and see what else we find."

"No, this is lovely."

He slid from his horse and removed Beast from his carrier. After setting the pup on the ground, he assisted Lindy from her mount. Though her weight had increased considerably in the five months since their wedding, Richard found the changes more alluring than he'd ever have guessed. There was something about his wife that had him convinced she could bathe in mud and chicken feathers and he'd still want to kiss her.

The moment her feet touched the ground, he leaned forward and did just that.

She gave a small squeak. Her lips curled upward beneath his, and she kissed him back with as much passion as he was giving.

His hands slid from her waist to her back, pressing her as close as possible with the child wedged between them. He shifted to one side and pulled her closer still, his lips never leaving hers.

Never in his life had he imagined the ecstasy of kissing the woman you loved, knowing she loved you in return. Every fiber of his being wanted to join with her as only a husband and wife should. Instead, he forced himself to slow his kisses.

She wasn't ready.

Was she?

He thought of the blankets he'd stowed in their saddle bags and the relative seclusion of their location. His lips still pressed against hers, he dared voice his hope. "Lindy?"

She froze.

He swallowed the words his mama wouldn't be proud he knew. He'd done it again. Pushed for too much. Why couldn't he enjoy the affections she offered without wanting more?

She tried to pull away, but he held her close.

"Forget it." He murmured against her lips. "Forget I asked anything." He kissed her. "Forget I said anything." He kissed her again, one hand stroking her back as the fingers of his other played with the hairs at her nape. "Let's just keep doing this for a while. It doesn't have to lead anywhere. I know you don't want—"

"It isn't that. I—" The loud rumble of her stomach cut off her words. Her mouth rounded along with her eyes. "I beg your pardon."

The volume of her body's demand for food forced a chuckle from him. "Hungry?"

She peered up through her lashes and nodded.

He heaved a sigh and studied her. Was now the time to press for more answers? Or should he set up their picnic and hope she opened her heart to him as they ate? *Lord?* His one word prayer for guidance was rewarded with another loud complaint from Lindy's abdomen. Food it was.

Several minutes later, most of the food they'd packed was consumed and Richard leaned against the trunk of an oak, Lindy's shoulder pressed against his. Beast played nearby as Richard adjusted his grip on their hymnal to angle it away from the glaring sunlight bouncing off the white page.

Lindy's voice filled the wide space beneath the trees with a beauty that only enhanced the ethereal feel of their surroundings.

> *All things bright and beautiful,*
> *All creatures great and small,*
> *All things wise and wonderful,*
> *The Lord God made them all.*

On the day Richard had brought the hymnal home and requested that Lindy sing for him, she agreed on two conditions. First, that she was permitted to choose the songs, and second, that he sing with her. So sing he did, though he managed to keep his voice a tad quieter than hers so he could hear her clearly.

> *He gave us eyes to see them,*
> *And lips that we might tell,*
> *How great is God Almighty,*
> *Who has made all things well.*

Did she include herself in those words? Did she know how well God made her?

They sang the final round of the chorus and Lindy began flipping through the hymnal. A title caught his eye and he placed his finger on the page. "What about this one?"

"God Moves in a Mysterious Way?" Her nose scrunched. "I don't know that one." She reached for the corner of the page to turn it, but he kept his finger in place.

"What if I sing it first and then we sing it together?"

Her brows lifted. "You'll sing it to me?"

Although his singing voice wasn't anything he was ashamed of, it didn't compare to the beauty of hers. So he'd never offered to sing for her before. He wasn't sure what had prompted him to do so now, aside from a strong urge to hear her sing this particular song.

He pulled the book closer and cleared his throat. With a nervous glance at his wife, who gave him an encouraging nod, he recalled the tune in his mind and began to sing.

> *God moves in a mysterious way,*
> *His wonders to perform;*
> *He plants his footsteps in the sea,*
> *And rides upon the storm.*

Lindy adjusted so she sat in front of him. A soft smile graced her lips as she watched him.

He returned his attention to the page. Thankfully, childhood memories kept him singing as he struggled to find his place.

> *Ye fearful saints fresh courage take,*
> *The clouds ye so much dread*
> *Are big wi—*

Loud crashing came from the brush to Richard's left.

Beast growled.

Lindy gasped and Richard jumped to his feet.

A skinny, blond-haired man stumbled from the bush, a large knife in his hand.

"Here now." The stranger staggered toward them. "Quit that noise you're making and let the lady sing."

Beast charged, but Richard scooped him up. The tiny warrior could do little more than agitate the intruder.

The man stopped several feet short of them. "You've the voice of an angel, ma'am."

His words were sweet, but he looked Lindy up and down in a way that made Richard want to punch him. How long had the man been listening?

Richard adjusted his grip to keep Beast from wiggling free. Why had he left his rifle sheathed on his horse?

"Thank—" Lindy gagged. No doubt the smell was upsetting her stomach.

The stench of whiskey and what must be several weeks of caked-on grime and sweat wrinkled Richard's nose. Was this man part of those bandit gangs he'd read about in the paper? A rustler? Were there others nearby?

"So, go on." The man waggled his knife. "Sing."

Richard scanned the surrounding brush. No movement. His attention snapped to the man with the knife. Whoever he was, this stranger was clearly off in the head, and with that blade in his hand, his intentions couldn't be good.

Perhaps if Richard remained calm, the stranger would as well. *Please, Lord.*

Richard shifted Beast to one arm and lifted his free hand to show the stranger he posed no threat. "Would you mind putting the knife away? I don't think my wife can sing if she's frightened."

The man turned his glossy-eyed glare on Richard. An unpleasant sensation for sure, but at least he wasn't ogling Lindy any longer. A thick scar ran along his left jaw and another crossing his temple. Whoever'd done the stitching had been in a hurry. The skin puckered and bunched all along the jagged lines.

The man took a step closer to Richard, his knife raising. "What'd you say?"

"I, uh..." What would calm this man and convince him to leave? "Is there something we can do for you? Do you need help?"

The stranger flung his head back and roared with laughter. "You think I want your help?" The man continued to cackle, clutching at his sides as if Richard's question were the funniest thing he'd ever heard. The flat of his blade bounced against his heaving ribcage.

Richard inched sideways, closing the gap between himself and Lindy. He clasped her trembling hand in his and urged her behind him.

Beast continued his furious barking and attempts to break loose.

Holding his breath, Richard took a step away from the hysterical man.

Behind him, Lindy shuffled backward, pulling Richard along.

The man's laughter ceased. He straightened and pointed his knife at them. "Where'd you think you're goin'?"

Richard froze. The horses were so close. This man was on foot. But it would take Lindy too long to mount.

The rifle butt protruded from its saddle holster. Tempting him. But he didn't think he could pull his rifle faster than the man could attack with his knife.

Especially with Beast still fighting for freedom.

Richard offered the first excuse that came to mind. "My wife's thirsty. She can't sing with a dry throat. There's water in our—"

"Thirsty, eh?" The man pulled a flask from beneath his leather vest. "I's got something that'll wet your whistle, lady." He took several staggering steps forward.

Beast snarled.

Was that hoofbeats galloping closer?

They all turned toward the trail.

"You s'pecting comp'ny?"

Richard shook his head. "I don't know who that is." *Please, God, let it be one of our men.* The flock was at least two miles from where they stood, but with the way the hills bounced sound, it was possible the vaqueros had heard Beast's clamoring and come to investigate. Everyone was on high alert since a neighboring ranch lost thirty sheep last week.

"Liar!" The stranger lunged at them, his knife swinging wildly.

Richard shoved Lindy out of harm's way. He lost his grip on Beast. The fierce bundle of black fur leaped from his arms and clamped his jaws around the man's leg.

"Ow!" The man howled and shook his leg, trying to break free.

Richard surged forward just as the man's blade swung downward.

CHAPTER 28

*C*larinda slammed through the front door and pointed to the kitchen table. "Hurry. Lay him there."

Richard stepped in to do her bidding. He'd cradled Beast's tiny, whimpering form the entire way home. Blood soaked his hands as he lowered his precious cargo onto the table's surface.

Clarinda set her largest pot on the stove and stoked the fire. "I hope the vaqueros find that ratbag and arrest him." At the intrusion of four Grand Valley Ranch vaqueros, the drunkard had dashed into the brush. Richard had ordered the men to give chase.

"I'm praying they're able to do so without more bloodshed."

She paced to the door and searched the yard. Manuel was still at the well, fetching the water she'd requested. Two other vaqueros stood at opposite ends of the yard, rifles ready. Her hand flew to her belly. "You don't think he'd come here, do you?"

"Not with all the guards we have."

Manuel rushed inside, a fresh bucket of water in each hand. He set one beside the table and dumped the contents of the second into the pot. "Do you need more wood?"

She checked the metal box beside the stove. "I think we have enough." What else did Beast need? Thread? A needle? Should she make a poultice? "Can you fetch Teodora? She'll know what to do." Why hadn't she sent for Teodora first?

"Of course." The boy dashed outside, disappearing toward the main house.

Clarinda joined Richard at the table. She stroked Beast's side, ignoring the metallic scent of blood. Blessedly, the knife had missed his tiny body and passed through the poor boy's right ear, but the thin flesh continued to stream blood. Beast whimpered.

The image of another wounded dog flashed in her mind.

She yanked her hand away.

Richard's arm wrapped around her waist. "He's going to be all right."

"Are you sure? He's lost so much blood."

"I don't think it's as bad as it looks. Ears bleed a lot."

"What if Teodora can't stitch such a tiny thing back together?" The older woman had tended many of the vaqueros whose injuries were deemed not serious enough for a doctor's attention, but she'd always done so in the bunkhouse—a place Clarinda had never set foot in. She had no idea how the dog's injury compared. All she knew was that whenever a man was hurt, the first thing Teodora wanted was hot water and clean rags.

Clean rags! Clarinda glanced toward her stash of rags in a basket in the far corner of the room. She didn't want to leave Beast.

Richard must have sensed something, because his arm tightened around her waist. "What do you need?"

Before she could answer, Teodora rushed into the house, Manuel on her heels. "Stand aside, girl, and let me see."

Clarinda jumped out of the way. Richard's warm hands came

to rest on her shoulders. His thumbs stroked a soothing pattern across her shoulder blades.

Teodora glanced up. "He'll live, but what's left of this ear has got to come off. There's no saving it."

⌒

By the time the vaqueros returned the next day, Clarinda was beginning to think she'd have to tie her husband to a table leg to keep him from going after them. It turned out the ratbag had a horse hidden in the brush. The men gave chase for several hours, but eventually they'd lost his trail.

Despite the long night's chase, the vaqueros set about their duties—visibly twitchy—and avoided retiring to the bunkhouse until Richard ordered them to rest. A night guard would be needed. For the rest of the day, the tension among those left awake was palpable and contagious. By nightfall Clarinda was ready to collapse.

The next morning, she awoke to someone banging on the front door. Richard went to answer it while she listened from her position in bed.

"Sorry to disturb you, Senor." Fernando's voice carried easily through the open door. "Twenty sheep went missing last night and four of our men were attacked."

Clarinda smothered her gasp with her hand.

"Are they all right?" Richard's voice took on an edge.

"They were hit pretty hard, but they'll be okay. Teodora's fixing them up. Fernando wanted your permission to take a group of vaqueros in search of the stolen sheep."

"Give me a minute." Richard returned to the bedroom. "Did you hear?"

Clarinda pressed her hands against the tick and levered herself vertical. "You should go." She hated the idea of him out there searching for rustlers, but waiting for the men to return last time had nearly driven him mad.

He kissed her fingers. "I don't want to leave you."

"I'm perfectly safe here. If anything changes, I'll send Manuel to fetch you." She squeezed his hand, then released it. "Go."

"All right, but I'm sending Teodora with your morning meal, first."

"She's tending the men."

"She can come when she's done. You still need to eat, and she can stay with you while I'm gone."

A few minutes later, the front door closed behind Richard, and Clarinda swung her feet over the edge of the bed. A practice pain seized her belly, but she refused to waste the day. By the time Teodora brought Clarinda's meal, the tightness had subsided and she'd dressed for the day.

Three hours later, she sat in her chair at the table, dicing a potato. She paused and sucked in a deep breath as another pain squeezed her middle. This one felt different than those she'd previously experienced—almost wave-like in how the intensity surged and retreated. And it was much stronger. She should ask Teodora if worry could change how they felt.

Not that she could stop worrying while Richard wandered the hills with that crazy man still on the loose. Was the ratbag behind the missing sheep?

As the pain eased, she smiled down at the tiny protector snoring by her feet. Fur tickled her bare toes with each rise and fall of his chest. Despite losing most of his right ear, Beast seemed to be healing well and was even more protective.

Richard said Beast had slept by her side all day yesterday. Since she got out of bed this morning—against Teodora's protests—he'd followed her around like a little shadow and kept threatening to trip her. After one painful stumble, in which she barely managed to avoid squashing the pup, Teodora wanted to move Beast to Lupe's pen. Clarinda wouldn't hear of it.

Much to her surprise, she'd grown attached to the little fur ball and enjoyed his constant presence. Beast was one of the few living creatures to ever accept her and wholeheartedly love her without reservation. His injury, gained in the attempt to protect her, only further endeared him to her.

Another constricting pain stole the air from her lungs and she waited for it to pass. That made four in the past hour. The most she'd ever experienced in such a short time. Could this be the beginning of true labor? Should she send someone to fetch Mother? What if she sent for Mother and it turned out to be more practice contractions?

Better to wait and see if the tightenings continued. Teodora would return from checking the oven in the main house soon, anyway. She'd know if it was time.

Clarinda finished preparing the potatoes and tossed them into the pot of boiling water filled with onions, beef, and herbs. The carrots were next. By the time she'd finished peeling, slicing, and adding them to the pot, she'd counted two more contractions—each stronger than the last.

With the stew complete, she turned to study their front room. If the babe *was* coming today it would arrive to a clean home. She grabbed a pail and headed for the well.

Halfway there, another contraction took hold. Hands on her knees, she breathed deeply, waiting for the pain to subside.

The crunch of dirt grew louder as someone rushed toward her. Teodora's house slippers came into view.

"What are you doing out here?" She didn't wait for Clarinda's answer—which was good because Clarinda couldn't speak. Teodora placed two hands on Clarinda's belly and gently pressed. "Ah, yes. As I suspected this morning. Your time has come." She grinned as the contraction passed. Her voice rose to a shout. "Manuel, come quick!"

Never far from the main house these days, Manuel came

charging around the corner of the barn and across the bridge. "Sí, Señora?"

"Send one of the men to tell Mr. Stevens his wife's time has come."

The boy gaped at Clarinda, unmoving.

Teodora huffed. *"¡Vámonos!"*

Manuel dashed toward the barn.

"Wait!" Clarinda gasped, but Manuel didn't appear to hear her. She looked at Teodora. "What about Mother?"

Teodora patted her shoulder. "I sent one of the other men to get her two hours ago. She'll be here soon."

"How did you know?"

"I've seen many women in labor. I know the signs. Now"— Teodora took Clarinda's arm and turned her toward the house —"let's get you inside."

She lifted her still empty pail. "But—"

"Whatever you were about to do can wait. You've got a baby to deliver."

Clarinda wanted to argue, but another contraction stole her breath.

∿

*R*ichard glared at the incriminating tracks leading away from the easternmost pasture. Rustlers were targeting the Grand Valley Ranch. Just what they didn't need with Lindy's time being so near.

He didn't like being this far from her. If it weren't for the thieves, he'd be at home now. His plan had been to spend the morning catching up the ranch's ledgers and the afternoon coaxing Lindy to sing for him. From the comfort of her bed. He hoped his stubborn wife was relaxing as she'd promised.

He scuffed his boot across the prints. "They've been gone for hours at this point."

"Sí. We'd better get going, don't you think?"

Richard scowled. It'd take them all day and then some to find these rustlers. *If* they could be found.

He'd have to get Lindy to sing tomorrow. She still wouldn't sing for others, but at least she sang for him. Someday, he hoped to convince her to perform again. Not regularly, and probably not for a big crowd, but at least once in front of an audience without her veil on. Her talent was too rare to remain a secret, and the sheer joy in her expression as she sang was too beautiful to remain his alone to behold.

As much as he treasured the honor of her trust, she needed to perform for others so she could receive their praise and feel their acceptance. Perhaps then she could begin to believe in God's acceptance and love for her as well. He'd have to choose her audience carefully—ensure only those who'd love and support her were present—and the timing would need to be perfect, but—

A lone rider approached from the west at a fast clip.

Richard pulled the rifle from its saddle holster.

As the man neared, Richard recognized Eduardo and broke into a sprint. "What is it? What's happened?"

Eduardo reined his horse to a halt. "Mrs. Stevens. Her time has come, sir."

Before the man was finished speaking, Richard was astride his horse. He shoved the rifle into its holster and kicked the mare's sides, setting off at a gallop across the pasture.

His chest tightened. No less than three of Mother's friends had died in childbirth as he'd grown up. *Lord, I can't lose her. Please protect Lindy and our babe.*

The trail grew narrow in the dense brush that separated this pasture from the next. Richard gritted his teeth as he slowed the horse to a near walk. Once through to the other side, he spurred his horse.

It seemed like days, but was only two hours before he reached the ranch yard.

"Take my horse." He ordered Manuel as he vaulted from the saddle and sprang up the porch steps.

Richard wrenched open the front door.

Inside, Mrs. Humphrey hustled from the chamber as Lindy's scream ripped the air.

He strode in that direction.

His mother-in-law changed course, blocking his path. "It's best you wait out here. It won't be long now."

Another gut-wrenching cry echoed in the room beyond.

He fisted his hands. He wanted to charge in and—and what? What could he do for her? He didn't know the first thing about birthing a child.

His knees wobbled, and he braced himself against the nearest chair. "How is she?"

"She's doing just fine. Don't you worry." The older woman patted his cheek with a soft smile, sweat beading her brow. "Everything seems to be going well."

Another yell brought his gaze to the closed chamber door. "You mean, she's *supposed* to sound like that?"

His mother-in-law laughed. "Many women do at this stage." She crossed to the stove where she snatched a cloth from its hook and lifted a pot of boiling water from the stove's surface. She scurried toward the chamber door. "You're welcome to wait in the main house, if you prefer. I can send Teodora for you when it's over." She twisted the doorknob.

"No." He may not be of any help, but he didn't want to be any farther from his wife than where he stood right now. "I'll stay here. Let me know if I can do anything."

"I will." She slipped into the chamber, affording him the briefest glimpse of his wife. She stood beside the bed, sweat-drenched and panting, her hands braced on the mattress as Teodora stroked her back.

As the door shut, Clarinda's head tipped back in another ghastly scream that ripped through Richard's heart.

CHAPTER 29

A loud noise jolted Richard from sleep. He peeled his cheek from the hard surface of the kitchen table and peered toward the window.

Pitch black. How long had he slept? He hadn't intended to drift off at all—only to rest his head as he prayed—but somehow sleep had overcome him. His gaze moved toward the chamber door.

All was quiet. What had awakened him? Rubbing his eyes, he mentally replayed the sound that had only half-registered in his sleep-addled mind.

A babe's cry.

Richard rose and stumbled across the room. He paused outside the chamber door and pressed his ear to its cool, smooth surface. Soft feminine voices murmured within, but he couldn't make out their words. Bright light streamed through the gaps surrounding the door.

He knocked softly.

A moment later, the door swung open to a grinning Teodora. "Come in, Papa. Come in and meet your new son."

A son. Richard floated somewhere between dreamland and

reality as he entered the chamber. More than half a dozen lanterns lit the space as Lindy reposed against a mound of pillows and blankets. Her sweat-drenched hair was splayed around her bare shoulders, and a small bundle nestled in her arms. She glowed as her face lifted to his, though her cheeks pinked as she checked that the blanket was tucked snuggly beneath her arms.

Richard blinked. He was seeing his wife in a greater state of undress than he'd previously been permitted. His steps faltered. "May I?"

"Yes, come."

He reached her side in a heartbeat and knelt to better see the cherubic face. "A son?" He stroked the child's cheek with his finger.

"Yes. Isn't he wonderful?"

Richard took in the babe's wee features, noticing a similarity to Lindy's brow, but a difference in their noses. Did the lad's nose resemble Arnie Walker's? What about his eyes? They'd remained closed since Richard had entered. "Has he opened his eyes?"

Teodora fussed with the blankets around Lindy's legs. "Only for a moment when he cried, but that's normal."

"Did you see their color?"

"It was too quick to tell"—Lindy smiled—"but I thought they might be blue."

Richard grinned. He liked the idea that the child might have Lindy's eye color.

Mrs. Humphrey began extinguishing the extra lanterns. "Of course, that could change, though."

"It could?"

She moved to the next lantern. "It's fairly common for their eye color to change during the first year of life."

"So we won't know for sure until his first birthday?"

Lindy adjusted her hold on the bundle, eyes worried. "Does it matter?"

He cupped her cheek. "Of course not. I'm only curious." He grinned at her. "I've never had a son before. There's a lot I don't know."

A breath of air escaped her, brushing across his wrist and—mother-in-law watching or not—Richard couldn't resist pressing a kiss to his tired wife's lips.

Behind him, the two women giggled.

"Well, I think that's our cue to give you two your privacy." Mrs. Humphrey lifted a basket of soiled rags and exited the room.

Teodora paused in the doorway to point at Richard. "Just remember, she worked hard to bring that child into this world. She needs her rest. So don't be keeping her up."

"Yes, ma'am."

∾

The night was a long one, with the babe noisily waking every few hours to feed. Not that Richard could help with that task. But who could sleep through such caterwauling?

As dawn lightened the sky, the infant's hungry noises again brought him to consciousness. Grateful Lindy didn't shoo him from the room, Richard turned his back once more to give her privacy. The child's quiet sucking filled the stillness of early morning.

For several minutes, he focused on stretching muscles that were sore from trying not to move, lest he disturb the sleeping babe or mother. "Have you settled on a name?"

They'd discussed a few options in the previous weeks, but hadn't made a final decision. The last they'd spoken, she'd been considering Lawrence or Chase. Either would be fine with him and he'd told her so, but she hadn't seemed satisfied with either choice.

The bed jiggled as she shifted behind him. "What do you think of Zane?"

"Zane?" He hadn't heard the name before. "Where'd you hear that one?"

"I read it in a list of passengers in the *Daily Alta* that mother brought last week. It stood out to me. I like how it sounds with Stevens and it's unique, like our son."

"Zane Stevens." He punched his pillow to adjust its shape. "I suppose it does have a nice sound to it and I like the idea of him having a unique name."

"Then you're agreed?"

"Well..." He listened, but didn't hear any more suckling. "Is he finished eating?"

"Yes."

"Can I turn over?"

The blankets moved higher. "All right."

He rolled over and angled his face to get a good look at the sleeping infant. "What do you think?" he whispered. "Do you like the name Zane?" He studied the child's sleeping face, trying to picture him as a five-year-old, a ten-year-old, at sixteen, and finally as an adult. Would the name suit him for the rest of his life? It was a big decision.

Careful not to disturb their child, he took Lindy's hand in his, and closed his eyes. "Lord, we thank You for this most precious gift. In so many ways, this child, though he is just beginning his life here, has already changed his world. You used his existence to bring us together, and for that, I am eternally grateful. Thank You for the wondrous gifts of life and love You've bestowed on us. Please, bless Zane as he grows. Help him to know how much he is loved by us and by You. We thank You for Your incredible grace and mercy. In the name of our Lord Jesus Christ, Amen." Richard opened his eyes.

Tears trailed down Lindy's cheeks.

"What'd I say?" He used his thumbs to wipe away the moisture.

She smiled at him. "These are happy tears."

"They are?"

"You make me so happy."

Richard raised himself onto one arm and reverently touched a kiss to his wife's lips. "The feeling's mutual."

"I'm glad." Though she said the words, something like doubt flickered in her eyes.

"You don't believe me?"

She looked down. "It isn't that, I just..."

He waited for her to continue, but silence reigned. "You just what?"

"I know that a husband expects...is entitled to...certain privileges, but I..."

He sank onto the bed beside her. After the way she'd kissed him in Sacramento, and again in the oak grove, he'd thought...hoped... Remembering the doubt he'd sensed in her that day, he braved the question he'd been avoiding for fear of its answer. "You don't want...that sort of closeness with me?"

"No, I do...I mean, I want to make you happy but...oh, I don't know what I want." She turned her face from him.

He didn't want their union to be about her making him happy. It should be about both of them making each other happy.

There was no denying the attraction that had sizzled between them since Sacramento. So why didn't she want to move to the next step? She said she loved him, but did some part of her still hold tender feelings for Arnie?

He frowned as his thoughts turned in a new direction. Had Arnie done something to make her think marital intimacy wouldn't be a pleasurable experience?

How could Richard broach such a subject?

"Is there something..." He paused, searching for the right words. Was there any delicate way of phrasing it? "Is there something that happened...before...that makes you think you won't enjoy it?"

She mumbled something into her pillow, but he couldn't make out the words.

He lifted onto his elbow, praying Zane would remain asleep for this awkward conversation. "I'm sorry, I couldn't understand you."

She turned enough to free her mouth from the pillow. "I'm more afraid that *you* won't like it." She peered at him from the corner of her eye, as if anxious for his reaction, but too fearful of it to fully face him. "That I won't please you."

Richard blinked at her. "Honey, why on earth would you think that?"

She closed her eyes. "Because last time..."

She didn't finish the sentence, but she didn't have to. How had he not figured it out sooner? Arnie left her immediately after their disastrous encounter. "You think he left because you didn't please him?"

She lifted one shoulder. "Maybe."

Gently cupping her face, he turned her to look at him. "There is no possible way that is true."

"How do you know?" Her eyes begged him for reassurance.

"I just know." He stroked a tendril of hair from her face. "You are loving and passionate and gorgeous and I have no doubt..." He held her chin, willing her to feel and believe his conviction. "No doubt—do you hear me?— that you and I will find every kind of pleasure in each other. All we need to do is trust each other and be open and honest with how we're feeling at every step."

A spark of hope battled the darkness of doubt in her eyes. "How can you be so confident?"

"Because I know you and me. And when two people love each other as much as we do, God blesses that in every way."

Her face flamed red. "You think God pays attention to..."

He laughed, startling Zane, who began to cry. Richard took the boy in his arms. Standing, Richard began to rock side-to-side, not knowing what he was doing, but letting instinct guide him.

Zane quieted again and Richard looked at Lindy. "Yes, I do think God pays attention to"—he winked at her—"*that*. God *created* us to be united in this way. The Bible says physical intimacy is a gift and a blessing to be shared between a husband and wife, and God's gifts are always good."

She pushed up to a sitting position. "But I didn't wait. I sinned and—"

"And have you asked God to forgive you?"

She shook her head.

"Do you want to?"

"I know I need to be forgiven but..." Her lips trembled as her eyes filled.

He shifted Zane to one hand and sat on the bed, taking her hand. "Honey, if you ask Him to forgive you, the Bible says He will be faithful and just to do exactly that. All you have to do is ask."

"It's really that simple?"

"Jesus Christ *died* to forgive you of your sins. He's already done the hard part. All you have to do is accept it."

∼

Five weeks later, wearing only his trousers, Richard held his breath as he lowered Zane into the cradle beside Lindy's chair. Carefully sliding his hands free, he didn't dare exhale until he'd tiptoed several feet away. Thankfully, the afternoon sunlight peeking around the closed curtains was enough to keep him from bumping into anything.

He grinned at his wife standing in her shift in the chamber doorway. The weeks of waiting for her body to heal had been an exquisite adagio. Now, with the doctor's approval this morning, they could finally enjoy a melodious resolution.

A shy smile lifted her lips as she whispered, "Are you sure?"

He crossed the room in four quiet strides, his feet padded by the socks he wore. Taking her by the waist, he drew her close and wrapped his arms around her. Pressing his forehead to hers, he held her gaze. "Honey, I've been waiting weeks and months for this moment."

She giggled until his lips pressed against hers. Her arms slid around his neck and she arched up onto her toes, returning his kisses with a passion that set a fire inside him.

Suppressing a moan, he steered her backward into their chamber and toed the door shut. As his lips followed a trail along her jawline and down her neck, he directed her toward their bed. Her fingers ran through his hair. He brushed a kiss on her collarbone and she released a soft sound of pleasure.

At the bed, he lowered her and paused. He searched her eyes for any lingering doubt or hesitation—though he hadn't seen it since the day she'd asked the Lord's forgiveness. "I love you, Lindy."

"I love you, too."

Satisfied that she'd have no regrets, Richard lowered himself beside her.

Pounding sounded on the front door and he froze.

CHAPTER 30

*A*t the loud sound, Zane bawled. Lindy rushed to Zane's cradle and attempted to soothe the child. Richard jumped from the bed.

He stormed across the front room. Whoever was on their front porch ought not to be so careless about knocking on the doors of families with infants. The vaqueros all knew better. Which meant the knocker was not only rude, but an uninvited guest. Richard had a good mind to greet them with his shotgun.

He positioned his body so whoever was there couldn't view Lindy and cracked open the door. A man he vaguely recognized as one of the Franklin House's employees stood there. Richard glared at him. "What do you want?"

The man wrung the brim of his hat. "Sorry I woke the baby, Señor. I have a message for Mr. Richard Stevens."

"That's me."

The man handed Richard a note, tipped his hat, and turned to go as Zane's wails doubled in volume. "Sorry!"

Richard gave the man's retreating back a final glare before looking down at the missive.

He froze.

It couldn't be.

He shut the door and hurried to his study. Lifting his letter-opener, he broke the wax seal.

September 30, 1858

Dear Richard,

I am pleased to inform you that recent business opportunities in San Francisco have necessitated my travel to that city, and fair winds and amiable weather have delivered me to the California coast ahead of schedule. As such, I am now ensconced at the Franklin House in San Diego with the greatest hope of seeing you.

I understand you are busy with your new family and ranch, but it would greatly please me if you were able to meet me here as soon as possible. I must leave the morning after tomorrow to continue my journey north, and there are issues we need to discuss at length which should not be conveyed in a letter.

Warmest Regards,
Simeon Childs

Lindy joined him, bouncing Zane in her arms. "What is it?"

"A letter from my uncle. He's in San Diego and wants to see me."

She puffed a lock of hair from her forehead, shifting from foot to foot as she rocked Zane. "Is that what *you* want?"

What he wanted was to return to their chamber and continue where they'd left off, but the paper weighed heavily in his hands. His uncle would only be here for a single day. Who knew when Richard would again have the chance to meet him?

Richard tried to picture the man in his mind. Did he dress as the fine gentlemen of his parents' acquaintance or in merchant's clothes, or perhaps sailor's? Did his nose share the same peculiar bump as Richard's? What was it Simeon wished to discuss that he didn't want to put in a letter?

Lindy's hand settled on his chest. "I think you should go."

"But..." His gaze flicked from her to their chamber door and back.

She smiled. "I'll be here tomorrow. Your uncle may not be." She gave him a gentle push. "Go."

~

*R*ichard sat with his uncle in a wagon near the river's edge. The man's slight limp had made Richard glad he'd brought the vehicle along to cart supplies back from the store. They'd needed a private place to discuss personal matters —something not easily found in town—and the wagon provided the perfect solution without requiring the older man to walk far.

Now, though, Richard couldn't stop staring at Simeon's profile. His nose was exactly like Richard's. He'd recognized that fact the moment he spotted his uncle descending the stairs of the Franklin House. If there had ever been any doubt of the truth behind Richard's birth, Simeon's appearance laid it to rest.

The nose was just the beginning of their resemblance. Though Richard's mother had also had blue eyes, Simeon's were the exact same shade as Richard's. His hair had the same cowlick, too. Even Simeon's broad shoulders and the way he held himself made Richard feel he was looking in a mirror. Or at least seeing what his mirror might show him in another twenty years.

It was uncanny.

Simeon caught him staring and grinned. "Perhaps it's a good

thing we're meeting here instead of Boston. I had no idea you looked so much like your father."

Richard's cheeks warmed. "You see it, too?"

"Of course." Simeon cocked an eyebrow. "You may need to don a disguise when you come to visit or people will think you're *my* son." He shook his head. "What it must have been like for poor Abner."

"My face was a daily reminder of Mother's betrayal."

"Which was hardly your fault." Simeon set a hand on Richard's shoulder. "I wasn't told much about your upbringing. I hope he was good to you and your mother."

Richard looked away. "He provided for me. Gave me his name."

"But he didn't love you as his own."

Richard stared at him. "How…?"

"The way you turned away before. And I can see it in your eyes now." Simeon tapped his temple. "I've learned the truth is more often found in what we don't say, than in what we do." He cleared his throat. "Well, you may not have had a loving home growing up, but I can promise, you'll find one in Boston, should you choose to return. Scandal or no, we stand by our own. Only your mother's wishes kept us away all these years. I'm afraid you'll not get rid of us now."

Richard laughed. "And who is us? You wrote of your eldest son, David. I know he helps you with the company. But who else is there that knows about me?"

Simeon spent hours filling Richard in on all the family connections and stories he'd missed growing up. Eventually, Richard drove the wagon back to the hotel where they enjoyed a fine meal in the hotel's dining room.

Silence descended on the table as they awaited their dessert, and Richard sensed his uncle was working up to whatever it was he felt uncomfortable putting in a letter. Most of what they'd talked about so far, while interesting and answering many of Richard's questions, could have been shared in a letter.

Finally, Simeon cleared his throat. "I don't want you to think what I'm about to say is in any way my attempt to distance our family from you. It's not. We've been waiting a long time to welcome you into our midst. However..."

Richard leaned forward. "Yes?"

"David, is anxious to move up in the world and he wants...well, he's hoping you'll consider letting him buy out our eastern contracts and set up his own business. You'd still own the contracts along the gulf and everything here in the west, as well as our contracts in Asia. He's also hoping you'll let him have one or two of our European contracts, but I told him that may be asking too much."

Unprepared for such a request, Richard tipped his head to the ceiling. How much were their eastern contracts worth? What portion of the company's revenue would he be losing if he let those go?

"Of course, it's your company and you're under no obligation to sell any of it. Though he is prepared to offer you a fair price."

His cousin must have been saving for years to have that amount of funds available. Richard smiled at his uncle. "Don't worry, I'm not offended by the request. Only unprepared to answer. I feel I need to know more about our company before I can make any decision to sell."

Simeon visibly relaxed. "Of course, of course. That makes perfect sense. I'm grateful you're willing to consider it at least. Thank you."

"After all the work you've put into making the company what it is, I'd be the worst kind of man *not* to consider such a request." Running his hand through his hair, he sighed. "Although, I have to admit, I'd rather find a way to promote him within the company—maybe look into a partnership or even make him a co-owner—so we can keep it all in the family."

Simeon laughed. "You certainly are your father's son. He would be so proud of the man you've become. I only wish he were here to see it."

A lump lodged in Richard's throat, and he forced himself to clear it. "And what would my father think of the contract I proposed for shipping our wool east?"

~

*A*n hour after Richard's departure, Clarinda woke to another knock at the front door. She slipped from bed and peered into the cradle she'd moved to the bedroom. Zane's tiny lashes didn't flutter, so she crept from the room and closed the bedroom door. She checked the buttons on the wrapper she'd fallen asleep in as she shuffled across the front room.

More knocking shook the door. Cringing, she reached for the knob. They ought to have a sign made and set outside to keep people from pounding when the baby was sleeping. It was difficult enough getting Zane to—

Arnie?

She slammed the door shut and threw the bar into place. Her heart beat in triple time.What on earth was he doing here? And now, of all times, with Richard away in town? How had he gotten past their guards? She looked down at her dressing gown, a hand moving to her hair.

"Clarinda?" Arnie's voice penetrated the thick wood. "I came all this way to speak with you, the least you can do is let me in."

Pressing her mouth to the crack, she whisper-shouted, "Would you lower your voice? The baby is sleeping!"

"Then open the door so we can speak like civilized people."

Of all the nerve. How dare he show up at her home, making demands? She pictured Zane's peaceful expression. If she ignored Arnie, he was bound to cause a racket and wake Zane. "Wait there. I'll be out in a minute."

Minutes later, she checked that her veil was tucked into the high neck of her dress. Satisfied that she was covered, she slipped out the front door and closed it behind her.

Beast charged up to greet her, but Arnie was nowhere in sight. Had he given up and left?

Teodora hurried across the yard. "I saw him go around back. He told the guards he was a friend of yours from school."

"And they believed him?"

"It was one of the new men. He didn't know you went to an all girls school.

Dirt crunched near Lupe's pen.

Clarinda turned in that direction, but Teodora caught her arm. "Do you know him? Should I call the guards?"

Clarinda patted the housekeeper's hand and pulled free. "He's no one and he'll be leaving soon. There's no need to call the guards." The fewer people who knew about Arnie, the better.

She followed the noise toward the rear of the house.

"He's *that* man, isn't he?"

"All right, yes. But I can handle him." *I hope.* "Just please go back to the main house. He'll only act worse if he thinks he has an audience."

"Worse? What do you think he'll do with no audience? No. I'm not leaving you with him alone."

"He won't do anything. That's not what I meant."

Teodora crossed her arms.

"Just give me ten minutes. If you don't see him leave in ten minutes you can send for the guards, all right?"

The housekeeper didn't budge.

"Please. For Zane's sake. Nobody can know the truth, and the quieter Arnie leaves, the less chance there will be of it getting out."

"Ten minutes." She pointed at Clarinda. "I'm going to put the clock next to the window." Teodora muttered in Spanish all the way back to the main house.

Clarinda ignored her and rounded the corner of her house to the backyard. She'd bought herself ten minutes.

Arnie leaned against a rail, watching the lamb nibble hay. "Why's this one back here instead of in the pasture with the others?"

Clarinda crossed her arms. "What do you want, Arnie?" *Please, don't let it be Zane.*

Arnie turned to study her. "You've changed, you know."

"What do you mean?"

He pushed off the rail and closed the distance between them. "When you answered the door just now, you weren't wearing this." He fingered her veil, his gaze holding hers through its thin film. "You'd never have done that in Benicia. There's a new confidence in the way you carry yourself. I noticed it in Sacramento." His voice lowered in the way it had when they'd been alone in the garden. "You're more beautiful than ever."

Hating the thrill that jolted through her with his compliment, she lifted her chin and stepped away. "A lot has changed since then." Was that a tremble in her voice? Surely his words couldn't still hold such sway over her. Not anymore.

He stepped close again, splaying his hand over her stomach. "Clearly."

She lurched backward and bashed into the side of the house. She shoved his hand away. "What are you doing here, Arnie?"

He cupped her cheek. "I've come for you, Clarie. I never should have let you go."

Rather than pleasure, his touch left her cold and uncomfortable. She twisted away, squeezed past him, and spun to face him. "It's far too late for regrets, Arnie. I'm not the naïve girl you fooled before."

"I know that. I told you, I can see that you've changed and I love it. All I'm asking is for a second chance."

"I'm married."

Arnie scoffed. "We both know your marriage is nothing but a sham to legitimize *my* child." He turned toward the house. "Where is he, anyway? I want to see the boy."

"How do you know about Zane?"

"Zane, huh? What kind of name is that?" He started toward the rear door. "People in town were more than happy to tell me all about the new little *Stevens* baby"—he sneered Richard's name as if it were something vile—"but I was hoping they were wrong about the name. Did your *husband* come up with it?" He reached for the doorknob.

She knocked his hand away. "Zane's sleeping. You can't go in."

"Then bring him out. He's my son and I want to see him."

"He's not your son. You gave up that right when you abandoned me in the middle of nowhere."

Arnie cringed. "I'm sorry, Clarie. You know I am. But Father—"

"Yes, what about your father? You say you've come to claim me, but what would your father say to that?" Though her conscience pricked like needles, she couldn't resist adding, "Or have you suddenly grown a backbone?"

"It wasn't about backbone. He found out about us and threatened to cut me off. That's why I was late." He shoved both hands into his hair and pulled. "I thought I could do it—that I could marry you anyway, but without money, how was I to care for you? Where would we have lived? How would we have eaten?"

Clarinda resisted the urge to laugh. Heaven forbid he get a job. "If you'd cared enough, been brave enough, you'd have found a way. We'd have figured it out together." Then again, if he'd been the brave sort in the first place, he'd never have suggested they elope. Why hadn't she figured that out before? Why had she made so many excuses for him? From the first day he asked her to meet in secret, she'd been blind to who he truly was. A selfish coward. "You need to go, Arnie. You don't belong here."

"Neither do you." He grabbed her and tried to draw her close, but she pulled away. "Come with me. You and the boy deserve better than life in this back-hole excuse for a ranch."

"I love this ranch and I love Richard. I'm not going anywhere with you." She tried to push him away from the house, but he wouldn't budge. Her ten minutes had to be almost up. How could she convince him to go? "Besides, your father will still cut you off and—"

"Father's dead."

She stilled. "What?"

"He got himself killed in a duel a week after I saw you in Sacramento."

"I'm so sorry."

"I'm not. The old fool deserved what he got, and now I'm free to live my life how I see fit." His strong arms pulled her close, his lips mere inches from hers. "And I want you with me. You're the only one for me." His mouth lowered.

She twisted her head and his lips landed on her cheek.

With a firm stomp of her booted heel onto his foot, she finally gained her freedom.

He hopped up and down, howling as he held his boot. "What'd you do that for?"

"I told you, I'm married! And I love my husband." She pointed toward the drive. "Now get out of here before I scream and one of the vaqueros brings a gun to *make* you leave."

Straightening, he scowled at her. "Fine. I'll go, but this isn't over." He plucked his hat from the fence. "I don't know what he's done to turn you against me, but I know you'll regret this."

His eyes took on the gentle yearning quality that had once

made her insides turn soft. Now, though, she saw the sentiment for the manipulative mask it truly was.

"Come with me, Clarie. Leave this place and come back to Benicia. We can be a family. The three of us. I've got the mansion now and there's talk of my taking Father's place in next year's mayoral election. After that, who knows? Maybe I could be governor someday. Think of the opportunities that kind of life would give our boy."

A life spent in the public eye, constantly worrying about what others thought of her. That was the last thing she wanted and the last thing she wanted for Zane. "I said for you to go."

"All right. I'm going." He pointed his hat at her. "I'm giving you the night to think this through." Arnie slapped his hat onto his head, stomped around the house to an unfamiliar horse tethered in the yard, and mounted up. "I'll see you tomorrow." Without waiting for her response, he urged the horse into a run and disappeared down the road.

CHAPTER 31

$\mathcal{I}$t was well past midnight by the time Richard returned from town that evening. After taking care of his horse, he hurried toward the house. Hopefully, Lindy wouldn't mind being woken. The conversation with his uncle had gone better than he'd expected. Although Simeon had wanted to negotiate certain points in the contract, his uncle was in favor of shipping the wool. Richard could hardly wait to tell Lindy. She'd want to know all the details.

After caring for Zane all day, was there any chance she had enough energy left to pick up where they'd left off? He toed off his boots on the front porch. Gently turning the knob, he eased the door open. If Zane was asleep, Richard had no intention of waking him.

No light illuminated the dark interior as Richard lowered his boots to the floor beside the door. His eyes still adjusting, he crept across the front room toward their chamber. The door stood open, so he continued to the bed, giving the cradle a wide berth. Zane's soft snoring brought a smile to Richard's face. He knelt on his side of the bed and reached toward Lindy.

Instead of his wife's feminine curves, he found rumpled blankets.

He ran his hands up and down the mattress. Their bed was empty.

He tiptoed back to the front room and scanned the darkened interior. The silhouette of Lindy's chair wasn't quite right.

He padded across the wood flooring.

His wife was slumped in her favorite chair, her head at an awkward angle. Her gentle, rhythmic breathing let him know she was in deep sleep.

Had she tried to wait up for him? He couldn't decide whether to shake her or kiss her. Instead, he slid one arm behind her back and the other beneath her knees.

"Arnie?"

Though her eyes remained closed, the mumbled name walloped him. After all this time, did she still think of the man? Dream of him? Were they good dreams or bad? It was impossible to tell with the single word. He squeezed her tight as he carried her to bed, murmuring in her ear. "It's me, honey. Richard, your husband."

"Mmm," was all the response he got as her body grew more limp in his hold.

He set her on her side of the bed and tugged the blanket to her chin. Sitting on his heels, he stared at her sleeping form. Clearly, his wife was exhausted. It seemed their conversation and everything else would need to wait for tomorrow.

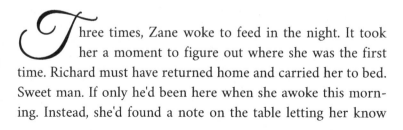

*T*hree times, Zane woke to feed in the night. It took her a moment to figure out where she was the first time. Richard must have returned home and carried her to bed. Sweet man. If only he'd been here when she awoke this morning. Instead, she'd found a note on the table letting her know that he'd promised to give his uncle a tour of the area and to expect them both for the evening meal.

She pulled an apple pie from the oven. What would Simeon Childs think of the Grand Valley Ranch and their home here? She considered the rag rugs, homemade curtains, and pillows she'd embroidered herself. The hardwood floors gleamed from her morning scrubbing, the windows shined, and a clean linen graced the table. Though far from impoverished farmers, their style of living was vastly different from what she recalled of the fancy parlors and grand drawing rooms of eastern society.

She could have recreated those rooms if she'd wanted. Richard had offered to buy her anything she desired for the house when they first moved in. But fancy things reminded her of a time she preferred to forget, and she hadn't expected they'd entertain guests. So she'd picked beautiful, but simple, pieces to suit their life. Would Richard's uncle look down on them for their differences or appreciate the hard work it took to make a comfortable home here?

She set the pie on the side table to cool. Zane's happy gurgle drew her to the blanket in the middle of the floor where he lay. She knelt beside him and pressed her finger against his tiny fist. He opened his fingers to close them around hers. Warmth flooded her as she gazed at his cherubic face. His innocent smile was the light of her days. She scooped Zane into her arms and pressed her cheek against the soft down of his fine, blond baby hairs.

Hoofbeats grew louder outside.

She hurried to the window. *Don't let it be Arnie.* What if he were here when Richard returned with his uncle? She hadn't had a chance to warn Richard of Arnie's presence.

What if they met in town? Her hand flew to her mouth. They wouldn't recognize each other by appearance, but they knew each other's names. Might there be a reason for the two to be introduced?

She needed to speak with Richard and explain she wanted nothing to do with Arnie's plans.

She shifted Zane to one arm and lifted the curtains. No dust rose from the south and the road toward town.

She stepped outside and followed the growing thunder toward the northeast and finally spotted a trail of dust. Who would be riding so hard from that direction? It couldn't be one of the vaqueros. The flock was to the south right now.

She tightened her hold on Zane. Without turning her head, she shouted toward the barn. "Manuel!"

"Sí, Señora. I see it."

She jumped at the nearness of the lad's voice. He stood less than ten feet away, gun in hand. Behind him, Teodora sprinted from the main house.

A single horse and its rider barreled into the yard. They came to a stop mere feet from where she stood. The horseman was one of the young men she'd seen in the village where Teodora's daughter lived.

As he panted, Teodora spoke in Spanish too rapid for Clarinda to follow. The man's response was just as quick, but she caught Richard's name in the flow of words.

"What's he saying?" She rubbed Zane's back, though he wasn't fussing. "He said something about Richard. Is Richard injured?" No, that didn't make any sense. Richard was in town giving his uncle a tour. This rider had come from the northeast.

"He was hoping Mr. Stevens was here. Something's happened at the village and the captain wants Richard's advice."

Clarinda gaped at Teodora. The leader of Graciela's village was seeking Richard's advice? "What on earth happened that they would ask for Richard's help?"

Teodora threw her hands up. "That's what I keep asking him, but he doesn't want to tell me."

Again, Teodora spoke in rapid Spanish.

The young man shook his head.

The housekeeper took two steps forward and seized the young man's ankle. She gave it a firm shake and uttered what must have been some form of threat because the man's eyes widened and he kicked his limb free.

He spoke again, and Teodora's whole face drained of color. Her body wavered.

Clarinda rushed to steady her with one hand, her other still cradling Zane. "What did he say? What's wrong?"

Teodora blinked and her shoulders squared, though tears pooled in her eyes. "It's Graciela. I must go!" She dashed for the barn.

Manuel chased her. "I'll go with you."

Teodora stopped. "No. You go to town and find Mr. Stevens. Tell him he must come at once."

"Yes, ma'am." Manuel raced past Clarinda and into the barn.

Teodora sprinted on his heels.

By the time Clarinda caught up with them, Manuel was mounting up and Teodora had almost finished saddling one of the ranch's spare horses.

"I'm coming, too." She didn't know what had happened, but if it involved Graciela, Clarinda would do whatever she could to help.

"No. You have the baby and—"

"Is it disease? Is Graciela sick?"

"No, she..." Teodora couldn't seem to find the words.

"Would Zane be in danger?"

Teodora shook her head. "But—"

"Then I'm coming. Just let me grab some nappies and my rebozo for Zane." She'd need the shawl-like garment to carry Zane as they rode. "It'll only take a moment." She sped toward the house, pausing at the barn door. "Wait for me!"

~

*A*s they approached the village, Clarinda could feel tension radiating off every person present. Several men stood guard around the village's perimeter. Here and there, women were gathered together, many weeping.

As they neared Graciela's dwelling, half a dozen grave-faced men stood near the entrance. The loud wailing of women and children escaped through the bark-covered walls.

Clarinda's breath caught and she looked at Teodora. The housekeeper didn't spare her a glance as she leapt from her horse and disappeared inside.

Clarinda dismounted gingerly with Zane tucked into the rebozo she'd tied him in before leaving the ranch. She took in the somber faces of the men watching her. The captain was among them—the cheerful face she remembered from her previous visits nowhere to be seen. She approached the entrance.

The captain stepped into her path. He spoke something in Spanish that she thought included the words *wait* and *speak*, but his accent was thick.

"I'm sorry." She recited the phrase Teodora had taught her for getting people to speak more slowly. "¿Puedes hablar más despacio?"

The captain nodded to one of the other men, who disappeared inside. He reappeared a moment later with Teodora.

The captain repeated his words to Teodora who translated them for her. "He says that since your husband is not here, he wants to know what you think they should do."

Clarinda tensed. Why would the captain care what she thought? "Do about what?"

Tears poured from Teodora's sparking eyes. "My daughter was attacked and almost raped by a white man."

Clarinda's knees wobbled, and she clutched Zane as Teodora continued to speak.

"He was herding sheep in a canyon not far from here. She was collecting herbs. She didn't know he was there until it was too late and he attacked her. Alvaro, her husband, heard her screams and came running. He killed the man who did this to her."

"I don't understand. What was this man doing so close to the village with a herd of sheep?"

"One of the men says the scoundrel is one of the new guards for the Smith Ranch. They hoped Mr. Stevens would know for sure."

Clarinda frowned at Teodora. "But how would Richard know if the man worked for Smith? Richard's only met Smith once and only a few of Smith's vaqueros were there. Richard's never been to Smith's ranch."

Teodora shrugged as she wrung her hands. "I don't know, but the captain is afraid that when the ranchers learn of the white man's death, they will be angry, accuse the village of trying to steal sheep, and bring violence to the village. He wants to know what punishment of Alvaro you think will satisfy the ranchers."

Clarinda gaped at Teodora. She replayed the housekeeper's words in her mind as crying continued inside the dwelling. Graciela had been attacked and almost raped. Alvaro had defended her. And they wanted to punish him for it? If the man who'd attacked Graciela worked for Smith, it was no wonder these people were frightened. But still...

"No punishment." The words burst from her lips before she'd even fully processed her decision. "He was defending his wife. The ranchers will surely understand that. They must." Even Clarence Smith had to understand a man's need to protect his wife...didn't he?

Teodora relayed her words to the captain, who frowned. He shook his head as the other men joined in the conversation. It was clear from their body language that some agreed with her while others did not.

Finally the captain held up his hand, drawing the debate to a halt. He spoke something to Teodora. The dear woman's face contorted.

"What is it? What have they decided?"

"He says Alvaro is to be whipped and then banished from the village for one year."

Clarinda stared at the captain. "No! It isn't right."

Though his brown eyes held deep sorrow, there was no sign of yielding.

"Please!" She looked from face to face. "At least wait until my husband comes." She turned to Teodora. "Ask them to at least wait until Richard comes. Maybe he can persuade them." Men were always more willing to listen to other men. Surely Richard could convince them not to do this.

She held her breath as Teodora translated her plea.

CHAPTER 32

*R*ichard steered his horse to a ridge overlooking their southern pasture. His uncle reined his horse to a stop beside him. Fatigue showed in the older man's expression. They should probably head for home soon.

"This is magnificent land you've acquired for yourself." Simeon gestured to the view. "It can't be easy keeping track of so many animals on such a vast piece of land. Quite different from our farms back home." He glanced at Richard. "I heard a man in town complaining of livestock being stolen. Have you had any trouble of that sort?"

"Some. Though not as much as those north of us. The night before Zane was born we lost twenty head. We've hired a few more men to keep watch since then—trusted relatives of the men we regularly employ. It seems to be keeping the wolves at bay, though I've no doubt they're still on the prowl."

"The sheriff hasn't caught them?" Simeon surreptitiously rubbed his weak knee.

"He's tried, but whoever they are, they never attack the same flock twice." Richard scanned the landscape for signs of two-legged trespassers. Nothing stirred. "There's too much land to cover. Too many places for snakes to hide."

"Thought you said they were wolves."

Richard laughed. "Snakes, wolves, whatever you want to call them, they're predators waiting to take what's ours. That's why my partner, Thompson, suggested we hire an investigator, and I agree. He's written to a man he knows in San Francisco to see if he'll take on the challenge."

The man Mr. Humphrey'd hired to investigate Richard had declined the job, explaining he dealt with information and didn't have the necessary skills to hunt rustlers. Thompson's man was supposedly experienced as a former Texas Ranger. If that was true, they ought to have results soon. Assuming he accepted the position.

"That's good." Simeon surveyed the land in silence for several minutes. "Despite the trouble, you seem happy here."

Thinking of Lindy waiting for him at home, he wondered if Zane was letting her get any rest. "I am." A grin lit his face. "Are you ready to meet my wife and son?"

"Certainly."

Just short of an hour later, they rode into an eerily quiet yard. Manuel didn't run out to greet them. A strange horse stood tethered to the pole in front of his and Lindy's house, still saddled. The horse's rider was nowhere in sight.

Simeon glanced at him as they dismounted. "You expecting company?" The older man's knee wobbled, but he recovered.

"Only you."

At that moment, the front door swung open and a man Richard didn't recognize stepped onto the porch.

"Who are you?" Without waiting for the stranger's answer, Richard pushed past him into the house. "Clarinda!" She wasn't in the front room. He strode into their chamber. She wasn't there either. He stormed back to the stranger on his front steps. "Where is she?"

"Whoa, hold on now. First things first." The man offered his hand. "My name's Arnie Walker."

Richard started to accept the handshake. *Wait, Arnie Walker?* He jerked his arm back. "What are you doing here? Where's my wife?"

"Your wife." The man sneered, all semblance of civility gone. "You don't have one. Not for long, anyway. I intend to bring her back with me. Her *and* my son."

White-hot fury fisted Richard's hands at his sides. "What have you done with them?"

The man had the good sense to take a step back. "I haven't done anything with them. Yet. I only arrived a few minutes ago and she wasn't here. But I promise you, when she returns, I'm helping her pack her bags and leave this backwoods—"

Richard's arm jerked with the urge to swing, but he kept his fists lowered.

Blessedly, the movement was enough to cut short the fool's words.

Simeon stepped toward Richard. "Is there anywhere she might have gone?"

"No. She knew we were coming for the evening meal. I left her a note..." Unless she hadn't received it. Was there a chance it fell from the table? Where could she have gone?

◇

*T*his couldn't be happening. Feet dragging, Clarinda followed the small crowd to the edge of the village where Alvaro's shirt was removed and he was bound to a post. This was wrong. Alvaro shouldn't be beaten and he definitely shouldn't be banished. His wife needed him at her side more now than ever.

She stifled the urge to shout at the men to stop. It would do no good.

324

Growing up, she'd witnessed the irrational hatred some of the ranchers held for these people. Especially Clarence Smith. Even if the captain's orders were unjust, his concerns were valid. There was nothing more she could do.

Hours had passed since her conversation with the captain, but Richard had not arrived. The captain would wait no longer. He ordered that the punishment be carried out.

The whip cracked the air and Clarinda flinched.

The next strike tore flesh from Alvaro's bare back. A red-hot line scored his olive skin.

He emitted a low groan.

Another blow. A loud cry. Blood dripped down his back.

Still another crack of leather ripped more skin away.

Clarinda's stomach churned. She averted her gaze as tears coursed down her cheeks.

One of only a few women present, she'd come to bear witness—hoping her presence might be of some comfort. That was foolishness. Alvaro barely knew her. She could do no good here.

She dashed back to Graciela's home and ducked through the low opening. She accepted Zane from the arms of Teodora's aunt—the woman who'd raised Graciela in Teodora's place.

Clarinda's gaze drifted to five-year-old Noemi and one-year-old Modesto. They were curled on a nearby blanket, having cried themselves to sleep. When they awoke, their father would be gone. They'd not see him again for a full year.

Assuming he survived. What would become of him away from this village? Where would he go? She had no idea how these people survived apart from their village life and gaining work at the local ranches. What would Graciela tell her children when they awoke?

She studied Zane's slumbering face. Bits of Richard's description of his childhood played through her mind. Then memories of her own isolation on the ranch. Now Noemi and

Modesto were losing their father. So many children separated from their parents. It wasn't right. Why did God allow it all?

A moan from across the fire pit drew her from her melancholy thoughts.

Drifting in and out of consciousness, Graciela seemed barely aware of what was happening.

When Clarinda had first entered the home, it took every ounce of her courage not to turn and run from the village. The jagged wounds marring Graciela's once beautiful face were painfully familiar. Though delivered by different means, the result was no less horrific. More so, really. Graciela would need to overcome far more than Clarinda had suffered. She pressed her eyes closed against the sight.

After so many Sundays spent studying the Bible with Richard, Clarinda had begun to hope there might be some truth to his claims that God cared about His people—that He made plans for their good. But what good could come of this?

~

"Look." Simeon pointed toward the road.

Richard followed his finger to a trail of dust. Someone was coming from town. And they were in a hurry.

Richard mounted his horse and raced down the driveway, intercepting a sweaty, frantic Manuel. "Oh, Señor! I've been looking for you." The lad gasped for air. "The Señora. Went to the village. Sent me to find you. You must go. Hurry!"

"Wait a minute, Manuel. Take a breath. Slow down. Do you mean Mrs. Stevens?"

The boy nodded.

"Does she have Zane with her?"

Again he nodded. "Sí. You must go!"

"Go where? What village did she go to and why?"

"Graciela was attacked. The man who came said the captain sent for you, but you weren't here."

The captain had sent for Richard? No, Manuel must have misunderstood. The man from the village must have come for Teodora.

Either way, he now knew where to find his wife and child. "Thank you, Manuel. You've done well. I'm going to change horses before I head out. Can you see that this one is well cared for?"

"Sí, Señor."

A horse nickered behind Richard and he turned.

His uncle and Arnie had followed him.

Simeon nodded. "Shall I come along?"

It was a valiant offer, but the tired man could barely stand upright. "No, you stay. I'm sure Clarinda and Zane are fine. I just want to see for myself."

"Are you certain?" Though he tried to disguise it, Simeon's relief showed itself in his sagging posture.

"Yes, but thank you for offering."

Arnie huffed. "Well, wherever you're going, I'm coming along."

"There's no need. Whatever you think you have to say to my *wife* can be said when we return."

"I said I'm coming."

Richard clenched his jaw. He didn't have time to argue. He needed to reach Clarinda as quickly as possible. Without a word, he spurred his horse to the barn.

Within minutes, he'd saddled a new horse and the two of them were pounding dirt along the northeastern trail.

CHAPTER 33

$\mathcal{T}$he startled scream of a child jolted Clarinda from sleep.

In the flickering light of glowing embers, Modesto scrambled backward in a terrified attempt to escape his mother's outstretched arms.

No! Clarinda's nails bit into her palms.

Modesto's cries mixed with the screams in Clarinda's memory.

This couldn't be happening again. She couldn't breathe.

Graciela whispered to her son while tears streamed down her cheeks.

Clarinda's whole body turned numb.

Noemi held her hands out to her brother and joined in the quiet pleading.

It was hopeless. He'd never come.

But Clarinda couldn't look away.

Then he stilled. He quieted.

She felt dizzy, her eyes blurring. She blinked hard, forcing them to focus.

Modesto's eyes darted back and forth between Noemi and

Graciela. Noemi gestured for him to go to their mother. Modesto shook his head, eyes still wide.

Bile churned in Clarinda's gut.

Graciela's wounds glared red in the firelight. Swelling distorted her features. She was unrecognizable. Of course Modesto was afraid. His mother looked like Clarinda, but she—

The extra veil! She sucked in a breath. Uncertain how long they'd be gone, Clarinda had crammed spare clothes into a bag before leaving the ranch. She withdrew the creamy cotton voile she'd packed and held it up. "I can loan you this, if you like. Maybe it will help."

Graciela's eyes sparked between her swollen eyelids. She said something in Spanish with a firm shake of her head.

"I'm sorry, I don't understand."

Teodora lifted her head from where she'd been sleeping. "She says she won't hide her wounds. Her son will get used to seeing her like this. He just needs time."

Teodora pulled a sweet roll from Clarinda's bag. She handed the paper-wrapped treat to Graciela who offered it to the boy. After only a moment's hesitation, he scooted forward and accepted the food. Graciela pulled him into her embrace, and this time he didn't withdraw.

On his blanket beside Clarinda, Zane began to squirm. The noise had disturbed him. He'd be hungry soon. She tucked him against her side and ran her fingers in soothing circles on his back.

Modesto stretched two fingers to touch his mother's face. Though the contact must have pained her, Graciela didn't pull away.

Clarinda held the veil out to Teodora. "Tell her she can still have this. I'm sure she'll want it later, when she's ready to go outside."

Teodora scowled, but seemed to relay Clarinda's offer.

Again, Graciela shook her head as she spoke.

Clarinda looked to Teodora for confirmation. "She doesn't want it?"

"She says she intends to bear her scars with pride. They are proof that she did not give in to that monster's wicked ways, and a symbol of her courage and survival."

A symbol of her courage and survival. Hadn't Fletcher always encouraged Clarinda to see her own scars in the same way? Her fingers slipped beneath her veil to trace the scars that ran across her cheek. Did Richard see courage and strength when he looked at her?

~

*R*ichard slowed his mount as they neared the village, not wishing to alarm its occupants. The wisdom of this decision was confirmed when they were greeted by twice the usual number of guards.

Beside him, Arnie reached for his rifle.

Richard waved for him to stop. "Do you want to get us killed? Get your hand away from your gun."

"Seems to me you're the one with a death wish. Why'd you bring us here?"

Maybe Richard should have told Arnie where they were going. But talking to his wife's former beau was about as appealing as walking barefoot through a forest of cholla cactus. He narrowed his eyes. "Move. Your. Hand."

Arnie glared back at him, unmoving.

A full second passed.

Then another.

The guards adjusted their stance.

If Arnie didn't comply soon, there'd be trouble.

Finally, Arnie lowered his arm, letting it hang by his side.

Richard surveyed the group of men facing them. Each one was armed and their posture rigid. What had happened here?

Where were Lindy and Zane? Didn't these men recognize Richard? "I'm Richard Stevens. I believe my wife, Clarinda, is here with our child."

Arnie scoffed, but thankfully made no other comment.

One man stepped forward and nodded toward Arnie. "And this man?"

"He's..." Richard fumbled for a way to explain Arnie's presence.

Arnie rolled his eyes. "I'm a friend."

"Uh...yes." *Please, Lord, don't let this man do anything foolish while we're here.*

The man who'd stepped forward waved for Richard and Arnie to dismount.

"Leave horses." He pointed to a nearby tree. "And guns."

Arnie's hand went for his rifle again. "No way."

"Then wait here." Richard dismounted, leaving his own rifle in its saddle holster. "Just don't cause any trouble."

"You're a fool. They're going to shoot you in the back and steal your horse."

"I've been here many times. These people are hard working and honest." Richard tethered his horse to the tree indicated and looked to the guard who'd spoken. "Can someone bring my horse water?"

The Indian nodded and Richard stepped toward the group. "Where's Clarinda?"

Arnie leapt from his horse. "Oh no. You're not going without me." He hurried to tether his mount and joined Richard—without his rifle. The man probably had a knife stashed somewhere. Maybe even a small pistol. He'd better not cause any trouble.

The guard who'd spoken waved for them to follow him into the village.

Halfway to Alvaro and Graciela's home, their guide took an unexpected turn. He stopped beside something long, lumpy, and covered with a blanket. Two boots stuck out the bottom.

Richard's gaze shot to their guide's. "Who's this?"

"Captain ask you tell us." He lifted the blanket to reveal the gruesome remains of a man who'd suffered a painful death.

Richard sucked in a breath. The man was nearly unrecognizable, but his grungy blonde hair and skinny frame were horrifyingly familiar.

"You know him?" Their guide studied Richard.

"Yes." Richard shook his head. "I mean, no. I don't know his name, but he trespassed on our land recently. He attacked our dog and..." What more might he have done had the vaqueros not come to their rescue? Manuel's explanation for Richard's summons to the village echoed in his memory. "Is this the man who attacked Graciela?"

"Sí. Alvaro kill him. Now he gone."

"Alvaro is dead as well?" Richard's throat tightened. If only they'd been able to catch the man after he attacked Beast. None of this would have happened.

"No. He...gone. Captain say..." The man scratched his jaw, staring at the sky. "'No come back for many moons.'"

For the hundredth time, Richard rued his inability to speak fluent Spanish. Though he'd been working to learn the language, his understanding was nowhere near enough to bridge the gap in this conversation. "Alvaro's been banished? Why?"

"He kill white man." The Indian gestured to the body as if that explained everything.

"But he was defending his wife."

The Indian shrugged. "Smith not care."

"What's Smith got to do with any of this?"

The Indian pointed to the body again. "Maybe work for Smith."

Richard had asked Lindy's father about Clarence Smith, and

the older man confirmed Lindy's assessment of the man as brutal and hateful toward anyone he considered his lesser. And the man viewed Indians as lower than animals. If the dead man *had* worked for Smith, the rancher would want revenge. "So send Alvaro to my ranch. I'll protect him."

Arnie blinked. "Why would you do that?"

Richard ignored him. "He shouldn't be punished for defending his wife."

The Indian shook his head. "It done." He turned away. "Come." This time their guide led them to the captain, who asked Richard about the dead man.

Richard conveyed what little he knew and tried to persuade the captain to send someone after Alvaro. The captain insisted Alvaro's presence would cause too much trouble. He instructed Richard to seek his wife and let the matter drop.

Seconds later, Richard and Arnie were approaching Alvaro and Graciela's home as Lindy emerged.

"Richard!" She threw herself into his embrace.

He squeezed her tight as sobs shook her body and tears soaked his shirt. He pressed a kiss to her forehead, relishing the feel of her safe in his arms even as his heart ached with hers. After a moment, he pulled back far enough to see her face. "Are you all right? Where's Zane?"

She took two shuddering breaths and shook her head. "Zane's fine. I'm not hurt, but Graciela and...Alvaro..." Her sobs took over again.

He held her close, stroking her hair. "Oh, honey, it's all right. Everything's going to be all right." He let his eyes fall shut as her tears subsided. *Thank you, Lord, for keeping them safe. Please comfort Graciela and her family as they find their way through these tragic events.*

Arnie shuffled his feet.

Richard glanced up. The man appeared delightfully uncomfortable. Lindy hadn't noticed him yet. Richard smirked.

Arnie cleared his throat.

Lindy finally looked up. And glowered.

Richard resisted the urge to crow.

His wife's arms tightened around his ribs as she twisted to face the intruder. "What are *you* doing here?"

"I came to see if you were all right, Clarie." Arnie took a timid step closer. "I...I thought you might need me." His gaze flickered between Richard and Lindy.

"As you can see, I don't. So just leave like I told you to yesterday."

Yesterday? She'd seen him yesterday? Arnie must have come to the ranch. Exactly how long had he stayed? Maybe Richard should have woken her when he'd come home last night. Was that why she'd been waiting up for him?

Teodora came out, Zane in her arms. "Ah, Mr. Stevens. I'm so glad you've come."

"I'm so sorry about what's happened." He scooped Zane from her and tucked his son against his chest. "How's Graciela? Is there anything I can do?"

Teodora paused. "May I stay here? Only for a night or two. My daughter—"

"Of course." Lindy beat him to answering.

"Absolutely." He nodded. The pain of the day's events had etched new lines in her expression. "Is there anything you need from the ranch? I'm happy to bring it for you tomorrow."

"I can't ask you to do that. People here can provide what I need."

Lindy took Teodora's hands in hers. "Don't be silly. You know you'll be more comfortable in your own clothes and with your own things. What about your Bible?"

Richard's brows rose. Was Lindy's suggestion a sign she was beginning to mend her relationship with their heavenly Father?

Arnie scoffed. "You mean the Indian can read?"

If Richard weren't holding Zane, he'd be hard-pressed not to punch the man. *Lord, help.* "I believe you were asked to leave. I strongly suggest you do so."

"And how am I supposed to do that? You rode so fast I haven't the first clue how to find my way back."

Not my problem. Richard bit back the retort. *God wants us to love our enemies.* Arnie was a pampered rich boy. Leaving him to get lost and die in the wilderness couldn't be considered loving. "Fine. We'll show you the way back, but then you need to leave and never return."

Arnie's expression was inscrutable as he crossed his arms, but he didn't argue.

Richard pulled a small notepad and pencil from his pocket. He handed them to Teodora. "I'm happy to bring you whatever you need. Just make a list so I won't forget anything."

~

A full moon shone low over the western horizon, its bed of twinkling stars fading as the four of them rode into the ranch yard. Clarinda slumped in the saddle. Dawn wouldn't be long in coming. She reined to a stop beside Richard in front of their house. He slid from his horse and assisted her from the saddle. Zane shifted in the rebozo.

Arnie reined his mount to a stop beside them. "Who's that?"

Mother rushed toward them. "There you are!"

"Where have you been?" Father demanded.

Lucy ran behind them. "We've been so worried!"

Clarinda'd completely forgotten today was Friday. Her parents must have arrived shortly after Richard left. She glanced at Richard. "Where's your uncle?"

Father stepped forward. "He told us what happened and we invited him to stay, but he decided to return to the hotel when it got late. Said he had a ship to catch in the morning."

Clarinda clutched Richard's arm with both hands. "Oh, no. I spoiled your evening meal and now I won't get to meet him."

Richard ran his free hand through her disheveled hair. "You haven't spoiled anything. It wasn't your fault things worked out the way they did. I'm sure there'll be another opportunity to meet him."

"But I know how much his visit meant to you and now—"

He shook free of her grip and took her hands in his. "Shh. There'll be plenty of time to talk tomorrow after I've taken Teodora her things."

"Yes, where is Teodora?" Mother looked past them. "I expected her to return with you."

Clarinda crossed her arms. "I told her to stay with her daughter. I'm sorry if that upsets you, but—"

"Don't be ridiculous. Under the circumstances, of course she should stay with her daughter."

"But she said you refused to allow her to visit her daughter."

"What?" Mother's hand fluttered over her chest. "I can't imagine why she...oh. Well, I suppose there was that one time..." She gave a stilted laugh. "But of course I didn't mean it. I was just—"

"Aren't you going to introduce me to your parents?" Arnie slid to the ground.

"Yes, who is this?" Mother eyed Arnie. "Is he a friend of yours, Richard?"

Arnie stuck his hand out, a wicked grin stretching his cheeks. "I'm Zane's father."

"I beg your pardon?" Mother shrank from his outstretched hand.

Father's brows drew together. "I must have misheard you. *Richard* is Zane's father." He turned to Richard. "Isn't that right?"

Richard glanced at her with a pained expression. He'd warned her he wouldn't lie for her. And for the first time, she didn't want him to.

"Richard is Zane's father in every way that matters."

Father's eyes narrowed. "But he isn't the boy's natural father." It was a statement, not a question.

"No." She whispered.

Arnie grinned. "Now that we have that cleared up, I'd like a moment to speak with Clarinda in private."

Richard tugged Clarinda closer. "I don't think so."

Clarinda tightened her grip on Richard's hand. "There's nothing for us to talk about. I told you, I love my husband and you need to leave. Now."

Arnie's mouth opened and closed several times. "Fine. Then I'll be taking my son." He reached for Zane's sleeping form, still cradled against her chest.

CHAPTER 34

Clarinda lurched backward as both Father and Richard jumped between her and Arnie.

"Over my dead body." Richard's fists clenched and unclenched.

Father jabbed a finger toward the drive. "I think you'd better leave."

"But he's *my* son!"

"Quit saying that." Richard fisted Arnie's shirtfront. "You gave up that right the day you abandoned Clarinda at dawn in the middle of nowhere."

"He did what?" She'd never seen Father so furious. His face was a frightening shade of red in the lamplight.

"You get off my property this instant"—Mother pulled a Deringer from her pocket, and Clarinda's knees wobbled. When had her mother started carrying that?—"and don't you ever let me hear that you've come near my daughter or my grandson ever again. Do you hear me, young man?"

Arnie's hands flew into the air as his feet propelled him backward. "Yes, ma'am. I hear you."

"Good." Mother gestured with her weapon toward his horse. "Now get."

In seconds, Arnie had mounted up and disappeared through the trees lining the drive.

Clarinda faced her parents. "I don't know what to say."

"Say you won't ever lie to us like that again." Father's stern expression was laced with pain.

Mother tucked her pistol away, her features pinched. "Why didn't you tell us?"

"Because you said"—tears clogged Clarinda's throat—"no man would ever love me enough to see past my scars. I thought Arnie did, and when he left me, I was too humiliated to admit how foolish I'd been."

Mother gasped. "But I never said that!"

Clarinda's hands fisted. "You did. It's why you sent me to Benicia."

Father frowned. "You misconstrued what we said, entirely."

"Yes." Mother nodded. "We sent you to Benicia because you were wasting away out here. We were afraid you'd never meet a man who could love you if you kept hiding the way you were."

Her sister piped up. "That's right. I'm the one who suggested the school because I was worried you'd have no way to support yourself if you didn't find a man to marry. And who were you going to meet to marry way out here?" She gestured to the ranch yard which was slowly brightening with the glow of dawn.

Clarinda's mind reeled. Could she have misunderstood them so terribly? She'd been so upset that day, all she remembered hearing was *you'll never meet a man who can love you*. Could she have missed so much of what they'd said? "But...but the attack. The reverend. All your friends who wouldn't come to see you. We had to leave our home, give up everything, and come to California because of me. I thought—"

"It's true we moved here partly because we could see what

the rejection back east was doing to you"—Father spread his hands wide—"but I'd been thinking about making the change since my sister relocated here the year before. Truthfully, the only reason we stayed in D.C. as long as we did was because of your singing career. When it became clear that was over...well, it freed me to make the move I'd been wanting to."

"But you never said—"

Father smirked. "You were a child. Such worries were beyond your years." He shook his head, the smirk fading. "I never imagined you'd take our move the way you did."

Clarinda's gaze flickered from face to face, scrambling for any bit of truth as her world tilted around her. "But the scandal. If everyone knew about Zane...who his father really is—"

"*I'm* his father." Richard wrapped his arm around her waist.

Grateful for his comforting touch, she leaned into him. "You know what I mean." She caught her father's gaze. "People would stop coming to your store again like they did after...after..." She gestured toward her hidden scars.

Father reached for her hand. "It's true people can be petty and cruel, but what happened in D.C. wasn't your fault."

"But you wouldn't let me help in the store. I scared the customers away."

"Not any customers we cared about." Father's eyes filled with tears. "We stopped asking you to help because we knew how much you hated being stared at. We thought we were protecting you."

"Then why did you leave me out here?" She pulled her hand free to wave at the darkened ranch yard. "I thought you didn't love me anymore. That you were ashamed and—"

Mother cupped Clarinda's cheek and held her gaze. "Sweetheart, I'm so sorry you ever thought we stopped loving you. We didn't move you to the ranch because we were ashamed of you. We thought we were protecting you—that it was what you needed.

We love you so much. And whatever you've done or been through, and whatever the consequences of your mistakes, we're still your family. We'll always be your family and we'll always love you and be here for you. Even if we don't know exactly how to help you."

Warmth radiated through Clarinda's entire body as she collapsed into her mother's arms. Her father, sister, and darling husband joined in the embrace.

Between them, Zane gave a tiny protest at being pressed so snuggly, and everyone laughed, loosening their grip.

"Well." Mother sighed. "It's been a very long night. I think it best that we all get some sleep and then perhaps"—she wiped at her damp cheeks and sniffed—"we can all enjoy a leisurely morning meal and continue talking. It seems we haven't been doing enough of that." Her speculative gaze bounced between Richard and Clarinda's. "And there seems to be a lot to catch up on."

~

*C*larinda's eyes popped open to bright light streaming through the thin curtains. What time was it? Urgent pressure in her bladder forced her to rise, despite the stiffness in her limbs. Had she moved at all as she slept? She glanced at Zane in his cradle beside the bed. Still sleeping. Good.

She slipped from bed and dressed as swiftly and silently as possible. Leaving the door cracked, she tiptoed to the back door. Richard's coat and hat were missing from their hooks. He must have left to take Teodora the things she'd requested.

Once outside, Clarinda hurried to the privy.

As she straightened her skirts a few minutes later, faint hoof beats sounded through the rough wood walls, then faded away. She exited and scanned the yard. It was quiet and empty. No sign of the rider she'd heard. It must have been one of the vaqueros riding out to take his morning shift guarding the sheep.

Glancing up, she frowned at the gloomy clouds above. It seemed fall was fully upon them. At least it wasn't raining.

Back in the front room, she paused to listen. No sounds of stirring came from the bedroom so she strode toward the kitchen.

It must be near midmorning. Had her parents also slept late or had they managed a morning meal for themselves? With Teodora gone, Clarinda had volunteered to cook everyone the morning meal. To her knowledge, neither Lucy nor Mother had ever prepared a meal. She stoked the fire in the stove. Most likely they were still asleep after last night's ordeal.

We'll always be your family and we'll always love you and be here for you. Clarinda smiled as she greased a pan for eggs. Richard was right. She'd never truly understood her parents, and they'd struggled to understand her. Why hadn't she confronted them with her hurt years ago? How much time had been lost to her prideful silence?

Well, no more. This was a new day and a new beginning.

She looked out the window as the bacon sizzled. Richard had surely made it to Graciela's village by now. How did the young mother fair in the light of day? Did she still believe her wounds were something to be proud of?

Clarinda recalled the many times she'd been shunned for her scars. Maybe things were different in an Indian village. But what about Richard? He loved her with her scars. And her family. All this time, she'd thought they hated her for her scars, but she'd been wrong. Could she have misunderstood others as well? What if the girls at school hadn't been laughing at her as she thought they had? What if they stayed away because she'd made it clear she didn't want friends?

She turned the bacon. There seemed to be a lot of misunderstanding going on. Mother and Father had fully supported

Teodora's decision to remain with her daughter. So it seemed Teodora had also misjudged Mother.

Several minutes later, eggs, bacon, potatoes, and gravy sat warming at the back of the stove as Clarinda finished slicing bread. She set the platter aside and went to the cellar for some jam.

As she reentered the house, she glanced toward the bedroom door and froze. Hadn't she left it cracked?

Yet now it was closed.

She scurried across the room, dropping the jam on the table as she passed it.

Not bothering to be quiet, she threw the bedroom door open and rushed to the cradle.

It was empty.

"Zane!" Her eyes scanned the floor, the bed, and even the walls. "Zane!" She whipped the veil up to rest atop her bonnet, dropped to her knees, and peered beneath the mattress. As if a child who couldn't so much as turn over had somehow crawled away.

But the suspicion clawing at her mind couldn't be true. It was too terrible.

Dashing into the front room, she scanned the area.

Large dusty boot prints traversed the wooden floor, leading to the front door.

Those hadn't been there when she'd gone to the privy.

CHAPTER 35

*C*larinda yanked her veil into place as she flew out the door and across the bridge. In front of the barn, one of the vaqueros was preparing to mount his horse. She snatched the reins from his grasp.

"Fetch Richard!" She grabbed the pommel and hoisted herself into the saddle. "He's gone to Graciela's village." She threw her leg over and secured her feet in the stirrups. "Tell him Arnie stole Zane!"

Without waiting for the man's response, Clarinda kicked the horse into a run, then a gallop. No stages left on Saturday, but there might be a ship sailing for San Francisco. Flying beneath the trees lining their drive, she glanced through their branches to the darkening sky. It looked thick with swiftly moving clouds. Would the ships set sail in such weather? Perhaps. Depending on the captain and his sense of urgency.

Please, Lord, let me get there in time.

*G*usts of wind kicked bursts of dust clouds into the air as Clarinda reined to a stop in front of the Franklin House. Her winded mount heaved with the effort of their journey. "Sorry, girl." She threw the reins around the porch post.

Storming inside, she spotted a man standing behind the desk. "Which room is Arnie Walker staying in?"

She darted toward the stairs.

Sputtering, the man chased her. "You can't go up there!"

"Which room?"

"He's not here."

She spun to face him. "What do you mean?"

"He checked out hours ago."

"Where did he go?"

The man's nose lifted. "I didn't ask, and that isn't the kind of information—"

"But there aren't any stages leaving today, and with this weather, surely no captain would set sail."

The man shrugged. "I heard the *Teresa* might try to beat the storm. Perhaps Mr. Walker purchased a—"

"Do you have someone who can tend my horse?" She glanced through the window. "She's just outside and been ridden hard."

"There's a livery across—"

"Yes, I know that. I don't have time to take her there." She plucked a coin from her pocket and set it on the desk. "See that she gets there."

"But—"

Ignoring the man's protest, she shot outside. Another gust of wind shoved her backward. Her veil pressed against her lips. Sand pelted her neck where the fabric had come loose from her collar. The storm had worsened in only the few minutes she'd been inside. What was going on?

Her horse whinnied and pulled against her tether.

Clarinda glanced at the hotel door. It didn't open. Was the man refusing her request?

She squinted against the wind in the direction of the bay. She needed to get to the ships. If the captain of the *Teresa* were foolish enough to set sail...

No. Don't even think about it. You will find him.

⌒

*L*indy's beautiful sleeping form had tempted Richard not to leave that morning. Nearly home now, he urged his mount into a trot. Would she and her family have finished their morning meal yet? As late as they'd all gotten to bed, they might still be sleeping when he returned. Only his promise to Teodora and an urgency to check on Graciela had moved him from the warmth of their bed.

Blessedly, Graciela's village had rallied around her. The people were doing what they could to comfort the grieving woman and her distressed children. Modesto was too young to understand his father would not be returning for a long time, but he'd picked up on the somber expressions of those around him. His elder sister cried through most of Richard's time there. Even the sweet roll he'd brought hadn't cheered her. Teodora and her sister were doing their best to comfort the family, but nothing they could say or do would erase the tragedy that had befallen them. He prayed God's comforting hand would draw them close and help them find peace.

The pounding of hooves grew louder as he crested the final rise before the ranch came into view. Just yards away, Eduardo rode fast in Richard's direction.

Worry slid up his spine, tensing his shoulders. Something was wrong. Richard urged his horse to close the distance. In moments, they drew alongside one another.

"What is it?" *Please let Zane and Lindy be safe.*

"Mr. Walker came back. He stole Zane, and Mrs. Stevens went after him."

Richard kicked his horse into a run.

Eduardo raced up beside him.

"How long ago did this happen?"

"Not sure when he took the boy, but Mrs. Stevens left maybe an hour ago. I was on my way back when I saw her race out. I came to get you right away."

"What about her parents?"

"They went after her, but they took a wagon."

Richard reined to a halt in the yard and jumped from his horse. The wind whipped with unusual strength as he raced toward the corral for a fresh mount.

～

*C*larinda's horse made another distressed sound, so she turned toward the porch post instead of the bay. She yanked the reins free, sped across the plaza, and pounded on the livery door. What seemed like hours, but was probably only seconds later, the door cracked open.

The liveryman frowned at her. His lips moved, but the wind stole his words.

"What?" She leaned closer.

"I asked what you're doing out in this weather?'"

She shoved her reins into his hands. "I need you to see to this horse. I'll pay for her care when I return."

Not waiting for the man's reply, she spun and ran toward the bay.

Or tried to.

With the wind pushing against her, her run was like a crawl. Her lungs burned with the effort. More and more sand stung her skin wherever it wasn't protected.

The veil forced itself into her mouth and she choked. She yanked it free. A gust stole the cloth from her grasp. In a blink, the sheer fabric was gone.

Sand stung her cheeks, her chin. She closed her eyes against the onslaught. Still pressing forward, her progress was slow.

Had they ever had a storm such as this?

Her bonnet blew free, and its strings strangled her for a moment. Then they, too, gave way. She glanced back. Her hat sailed high over the roof of the Morenos' house.

Facing forward again, she could see no more than a few feet ahead. The world was nothing but a thick cloud of whirling dust. It filled her nose, her mouth, her ears. It shoved her backward like an enemy determined to keep her away.

She could not—would not give in. Zane was out here somewhere.

She spit the dirt from her mouth. Covering her nose with her gloved hand, she forced one foot in front of the other.

CHAPTER 36

*T*he plaza swirled thick with dust as Richard rode into its center two hours later. Something about this storm didn't feel right. He'd passed Lindy's family on the road and urged them to go back. They'd refused.

So he'd raced on. If he could locate Lindy and Zane quickly, they could all return to the ranch to ride out the storm.

Rain began to fall as he dismounted in front of the livery. Huge, muddy droplets pelted him. He pounded a fist against the closed door.

Across the road, a tree bent at an alarming angle. Its roots were breaking free of the earth. A long second passed, then two. With a thunderous tear, the tree ripped loose and flew down the street. It crashed into a fence.

Richard's horse reared. He wasted precious time calming the animal down. Eventually, confident the horse wouldn't bolt, Richard grabbed the door handle and pried. The wood slab wouldn't budge.

He pounded until a loud scraping informed him the locking bar was being lifted.

The door cracked open.

Richard shoved his reins at the glowering liveryman and shouted, "Can you take my horse?"

The man accepted the reins and shouted back, "Though I can't know why you'd be out in a storm like this." He pushed the door wider to admit the horse. "You and that woman ain't right in the head, if you ask me."

Richard helped him hold the door open against the gusting squall. "What woman?"

"That one with the funny coverings who—"

"Which way did she go?" Richard tipped his head so the rain streaming down his forehead would bypass his eyes.

The man pointed toward the road leading to the bay. The sheeting rain made it impossible to see the ships' masts.

With the horse and liveryman finally inside, Richard let the door slam. He held it closed until the bar scraped into place. With the door secure, he turned and shoved his way through the angry downpour.

∾

*R*ain battered the fabric of Clarinda's dress as she pressed toward the bay.

A huge shadow, more than twenty feet tall and at least as wide, darkened the space before her. *What on earth?* There were no houses here.

Another gust knocked her to her knees.

Rain pounded her as the winds howled.

Wood groaned and creaked. She squinted at the shadow. Could it be a ship? Was she closer to the water than she'd thought?

The shadow lunged forward. It formed into a schooner as it surged toward her, driving a gouge into the muddy earth.

A scream ripped from her throat as she flung herself out of its path. She curled into a ball. Covered her head with her arms.

Debris sailed overhead and kicked around her.

She tried to rise but wasn't strong enough.

Crawling through the mud, she retreated from shore. It was too much.

This storm was like nothing she'd ever seen. Though it was the middle of the day, black clouds blocked the sunlight, shrouding the world in shadows as dark as night. It was as though the devil himself had charged into their small town.

Lord, protect my child. Please. Where had Arnie stopped to wait out the storm? Surely not on a boat. Tears formed in her eyes, but the wind whipped the drops away before they could touch her cheeks.

Her head bumped into something solid. Reaching up, her fingers grazed the rough exterior of an adobe wall. Where was she? It took all her strength to raise onto her knees. Still, it was impossible to see through the swirling mud and rain. Trailing her hand along the wall, she searched for an opening—some way to escape the storm.

A section of torn-up fencing shattered against the adobe, inches above her head.

Screaming, she ducked.

Another huge shadow loomed near the shore. Groaning, splintering wood filled the air. *Dear Lord, is anyone aboard those ships? Where are Arnie and Zane? Please, God. Please, keep them safe!*

A chunk of debris slammed into her legs, bruising her shins through the fabric of her skirts. She cried out in pain. The wind whipped the shattered wood away.

Please God, save me and Zane. Not even Arnie should die like this. Please, Lord. Save us all. Was God listening? Did He really care as Richard said He did—as His Word promised?

Warm hands grabbed her shoulders.

Her head flew up, eyes popping open. "Richard!" Her limbs wobbled, threatening to give way.

He pulled her onto her knees beside him. "Come on!"

Placing his body between her and the worst of the wind, he led her along the wall.

They reached a corner and a gust of wind slammed into her. Without the support of the wall, the storm's fury almost toppled her.

~

*R*ichard tugged on Lindy's arm. "Come on!"

She shook her head, trying to curl into the ball she'd been in when he'd found her.

The shape of a door darkened the center of the next wall. He pointed at it. "Look!"

She squinted and must have seen it, because she started inching forward again.

With their backs to the thrust of the storm, he nearly fell on his face. His arms shook with the effort of remaining upright. How was Lindy managing it?

Finally, they arrived at the door. Richard pulled the lever. The door slammed open and they toppled inside, his body collapsing onto hers.

He rolled off. "Are you all right?"

"I'm fine."

Together, they shoved until the door latched into place.

Richard stood on shaking legs and felt around in the dark. They were in some kind of shed. The place was filled with barrels, crates, and other stored items. He grabbed Lindy's hand and placed it atop the nearest barrel. "Help me move this."

With the barrel pressing the door shut, they sank to the ground. *Please let it hold.*

Faint, gray light filtered through gaps near the shuddering roof, illuminating the tears coursing down Lindy's cheeks. His hand sought hers and squeezed it. "Are you sure you're all right?"

She nodded and threw herself against his chest. "Oh Richard, I'm so scared! Where is Zane? What if he's out there?"

Something crashed against the shed as he stroked a hand across her back. "Wherever he is, I'm sure God's watching over him. And He loves Zane even more than we do."

She stared at him, eyes wide. "He heard me."

He rubbed the tears from her cheeks with his thumbs, leaving dirty streaks in their wake. "What do you mean?"

"I prayed. I asked God to save me, and the next moment you were there. How did you find me?"

He smiled. "I prayed too."

"You did?"

He combed his fingers through her disheveled hair, needing the feel of her to reassure him she was safe. "I was terrified for you. Especially when I saw that ship crashed so far on shore and with so much debris flying around. I nearly turned back, but I knew you were out there. I knew you wouldn't stop unless you had no choice. But there was so much rain and mud, I could barely see a thing." He cupped her cheek. "I begged God to help me find you, and He did. Just like He brought me to you that day on the wharf, and how He brought me to San Diego."

"What do you mean?"

A fierce gust rattled the door and shook the rafters, drawing Richard's gaze. Would the roof hold? If the winds could force full-sized schooners ashore, would this tiny shed withstand the fury?

He pressed Lindy closer. "When you took off running from that dog. I lost sight of you, but then the Lord parted the crowd and I saw that pup sniffing at the pile of crates you'd hidden in."

"And San Diego? What do you mean, He brought you here?"

He swallowed, sensing that the time had finally come to tell her the whole truth. Would she have faith in God's guidance or dismiss Richard's dream as only that—a dream?

CHAPTER 37

Clarinda gaped at him. "You heard my name in your dream?" She'd never heard of such a thing.

"Yes, *Clarinda*. It was perfectly clear."

"But—"

The roof sheered away from the walls, ripping into the sky like a sheet of paper. Wind drove rain down on them like a thousand stinging bees.

"Quick." Richard reached for a barrel. "Help me move this."

The four thick walls of the adobe shielded them from flying debris as they worked to arrange barrels and crates to form a makeshift cave. Once finished, he gestured for Lindy to duck beneath them. Raised from the flooding floor by a layer of smaller crates, she stretched her body between two rows of barrels, with larger crates lined across the top. The makeshift roof leaked, but it was better than nothing. Thankfully, the height of the walls kept the wind from swooping in to blow the heavy barrels and crates around.

Richard knelt near her feet and peered in. "It's a bit tighter than I hoped. Can you roll on your side?"

Once there was room, he slid in beside her and wrapped her

in his arms. She returned his embrace and their legs intertwined as he pulled her closer still. His warmth flowed through her.

She tapped his back. "I don't remember Fletcher telling you my Christian name."

"He didn't." Richard used his nose to wipe a drop trailing across her temple. "Not directly. But he called you *Clarinda* when he found you upset and missing your veil."

She'd forgotten about that. "Then what happened? In your dream, I mean."

"I woke up knowing the name and the dream had meant something important, but not sure what. God led me to the first book of Matthew, specifically the verses about an angel appearing to Joseph in his dreams."

She cocked a brow at him. "You didn't think I was an angel, did you?"

The door of the shed rattled.

"Of course not. But the verse about Joseph waking up and taking Mary as his wife stood out to me. And I knew. God had given me my wife's name." He smoothed some of the mud from her cheeks. "It took me a while to remember where I'd heard your name. When I did, I searched all over San Francisco for you."

"So that's why, when you proposed, you said God had chosen me to be your wife." Water dripped into her eye and she blinked it away. "I thought you were a crazy zealot, but I was so desperate." She managed a small shrug in their cramped space. "I figured a man that passionate about religion wouldn't beat his wife or come home drunk."

Richard cringed. "I wish I could say that were true of anyone calling themselves a Christian, but even the saved still struggle with sin."

"That's true. Which was why I also considered the other things I knew about you."

"But what could you have known?"

It was her turn to stroke mud from his cheek. "I knew you were compassionate and generous, because you noticed my sickness and offered me the candy you'd obviously purchased for someone else. I knew you were brave and loyal, because, though I was almost a stranger, you ran all the way down the wharf and shooed that dog away from me."

Something clattered against the roof of their cave and she gasped.

Richard stroked her hair. "Are you all right?"

She nodded and bit her lip. What had she been talking about? Oh, right. "From your conversation with Fletcher, I knew you were intelligent, hard working, and successful. I knew you were respectful because you didn't pursue continuing our acquaintance when I dragged Fletcher away that day, instead of letting him invite you to dine with us. I knew you were self-controlled and forgiving because you didn't lash out when I kicked you in the face as reward for trying to help me."

Richard winced. "That did hurt."

"And most importantly, I knew you were kind, patient, and considerate because you didn't immediately reveal my deception to my family, but gave me a chance to explain myself." Three attributes she'd come to realize described the core of who Richard was and why she'd fallen in love with him.

"All that, you learned from seemingly miserable, terrifying circumstances." Richard shook his head. "Imagine if you hadn't gotten seasick that morning. Or if that dog hadn't chased you."

"You're right." Tingling ran over her skin. "If those things hadn't happened, I'd not have known any of that." But what did that mean? "Do you think—?"

A crate they hadn't used toppled to the floor with a thunderous crash and Lindy startled.

Richard tipped his head. "Do I think what?"

She swallowed. "Do you think God made those things

happen so I would know what to do when you showed up?" Was that something a loving Father would do?

"I think God used those unhappy circumstances to bless you. I think God works all the details in our life together for our good, though it's often difficult for us to see it."

That made more sense.

Something crashed through the open roof to the floor of the shed and Richard shifted his body so he was slightly above her. If their cave collapsed, he'd protect her. Her husband was incredible.

"It's like this storm." Richard stroked her arm. "He didn't prevent it from coming and He hasn't made it stop. But He used it and me to demonstrate His love and care for you, by helping me find you at exactly the right moment and by providing us with this shelter." He gestured to the walls protecting their cave from the worst of the tempest.

It was so much to take in. Did God truly care so much about everything in her life? About her? Was He watching over her not just today, but always?

A thick splinter jabbed Clarinda's back. She shifted away from it. "But what about San Diego? You said He brought you here."

He told her about his conversation with her friend Katie and receiving the letter from Henry.

More water dribbled through the cracks onto her face, and she wiped it away. "So you knew? Even before I saw you that day on the plaza, you knew I was here?"

"I knew your family was here." He squeezed her gently. "I hoped you were, too."

She wiped a wet lock of hair from his forehead. "You sure weren't expecting what you found, though."

He smiled. "That's for certain."

His lips brushed hers and for a moment the world drifted away.

Her chest ached with the need to feed Zane. *Lord, where is he?* Richard's eyes softened and he touched his forehead to hers. "He'll be all right, Lindy. God's with him just as He's always been with us. But I promise, we'll go look for Zane as soon as it's safe to go out again."

It was incredible how many things God had worked out to bring Richard into her life. Like her veil being lifted, Clarinda's memory flooded with other ways God had used negative events for her good.

The day she'd been attacked by that dog in the back alley, everyone was supposed to be at the front of the house where they wouldn't have heard her screams. But their maid had broken a valuable vase and come out back to dispose of the evidence. It was she who'd sounded the alarm that spared Clarinda's life that day.

Though her aunt and uncle's move north meant the loss of Fletcher's companionship in San Diego, it meant her cousin was close enough to render aid when Clarinda needed it most.

Even her misguided, sinful choice to cross that line with Arnie, God had used to bring her Richard and give her Zane.

"You're right. I can see it now. He's been with me all along. I just didn't believe it." Hope pierced her fear like a beacon in the storm. "God really does care about me."

He pulled her close and pressed a kiss to her wet hair. "He does."

Closing her eyes, she snuggled against Richard's shoulder. He'd said before that she could pray in her mind as if she was talking out loud to God—that God just wanted to hear what was on her heart. She took a deep breath. *Thank You for taking care of me all these years. I'm sorry I didn't see it before. Please keep my child safe and help me to find him as soon as possible.*

CHAPTER 38

*N*ight had truly set in by the time the storm calmed enough for them to venture from their shelter. Though rain still gushed to the ground like the Lord was emptying His bathtub, the wind had ceased its violent assault. Clarinda clung to Richard's hand as they scurried through the deluge, picking their way around piles of roofing, downed fences, shattered wagons, and the remains of a windmill. They had to climb over a large tree to reach the front steps of her parents' store. Light glowed through the gaps around the shuttered doorways.

Richard tried the latch but the door was locked.

Father answered Richard's knock.

"Clarinda!" Father pulled her into his arms as Mother crossed the crowded store.

"Oh thank the good Lord, you're both safe!" Mother's arms joined Father's in holding her close.

Clarinda returned their embrace. Two hugs in as many days? And in public. It was more than she could fathom.

Wait. Her bonnet and veil were probably halfway to Los Angeles by now. She was uncovered.

She buried her face in Father's coat. Had he noticed her scars?

A symbol of courage and survival. Graciela's words stiffened Clarinda's spine. It was time to stop hiding who she was.

Clarinda lifted her chin.

Father beamed at her, and Mother cupped her cheek. "It's so good to see your beautiful face."

Mother thought she was beautiful? Clarinda forced words past the lump in her throat. "Where's Zane?"

Richard wrapped his arm around Clarinda's shoulders. "We weren't able to find him in the storm. We were hoping you might have some news."

Clinging to the arm of her fiancé, Lucy joined them. "We barely made it to the store, but as soon as the wind died down, Father went to the hotel to see if Mr. Childs had seen you."

"My uncle?" Richard straightened beside her.

A man who looked strikingly like an older version of her husband stepped forward. "Of course, I had to tell them I hadn't seen you." He held his hand out to Richard. "I'm so glad you're safe."

Richard accepted the man's grasp. "I thought you'd sailed."

"I planned to until I saw the sky this morning." He tapped his weak knee. "And my bones told me not to board. I'm glad I listened. Your father-in-law tells me that man, Walker, has taken your son. Is that true?"

"Yes, and if he's not here, we need to keep searching. Perhaps—"

"I've been asking the neighbors." Father gestured to a small crowd of people filling the store's aisles behind Lucy and her fiancé. "No one's seen Mr. Walker or Zane, but they're all willing to help."

Clarinda braced herself for the gasps and whispers before turning to fully face the others in the room.

The usual reactions didn't come.

A few studied her with open curiosity, but not one person turned away or showed any sign of fear or disgust.

She glanced at Richard. He gave her shoulder a squeeze and lifted his voice. "We appreciate any help you're willing to give. We don't believe the man who took Zane intends to harm him, but he does intend to take him away from us. We're told he checked out of his room at the Franklin House sometime this morning. Most likely, he's on board one of the ships in the bay, or else hiding out somewhere here in town. I don't think he'd have tried to leave by horseback, but if someone wants to check with the liveryman, that would be appreciated. I'll be starting at the bay."

Father strode toward the door. "I can speak with Mr. Gladstone at the livery."

"I'll come with you." Mr. Childs followed Father. "If the man has taken to the road, we can set off after him together."

The two men disappeared outside as Lucy's fiancé stepped forward. "I'll check the hotel again. Maybe with the storm he came back."

Everett Thompson came forward next. "I can go with you to check the ships. Most of them were emptied when we knew the storm was coming, but I don't think everyone returned to town."

More men volunteered to search other locations, and soon every man in the place had set off into the rain, in search of Zane.

Richard drew her into a tight hug. "I'll find him. Don't you worry." He let go and stepped toward the door where Mr. Thompson waited.

"I won't"—she lifted her chin—"because I'm coming with you."

He frowned. "Don't you want to wash up and change into something dry? I don't want you getting sick."

"Do you honestly think I'm going to stay here and take a bath while my baby is missing?"

He sighed. "Not really, but I had to try." He took her hand. "Let's go, then."

"Wait!" Mother hurried forward, two wool-lined coats in her hands. "At least take these."

~

*R*ain continued to fall as they dashed through the main section of town and crossed the mostly barren land separating the settlement from the bay. Like toy ships tossed in the fit of a toddler's tantrum, the *Plutus* and the *Lovely Flora* sat high and dry on the shore. Clarinda's gaze followed the long gouge marking the *Plutus's* path across land. If she'd stood four feet to the left... A shudder passed through her.

Richard cast her a worried glance. "You all right?"

"By the grace of God."

His gaze moved between her and the *Plutus*. He wrapped an arm around her waist and kissed the top of her head. "Praise God."

Farther on, another ship listed sideways in the dock where it'd been under repair. Only two schooners appeared to have ridden out the gale without harm—the *Clarissa Andrews* and the *Teresa*.

"Thank you, Lord." Richard's whispered prayer matched her own as they hurried toward the farthest ship.

It took several minutes of shouting and waving to get the attention of the crew aboard the *Teresa*. But it was soon clear the crew had no intention of rowing to shore for them.

"Look there." Mr. Thompson pointed to a dinghy more than a hundred yards away. It lay upside down beside the nearest building.

They ran for it. Blessedly, the oars were hidden beneath its hull.

It took all three of them several minutes to half drag, half shove the small boat to the water.

Mr. Thompson held it still and Richard deposited Clarinda inside. He and Mr. Thompson gave the dinghy a shove, then leapt aboard. They grabbed the oars and rowed hard toward the *Teresa*.

When they drew near, several sailors and a man who appeared to be the captain gaped at them from the deck. "Are ye mad? Why'd ye be wantin' to board in this foul weather?"

Quickly, Richard explained the situation. As soon as the sailors understood a small child was in danger, they threw a rope ladder over the side of the ship.

Mr. Thompson climbed up first.

Richard gripped the ladder as their dinghy swayed with the waves. He shouted at the crew watching them from above. "Can you anchor a rope and toss the other end down for my wife?"

Moments later, Richard finished securing the rope around her waist. "Now you go."

The ladder felt slick beneath her hands. "What if I fall?"

"I'll be right behind you."

Clarinda tested the bottom rung with her boot. It slipped. She swallowed against her rolling stomach. *Zane might be up there.* She tightened her grip. *Just start climbing and don't look down.*

In both an eternity and a blink, she was standing on the deck with Richard beside her.

The captain shook his head at them. "I havn'a seen any babes aboard. But if he's wee as you say, mayhap the caitiff smuggled him in his luggage." He ordered all passengers to present themselves above deck.

Clarinda held her breath as man after man emerged to stand in the driving rain. It wasn't fair to those who'd done no wrong, but were forced to shiver as they waited for Arnie to appear. But it was the captain's orders, and she'd do anything to find Zane.

As the minutes passed, Clarinda's knees weakened. What if he wasn't here?

Richard's arm came around her waist, steadying her.

A man with slicked-back, wavy-brown hair and a pointed goatee emerged from below.

"There he is!" She charged across the deck.

What looked like a small package wrapped in brown paper peeked from beneath Arnie's coat. *Zane?*

Arnie's gaze darted around as his hands covered the bundle. He broke right, making a beeline for one of the ship's dinghies.

CHAPTER 39

a sailor caught him by the arm and dragged him to Clarinda. "This him, ma'am?"

"Yes." She pointed to the paper-wrapped bundle. "I think that's my baby."

Arnie tried to shake loose of the crewman's tight hold. "It's just my breakfast. I haven't eaten yet. The seas are too—"

A loud cry erupted from the package, making any further protest pointless.

Richard grabbed Arnie's other arm and held him firm as Clarinda pried her son from Arnie's grasp. Zane's scrunched up face wailed at her from an opening in the damp paper.

She hugged the babe to her and dashed for shelter from the rain through the doorway the passengers had been exiting from. A steep set of stairs descended to a long, narrow hallway. Out of the weather, she stopped and peeled the paper disguise from Zane. She pressed her back to the wall and sank to the floor so she could set him in her lap and unwrap the blanket Arnie had bundled him in.

"Shh, my sweet boy. Mama's here. I'm here." Beneath the blanket, Zane wore the same nightgown he'd been put to sleep in, and his napkin was soppy wet, but his little hands and feet, arms and legs seemed to be as healthy as they'd been that morning. "Thank you, Jesus!" She pressed kiss after kiss over every inch of his skin as he wailed his protest of being undressed.

"Here." Richard's voice brought her attention to where he stood offering her a clean napkin. "Your mother handed it to me as we left."

She changed Zane into the fresh cloth, removed the soiled gown, and rewrapped him in the warm blanket. His crying subsided as she tucked him beneath her coat and his body warmed. "I hope my wet bodice doesn't soak through his blanket."

Richard lifted the collar of her coat. He leaned in to give the boy a kiss and stroke his cheek. "He's all right? No harm done?"

She raised her gaze to meet her husband's face. "He seems well."

Richard exhaled. "Thank you, Lord."

"Here." Behind Richard, Mr. Thompson held out his frock coat. "Wrap him in this."

Richard took it and handed the garment to Clarinda, but she hesitated. "Won't you be cold?" His overcoat didn't look as snug as the coats she and Richard wore.

Mr. Thompson waved her concern away. "I'll be fine, but we've got to keep that tiny one warm and dry. He's been through enough today without suffering a chill."

"Thank you." She drew Zane out. The dampness of her bodice had indeed begun to dampen the outer layer of the blanket. She wrapped the loaned garment around her son and returned him to the warmth of her coat.

Passengers began filing down the stairs, and Clarinda stood to let them pass. The captain entered and led her, Richard, and Mr. Thompson to the dining salon. Two crewmen followed with Arnie in their grip.

He struggled as they dragged him inside. "You can't arrest

me. He's my son. Mine! You can't arrest me for taking my own son."

Mr. Thompson jabbed a finger at Arnie. "Quit lying. Everyone in town knows that boy belongs to Mr. and Mrs. Stevens."

"I'm not lying. Just ask her." Arnie's face was red as he turned his glare on her.

Mr. Thompson stepped forward, his fists clenched. "You shut your mouth, or I'll shut it for you."

Arnie's nostrils flared, his gaze bouncing between her and Mr. Thompson. "Tell them the truth. Tell them I'm Zane's father."

"You aren't his father." Clarinda wrapped her arms around Zane's tiny body. No matter what had happened between her and Arnie, he wasn't Zane's father. True fathers loved their children and protected them as Richard had done from the moment he learned of Zane's existence. No loving father would do what Arnie had done. "You stole him from me and took him out in a storm that could have killed him."

"You left me no choice. And how could I know about the storm? I didn't think—"

"That's just the point! You didn't think. You never think about anyone but yourself." As she spoke, her voice grew louder and Zane made small fussing noises. She shifted the angle of her arms and he settled.

Keeping her gaze on Arnie, she lowered her voice, though her tone remained firm. "There's always a choice, and you chose your own selfish wants and desires over those of Zane's. Just like you did"—aware of her audience, Clarinda chose her words carefully—"before. Just like you always do. That isn't love, Arnie. It's selfishness and pride." She tipped her head to the side. "What did you plan to do once you got him to Benicia? How were you going to care for him?"

Arnie lifted the canteen hanging from his neck. "I've got milk and—"

"Have you even considered the effect Zane's presence would have on your political career? You aren't married. If you claim him as your son, what does that imply? Think of the scandal that would cause. Do you really want to deal with that? You realize they'd call him a bastard. Is that what you want? For Zane to live with such a title?"

"They wouldn't dare. I—"

"True love means putting the good of those you love ahead of your own." She shifted Zane's weight to one arm and took Richard's hand. "Can you honestly say you'll do that for Zane?"

Silence reigned as she rubbed circles on her son's back through the coat. She felt the stares of everyone in the room, but kept her focus on the man who held Zane's future in his hands. If he chose, Arnie could expose them all to scandal. He could ruin Zane's future. Or, he could show the bit of goodness she still believed he harbored deep behind his arrogant exterior, and place his son's needs above his own. But she couldn't make the choice for him.

Please, God, let him choose Zane's good. Just this once, let him think of someone other than himself.

Arnie's shoulders slumped. "I..." His voice trailed off and he cleared it twice before continuing. "I suppose you're right. I'm not sure what I was thinking. Clearly I'm not..." He swallowed, his eyes darting around the room. "I'm not the boy's father. I guess I got confused for a while, but...I'm not a kidnapper." His hands trembled. "They're talking about turning me over to the sheriff. I can't go to jail. It'll ruin everything."

Richard's grip tightened in hers. "You should have thought of that before you stole my son."

Arnie scowled. "He's not—"

"No one's taking you to the sheriff." She couldn't let them argue. Arnie was close to agreeing to what was best for Zane, but if he felt threatened or humiliated he'd retreat beneath his arrogance.

Beside her, Richard tensed. She faced him, and his eyes seemed to search her soul. Finally, he nodded. He'd support whatever she decided.

Her attention returned to Arnie. His teeth were clenched, though his chin quivered.

She widened her stance. "You won't be taken to jail. Not if you promise to leave and never come back—to never try to take Zane from us again."

"I promise."

She turned her gaze to the crewmen still holding him. "You can release him."

The men looked to their captain, who looked to her. "Are you certain that's what you want, ma'am?"

"I'm sure."

The captain rubbed his beard as he eyed Arnie. "What'd you say your name was?"

"Uh, Arnold Walker."

"I've got friends up north. Seems to me they've mentioned a Walker family." He gestured to Clarinda. "She mentioned Benicia. That where you're from?"

"Yes, sir."

"Wait." Mr. Thompson eyed Arnie. "You're Mitchell Walker's son?"

"I...uh—"

"I got a letter a few weeks back saying he'd passed on and left everything to his son." The businessman eyed Arnie head to toe. "That's you?"

Arnie's Adam's apple bobbed. "Yes, sir."

"Sorry for your loss." The words were right, but Mr. Thompson didn't appear the least bit mournful as he crossed his arms. "I did a fair amount of business with your father. We've a large number of associates in common. I don't think those men would approve of—"

"No!" Arnie struggled against his captors' hold. "You can't tell them."

Clarinda gasped and Zane startled in her arms. "But—"

Mr. Thompson held his hand up to silence her as Zane began wailing, but the shrewd businessman kept his gaze on Arnie. "Oh, I assure you, I *can* tell them, and they'd trust what I had to say. But I won't, *if* you keep your word to Mrs. Stevens, never to bother them again."

Clarinda held her breath as she jiggled Zane.

Arnie nodded so vigorously, she thought he'd injure his neck. "I won't. I mean, I will. I mean, I'll leave them alone. I promise."

The captain finally gave the nod to his crewmen, and the sailors released Arnie.

He smoothed the wrinkles in his coat sleeves as he studied Mr. Thompson. "You really won't say anything?"

Zane's whole body writhed, his wails deafening. She undid enough coat buttons to slip her hand through the slit and pop her little finger into his mouth. His tiny lips latched on and started sucking. Her poor boy was clearly starving, but she couldn't feed him in front of all these men. "Just a few more minutes, darling," she murmured against his cheek as she searched for a means of privacy.

Mr. Thompson held out his hand. "I won't, if you don't."

As the two men shook, Zane spit out her finger and screamed.

All eyes turned on her and her cheeks warmed. "I, uh, need to feed him."

"Of course." The captain motioned for everyone else to leave. "You can have the room."

As Clarinda popped her finger back into Zane's mouth, the crewmen exited, followed by Mr. Thompson.

The captain was behind them, but stopped in the doorway. Arnie hadn't budged.

The captain crossed his arms. "Mr. Walker?"

"I'm coming. I just..." Arnie's attention was fixed on Zane. "Might you be planning a visit north, soon? I understand Mr. Stevens has a mine in Nevada City."

How did he know that? Had he been investigating Richard? She glanced at her husband, who shrugged, as if to say he was as surprised by Arnie's knowledge as she.

Arnie took a step closer to them. "Would you consider letting me come visit you, while you're up there?" Arnie rubbed his arms where they were likely sore from being held so tightly. "I promise, I won't cause any trouble. I just...now that I've seen him, held him...I can't stand the thought of never seeing him again."

Zane sucked noisily as Clarinda considered Arnie. She wanted to tell him no. He had absolutely no right to have any part in Zane's life, but... She looked down at her son. Would he hate her for keeping Arnie away?

Richard pulled her to the far corner of the room.

His voice was low as he leaned close. "It's up to you, but it might be something to consider. I know what it's like to wonder whether anyone in this world shares the same traits as you. I won't lie to Zane about his parentage."

"But when do we tell him? How? A young child can't be expected to carry such a secret."

Richard shrugged. "I don't know. Maybe we wait and see how he grows? We can wait for signs that he's mature enough to handle the truth and won't be tempted to share it with others until he's ready to handle the consequences. What do you think?"

"I think it's as sound a plan as any. But what about Arnie?"

"Zane's bound to have questions about him that we can't

answer. If we can find a way to keep Zane safe and still have Arnie around to answer those questions, it might be best."

Slowly, she nodded. As much as she longed to have Arnie out of her life and leave her past mistakes behind her, the little life nestled against her would forever bind them. If it was in Zane's best interest to be able to ask Arnie questions when he was ready, she needed to do what she could to ensure that was an option for her son.

She strode to stand in front of Arnie, Richard at her side. "We'll consider what you've requested. It won't be any time soon, but sometime...in the future...when *we* feel Zane's ready." She lifted one shoulder. "We can figure something out. For Zane's sake."

Richard jabbed a finger at Arnie. "But only if you keep your word not to cause any trouble or contact us. *We'll* reach out to *you* when he's ready."

CHAPTER 40

*C*larinda set the last of the pies on the kitchen table to cool and reached for her apron strings. Callous fingers brushed hers away and loosed the garment for her. Taking her by the hips, Richard spun her around. He tossed the apron aside and drew her into his arms. She lifted her chin to receive his kiss and reveled in the taste of him.

He maneuvered her against the wall and pressed his body against hers.

She broke their kiss with a scolding grin. "Husband! You know we have guests outside whom we cannot neglect."

He growled playfully, his lips following the curve of her neck. "Forget about them."

"You know we cannot." She laughed and pushed him away. "You're the one who invited every neighbor within a day's ride to celebrate Alwina's third birthday." Their second daughter, a golden-mopped cherub, had half the town wrapped around her little finger, so almost everyone who'd been invited had come to share in the festivities. "Not to mention Fletcher is bound to come looking if we disappear for too long."

Fletcher had arrived unannounced two days prior and made himself comfortable in the guest room Richard had built onto the back of their house. Her cousin claimed it was his right, as the "orchestrator of their domestic bliss," to arrive whenever he chose and stay however long he wished. And he'd been doing so for years.

"I suppose you're right." Richard's little boy pout was enough to rival seven-year-old Zane's. "Your mother sent me to find out what's keeping our son."

"What do you mean?"

Richard sighed. "She asked him to sing for everyone, and you know he adores her, so he promised he would. But while your father and I were moving the piano into the yard, Zane disappeared *somewhere.*" He gave her a pointed look.

She nodded. "I'll go and fetch him." She wiped the flour from her hands and scooped her "bit of sunshine" from the bowl she kept it in when she baked. The yellow diamond circled with tiny seed pearls was too precious to coat in dough. Richard had given her the replacement wedding ring on their one year anniversary, saying it was "a bit of sunshine for the light of my life." She slipped it onto her finger, checked her hair in the mirror, and hurried outside.

She wove her way through the gathering of folks over-flowing the courtyard. They spilled into the space between the main house and the home she and Richard occupied with their three children. Though it wasn't the first party they'd hosted at the ranch in the past few years, it still seemed strange to have so many people visiting the place where she'd lived so long in near isolation.

The visiting pastor's wife stepped into Clarinda's path. "There you are dear. Thank you so much for inviting us." She nodded toward her husband, who stood several feet away laughing at something two other men were saying. "I haven't seen him this relaxed in weeks." The woman turned to survey the happily milling crowd. "In fact, I think this is just what our community needed right now." She took Clarinda's hands and gave them a squeeze. "Thank you."

"It's my pleasure, I assure you."

It had been seven years since Thompson contacted the former Texas Ranger about investigating the livestock rustling plaguing their region. At the time, he'd been otherwise employed, so it took him over a year to arrive. Then he'd been shot his first month on the job. That took him six months to recover from. Since then, he'd been slowly rounding up locals involved in the thefts. All told, eleven men had been arrested, tried, and either hung or sent to jail—including Clarence Smith and three of his neighbors.

Clarinda had been horrified—though not surprised—to learn that the flock of sheep Graciela's attacker had been guarding all those years ago hadn't belonged to the Smith Ranch. The true shock had come in learning that the sheriff had been accepting bribes to look the other way. His had been the final arrest.

The entire affair had shaken their community, leaving a pall of distrust between neighbors. It was wonderful to see them chatting and happy again.

Clarinda returned the woman's squeeze and excused herself. She darted toward the small flower garden Richard had helped her start two years ago. Hedged with mesquite, the secluded space originally designed as Clarinda's sanctuary, had become her son's favorite place to retreat when he was feeling nervous or upset about something—which he often was when company was about.

Thank the Lord, Arnie had kept his word and not ousted Zane's secret. Her shy little boy would've shriveled in the face of such harsh scrutiny. He could barely tolerate public praise.

As talented as she ever was, Zane's soprano could hold the stage with opera sensation Charles Adams, should her son ever find the courage to perform publicly. Thus far he'd only performed for his siblings, herself, Richard, and her parents. This would be his first performance in front of anyone else. It was little surprise he'd gone into hiding.

She followed the narrow path between rose bushes, past her blooming lilies, and finally spotted his small form tucked into the shadows of the farthest corner.

Stooping beside him, she ruffled his hair. "What are you doing all the way back here?"

"Waiting."

"What for?"

"For everyone to go away."

"Oh, darling." She combed her fingers through his hair, setting it back into place. "I know you're nervous because your grandmother asked you to sing for everyone, but there isn't anything to be afraid of. Everyone here cares about you and wants to see you do well."

"But I don't think my throat will work."

"What makes you say that?"

"Listen." He took a deep breath and made a comical attempt at pretending to sing without making a sound.

"Hmm. I see." *Lord, give me wisdom to help my boy find his courage.* Her eyes traveled the garden. "I have an idea." She took his hand and led him out of the shadows into a sunny patch of ground. "Let's try singing here."

He squinted one eye at her. "You'll sing too?"

"I'll sing, too." She gave his hand a squeeze, then released it and stood, assuming her performance stance.

Mimicking her, he folded his hands at chest level and pulled back his shoulders.

She smiled down at him. "Ready?"

With a swallow so big she could see his throat working, he

nodded.

So she opened her mouth and together they sang "God Works in a Mysterious Way." It was Richard's favorite hymn and one they'd been practicing of late to sing for her husband's upcoming birthday. As they sang, several sets of footsteps pattered near, but she was too caught up in the music to care.

> *God moves in a mysterious way,*
> *His wonders to perform;*
> *He plants his footsteps in the sea,*
> *And rides upon the storm.*
>
> *Deep in unfathomable mines*
> *Of never failing skill;*
> *He treasures up his bright designs,*
> *And works His sovereign will.*
>
> *Ye fearful saints fresh courage take,*
> *The clouds ye so much dread*
> *Are big with mercy, and shall break*
> *In blessings on your head.*
>
> *Judge not the Lord by feeble sense,*
> *But trust him for his grace;*
> *Behind a frowning providence,*
> *He hides a smiling face.*

The words of the song poured peace over her soul as they sang the last verse

> *Blind unbelief is sure to err,*
> *And scan his work in vain;*
> *God is his own interpreter,*
> *And he will make it plain.*

As their final notes drifted into the branches, thunderous applause erupted from the other side of the mesquite bushes.

Zane lifted his wide blue eyes to hers. "My throat worked, Mama."

She laughed. "Of course it did."

"But why?"

"Because we, my darling, were never meant to hide in the shadows. We were meant to sing in the sunlight."

At that moment, guests began to trickle into the garden, led by her teary-eyed mother. "That was wonderful! You must come to the courtyard and sing another song for us so we can all watch you perform properly."

Zane's wide blue eyes pleaded with Clarinda as his fingers mangled the hem of his coat. "Will you sing with me?"

In front of all these people? Clarinda's heart stuttered, then calmed. She was a child of the one true King. She was chosen, she was loved, and she was beautiful. Smiling, she took Zane's hand and led him to the courtyard.

Richard took a seat at the piano waiting there and her heart surged with gratitude as she met his adoring gaze. God had gifted her with blessings beyond measure through that precious man.

Zane tugged her hand and whispered, "You ready, Mama?"

She nodded and cued Richard to play.

Together, surrounded by their family and friends, they sang in the sunlight.

Don't miss *Harmony on the Horizon*, book 2 in the Chaparral Hearts series!

Chapter One

June 30, 1865
San Francisco

A girl's terrified scream jerked Margaret Foster's attention from the mathematics formula she'd been rehearsing in her mind. Numbers fled as she focused on her surroundings.

Fog shrouded the buildings lining the cobblestone street. A chill shivered up her spine as she searched the wooden sidewalks. Not another person in sight. Who had screamed? And when had Margaret left the crowds of people headed to work?

The woman who owned the boarding house Margaret had checked into yesterday said to turn south at the milliner's shop with a large, glass display window. Margaret surveyed what she could see of the street through the fog. None of the buildings bore windows of any kind.

She squinted at the nearest sign. *Melodeon?* She stepped away. This couldn't be the right neighborhood. She must've been so focused on reviewing the formulas for the mathematics portion of her teaching exam that she'd missed her turn. And stumbled into a neighborhood she'd know better than to enter back home in Boston.

She pivoted. *Foolish woman! Knowing your lessons won't matter at all if you're late and—*

Another scream spun Margaret toward the alley she'd been passing. Tall buildings on either side blocked the early morning light. She ought to leave—run from this place. But if someone were in need...Margaret peered into the shadows. "Hello? Is someone there?"

Scuffling accompanied the movement of dark figures at the far end of the alley.

Frantic, feminine speech in a language she didn't recognize burst forth. Then was cut off. The words may have been foreign, but their tone was all too familiar—desperate, pleading.

Margaret fumbled for the weapon hidden within her skirt pocket.

A Chinese girl, who looked no more than ten years old, burst from the shadows, tears streaming down her cheeks. She sprinted past Margaret.

A scowling, red-haired man charged after the child and caught her. He dragged her, flailing and sobbing, back toward the muddy alley.

Margaret gave up searching for her pocket's opening. "Stop!" Margaret lunged forward and grabbed the girl's arm in both hands. "Let her go!"

The man took one arm off the child and back-handed Margaret across the face, breaking her hold on the girl. "Mind yer business, woman." He continued dragging the screaming child into the shadows.

Please, Lord. Margaret shoved her hand once more into her skirts and this time found the pocket's opening. She withdrew her brother Nash's pepperbox and aimed it squarely at the man's head. "I said, let her go."

He shoved the girl into the mud and raised his hands—one of which was missing a finger. His gray-blue eyes raged at Margaret with the fury of a hurricane at sea. He lunged. One strong hand shoved the barrel up while the other seized her wrist.

He squeezed until she thought her bones would break. With a cry, she relinquished the weapon. This was it. Nash'd been right. She was going to die for sticking her nose into other people's affairs.

But rather than turn the weapon on her, the man stuffed Nash's sidearm into the back of his trousers.

Margaret took a step back, but he caught her arm. She jerked hard, but his grip was strong. He dragged her toward the shadows. "Seeing as she's gone, thou'll take her place."

Margaret's gaze swung to where the child had fallen. The spot was as empty as the alley the brute was forcing her into. She dropped to the ground. The shoulder of the arm he held screamed as her free hand clawed for a grip on something, anything that would halt their progress into the darkness. It was no use. There was nothing to cling onto. In seconds they'd be out of sight.

She craned her neck toward the street. *There!* A tall figure emerged from the fog. She dug in her heels. "Help! Please, help me!"

A man at least ten years her junior sprinted toward them. "Hey, what do you think you're doing?"

The fiend dragging her reached for the pepperbox at his back, but her hero caught his arm. He stole the weapon and held it out of reach.

"I don't think so." The young man's lopsided grin flashed bright.

Her captor sent a fist toward the younger man's face.

Thankfully, her hero was quicker than the red-headed scoundrel who'd accosted her. He ducked several blows —though not all—before landing a solid punch against the man's temple that crumpled him to the ground. The swine tried to stand, but his senses must have been knocked sideways.

Her hero leveled the pepperbox at the man. "What're you thinking, Drogo? Can't you see this is a lady?"

Wait, her hero knew the fiend's name?

Drogo spit blood into the mud. "She stole from me." He attempted to rise again, but only made it to his knees and bent double. His last meal cast itself across the earth.

Her hero studied her.

"I did no such thing." She lifted her chin. "I merely endeavored to stop him from harming an innocent child."

Her hero's eyes narrowed on Drogo. "Didn't think that was your game."

Drogo wiped his mouth with a shrug. "Money's money." His glare speared her again, albeit a bit glassier than before. "And I don't let nobody take mine from me."

"Listen." Her hero scanned the empty street and alleyway, while keeping one eye fixed on Drogo. He was incredibly jumpy for a man holding a gun on a seriously injured opponent. "Clearly this lady doesn't have the good sense God gave her."

Margaret reared back. "I beg your pard—"

"But the kid's gone now and the longer you waste on this"—he tipped his head toward Margaret—"the longer it'll take you to find your merchandise again."

Margaret's jaw fell open. "You can't mean to let him go after her? Why aren't you shouting for someone to arrest him?"

Drogo laughed as if she'd said the funniest thing he'd ever heard. Finally, the red-haired blackguard lurched to his feet, his eyes fixed on her hero. "Thee'd better hope I find it, Johnson. I know where to find thou."

Margaret lunged for the pepperbox as Drogo staggered

away, but her hero lifted it out of reach. Curse her short stature. "You're letting him get away."

Johnson took a firm grasp of her elbow and started backing them away. His gaze didn't leave Drogo until the fiend had disappeared around a corner. Even then, he waited several more seconds before speaking. "There aren't many policeman brave enough to venture into this neighborhood. And none are dumb enough to try to arrest *that* man." He glared down at her as he hustled her up the street in the opposite direction Drogo had gone. "What were you thinking coming down here?"

Margaret dug in her heels and jerked her arm from his grasp. "Where are you taking me?"

"Somewhere it's safe for a lady like you."

"What about my gun?"

He lifted her pepperbox. "This is yours?"

She nodded and held out her hand.

He glanced over his shoulder, then pressed the weapon into her palm. "Just don't shoot me with it."

She stiffened. Did he believe all women incapable of handling firearms or was there something about her in particular that led to him to such an erroneous conclusion? *Well, you did foolishly wander into a dangerous part of town. You know better than to get so lost in your thoughts.*

The starch left her spine. "Thank you for saving me, Mr. Johnson." A shudder ran through her with the thought of what might of been had this young man not come to her aid. *Thank you for sending him, Lord.* She tucked the weapon away and offered her hand. "My name's Margaret Foster, by the way."

He ignored her hand and took her elbow again. "Come on. You're not safe yet, Miss Foster."

A minute later, they rounded a corner onto a street filled with the expected bustle of a city in the morning, and he released her.

The contrast with the previous lonely street was striking.

How had she not noticed the difference sooner? She clapped a hand over her eyes as heat seared her cheeks.

"Here."

She lowered her hand to find Johnson's hand thrust toward her, a stained handkerchief in his palm. She recoiled. "Oh. No, thank you. I'm fine." Did she *look* like she needed to blow her nose?

He shook his head and crammed the cotton square into his vest pocket. "Just figured you'd want to wipe the blood off, but have it your way."

"The wha—?"

"How many?" He held two fingers in front of her eyes.

"What?"

"How many fingers do you see?"

"Two, but—"

"Good." He dropped his hand. "Any dizziness?"

Did he think she'd suffered a brain injury? "I told you I'm fine, so—"

"Great. Now, look." He grabbed her shoulder and spun her to face the way they'd come. Speaking in the same tone she used when one of her youngest students was confused, he pointed. "That way's bad." He spun her back toward the bustling street. "That way's good. Try to keep them straight." With another flash of his grin, he released her and strolled away.

Margaret's fingers trembled as she pulled her clean handkerchief from her pocket and dabbed at the ache in her cheek. Sure enough, the fabric came away red. She pressed the handkerchief to the wound and peered down at her dress. Torn and filthy, as she'd suspected. She lifted her free hand to right her crooked fanchon bonnet. Two hairpins came loose in the process, and a curl of hair snaked its way down her neck. "Just wonderful." She rubbed at the muck coating her blue dress to no avail.

She'd kept this dress safely locked away for all the miserable months she'd spent sailing from Boston to San Francisco. Its special beauty was meant to give her the confidence she needed to see her through today's teacher examination and interview.

After disembarking yesterday, she marched straight to the boardinghouse San Francisco's School Board had directed her to in their letter, then spent the rest of her day bathing and pressing the wrinkles from her dress. Yet it was all for naught. Her best dress was ruined. Tears pricked at the corners of her eyes, but she firmed her lips and blinked away the emotion. *A lot more could have been ruined.* She lifted the chatelaine attached at her waist, sniffed the ball of lavender, and checked the timepiece. *Oh no!*

GET FOR HARMONY ON THE HORIZON AT YOUR FAVORITE RETAILER.

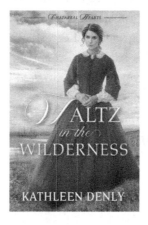

Book 2: *Waltz in the Wilderness*

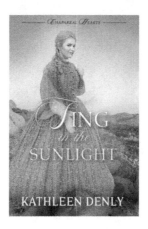

Book 2: *Sing in the Sunlight*

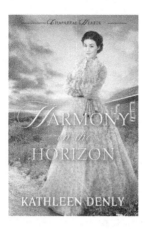

Book 3: Harmony on the Horizon

Did you enjoy this book? We hope so!
Would you take a quick minute to leave a review where you purchased the book?
It doesn't have to be long. Just a sentence or two telling what you liked about the story!

Receive a FREE ebook and get updates when new Wild Heart books release: https://wildheartbooks.org/newsletter

A special note from the author to members of the adoption triad—birth parents, adoptive parents, and of course, the children themselves:

When reading this story please do not view it as an opinion of how unplanned pregnancies should be handled or how adoption should be viewed. This is one character's unique story. It is not intended to represent the community in general. That task is too large for any novel. If you are part of the adoption or fostering community, you know there are an innumerable variety of reasons behind the decisions birth parents make and the same is true of adoptive parents. Each family's story is unique.

I'd also like to take this moment to draw attention to the conversation between Richard and Clarinda when he first arrives in San Diego. At one point she declares "I don't want my child to grow up wondering why his mother didn't love him enough to keep him." Please do not take this as me saying that a birth parent who relinquishes their child doesn't love them. That is not my intention at all. I *know* in many cases a birth parent makes that choice from a place of incredible sacrificial love. However, I also know that this is a fear many birth parents struggle with and a question many adopted children ask themselves. I didn't want to give a whitewashed version of Clarinda's story by removing her concern and struggle. I wanted the reader to feel her raw, uncensored emotions as best as I could portray them. I wanted the reader to witness her struggles in as real a way as possible. Yet, I know that I cannot convey with words the soul-deep ache of a birth parent's decision regarding the fate of their child.

In regards to the language surrounding unplanned pregnancy and unwed mothers, I have attempted to remain as true to the time period as possible without being unnecessarily offensive. I hope that I have struck the right balance.

I ask for your grace and that you view this story not as a political statement, but as my attempt to show God's love through Richard and Clarinda's story.

FROM THE AUTHOR

Dear Reader,

As always, I've sprinkled bits of history throughout this novel. There are also a couple hidden connections to book one in this series, *Waltz in the Wilderness*. Did you spot them? Read on to find out.

The Benicia Young Ladies Seminary was established in 1852 as the first school of higher education west of the Rockies. Despite the word "seminary" in its title, it was not a religious school but can be better understood as a women-only college. At the time, it was expected that Benicia would become California's state capital. The new school aimed to build character in a new country where ideals were needed, and to open the minds and hearts of their students to the searching influence of great thinkers, poets and musicians." It was established by a 12-member board of trustees—all men. However, the director of the school was a woman. The trouble was, these female directors had a habit of getting married and therefore needing to be replaced. That is, until Mary Atkins came along in the school's second year. She ran the school until 1865 when Cyrus and Susan Mills took over and renamed it Mills College. The school was relocated to Oakland, California in 1871 and is still in existence today.

I took some artistic liberty with the start date of the Overland Mail Company (today known as the Butterfield Overland Mail/Stage). It actually began in September 1858, but I have my characters riding it in January of that year. This was a conscious choice. I knew I wanted to incorporate both the new stage route and the San Diego hurricane in my story but their actual historical dates didn't work for my plot, so I decided to keep the true hurricane date and fudge the start of the stage route. That said, all other details of the stage experience are fully accurate, including the description of the fold-down benches, the style of coach, and the exact location where passengers disembarked in San Diego in 1858.

The Humphrey's store and home in San Diego was inspired by the Whaley House which has been restored and is now run as a museum in Old Town San Diego. And here's a little secret: In my mind, the store where Eliza and Daniel purchase their supplies in my novel, *Waltz in the Wilderness,* is the same place. So the man behind the counter serving Eliza & Daniel would have been Neal Humphrey. Another less secret connection is that there is a reference to young Clarinda Humphrey made during the pivotal conversation between Daniel and Alice near the end of *Waltz in the Wilderness.*

The Grand Valley Ranch was inspired by two places. The first, being Jamacha Rancho—which by 1853 was owned by five Americans: Colonel John Bankhead Magruder, First Lieutenant Asher R. Eddy, Eugene B. Pendleton, Frank Ames, and Robert Kelly. There is some mystery as to how the land came to be owned by these men which can be read about at https://sandiegohistory.org/journal/1984/april/jamacha/. However, I chose this ranch and these men as my inspiration because the men were brought together by the New San Diego project, otherwise known as Davis's Folly, which I mention in *Waltz in the Wilderness*. You may recognize that I used two of the last names of these men (Kelly & Ames) as minor characters in the novel (co-owners of the Grand Valley Ranch). The actual location of The Grand Valley Ranch as described in *Sing in the Sunlight*, however, is closer to the location of Rancho de los Coches in El Cajon, California. Incidentally, both Jamacha Rancho and El Rancho de los Coches were originally granted to Doña Apolinaria Lorenzana.

The incident involving the attack on Graciela was inspired by an actual historical event. A white man did attack a Native woman whose husband defended her and killed the attacker. The Captain did not send for a white man, however. According to the historical report printed in *El Capitan* by Tanis C. Thorne, they sought the advice of a white woman with whom they had a close relationship. (I changed that detail because I didn't think readers would accept it. Sometime truth is stranger than fiction.) According to the report given by a Native woman, the white woman's response was the same as Clarinda's—no punishment should be given—however, the whipping and banishment of the victim's husband did occur due to concerns of backlash from surrounding ranchers. There is some debate among historians whether the whipping was a traditional Native punishment or had been introduced by Spanish settlers.

The actual rustling scenario described in *Sing in the Sunlight* (involving local ranchers and the sheriff) was entirely fictional, however the departure of the military and local citizen's concerns about being unprotected were entirely factual and documented in the local newspaper. Further, rustling and raids by bandits from below the border were a regular occurrence. There are numerous accounts of such events throughout this time period. There are also some accounts of attacks/uprisings by Native Peoples, though by the late 1850s these events were the exception.

The account of a Category 1 hurricane striking San Diego on October 2, 1858 is shockingly true. In writing *Sing in the Sunlight*, I followed the actual timeline and I described the resulting destruction (including the ships blown onto shore) as given by numerous historical sources. To learn more about the only hurricane known to have struck California, visit https://www.aoml.noaa.gov/hrd/Landsea/chenowethlandsea.pdf. Actual newspaper accounts begin on page 1691 of that PDF.

The description of San Diego's economy at the time (depressed with several local ranchers going bankrupt) is historically accurate. Although the gold rush created an initial boon for selling both San Diego's cattle and sheep to the northern gold fields, competitors quickly began driving their livestock from the east and south of the border. This drove prices back down. To further complicate things, Southern California suffered such a long and severe drought it impacted the local flora in a way that made it nearly impossible for ranchers to keep their cattle fed. Those who could, drove their cattle to the local mountains to find enough food to keep the animals alive. However, for many, it cost more to feed the cattle than they could later sell them for. This, in addition to exorbitant court costs incurred by trying to confirm legal claims to their land grants after the American takeover, drove many San Diego ranchers to ruin. While sheep weren't selling for high prices either at this time, they were more drought tolerant and able to be kept alive for less cost. Several ranchers who survived this era did so by raising sheep and diversifying their investments. Americans were particularly adept at this, with many businessmen owning interest in a wide variety of industries .

I hope you've enjoyed learning more about the history of California and the connection between *Waltz in the Wilderness* and *Sing in the Sunlight*. In book three of my Chaparral Hearts series there will be more history, more connections, and you'll get to know more about Everett Thompson, Fletcher Johnson, and Clarinda's friend from school, Katie.

Blessings,

Kathleen

ABOUT THE AUTHOR

Kathleen Denly lives in sunny Southern California with her loving husband, four young children, and two cats. As a member of the adoption and foster community, children in need are a cause dear to her heart and she finds they make frequent appearances in her stories. When she isn't writing, researching, or caring for children, Kathleen spends her time reading, visiting historical sites, hiking, and crafting.

If you enjoyed this book, be sure to sign up for Kathleen's Readers' Club! KRC Members will be the first to know when Kathleen's next book is scheduled to be released!

QUESTIONS FOR DISCUSSION

Do you or someone you know struggle with self-worth? What does the Bible tell us about our personal value?

Have you ever experienced a misunderstanding similar to what Clarinda and her parents experienced? Is it possible you're currently misunderstanding someone? How can you help avoid/resolve such misunderstandings?

Have you ever struggled to find your purpose in life? What do you want people to say about you after you die?

Do you ever struggle to understand why God allows certain things to happen? What does the Bible say about such events? How can you use your personal experiences to bless others?

Have you ever committed a sin you felt was unforgivable? Read 1 John 1:9

Has anyone ever fooled or manipulated you? Have you forgiven that person? How can you use that experience to bless others?

Did any part of this story touch your heart?

What was your favorite twist/surprise in the story?

What did you think of Arnie?

Could you relate to Clarinda's struggles?

What would you have done in Clarinda's situation—unwed and pregnant?

Are you or anyone you know involved in the adoption and foster community?

What do you think of Fletcher Johnson? Who do you think would be a good match for him?

What do you think of Everett Thompson? Where do you think his story should go in book 3?

God uses a dream to direct Richard as He did for certain people in the Bible. Has God ever spoken to you in an unexpected way? How can you discern God's voice from your own thoughts/desires?

Have you ever eaten braised lamb? Do you have a favorite lamb/mutton recipe?

What makes this book different from other historical romance novels you've read?

What do you think of Clarinda's parents?

Did this story challenge you or your perceptions in any way?

Who was your favorite character in *Sing in the Sunlight* and why?

What most appeals to you about the book's cover?

What would you like to see in the next book?

If you love historical romance, check out the other Wild Heart books!

Marisol ~ Spanish Rose by Elva Cobb Martin

Escaping to the New World is her only option...Rescuing her will wrap the chains of the Inquisition around his neck.

Marisol Valentin flees Spain after murdering the nobleman who molested her. She ends up for sale on the indentured servants' block at Charles Town harbor—dirty, angry, and with child. Her hopes are shattered, but she must find a refuge for herself and the child she carries. Can this new land offer her the grace, love, and security she craves? Or must she escape again to her only living relative in Cartagena?

Captain Ethan Becket, once a Charles Town minister, now sails the seas as a privateer, grieving his deceased wife. But when he takes captive a ship full of indentured servants, he's intrigued by the woman whose manners seem much more refined than the average Spanish serving girl. Perfect to become governess for his young son. But when he sets out on a quest to find his captured sister, said to be in Cartagena, little does he expect his new Spanish governess to stow away on his ship with her six-month-old son. Yet her offer of help to free his sister is too tempting to pass up. And her beauty, both inside and out, is too attractive for his heart to protect itself against—until he learns she is a wanted murderess.

As their paths intertwine on a journey filled with danger, intrigue, and romance, only love and the grace of God can over-come the past and ignite a new beginning for Marisol and Ethan.

~

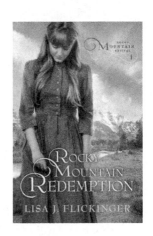

Rocky Mountain Redemption by Lisa J. Flickinger

A Rocky Mountain logging camp may be just the place to find herself.

To escape the devastation caused by the breaking of her wedding engagement, Isabelle Franklin joins her aunt in the Rocky Mountains to feed a camp of lumberjacks cutting on the slopes of Cougar Ridge. If only she could out run the lingering nightmares.

Charles Bailey, camp foreman and Stony Creek's itinerant pastor, develops a reputation to match his new nickname — Preach. However, an inner battle ensues when the details of his rough history threaten to overcome the beliefs of his young faith.

Amid the hazards of camp life, the unlikely friendship growing between the two surprises Isabelle. She's drawn to Preach's brute strength and gentle nature as he leads the ragtag crew toiling for Pollitt's Lumber. But when the ghosts from her past return to haunt her, the choices she will make change the course of her life forever—and that of the man she's come to love.

∾

Lone Star Ranger by Renae Brumbaugh Green

Elizabeth Covington will get her man.

And she has just a week to prove her brother isn't the murderer Texas Ranger Rett Smith accuses him of being. She'll show the good-looking lawman he's wrong, even if it means setting out on a risky race across Texas to catch the real killer.

Rett doesn't want to convict an innocent man. But he can't let the Boston beauty sway his senses to set a guilty man free. When Elizabeth follows him on a dangerous trek, the Ranger vows to keep her safe. But who will protect him from the woman whose conviction and courage leave him doubting everything—even his heart?

Made in the USA
Monee, IL
04 June 2022

97461807R00226